Pretty WHEN SHE Destroys

RHIANNON FRATER

PERMUTED PLATINUM

Published by Permuted Press
109 International Drive, Suite 300
Franklin, TN 37067

Cover art by Claudia McKinney, Phatpuppy Art

Follow us online:

Web: http://www.PermutedPress.com

Facebook: http://www.facebook.com/PermutedPress

Twitter: @PermutedPress

Dedicated with much love to Dru, who always knew that the Pretty When She Dies novels would find their audience when the time was right.

PROLOGUE

The Beginning of the End

April 2012

The promise of rain loomed in the gray early evening sky hovering low over the East Texas college. Bianca scurried along the cracked sidewalk, her petite frame dodging around the other students. As usual, no one took note of the girl with the pale hair and vivid blue eyes dressed in a flowered dress, old fashioned blue shawl covered in fluffy sunflowers, and heavy combat boots.

Ducking under the portico of one of the buildings, Bianca clutched her books tight to her chest and stared in anticipation out over the courtyard.

"Here it comes," she breathed.

Seconds later, the sky opened, sheets of rain washing over the people still on their way to class. Laughter and cries of dismay filled the humid air as people scrambled for cover. Bianca stepped behind one of the pillars to avoid the small stampede into the building. The reek of ozone, weed, body odor, and coffee floated in the air after the college kids disappeared inside.

The steamy air and patter of rain painted her surroundings with a dreamy brush, but Bianca felt apart from the world. The rain was of no real concern to her. Instead, her eyes traced over the pathway the girl with tattoos always traveled on her way to class at this time.

Ever since she had accidently bumped into the other young woman on the way to a lecture, Bianca had been obsessed with the beauty with the long black hair, inked skin, and vivid blue-gray eyes. Bianca had experienced an intense surge of power when their bodies had collided that had been so powerful it had knocked her off her feet. Instinctively, she'd known that the other woman was gifted - or was it cursed? - with the same power Bianca had inherited from her own mother, the famous medium Josephine Leduc. She'd been so startled she hadn't uttered a word as the other woman helped her to her feet before hurrying on to class.

It had taken a little sleuthing, but Bianca had uncovered as much information as possible on the other medium. Her name was Amaliya Vezorak, which sounded very exotic to Bianca. At first, Bianca had only wanted to speak to the other medium about the powers they shared, but then the terrible nightmares and visions had begun.

Brushing her blond hair from her face, Bianca shifted nervously. She'd been practicing what she wanted to say to Amaliya every day for a week. It had been difficult to fight through the storm of information filling her mind through her visions and dreams, but Bianca was certain that Amaliya was in danger. Recurring images of Amaliya covered in blood, somewhere beneath the earth, haunted Bianca. Since Amaliya was a medium, too, Bianca hoped she'd listen to her warning. There was a dark entity closing in on Amaliya, plotting to ensnare her, and Bianca hoped she could save her.

Bianca's heart raced when she saw the familiar silhouette of the other medium walking through the rain. Not even bothering to cover her hair with her book bag, Amaliya sauntered through the downpour, her heavy boots splashing through the puddles forming on the cracked sidewalk. Her curves were tucked into a tank top and jeans, her black hair in a loose bun, the inky tendrils clinging to her neck and cheeks.

Taking a deep breath, Bianca stepped out from behind the pillar. As always, when the other medium was near, her skin tingled and the voices of the dead strengthened. It was difficult to hear through all the noise, but she concentrated on the sound of the rain to focus her mind.

Amaliya started up the stairs, her eyes rising toward Bianca.

"Uh, hi, I'm Bianca Leduc," she murmured in a soft voice.

The door banged open behind her, making Bianca start.

"Amaliya! Just the student I've been looking for."

The crisp English accent sent chills racing down Bianca's spine. As if gripped in a dead man's hand, Bianca found herself unable to move. Dragging a quivering breath, she clutched her books tightly to her chest.

Amaliya stopped on the step below Bianca, her face lighting up with delight. "Professor Sumner, how can I help you?"

The air around Bianca grew thick and icy, making it difficult to take a breath.

The putrid reek of death and blood filled her mouth and nose. Bianca felt as though she was now invisible, even though she was standing within three feet of the two people. She could feel malevolent power pulsating out of the tall blond man and encapsulating Amaliya.

How could the other medium *not* feel it?

"What did I do now, Professor Sumner?" Amaliya asked, her eyes brazen, teasing, and flirtatious. How could she not detect what the man truly was beneath his cultured visage?

"Nothing at all," the man answered in his posh English accent. "I was wondering if you'd join me for coffee sometime. I have a special project I'd love for you to be a part of."

Professor Sumner's presence was a dark shadow that stole away Bianca's resolve. Terrified, she stared at the books in her hands, unsure of what she should do. A part of her wanted to blurt out to Amaliya all she suspected, but then wouldn't the creature just kill them both? His magic reeked of death and destruction.

"Anything you want me to be a part of has to be awesome." Amaliya's red lips turned up at the corners into a seductive smile.

The sexual energy between the man and his future victim sizzled between them in the balmy air, repulsing Bianca.

"Oh, it is, I can assure you. So is that a yes?"

Trembling, Bianca realized he was toying with Amaliya. Again, the image of Amaliya covered in blood bloomed in Bianca's mind. Biting her bottom lip, Bianca struggled to speak. She imagined grabbing Amaliya's hand and running off together, escaping the creature that was hunting the tattooed beauty. Yet she couldn't move. The malevolent power swirling through the air had her pinned where she stood.

"I'm heading home for Easter tonight after I do some laundry," Amaliya said, tilting her head to gaze with obvious yearning at the terrible being disguised as a mortal man. "Maybe after break?"

Bianca finally dared to raise her face to gaze upon the couple speaking just a few feet from her. The air around them was thick with darkness. It distorted their images, wavering like heat. The glamour disguising the man flickered under her scrutiny. His true face was even more handsome and cruel than she had imagined.

The umbrella blossomed into a black flower over their heads. "That would be lovely. Are you on the way to class? I can walk you there." The monster pretending to be Professor Sumner gestured out into the steady downpour.

"Actually, I think I'll skip it." Amaliya scrawled something on a piece of paper and gave it to him. "My number. For that coffee."

"Thank you. I have some errands to do. Can I walk you somewhere?"

"Yes, you can."

"Then after you."

Amaliya grinned as she walked into the curtain of rain with the tall man.

Bianca tried to call out after her, but her voice wouldn't come. On impulse, she dropped her books. The noise drew Amaliya's attention, her mesmerizing eyes barely skimming over the disheveled girl standing beside the pillar.

The professor didn't even look back.

Bianca tried to speak, but no words escaped her lips.

Amaliya gave her a curious look, then turned away.

Gathering her things, Bianca followed the two figures fading into the falling rain.

The voices of the dead whispered in her ears, their fingers clutching at her, urging her to hurry.

"Stop him! Stop him!" they chanted.

Again, flashes of Amaliya covered in blood filled her mind's eye. Flinching, Bianca stumbled off the sidewalk into the mud. She pressed a hand to her head, trying to still the internal violence of her visions. They pummeled her, physically jerking her about.

...Amaliya covered in blood...

...Amaliya bringing destruction...

...the world in darkness...

"Please stop," Bianca begged the powers hurling the warnings into her already overloaded mind. Lifting her hand, she drew a ward in the air. It lessened the onslaught, but still the one voice that always haunted her persisted. It was her mother, Josephine.

Stop him! Stop him! She'll destroy us all if he succeeds! He's going to lure her into his trap tonight. Go to the coffee shop! Hurry! Hurry!

Crying out, Bianca staggered forward. Her pale blond hair falling around her face, she knew she looked crazed. She was Cassandra in Greek mythology wailing prophecies that no one would heed. There was no choice other than for her to follow the vampire and Amaliya. Only she stood between the world and destruction.

Staggering through the rain, Bianca turned toward her dorm. She'd never catch up to Amaliya now and wasn't sure where she lived. There was only one coffee shop in town, so Bianca wasn't defeated yet. She just had to get the weapon she had bought to destroy the evil that had set his sights on Amaliya.

The café was warm and filled with the fragrant smell of coffee. Nestled into a chair in the corner, Bianca watched Amaliya and the professor as they chatted at a nearby table. Bianca could see the power of the vampire drifting in the air, tangling with the aura of the other medium. The writhing dark magic sickened Bianca. It was evil and full of death.

Reaching into the oversized bag on the chair beside her, she traced her fingertips over the sheathed silver dagger. She had to wait. If she struck at him in public and failed, it would be the end of everything; therefore, she had to wait until they were away from the public. The stillness around her was comforting after the cacophony of voices that had assailed her earlier. Maybe her mother's spirit was holding back the others, or perhaps they were silent now that they knew she would move against the monster that would be the end of the world.

Watching Amaliya, tears sprung to Bianca's eyes. Every aspect of her yearned to connect with the other woman, for Amaliya would understand what Bianca suffered. They would be like sisters, best friends, and, at last, Bianca wouldn't be alone.

The green tea in the chipped bright yellow cup was cold now. Bianca's fingers traced the lip lazily as she pretended to read the book she'd propped up before her. Whatever the two were discussing, it appeared to be upsetting Amaliya. PJ Harvey's voice sang hauntingly over the loudspeaker above Bianca's head, mournful and full of pain. It perfectly mirrored Amaliya's expression. Crossing her legs, Bianca inadvertently bumped the table with her knee, the mug crashing to the floor. Bianca slid off the chair, picking the pieces out of the cold liquid. A barista hurried over with towels, a broom, and dustpan.

"I'm sorry," Bianca said. "I can pay for the mug."

"It's no big deal," the male barista assured her, mopping up the tea with the striped towels.

Bianca continued to pick up the slivers of the cup, her trembling hands making it difficult to get the smaller pieces.

"Hey, it's okay. Let me get it. You might cut yourself." The young man smiled at her.

Bianca slid back onto her chair, her eyes straying to the table across the room. It was empty.

Gasping, she shot to her feet, grabbed her things, and darted out of the shop. The professor's Mini Cooper pulled out of the parking lot just as she stumbled down the steps to the warm asphalt still steaming from the earlier rain. In a mad scramble, she ran to her scooter, hopped on, started it, and pursued the car. The roads were still slick from the rain, but she exceeded the speed limit, and soon the Cooper was in sight. The dirty water kicked up by the car tires splashed over her skirt and boots, but Bianca didn't care. The urgency ripping through her kept her speeding along.

Bianca lost the Mini Cooper a short distance from the dorm buildings. Caught at a red light, she was forced to wait while the traffic congested the intersection. When the traffic light finally changed to green, her little scooter soared along the lane guarded by tall pine trees. Bianca fought against her growing panic and fear. The voices of the dead whispered out of the darkness, urging her to hurry. Reaching the dorms, Bianca scanned the nearly empty parking lot. Dread ate at her stomach as her scooter cruised up and down the rows. At last, she spotted the Mini Cooper parked near a dumpster. It was close to two dorms.

"How do I find them?" Bianca whispered a prayer to the universe.

Sliding off the scooter, she already knew the answer. The one ability she feared most would have to be put to use. Her front teeth burrowed into her bottom lip while she gripped the hilt of the dagger. Trembling, tears in her eyes, Bianca lowered her eyelids. The collapse of her carefully constructed mental walls left her panting in fear. Immediately, she could both feel and see the pitch-black trail of the dark powers of the false professor heading toward the far building. The inky remains of his passing smeared the air, writhing like snakes. Sucking a shuddering breath through her gritted teeth, she followed it into the gloom. The wet earth squelched beneath her boots as Bianca stalked resolutely after the monster she feared but had to vanquish.

Rounding the corner, she saw Amaliya and the false professor in a passionate embrace. For a second, Bianca faltered, abruptly uncertain. The scene was so intimate it was hard for her to believe that Amaliya was truly in danger. The man's face was hidden in the darkness of the other woman's hair, his hand tucked within her jeans, stroking her. Bianca pressed a hand to her forehead, wondering briefly if she'd lost her mind. Had all the people who'd accused her of being crazy been correct?

A heavy plopping noise drew Bianca's attention back to the writhing couple. A cloud slid from the face of the moon, the pale light illuminating the dark liquid pouring out of Amaliya's throat.

Bianca gasped.

Kill him! Kill him! Kill him! Kill him!

Dragging the silver dagger out of the sheath, Bianca dropped her bag onto the misty ground.

Amaliya slid from the professor's grip, her throat a bloody ruin.

"Yes, so very pretty as you die," the monster said.

Bianca raised the weapon and rushed him. He didn't even turn toward her. A mere sweep of his hand sent her tumbling to the ground. The dagger fell from her fingertips, disappearing into the murk. Rolling onto her stomach, Bianca's hands raked the grass, searching frantically. The voice of the vampire was a low murmur as he bent over his victim. The vampire's power surged. The night pressed down on her body. Bianca fought to raise the walls she had lowered to find him, but she sensed his aura seeping into her mind like ice-cold water. Sluggishly, she crawled across the rain-drenched ground, searching for the weapon.

Agony ripped through her scalp when he grabbed her by her hair and dragged her deeper into the shadows dwelling at the base of the dorm building. Only the tall pines with the wind writhing through their branches were witness to the violent scene. Bianca kicked her feet while her fingers scrabbled at his hand. When he tossed her onto the ground beside Amaliya, Bianca could smell the overwhelming coppery smell of warm blood.

The ancient vampire regarded her with glowing white eyes. Handsome in a cold, cruel manner, his fake face was gone. Pinning her with one hand, he squatted near her. "Now, now, my little Bianca, did you really need to interrupt my moment with our delicious Amaliya?"

Bianca's gaze slid to the other medium. Amaliya's eyes were wide, staring, her breath rattling in her throat. She wasn't gone yet, but close. Tendrils of the vampire's power punctured Amaliya's body, feeding her false life. The other medium's lips and tongue were stained with blood.

Tears blurring her vision, Bianca reached out to Amaliya, her fingers straining for the other woman's hand. So many regrets filled her. If only she had been wiser, stronger, and bolder, maybe she could have saved Amaliya.

"Why are you doing this?" she whispered.

The vampire didn't answer. Striking as swiftly as a viper, his fangs tore into her throat, her blood spilling into his mouth and onto the ground. Bianca tried to call out, but his power rendered her speechless. Even as the agonizing pain threatened to swallow her into unconsciousness, Bianca strove to reach Amaliya's limp hand. The vampire savagely tore at her flesh, the excruciating pain her punishment for interrupting him. She could feel his anger pouring into her, but she fought against the giant wave of his power. Death loomed ever closer, but she fought against it.

With one last great effort, Bianca managed to at last touch Amaliya's fingertips with her own. Or maybe Amaliya had reached for her? Just a spark of life remained in the other woman.

Find me, Bianca whispered into the dying woman's mind. *Find me. We will defeat him together.*

The vampire tore Bianca from Amaliya, dragged her into his arms, and forced her mouth against the wound he'd inflicted on himself. Cold blood poured into her mouth, gagging her as his dark magic infested her dying body, binding her to him forever.

PART ONE

The Return of the Summoner

CHAPTER ONE

July 2012

The aggravation Santos felt toward his sister, Etzli, was beyond the normal low-grade variety he usually experienced. She had simply vanished from the house earlier in the night, and none of the cabal knew where she had gone. Even Gregorio, who was obsessed with her, had no idea where Etzli may have slipped off to.

Pacing in his office, Santos clutched his cellphone in one hand. Every call he'd made had resulted in the knot in his gut clenching ever tighter. With all that was going on in the supernatural realm, he couldn't believe his sister would be so flagrantly inconsiderate. He didn't even want to entertain the idea that Cian and his necromancer-vampire hybrid may have taken her.

Dark hair falling over his brow, he rested his hands on the edge of his desk. Everything felt wrong. The takeover of Austin and the capture of Amaliya should have been easy. Instead, he had lost a valuable witch and was quickly losing face in the eyes of the other vampire leaders. Santos had fought hard to claim San Antonio, Texas, as his territory and meticulously created a strong cabal that was feared by the other vampire masters of Texas. He refused to lose their fear and respect.

For years he had left Cian alone in Austin. The most powerful of vampires, The Summoner, had created Cian. For that reason, Santos had not dared to move against him. Cian had lived a solitary life in his small college town for nearly forty years. The last decade had altered the state capital into a growing metropolitan area that was able to now support a greater vampire presence. The arrival of Amaliya had changed things further when she killed The Summoner.

Amaliya was pure power.

Santos loved power.

With The Summoner gone, it was time to kill Cian and claim Amaliya, but nothing had gone as planned. To make matters worse, Etzli, the one person who was supposed to be his unwavering supporter, had been elusive and contrary of late. Santos had already lost Irma, his black witch, and Manny, one of his guards, this week when he'd sent them to test Amaliya's power. He didn't want to lose anyone else, especially his sister.

Checking his phone again, Santos growled low in his throat. None of the people searching for Etzli were reporting in. This was not a good sign. What if she was dead? The thought terrified him. They'd survived for so long together he couldn't bear the thought of not having her near him.

There was a sharp knock on his office door, then it opened without his permission. Gregorio poked his narrow, craggy face through the gap.

"Since when do you just barge in, Gregorio?"

"My master, there's a situation developing. You must come quickly!"

"What is it?" Santos asked, his voice sharp with disapproval. Now his servants were disrespecting him in his own home. He'd deal with whatever was upsetting Gregorio then punish him.

"Etzli has returned, but not alone. It's..." The man hesitated. Beads of sweat dotted his brow and upper lip. Fear was in his eyes.

"Is she hurt?" Santos moved swiftly toward the human.

"They're with the blood minions. It's very bad," Gregorio muttered, lowering his eyes in submission. "Very bad."

Santos wrenched the door from the man and brushed past him into the long hallway. The heels of his highly polished black leather boots clicked sharply against the tiled floor as he swiftly strode toward the wing where he kept the humans that provided blood to his cabal. The blood minions were well taken care of and offered their throats and necks, and sometimes other choice spots, willingly and without complaint. They were addicted to the vampire bite. Santos kept them in luxury until either they died or were turned into new members of his vampire family. A few of them were his personal favorites and only fed him. There were very strict rules in place when it came to the minions. One was not to kill them without Santos's explicit permission.

The reek of blood, terror, and offal reached him when he entered the wing the minions inhabited. Screams, sobs, and moans assailed his ears, emanating from the large room used as a recreational room. Bursting into a sprint, Santos leapt the length of the hall. The footfalls of his cabal sounded in his wake. Word spread fast among his vampires when something was amiss.

The vampire hurtled through the arched doorway into the room.

Blood splashed the walls, stained the furniture, and puddled on the floor. The bodies of the minions were strewn about like debris after a Texas tornado. One his favorites, seventeen-year-old Ricky, lay in two pieces near his feet.

"Etzli!" Santos shouted, rage blinding him so that he didn't immediately see if she was among the broken, torn bodies.

"She was hungry," Etzli said calmly from the shadows.

Santos whirled about, glaring at his half-sister. Long black hair glimmered in the light, and her dark eyes burned like coals. Clad in a black dress that was slashed to the thigh, she held one of her bone knives in one hand. Blood was slathered across her full lips. Raising one arm, she revealed a twisted, stumpy hand.

"And I needed to regrow this."

Confused and frightened, Santos grabbed her mutilated limb. "Who did this to you?"

"Cian," Etzli answered.

"Cian?" Santos stared at her, not understanding. "You fought Cian?"

"And Amaliya."

"Where?"

"A graveyard in the Texas Hill Country." Etzli smirked, obviously enjoying feeding him only tidbits of information.

"Why did you go there alone?" Santos demanded.

"I wasn't alone." His sister turned adoring eyes toward the center of the room.

"Master, she's still killing," Gregorio said, his voice urgent.

Disoriented by all that was occurring, Santos whipped about to see a girl he didn't recognize crawling on her toes and fingertips toward a cowering female human. At first he thought it was a child but then realized it was a young woman, perhaps in her late teens. Blood soaked her pale blond hair, stained her white lace dress red, and dripped from her lips.

"Stop!" Santos ordered.

The girl hissed at him, baring long fangs, then grabbed the sobbing human by the collar of her dress and dragged her across the slippery floor toward her mouth.

"Stop! Don't touch her!" Santos hurtled toward the vampire.

Thrashing about, the chosen victim screamed for Santos. He was about to grab her hand and wrench her from the grip of the vampire when her throat was shredded by the fangs of the other vampire. Blood, hot and precious, sprayed over Santos, instantly soaking his blue silk shirt. The blond vampire plunged her face into the fount of blood to drink.

With a howl of rage, Santos lurched forward to seize the intruding vampire.

"Don't touch her!" Etzli's voice hissed, then Santos was jerked off his feet and slammed to the ground.

Striking out in anger, Santos knocked his sister away. She immediately kicked out, sending him sliding across the bloody floor. Landing against a pile of broken bodies, Santos snarled, rising swiftly to his feet. Etzli glowered at him, standing between him and the strange vampire who was feasting on the last of his minions.

"What's happening?" he shouted.

3

Santos was dimly aware of his cabal gathering in the doorway. At least twenty of his people were watching. None moved to interfere, clearly awaiting his order.

"She needed blood," Etzli answered coldly. "Lots of it, to fully restore her powers. Rachoń was keeping her only half-alive with her own blood."

"Who is she?" Santos voice was cold, clipped, and full of his fury. Not only were his blood minions destroyed, but he was being usurped by his own flesh and blood.

Etzli's response was a slow, cruel smile. "Your new master."

"*Jefe?*" one of his guards said in Spanish. "Boss?"

Santos raised a hand, quieting the murmurs among the vampires clustered together watching the bloody feast. Their eyes burned bright, their own hunger rising.

"Etzli, explain yourself right now."

Etzli's smile only broadened.

The girl behind Etzli dragged herself upright, drunk on the blood she had consumed. Swaying, she stared at Santos with bright blue eyes. She licked her lips with a bloody tongue.

"Who is she, Etzli?"

"Get on your knees, Santos," Etzli ordered. Directing her dark eyes at the vampires staring in shock at the scene playing out before them, she said, "On your knees!"

The eyes of the cabal turned to Santos. Fury enveloping him, he clenched his hands at his sides. "Etzli, I'm warning you..."

"No, *I'm* warning *you*!" Etzli snapped. "Your defiance will not be tolerated, Santos! Now on your knees! All of you!"

"What the fuck, Etzli?" one of the vampires said, his dark eyes menacing. "You can't talk to Santos like that!"

"Jorge, this is between me and my sister," Santos said, holding up one hand in warning. Though his anger was close to consuming him and sending him into a violent rampage, he stared at his sister with the last bit of hope he had inside of him. "Etzli, this is my house! My city! My cabal! What the fuck is this...thing," he gestured at distaste at the blood-soaked vampire, "doing to you?"

"I said on your knees!" Etzli screeched.

In a blur of shadow, she struck out at the cabal. Gasps of pain and shock rang out, mingling with the crunch of bone. Etzli's whirling figure slashed at the vampires with deadly efficiency. In seconds, they were on the floor, legs shattered, splinters of bone puncturing their flesh and clothing. Standing over the broken men and women, Etzli twirled her bone dagger in her one good hand.

Santos at last felt fear.

"On your knees, Santos," Etzli said calmly, her threat clear.

One of the male vampires made a grab for Santos's sister. She slashed off his head with one mighty blow. It rolled away with a meaty thump.

After all his years of hard work, all his plans, Santos was thunderstruck to realize he was losing his cabal to the one person he had loved and trusted above all others. "Etzli..."

The reek of death, blood, fear, and dark magic filled the room. Santos's eyes slid toward the pale, blonde vampire standing placidly among the corpses. The air grew frigid as the creature stared at him.

"Who are you?" he whispered.

The blue eyes flashed white, and the slaughtered minions started to squirm around him. Those who were able to stand rose to their feet, while the ones in chunks flailed like newborn babes.

"Where is that famous Latin temper, Santos?" the girl asked. She stepped over the writhing bits of human flesh, advancing on him.

"There is another one," Santos said at last. "And you have enslaved her, Etzli?" His dark eyes darted toward his sister.

"I *serve* her," Etzli replied, her voice filled with reverence.

Bloodied fingers gripped at Santos's legs. Glancing downward, he saw Ricky's upper half attempting to drag him to the floor while his legs flailed nearby. With disgust, Santos kicked the partial corpse away.

"I will not kneel," he said at last. "This is still my cabal. You will have to kill me to take it."

"I don't want to kill you," the blonde vampire said, laughing. "Not yet. I don't need to kill you to take your cabal from you."

Another vampire attempted to attack Etzli. She lashed out, and another head rolled across the floor.

Rippling waves of dark magic flowed out of the new vampire, a visible manifestation of her power. Resembling great wings, the darkness knitted the corpses into monstrous creations.

"No!" Santos gasped, at last understanding. "No! You're dead!"

"Do you really think a little thing like the death of my body would stop me?" The girl laughed with delight. "You're such a foolish little child."

The massive creatures made of human flesh, bone, and sinew roared. Teeth made of broken bones filled their maws.

Santos sought out his sister's gaze, desperate to understand her betrayal. "Etzli, why?"

"Because The Summoner is our future. We've become weak and complacent. The Summoner will restore us to greatness." Lifting her chin, she visibly dared him to argue with her.

The hulking monsters of flesh moved menacingly toward Santos. They disgusted him, and he took a step away from them.

"We're blood, Etzli. You can't betray me this way."

"I'm not betraying you, Santos. I'm saving you. You're weak. Pathetic. These little games you play are silly and childish. You want to be king of your own realm instead of realizing the greatness of what we are." Etzli resembled the

Aztec blood goddess she claimed to be as she stepped out from amidst the vampires she had crippled. "Our time is coming. Either you stand with us or die."

Santos shifted his gaze to the woman he now realized was The Summoner. How the ancient vampire had come to reside in the body of the slender blonde woman was of no importance. The glowing white eyes and cold smirk terrified him.

"The Summoner has returned to us. She will guide us to our true victory," Etzli proclaimed to all the vampires. "She is the purity of our power."

Stepping toward Santos, The Summoner raised her hands. "Kneel, Santos." A ring flashed on one finger, and Santos flinched, a sharp pain filling him. The monsters made of flesh and bone shambled forward, their gigantic arms made of the intertwined limbs of the dead tipped with massive claws made of bone. The blood splattered across the room slithered like red snakes across the floor, wrapping around the girl's body before sinking into her pale skin. As the bright red liquid vanished into the body of The Summoner, the death magic of the necromancer/vampire increased. Razor-sharp slashes of power shredded through Santos. At first he thought it was an illusion, then he felt his cold vampire blood oozing from the many wounds covering his body.

"I said...kneel." The smirk was gone. A cold, impassive face stared at him. The white glowing eyes compelled him to obey.

Shuddering, Santos locked his legs, refusing to fall to The Summoner's power. "No."

A corner of The Summoner's lips twitched, a ghost of a smile appearing.

One of the monsters swung its long arm, its claws glistening wetly. Santos fell as his leg was torn from his body. Gritting his teeth, he refused to cry out or reveal his agony. Willing his wound to heal, he felt his powers waning. Silence filled the room. Lifting his head, he saw the vampires of his cabal were all shifting their healing bodies into kneeling positions. Gregorio was already prostrate before Etzli.

Striding over to Santos, The Summoner planted her small foot on his chest, shoving him onto his back. "You will kneel before me willingly." Pressing down, she broke his sternum, driving it into his heart. "Do you understand me?" Applying more pressure, she cracked ribs.

Blood bubbling on his lips, Santos glowered up at The Summoner.

"Kill him," Etzli said, her dark eyes hard as obsidian.

"No," The Summoner intervened. "Chop his other leg off, drain his blood, and pack him away until he's needed." Tilting her head, her blonde hair stained red by the blood she had consumed, The Summoner said to the cabal, "You serve me now."

"Yes, Master," they answered in unison.

"Our time comes." Leaning down, The Summoner gripped a handful of Santos's hair and drew his face close to hers. "You will see my greatness. You were a babe playing the games of children. Soon you will see true power."

Amaliya shoved the silver dagger into the sheath in her boot and reached for a second one tucked into the foam of the weapons locker Cian had hidden in the base of one of the guest beds in their penthouse.

"I'm carrying the obsidian blade and the silver-plated sword." Cian squatted beside her, loading a clip with silver bullets for the pistols. He wore thin black gloves to protect his hands. "I'm going to put the silver stakes in the black bag, the white birch in the red. The silver will work on both vampires and weres. The white birch is for Etzli. It's even stronger than silver."

"Gotcha."

Amaliya was glutted on the blood of the residents of Cian's apartment building. As soon as she had awakened, she had slipped in and out of the fancy apartments sipping from the throats of the inhabitants until she literally couldn't drink anymore. Cian had taught her to drink without killing, but her anger and grief was so strong it had been a struggle not to drain her victims dry. Red-tinged tears streaked her face. She hated that she was crying, yet how could she not? Not only was she mourning, she was furious. Her grandmother had been incredibly important in her life, and now she was gone. Wiping at her face, she struggled to steady her nerves.

"As soon as we reach Santos's mansion, bring the dead up. Have them attack whatever moves. Santos keeps a lot of blood minions, so keep that in mind if you need more blood." Cian's accent was thick, deep, and dangerous. "Don't hesitate to kill the minions if you need more bodies for zombies."

Amaliya nodded.

"I'll concentrate on Etzli." Cian hesitated, then slapped a clip into one of the pistols. His hazel eyes met hers. "The Summoner is yours."

"I'll kill him," Amaliya said in a tough voice. Her sweet little grandmother lay in a mortuary somewhere in Eastland County waiting to be prepared for burial in a few days. Innocente had only been dead less than twenty-four hours and already the void that she had left in Amaliya's life was unbearable.

"Staking didn't work on The Summoner, so try decapitation." Cian tucked the pistol into a holster on his belt.

"And if that doesn't work?"

"We'll figure it out," Cian said with a wry smile.

Amaliya grabbed the collar of his shirt, dragged him close, and kissed him. His tongue and lips were flavored with fresh blood. He tasted like power. Releasing him, Amaliya experienced a surge of love so powerful it hurt. She loved him. He loved her. It was one of two truths she knew without a doubt. The other was that The Summoner needed to die.

"I fuckin' love you," Amaliya growled at him before rising and stalking out of the room. "Now let's go kill that asshole."

Cian grabbed the bags of weapons and followed her out into the main living area of the apartment.

The vampires were dressed alike in black jeans, t-shirts, and boots. They needed clothes that allowed them to move quickly and hopefully without detection until it was too late for The Summoner and his people.

After they had returned the previous night from Fenton, Texas, Amaliya had waited until their friends left for their own homes and their house guests - Cassandra, Cian's dhamphir daughter and her girlfriend, Aimee, a witch - had gone upstairs, before informing Cian that she was going to kill The Summoner. The death of Innocente ate at her viciously, but the demise of Pete, her childhood friend who had died trying to save her, inspired a rage so powerful it made her tremble. The Summoner had murdered people who loved her, and she was going to kill him. She had found a way to kill him once, and she would again.

Cian placed the bags in the front hall, then checked his jean pockets for his car keys. "We'll take the back route into San Antonio. It's longer, but there is less of a chance of one of Santos' people spotting us before we hit the mansion."

Amaliya nodded tersely. "Sounds good."

A wisp of fear threaded through her raw fury, but she ignored it. Maybe it was a suicide run going after The Summoner, but she didn't want to acknowledge that possibility. She hadn't even discussed her plan with Cian when she had awakened. Cian had simply anticipated her desires and started preparations immediately.

"When are we leaving?" Cassandra asked, coming down the stairs from the second level of the apartment. Her girlfriend was right behind her. Both were dressed in black clothing and carried messenger bags. Cassandra's chin-length chestnut hair was pulled up into a fake Mohawk with rubber bands while Aimee's was in a long braid wrapped around her head several times.

"You told them?" Amaliya asked Cian, narrowing her eyes.

Cian shook his head. "No, of course not."

"It wasn't too hard to figure out that you'd want to kill The Summoner as soon as possible," Aimee said as she reached the main floor.

"And since he's most likely with Etzli's brother, it made sense to attack tonight before they can move," Cassandra finished.

"We can use the help, Liya," Cian said, lifting one shoulder.

"Fine, but let's get going." Amaliya had to admit she felt a little relief at the thought of the witch and dhamphir coming along.

The doorbell rang a few seconds later. Cian checked the security feed on his computer monitors. "It's Jeff and Samantha with the others."

"Was there a memo?" Sarcasm dripped from her words as Amaliya lifted her eyes to the heavens.

When the front door opened, Jeff, the leader of the local supernatural hunter group, entered first. He was closely followed by the perky blonde phasmagus that was his girlfriend. Samantha grinned when she saw Amaliya's glower and gave her a little wave. Eduardo, the hunky were-coyote, filed in before the rotund Benchley and his boyishly cute younger sister, Alexia.

"I've been trying to call you," Jeff informed Cian.

"I have my phone off." Cian folded his arms over his chest and surveyed the people dressed in dark clothes and carrying bulky bags most likely crammed with weapons.

"You weren't going to go without us, were you?" Samantha narrowed her eyes and poked Cian in the chest with one finger.

"The thought did occur to me," Cian confessed.

"Okay, the gang is all here. Let's go!" Amaliya headed toward the door.

Benchley moved to cut her off, his round face grimacing. "Not so fast."

"Out of my way, Bench."

The man flinched under her glare, but the sexy coyote stepped in front of Benchley and put his hands on Amaliya's shoulders. "Listen to the man."

Amaliya shrugged off Eduardo's hands. "Fine. What's up? Time is a' wasting."

"I was checking the local emergency channels in both Austin and San Antonio to make sure we don't run into any issues," Benchley said, holding up his phone.

"Then we heard something you're not going to like." Jeff joined the cluster of people in the front hall. "There's no point going to San Antonio."

"I'm still going. You're not going to stop me," Amaliya declared, pushing past Benchley and Eduardo.

"Santos' mansion burned to the ground today. It also burned a lot of the surrounding woods and one neighboring house. It's smoldering right now. The San Antonio fire departments were fighting it all day."

Jeff's words cut through her and sent her mind spinning. Slamming her hand against the heavy metal door, she growled with frustration. "What?"

In the main room, she could hear Cian tapping away at his computer.

"It's all burned up," Alexia said, wincing.

"Cian has it on the computer!" Samantha called out.

Amaliya stalked down the entry hall and into living room. Cian was at his computer watching a video from the local TV station. Lightly stroking his chin with his fingers, his hazel eyes flicked toward Amaliya when she leaned over him.

"No!" Amaliya hissed. "No!"

"They probably left last night," Cian said.

"Fuck! No!"

"Maybe they're dead in the fire," Benchley said hopefully.

Aimee and Cassandra joined the group of people crowding around to watch the news report on the fire.

"It's not unusual for vampires to burn their abandoned havens," Cassandra remarked. "It makes it harder to find out where they've gone."

"Nothing left for a tracking spell," Aimee muttered.

"Maybe they're dead. In the fire." Benchley tapped Cian on the shoulder. "Right? Maybe it was an accident and they all burned? Right?"

Cian shook his head. "No. No. This is what Cassandra surmised. The Summoner and his people abandoned it last night and had someone burn it down during the daylight hours."

"I'm sorry, Amaliya," Samantha said, patting her on the shoulder.

"Fuck this shit!" Amaliya shouted, storming away from the looks of sympathy and pity. She launched herself out onto the balcony, her fingers closing around the rail. The scream that erupted out of her was torn away by the hot night wind. Grabbing fistfuls of her hair, she buckled over, weeping. When Cian took her in his arms, she sank against him.

"I'm sorry, Liya."

"I want him dead," she sobbed. "I want that fucker dead!"

"I know. I know." Cian kissed her brow and held her firmly against his body.

"It's not fuckin' fair that he killed her. It's not fuckin' fair! She was trying to save Bianca!"

"Innocente was a very good person," Cian agreed.

"I want to fuckin' rip his fuckin' head off!"

"And you will."

Clinging to Cian as her rage dissolved into despair, Amaliya shuddered. It was as if her body couldn't fully contain the strong emotions roaring through her.

"Liya, Jeff is going to research the rings that The Summoner wanted so desperately. Once we find out what The Summoner is planning, we'll find him and stop him. You'll take his head. You will avenge Innocente and Pete. I know it."

Lifting her head, she stared out over the Austin skyline toward the south. "Do you think he's still in San Antonio?"

"I have a feeling he picked that city for a reason. So, yes, I do think he's still there." Cian pressed his lips against her forehead, his hands rubbing her back to soothe her.

In all her life, only Cian could calm her when she felt like this. Only he felt like a safe harbor from her dark emotions. When she was at her weakest, he always made her feel strong.

"You *are* strong," Cian whispered against her cheek. "You're amazing. You will get your revenge. I swear it."

Nodding, she wiped her tears away with irritation. "I will."

"But we need to go now. Not to San Antonio, but my secondary haven. The Summoner is in hiding and we should be, too."

"It's all falling apart," Amaliya moaned. She had tried so hard to adapt to her new life, and just when she was finally settling into it, The Summoner had once again wrecked it.

"No, no. Not falling apart, Liya. Just changing."

Amaliya knew he was right, but all the recent changes were filled with blood, pain and death. The only way to stop it would be through blood, pain, and the death of The Summoner.

CHAPTER TWO

Two Weeks Later

"Lucifer's sword was found by the Mayans. They believed it was the weapon of a fallen god and built a temple to house it. The Spanish conquered the Mayans, took the sword and the myth around it, and delivered it as a gift to the Catholic Church."

Amaliya sat in the big back room of Jeff Summerfield's occult book shop listening to the information gleaned over the last few weeks by the young man with the soulful eyes and messy brown hair. Outside, the summer wind pummeled the side of the old house that was transformed into the bookstore. The tall pecan trees that bordered the building pelted the metal roof with nuts. The sound was a little distracting as Amaliya tried to pay attention to Jeff. The long oak table was surrounded by a strange assortment of people. Cans of soda and cups of coffee sat before the humans, while the spaces before the supernatural beings remained bare. Though Jeff and his group of friends called themselves vampire hunters, they were actually more along the lines of paranormal investigators. Amaliya liked all of them but wasn't too sure how effective they would be in the coming battle with the ancient vampire who had created her and infused her with his necromantic powers. Looking around the table, she wondered again if maybe she should just try to find The Summoner on her own. The people were definitely a motley crew of mortals and supernaturals.

Benchley and his sister, Alexia, were regular humans that had started off as paranormal investigators before becoming hunters. Samantha had been Cian's mortal girlfriend before Amaliya had landed in their lives and disrupted it. Now the perky blonde was a phasmagus – someone who could control the spirits of the dead – thanks to ingesting Amaliya's blood when the vampire had tried to save her life. Rachoń, the strikingly beautiful black woman next to Jeff, was Cian's vampire sister who ruled all of Louisiana and up until a few weeks before had been considered an arch enemy. Cassandra, Cian's dhamphir daughter, and her witch girlfriend, Aimee, sat snuggled at the end of the table. Amaliya liked both the women and was glad that they had decided to stay in Austin and join the fight against The Summoner. The man sitting near them was not so welcomed in her eyes. She wanted her cousin, Sergio, to go home and be with his wife and kids.

"They gave the Catholic Church Lucifer's sword?" Eduardo, the were-coyote and the last of their crew, let out a snort of contempt. "That's pretty stupid."

The geekily cute Alexia shook her head at Eduardo. "Actually, it makes sense. It would've been made in heaven. It may have been his sword, but it could've been considered a holy relic."

Amaliya rolled her eyes. The whole story sounded outlandish to her, but there was something up with the ring The Summoner had worn. It had to be important for him to recall an entire cemetery searching for it. She shivered, remembering how cruel the possessed Bianca had appeared. Though she hadn't really inter-acted with the girl when they were both attending college, Amaliya had always thought of Bianca as pretty, sweet, and very shy. She'd even suspected Bianca had a crush on her after often catching the younger woman stealing looks in her direction.

Jeff was talking again, so Amaliya attempted to pay attention. She felt rest-less. Sitting and discussing all of the information Jeff had discovered was not the action she craved. She wanted to find a way to kill The Summoner and be done with him once and for all. It still stung that she had not been able to kill him before he had slipped away into hiding.

"...someone in the Vatican decided that it would be a great idea to melt down the sword and create rings out of it. Well, originally, they wanted to make a crown, too, but when the blacksmith melted the sword, it lost mass. In the end, he only had enough gold for the rings. The jeweler made thirteen rings: one for the Pope and twelve for select archbishops."

"Does this sound like a horror movie in the making or what?" Eduardo winked at Amaliya. He was flirting with her to piss off Cian. She had to admit the coyote was very attractive with his sleek black hair and chiseled physique. There was also an aura of danger about him that Amaliya found enticing.

"Totally *Exorcist* material," Benchley mumbled from across the table.

"So what happened to the rings, Jeff?" Amaliya wanted to hurry up the meeting so she could get the hell out of the building and back to their new home. She and Samantha were going to practice using their powers together in prepara-tion to fight The Summoner. Sitting around and plotting was not Amaliya's forte.

"Well, they made the wearer go crazy. And realizing what was happening, the Jesuits collected the rings, divided them up among thirteen devout priests, and sent them out all over the world to hide the rings."

Cian raised his eyes toward the ceiling but said nothing. Amaliya could tell he wasn't liking what he was hearing.

"And somehow the vampires found out about them," Rachoń stated from where she sat near Jeff. Her maroon-colored eyes narrowed in thought.

Amaliya wondered if Cian and Rachoń had noticed anything odd about the ring The Summoner wore. Probably not, she decided.

"Yeah. About a hundred years ago, they became a hot commodity among the vampires," Jeff continued.

"About the time that The Summoner was holed up in some Mayan temples in the Yucatán Peninsula," Cian muttered to Amaliya significantly.

"That was when he kidnapped Etzli." Rachoń gave a slight shake of her head. Amaliya knew that Rachoń and The Summoner had been lovers for a very long time. Cian had said she was The Summoner's favorite. The Summoner, however, had mocked Rachoń's devotion to her human family and taken Etzli to be his cohort. If that hadn't happened, Amaliya couldn't help but wonder if Rachoń would still be on his side or theirs.

"She's been in on it all along," Cian said, his hazel eyes gazing into Amaliya's.

Amaliya nodded in agreement. She'd never liked Etzli. The tiny woman had taken way too much pleasure out of her brother Santos torturing Amaliya when she'd been dumped in their territory by Cian's duplicitous ex-mortal servant, Roberto.

Jeff straightened up the files on the table and cleared his throat. Amaliya wanted to shout at him to get on with it.

At last, Jeff concluded, "So, uh, well, lots of different hunter groups have been tracking down the individual rings over the years, but no one knew they were all connected. Not until now. The rings all ended up with different names and different legends, but when Cass and Aimee stole the ring from the Master of Dallas and then connected it to The Summoner, it all became clear."

"He wants the rings. All of them!" Amaliya said, trying to urge Jeff to hurry the hell up.

Cian's hand rubbed her knee affectionately, and he leaned toward her to whisper, "Let Jeff have his moment."

Lowering her own voice, Amaliya answered, "I'm about to lose it here."

The gentle squeeze of Cian's cool hand only made her more impatient. Now she wanted to go home, fuck Cian, and then practice her powers with Samantha.

Returning her attention to the conversation, Amaliya heard Benchley exclaim, "What if that date is significant for another reason? What if it has to do with these rings that used to be a sword? Think about it. What if the Mayans figured out that on that date if the sword is used properly, it could bring destruction down on us?"

Amaliya was so sick and tired of all the end of the world talk about 2012. People were so paranoid. "But why destroy the world? What does The Summoner get out of that? He seems real intent on living."

Cian's grip tightened a bit on her leg, and she felt the tension within him ratcheting up. "He has always been thwarted by the sun. Always. From the beginning of his existence as a vampire, he has always been confined to the night. Maybe he wants to eliminate his ultimate enemy – the sun."

Rachoń lifted her eyes, fear filling them. "Rip open the veil to the abyss and darkness consumes the earth."

"But he'll let out all the demons, the monsters of the pit..." Alexia sunk lower in her chair, looking overwhelmed by the idea. "Of course, he'd love that."

Cassandra finally spoke up. "So he wants to destroy the world. Great."

"So we stop him," the witch beside her said in a calm, determined tone.

"But how?" Sergio asked. "We're just a bunch of...uh..."

"Fuck ups? Rejects?" Amaliya grinned, lifting her eyebrows.

Eduardo frowned. "Speak for yourself. I'm pretty awesome."

Rachoń dismissed Eduardo's comment with the flick of her hand. "Some vampires will help him, you know."

"And you?" Cian's question was sharp. Amaliya knew Cian didn't trust her.

"I love my family, he was right about that. And some members of my family aren't vampires. I don't want them to die." Rachoń met Cian's gaze evenly and defiantly.

Sergio leaned his big body over the table to confront Cian. "What about you? Do you want an eternal night?"

"No." Cian gave Amaliya a furtive look. It was unreadable, but somehow she got the gist of it. The idea of an eternal night was alluring, but Cian would not sacrifice those he loved to obtain it.

Cassandra pounded the table with a clenched hand. "I say we send out what we know to the hunters and get a coalition going. We need to track down these rings and keep them from him."

Amaliya raked her fingers through her long hair, leaning back in her chair with exasperation and nervousness. "If we do that, he'll know that we figured out what he's up to. He'll come for us."

Beside her, Samantha reached out to touch Amaliya's shoulder. "He's going to come for you anyway. At some point, he'll come for you, because it's obvious he tried to make you and Bianca for a reason. Now that he's in her body, he's going to try to claim you."

"What do you mean?" Amaliya narrowed her eyes at the blonde, nervous that she was right.

"He must need another necromancer to help him pull off whatever he means to do." Samantha gave her arm a gentle squeeze.

Jeff nodded and shut the book he'd been reading from earlier. "She's right. Why else would he have tried to make you and Bianca? It makes perfect sense that he needs you."

Cian took Amaliya's hand. "So we have pieces of his puzzle that he will come for."

"Yeah." Jeff winced.

"Then we'll be ready for him." Cian's hand tightened around Amaliya's.

Rachoń gave a curt nod of her head. "We create a coalition then, and we stop him."

Cian also nodded. "We have no other choice."

Cassandra leaned forward in her chair. "We fight."

Eduardo grinned fiendishly. "Until we die."

The witch gave him a dire look. "Or win."

"Like Buffy and the Scoobies," Samantha said, sounding almost jovial.

"Nothing will take you from me." Cian stared into Amaliya's eyes, a vow in his words.

"I won't let him take me," Amaliya said, pressing her lips to his hand.

"So let's get to planning..." Jeff said.

"Any ideas on where we can find the asshole?" Benchley questioned.

"Too bad he burned down Santos's mansion," Alexia groused.

"He knew we would come for him there," Cian said.

They learned that the blaze had devoured the mansion and part of the surrounding greenbelt. The amount of burned bodies in the mansion had caused quite a stir in the media. Santos had created a fake persona for all his human dealings, so the police were after a serial killer phantom that didn't actually exist. Meanwhile, Santos had vanished, along with his sister, cabal, and The Summoner.

Benchley stared into his cup of cold coffee, looking grim and a little afraid. "I wonder where the psycho pixie is now."

"Poor Bianca," Alexia said in a sad voice.

"Poor Grandmama." Sergio's green eyes darkened with emotion. "She was trying to save someone who doesn't exist."

Amaliya shifted in her chair, uncomfortable with the subject of Bianca. Her memories of the girl were now mixed with those of The Summoner. It made it difficult for her to sympathize with the girl she had barely spoken to in college. Guilt ate at Amaliya. Why had she risen, but not Bianca? Why had Bianca truly died while Amaliya had turned into a vampire?

"Vampires don't rise after three days. When Bianca came out of the grave, we should have known it was him." The regret in Rachoń's voice and manner surprised Amaliya until she remembered that Prosper had died at the hands of the risen girl. "Though I cannot set the past right, I can send you help. A member of my family will be coming to Austin to assist you. His name is Baptiste. He's an elemagus."

"What's that?" Samantha asked.

"He can manipulate the elements," Alexia answered.

"Like an elementalist in *Guild Wars*," Benchley added, trying to be helpful.

"*I don't know what that is.*" Samantha squinted her eyes at Benchley, then understanding crept into her gaze. "*Oh! Is that a game?*"

Benchley opened his mouth to answer, but Alexia clamped her hand over it. "It's a game, but that's not important. Elemagus are very rare, so this kinda puts us ahead of the game."

"We're becoming a team of supernatural rarities." Jeff's tone didn't reveal whether he found this to be a positive or negative trait. He frowned at his cup of coffee, then got up to pour more.

"Phasmagus in the house!" Samantha said, holding up her hands.

"But we could use more help," Cian said pointedly to Rachoń.

Instantly the tension in the room increased. Amaliya set her hand over Cian's, hoping he'd keep his temper in check. Jeff hesitated where he stood with the pot of hot coffee in his hand.

"I have Louisiana to take care of." Crossing her legs, Rachoń rested her hands on her lap, her maroon eyes never wavering from Cian's gaze. "Baptiste is powerful. He's already asked to come to Austin to join the fight. Prosper was his great-grandfather. He wants revenge against The Summoner."

"And we appreciate you sending him," Samantha said swiftly, shooting Cian a look that basically told him to shut up.

Cian frowned but didn't speak.

"Cian, why don't you just make vampires?" Sergio asked. "Seriously. I'm sure there are a whole lot of *Twilight* fans who'd love to be a vampire."

"I would be creating cannon fodder," Cian answered. "They'd be low-powered and easily killed."

"And we're not?" Benchley scowled as he pointed to his sister, Sergio, and himself. "We're human. We're not super-peeps."

"But you're well-trained vampire hunters who work for The Assembly." Cassandra shifted in her chair, the wood creaking in protest. She looked a little uncomfortable with the topic. Amaliya had been observing Cian's daughter for the last two weeks, and it was obvious that she tried to live as a mortal as much as possible. Amaliya was starting to suspect Cassandra wasn't always comfortable with the vampire side of her nature.

Rachoń filled the awkward silence by speaking up. "New vampires are unpredictable, weak, and have to be under constant watch by their creators. If Cian made a bunch of vampires, he'd have to exert his control over them constantly."

"Which would be draining," Cian said, agreeing.

"Which would make you weaker instead of being at full strength." Amaliya felt the need to defend Cian. He was dealing with enough without being reminded that he had screwed up by not building his cabal. But then again, he couldn't have anticipated all that was happening. Cian had wanted a low-stress life without vampire politics. Obviously, that had not been in the cards for his life.

Cian squeezed her hand lightly. "Exactly."

Amaliya loved the feel of his skin under her hand and the way his gaze made her feel. They were united in this battle.

"What if Amaliya makes a vampire?" Sergio dared to ask.

"I wouldn't," Amaliya said swiftly. The mere thought terrified her. "I can barely control what's happening to me. And look at what my blood did to Sam..."

Samantha winced but had to bob her head in agreement. "She totally fucked me up."

Amaliya stuck her tongue out at her former rival. Samantha returned the gesture.

"What if she makes another one just like The Summoner?" Rachoń interjected. "There's no assurance that the fledgling would side with us. The Summoner made all of the vampires in this room. His blood is within us." She pointed at Cian. "You and I know that the only reason we can stand against him is because of our age."

"But Amaliya can stand against him." Samantha cast a big smile at Amaliya. "She can totally kick his ass."

A shiver ran through Amaliya at the thought of how hard it was to defy The Summoner when her creator's power mingled with her own. It was very difficult to admit how much sway he still had over her whenever she was near him.

Cian looked at their combined hands while Rachoń lifted her eyebrows slightly.

Jeff abandoned his seat at the end of the table to pull another chair close to Samantha. Sitting down, he gazed at Amaliya pensively while nursing his hot cup of coffee.

Benchley and Alexia stared at Amaliya with open curiosity. They had not been in the graveyard to see the last battle between Amaliya and The Summoner.

"Well, she can!" Samantha looked defensive. "We all saw her do it!"

Settling back in her chair, Rachoń regarded Amaliya thoughtfully. "How hard was it?"

Amaliya shrugged, not enjoying the feeling of being put on the spot.

"You missed the make-out session," Cassandra said to Samantha under her breath. "Amaliya totally lip locked with The Summoner."

Cian gave his daughter a sharp look, his hazel eyes cold.

"Well, she did," Cassandra said.

Amaliya met Samantha's stare with a defiant tilt of her chin. She didn't feel she should be judged for something she had no control over. Whenever she was around The Summoner, his magic called to her in a way that was difficult to fight.

"Really?" Samantha was clearly grossed out. "*Really?*"

"It's a vampire thing," Amaliya answered. "He created me. We're connected. It's hard not to..."

"Did *you* make out with him, Cian?" Samantha leaned forward to peer past Amaliya at her former fiancé.

This brought a surprisingly girlish giggle from Rachoń.

Cian ignored the question and his sister's laughter. Remaining silent, his fingers played with the rings Amaliya wore.

"Ha! You were his bitch!" Eduardo's laugh was more like a bark than a human sound.

"Do you want me to kill you that badly?" Cian asked the coyote.

"Look! Everyone knows how hard it is to break free from a vampire's blood bond." Cassandra pounded her fist on the table to get everyone's attention. "It fucks your brain up hardcore. So it's not her fault."

Sergio let out an explosive sigh.

Amaliya glowered at her cousin across from her. "What?"

"Your life is so fucked up," he said sadly.

Aimee set her hands on the table and took a deep breath. "Everyone leave her alone. I was bonded to a vampire. It's not easy to defy them. I'm a true witch and not a mortal so I had a certain amount of immunity, but it was still very, very difficult to break free."

"How did you do it?" Sergio asked. "Can you do the same for Amal?"

Pressing her lips together, Cassandra appeared uneasy. Aimee gave her a significant look, but Cassandra responded with a short shake of her head.

Aimee sighed, her fingers fidgeting with the bracelets she wore on one wrist. After a long pause, she said, "I don't know if I can help a vampire. It was a spell I had to cast. It was complicated."

Curiosity gripped Amaliya. She had a feeling the dhamphir and witch were hiding something significant and not willing to divulge the information. One look at Cian revealed that he thought the same, but he gave her hand a light squeeze to keep her from saying anything. They'd talk to the women later.

"So if you can't make vampires, what are you going to do?" Sergio asked Cian, his eyes narrowed. "Without more people how the hell do you plan to take on The Summoner?"

"That's the thing," Jeff said, speaking up. "If we can keep him from getting all the rings, we may not have to fight to keep him from tearing the veil. The Assembly is going to help us track down the rings and claim them. I've been on the phone most of the last few days trying to get some sort of plan going among all the various groups."

"And we have one hidden," Cassandra muttered.

"That puts us ahead automatically, right?" Aimee ventured a small encouraging smile.

"Except he will still come for Amaliya." Rachoń tilted her head and regarded the tattooed woman with a quite serious expression. "You're unique. He'll want you at his side even if he fails to rip open the veil."

"That's their fight," Eduardo said, gesturing toward Cian and Amaliya. "Not mine."

Samantha glowered at the coyote. "Do you have to be such an asshole?"

"I'm stating the truth. We're all here to save the world, not her. Even if she is pretty fuckin' hot and I'd love to bend her—"

Cian kicked Eduardo's chair over. The coyote hit the floor, rolled, and came up growling. Instantly on his feet, Cian bared his fangs, eyes flashing red.

Amaliya rolled her eyes. "Oh, my gawd! Calm the fuck down, boys!"

"Don't push me, vampire," Eduardo said around a mouthful of sharp teeth.

"You're in my city because I allow it," Cian answered. "Amaliya is mine, not yours."

"Excuse me?" Amaliya slammed her high heels onto the floor and stood with her hands on her hips. "I'm my own person, Cian, and your girlfriend. You don't own me."

Rachoń laughed with delight. "And you wonder why I won't send more of my people to help you."

Back me up. He's challenging my authority, Cian's voice said clearly in Amaliya's mind. *Don't weaken me.*

"But Cian is totally the boss of the city, and what he says goes," Amaliya said quickly, her brow furrowing. Had she really heard Cian's words in her head? She didn't want to undermine him, so she decided to act as though she had somehow really heard him. "I'm totally in his corner, so back your shit down, Eduardo."

Eduardo narrowed his non-human eyes at her.

"So if I tell you to help me defend Amaliya, you will do exactly that or you will leave my city." Cian met the coyote's gaze. His lean muscled body was tensed for battle.

Using the tip of his boot, Eduardo up righted his chair, slumped into it, and nodded. "Fine."

"The truth of the matter is that we all have a role to play," Cian said, turning to face the people gawking at him from around the table. "Jeff, coordinate with The Assembly. Aimee, find a way to set up strong wards against any form of attack and we need the most powerful defensive and offensive spells you can mix. Alexia, you need to start building a communication center so we can keep track of what is going on. Rachoń, send Baptiste, but you better prepare your people to fight if the veil does come down. Benchley, you know a lot about ghosts and mediums, so help Samantha. Samantha, you need to be at full power, so you'll need to practice, and often. Amaliya, I expect you to do the same. Cass, I will need you to build an arsenal that will be able to take out supernaturals. Sergio, go home. This isn't your fight."

"I'm invested in this, too! I have a family," Sergio exclaimed.

"You're also a liability. You're not trained for this." Cian remained standing, arms folded over his chest. Amaliya remained at his side, trying to look supportive and imposing.

"Then train me!"

"Go home," Amaliya said, tired of the fighting. "Sergio, I already lost Grandmama. Do I have to lose you, too?"

With a grunt of frustration, Sergio looked away from her. "Fine."

"What will you do, Cian?" Jeff ventured to ask.

"Talk to the other vampires and hope I can convince them to side with us," Cian answered.

"Any chance they'll do that?" Cass asked.

Cian lifted his shoulders. "I don't know."

"So we're done," Jeff said.

"We know what we need to do," Cass agreed.

Cian shoved the chair he had been sitting in back under the table. "Let's get to work."

As the group split apart, forming small pockets scattered across the room, Amaliya followed Cian along the short hall into a smaller room filled with bookshelves. Taking hold of her wrists, he tugged her close, kissing her deeply.

"You heard me in your mind," he said in a soft voice when they parted.

She nodded.

Cian grinned. "Finally. I've been trying to break through that tough head of yours for months."

"You hear my thoughts, don't you?" Amaliya asked. She had always wondered but was afraid to ask.

"Yes. Not always, but sometimes." Cian slid his hands up her arms to rest on her shoulders.

Did you notice Aimee and Cassandra when talking about the blood bond?
Cian nodded.

Amaliya was both unnerved and impressed by their new connection. *They know how to break it, don't they?*

Maybe. I don't want to push too hard...yet.

"Still trying to connect with her?" Amaliya said aloud. She pressed her hand to his cheek, and he turned to kiss her palm. The pulse of his power enraptured her. She loved him so much.

"Yes, but it's not easy. Though getting better."

"Sorry to interrupt, but I'm leaving. I have much to do," Rachoń's voice said from behind them.

Cian turned and nodded. "We'll be in touch."

"You do realize that most vampires have no reason to side with us, don't you, Cian?"

"I can try to convince them otherwise."

"You'll most likely fail," Rachoń said.

"We'll prepare for the worst." As always, Cian sounded reassuringly calm and confident.

"That's good. Because the worst *will* probably happen." Rachoń's maroon eyes settled on Amaliya. "Unless you have any ideas of what to do?"

This comment surprised Amaliya. "Why me?"

"Because you're the closest thing we have to The Summoner. You're more like him than any of us. If anyone can figure out how to destroy him and win this, it's most likely you." Rachoń's gaze was unwavering.

Maybe Cian sensed her sudden panic, for he took her hand once again. As always, her first instinct was to run, but she knew it wasn't an option anymore. She cared too much about the people willing to fight with her against The Summoner. She loved Cian too much. And, if she was honest with herself, what Rachoń said made perfect sense.

"I'll see what I can figure out," Amaliya said at last.

Rachoń's lips turned up at the corners just a bit. "You do that."

Then she was gone.

Facing her again, Cian kept a firm hold on Amaliya's hand. "We have time. Don't stress yourself."

"Maybe," Amaliya answered. "But if our luck stays the way it's been going, we may end up scrambling right up until the big deadline."

"December 21, 2012." The words were spoken with distaste. "Wouldn't it be amusing if at last one of the dire prophecies got the date right?"

Amaliya sneered at the thought. "I just don't want to be scrambling with our backs against the wall up until the very end. I'd like for us to have a real life one of these days."

"A real life would be nice." Cian kissed her again, making her shiver with love and lust.

"Can we go home now? I really want to get you naked."

With a chuckle, Cian said, "My thoughts exactly."

CHAPTER THREE

When Cassandra observed her father and Amaliya slip out of the room into the hallway, guilt gave her conscience a little nip as relief swept over her. Though she was definitely warming to Cian and they were making strides in their father/daughter relationship, she wanted to speak with Aimee alone before he inevitably questioned them about possibly breaking the blood tie between Amaliya and The Summoner.

Warily watching Rachoń as the vampire spoke with Samantha, Cassandra gripped Aimee's hand and drew her girlfriend away from the others. Rachoń's curious looks in Cassandra's direction had her on edge, and there was no way Cassandra wanted Rachoń to overhear what she had to say to her girlfriend. Aimee, as she tended to do with incredible ease, appeared to understand what had Cassandra so concerned and gave her a slight nod.

Fingers tenderly brushing over Cassandra's palm, Aimee gave her a reassuring smile while her eyes darted to the doorway to Jeff's office. Together, they slipped through the threshold, and Cassandra shut the door behind them.

"Ugh!" Cassandra exclaimed, clutching her head in her hands. "Vampires! They give me such a headache."

"Cass, it's fine. Don't be nervous." Aimee's touch against her cheek was gentle and soothing.

"Well, vampires tend to make me nervous. You know they kill my kind," Cassandra groused but leaned into Aimee's tender ministrations.

"No one touches my girl." Aimee gave her a brief peck on the lips. "Plus, Cian won't let anyone hurt you. You already have him wrapped around your little finger."

"Yeah, dear old vampire dad." Cassandra rolled her eyes even though the comment pleased her.

She wanted to have a real relationship with Cian, but whenever she was around him, she felt apprehensive, which prompted her to flip her sarcasm switch and keep him at arm's length. He had already made it clear that he wanted to forge a close relationship with her, but it scared her as much as thrilled her. Every time she looked at him, she could see herself reflected in his face. And sometimes what she saw scared her. Cian was a powerful and sometimes terrifying vampire. What did that say about the vampire side of her nature?

Aimee cocked her head and studied Cassandra with a gaze that always made Cassandra feel like Aimee was peeling away all her carefully constructed layers until the witch could peer into her soul. "You're not a vampire. You may be like him in some ways, like your mannerisms and looks, but his vampire nature makes him very different from you."

"Are you reading my mind?"

"No, I just know you very, very well, Cass. There is a darkness in Cian that you don't have."

"And yet here we are hanging out with him like he's one of the good guys."

Aimee shrugged her delicate shoulders. "Compared to The Summoner, he *is* a good guy."

Cassandra perched on the edge of Jeff's desk, mindful not to spill anything onto the floor. "Aimee, he's going to want the bond between Amaliya and The Summoner broken. And since he now knows we broke your blood enslavement, he's going to want us to do the same for her."

"And you're freaking out why?"

"It's *my* blood that broke the bond between you and that asshole!"

Cassandra hated even to think about Frank, the vampire who had kept Aimee as a slave. Though she had gone to Aimee's rescue, in the end, they had saved each other from Frank's clutches. Knowing that Aimee had been at the mercy of Frank for so long still angered Cassandra, but at least her dhamphir blood had been able to break the bond between them. Aimee was strong, fearless, and the more level-headed one in the relationship, but Cassandra held her at night when the witch thrashed about in her sleep, still attempting to escape Frank in her nightmares.

"But I'm a witch," Aimee said. "It's different."

"How?"

"Frank's blood was poisoning me, binding me to him like that. It was like an infection. An illness. Your blood cured me, and it would cure a human who was under the same type of thrall. But Amaliya was *created* from The Summoner's blood. She's a new creature because of him. She's *infused* with his power, his blood, his everything. In some ways, she's a piece of him. Probably more so than his regular vampire offspring like Rachoń and Cian. Maybe your blood could dampen *their* bond to him if it was an issue, but Amaliya..." Aimee's brow crinkled even more. "She's all tangled up in The Summoner."

"So she's fucked?" Cassandra liked the idea of her blood staying in her own veins, but at the same time she felt terrible for any person bound by a vampire.

"I could try to figure out if there is a way, but..." Aimee averted her eyes, her fingertips lightly thrumming against her bottom lip.

A chill flowed down Cassandra's spine, and she shivered. "You're thinking she'd have to drain me totally to get free, aren't you?"

Aimee flinched. "That's a distinct possibility."

"I vote we find another way. I have no desire to die." Cassandra folded her arms across her small breasts and stuck out her chin defiantly.

"Babe, no one is going to ask that of you. Especially your own father." It was Aimee's turn to roll her eyes.

Cassandra's heels thumped against the desk as she swung her legs. "Yeah, yeah, but still. This is why my kind keeps under the radar. The big bad scary vampires are total dicks when it comes to dhamphirs."

Aimee set her hands on Cassandra's thighs and leaned toward her. "Babe, listen to me. You're freaking out because of the shit that went down with Frank. I get it. But we made it through all of that. We *will* make it through this, too. I'm a badass witch, and you're a hot sexy ass kicker. We can do anything we put our minds to. I know that."

Staring into the face of the woman she loved with all her heart, Cassandra's heart skipped a beat and she found it a little hard to breathe. Aimee was not only beautiful, she was pure power. Her inner strength was undeniable and sometimes a little scary.

"We're ahead in the game, right? The ring is safe."

"The ring is safe, Cass. The Summoner has no idea where it is. We're going to do everything in our power to keep him from succeeding. We're going to win."

Cassandra rested her hands on Aimee's, caressing the slim fingers adorned with layers of rings. She could feel the power pulsing inside the stone amulets. "We just can't lose. I think of what my mom went through when she lived with the vampires and what it did to her. I don't want that to happen to everyone in the world."

Galina, Cassandra's mother, struggled to retain memories, often slipping into the past when not grounded in the present. She kept a notebook full of tidbits she needed to remember, which included information about her own daughter. Cassandra had to place updated photos of herself alongside the recent entries so her mother would remember her daughter was now an adult. There was only one thing that Galina seemed to be able to remember without her notebook: Aimee. From the moment Galina had met Cassandra's true love, her mother had full recall on her interactions with Aimee. At first it had hurt Cassandra's feelings, but then she realized it was Aimee's inner light that anchored Galina's mind. Maybe it would slowly heal her until Cassandra's mother wouldn't need a notebook to remember that she no longer lived in Austin with a vampire cabal that used her for sex and blood. Maybe at last Galina would stop pining for Cian and waiting for him to come for her.

"A world ruled by The Summoner, vampires, and demons is not one I want to live in either," Aimee said.

"Cian's going to ask about the blood bond. What are you going to say?"

"I'm going to ask for Amaliya's blood. Then I'll see what I can figure out."

"But he can find out about the myth about my blood. You found out."

"There are a lot of myths about dhamphirs, including that you're boneless."

"Well, I *can* do that creepy compression trick," Cassandra reminded her. It unnerved her, but Cassandra could fit through very small openings. Her body just folded up at her will, allowing her to squeeze through the tightest of spots.

"My point is that there are a lot of rumors about your kind, but not much is absolute fact. Cian's aware of that. Hell, you aren't consumed with the unyielding desire to kill him, are you?"

"Well..."

Aimee's eyes narrowed.

"I'm joking! No. No. And I don't have the unhealthy desire to drink my mother's blood." Cassandra made a face. "I see what you're saying though. He doesn't know any more than the rest of them when it comes to what I can and can't do."

Her girlfriend gave her a brief nod. "We control the information when it comes to what you can or can't do."

"I feel like I'm lying."

"Well, you sorta are," Aimee said. "We have to take care of ourselves. They don't know everything that I'm capable of. Heck, *I* don't know everything that I'm capable of. And, if you want to be perfectly honest, most of the people in this makeshift cabal don't either. Amaliya is still growing into her power. So is Samantha. Out of all of us, Cian is probably the only one who has a handle on his nature."

"And then we have the mortals." Cassandra sighed.

"It's good that Sergio is going home."

"Maybe Benchley and Alexia should stay out of this, too."

Aimee shook her head. "They've been a part of this for too long. They know what's up."

Cassandra drew Aimee closer, her hands resting on her waist. Peering up at her, Cassandra said, "If you want to go, we can get my mom and try to go find a place to hide."

Setting her slim fingers against Cassandra's neck, Aimee leaned her forehead against Cassandra's. Her bronze-colored hair fell around them like a fragrant veil. "We can't hide from this."

With a heavy exhalation of surrender, Cassandra acknowledged this truth. "Yeah."

"Just let me do the talking about the blood issue and trust me to deal with it. Okay?"

"Okay."

"And don't freak out." Aimee kissed Cassandra's lips tenderly.

"Keep doing that and the last thing on my mind will be freaking out," Cassandra whispered, then returned the kiss.

"So what do you think they're doing in there?" Benchley asked, spearing the office door with an annoyed look.

"Making out," Eduardo decided.

"Yeah," Alexia said wistfully. She rocked back and forth on her heels, coming across a tad forlorn.

Jeff gave her a little side hug, striving to comfort her. Alexia's latest boyfriend had turned out to be a bit of a jerk, and the break up was fresh. With a little sigh, the tomboy gave him one of her scarily strong, tight squeezes. She was small but tough. For the last year she'd been taking *krav maga,* the Israeli martial arts, and he could feel it in her grip. Letting go of him, Alexia hopped away and sat on the edge of the table.

Jeff glanced over his shoulder to check on Samantha. She was still talking to Rachoń and seemed not to be intimidated at all. The female vampire's imposing demeanor and keen intelligence made Jeff uneasy. Although Cian had accepted Rachoń's offer of support of their endeavors, she was still a notorious vampire with a long history of not so pleasant exploits. Perhaps she was good to her family, but she was ruthless where all others were concerned. Jeff couldn't help but worry about her playing them all for fools and plotting behind their backs. Stupid vampires were easy to deal with. Smart ones were terrifying.

Benchley must have noted his interest in the conversation across the room, because he said, "What do you think they're they talking about?"

"Rachoń wants to know if Samantha saw Prosper's ghost in the graveyard," Eduardo answered, yawning dramatically and flashing his sharp canines.

"Oh." Benchley obviously hadn't considered that Rachoń might be interested in such a thing. "I guess that makes sense."

"I'm sure Amaliya has asked Samantha about Innocente." Alexia sighed and plunged her hands into the pockets of her hoodie. "Hell, I was tempted to ask about Mom and Dad."

The siblings' parents had died in a car accident, and only the two kids in the back seat had survived. Their parents' death was the main reason Alexia and Benchley had come into Jeff's bookstore seeking answers about the afterlife and how he'd ended up befriending them.

"Well, I don't like her talking to Sam. We should go over there." Benchley folded his arms over his chest, set his feet apart, and glowered at the vampire.

"We're in the same room, Bench." Jeff was uncomfortable, too, but Samantha looked calm and interested in whatever Rachoń was saying.

"And she's a phasmagus," Alexia added.

"And I'm here," Eduardo said, pretending to stretch so he could flex his impressive arms.

Alexia feigned gagging.

Eduardo grinned.

"Still..." Benchley frowned, ignoring the moment of lightheartedness.

Jeff's best friend tended to be overly protective of Samantha due to his still-unresolved crush on her. Jeff didn't mind it. Benchley had a terrible track record when it came to dating and tended to be infatuated with unattainable women. Jeff wasn't too surprised that Benchley mooned over Samantha, but he was hoping he'd be over it soon.

Sergio emerged from the nearby restroom and strode over. Amaliya's cousin was tall, muscular, and a little imposing until he smiled. He was loyal and good-natured, but tonight he was scowling almost as much as Benchley.

"I guess this is where I call it," Sergio said. The man was obviously still grumpy about his dismissal.

"It's for the best, man." Benchley clapped the other man on the shoulder. "Shit is going to go down and you've got kids."

"Yeah, which is why I should help," Sergio groused.

"I know it's not much of a consolation, but I'm not completely in agreement with Cian on not having you involved." Jeff tried to watch his words carefully, but it stung that Cian had basically taken over the group tonight. "I think you could be an asset, but at the same time, you have more to lose...and so does your family."

"Cynthia would kill me if I got injured, or worse, died," Sergio admitted, sighing wearily. "She didn't even want me here in Austin tonight. She wants to take Cian's offer."

"Cian's offer?" Jeff arched an eyebrow.

"Yeah, Cian's been trying to throw money at us since Grandmama died." Sergio's green eyes were rimmed with red and a little watery. Like Amaliya, he had been close to his grandmother, and her death had hit both of them very hard.

"Money? Really?" Alexia cocked her head. "What for?"

"He wants us to go into hiding. Somewhere far away. He's been on me almost every night. But tonight, when Amal said what she did..." Lowering his head while shuffling his feet, Sergio let out a slow exhalation. "Well, I get it. When I thought she had been murdered, I was so angry, so full of despair. I would have done anything to have changed her fate. When I found out she was still alive - well, sorta alive - I was so relieved. Then we lost our grandmother, and all those feelings came flooding back. I understand how she would feel if something hap-pened to..." He pointed to himself.

The group around Jeff remained silent. Jeff caught the swift look between the two siblings. They had yet to actually lose someone close to them to the world of the supernatural. The brutality of the hidden world was something he understood very well. Jeff had lost his mother and his leg. Innocente had been someone they had known and liked but not actually loved.

Eduardo, meanwhile, seemed completely unconcerned.

There was a subtle shift in the air, and Jeff glanced over to see Rachoń was no longer in the room. Samantha was checking her phone while sauntering over to the group. She had a distracted air about her.

"Everything okay?" Jeff asked.

Samantha shoved her phone into her purse. "Yeah. Mom's bugging me about Sunday dinner."

"I meant about Rachoń?"

Shoulders sagging, Samantha toyed with one of the curls at the nape of her neck. "Uh, I suck as this phasmagus thing. I couldn't answer any of her questions."

"Told you." Eduardo nudged Benchley with one elbow. "Talking about Prosper."

"Well, I wasn't much help. I am still struggling with the whole ghost thing. I can't control which ghosts I see. They just show up randomly."

"I'm totally going to help you with that," Benchley promised. "I'm already chasing down some leads to get some really primo information."

Jeff slid an arm around Samantha as she snuggled into his side. "You'll catch on. You're the first phasmagus in a very long time."

"I suppose asking you if you saw my grandmother recently is not the best idea?" Sergio said, hope in his voice.

"I haven't seen her since that night," Samantha answered sadly.

Sergio bobbed his head, already surrendered to that possibility. "That's good though, right?" Sergio looked between the ghost hunting siblings. "It means no unfinished business?"

"It means she went into the light," Alexia assured him. "She's on the other side."

Benchley appeared to be about to say something, but Jeff lightly kicked his ankle. Sergio needed to be comforted, not overwhelmed with Benchley's many theories about ghosts.

Sergio didn't notice, or chose not to. The big guy nodded, then looked toward the hallway. "I guess I should say goodbye to Amaliya. Do you think Rachoń is still around?"

"You think she's scary, too, huh?" Benchley grinned.

"I think she's nice," Samantha said. "In a scary sort of way. She really does care about her family."

"But we're not her family," Jeff reminded his girlfriend, giving her a significant look. "She'll put them first, every time. Even if it means letting us die. Or killing us."

"I wouldn't go as far as saying I would kill you," Rachoń said from the entrance of the hallway, a slight smile upon her full lips. "We're allies now. I take that fact very seriously. And I'm trusting you with Baptiste."

"I didn't mean any offense," Jeff said, wishing he'd chosen his words a bit better.

"None taken. You were speaking the truth." Rachoń drew closer to them, her maroon eyes examining each one. "I'm about to take my leave, so I thought I'd impart some wisdom before I depart."

Jeff sensed his crew tensing around him. There was something definitely unnerving about Rachoń's manner. She moved like a snake, each movement measured and graceful.

"Okay," Benchley said, his voice cracking.

"Treat each other like family. Don't let what comes next drive a wedge between you." Rachoń gave them all a significant look, then vanished in the blink of an eye.

It was the first time any of them had seen a vampire disappear into thin air. They were all stunned.

"Did that scare anyone else?" Benchley was several shades whiter than usual.

"Totally," Aimee said from where she stood with Cass near Jeff's office.

"Vampires and their dramatic exits," Cassandra grumbled as she stalked over to join them.

"Well, on that note, I'm making my own," Sergio announced.

Jeff extended his hand, wishing that Sergio could stay and fight but knowing that it was probably wise if he took Cian's money and went into hiding. His own father had fought when others had told him to flee and he had lost his wife and almost his son. Sergio ignored his hand and gave him a bear hug instead. When the big man embraced Samantha, they spent several moments whispering to each other before parting. Benchley gave him a fist bump while Alexia deftly avoided a hug and shook his hand. With some consternation, Jeff realized Eduardo had slipped out when no one was looking.

By the time the group located the two vampires (who were kissing in the stacks) and finally locked up the bookstore, Jeff had an ugly knot of worry forming in his stomach. The only thing around him that felt stable and certain was Samantha. Her arm around his waist was his lifeline to sanity. Aimee and Cassandra stood to one side sharing worried looks while Benchley appeared just as gloomy as his jilted sister. Amaliya and Sergio's goodbye was terse despite the affection they obviously had for one another. Cian forced a check into Sergio's hand, his look steely.

No wonder Rachoń had departed after tossing her pearl of wisdom at them. She could see that they were already splitting along the seams, breaking into small clusters.

Jeff pressed a kiss to the top of Samantha's head and inhaled the sweetness of her scent. Maybe he wasn't cut out to lead any of them for he had no idea how to rally the troops and find the unity they would need to defeat The Summoner.

Tangled up in the bed sheets, Amaliya listened to the absolute silence that filled the bedroom during the day. The soundproofing kept the neighborhood noises at bay but also created an aura of sterility within the room that made Amaliya uneasy.

Cian was perfectly still beside her. The daylight plunged him into the deep vampire sleep that robbed him of all signs of life. During the day he was nothing more than a corpse, and Amaliya hated that fact. She also hated that when she was asleep, she was just also a dead body waiting to reanimate. It was the only part of being a vampire that she truly disliked.

Though Cian was jealous of her ability to awaken in the early afternoon, Amaliya disliked slipping back into consciousness only to be trapped inside the darkened room with Cian's unmoving form. She was not like other vampires, and she often resented that fact. The Summoner had made a new type of vampire when he had created her. Her early awareness was just another part of the curse he had inflicted upon her. She wondered if Bianca would have suffered the same way if she had survived the transformation and risen as a vampire. How much would she have been like Amaliya?

Bothered by her thoughts, Amaliya rolled onto her side in the large bed, putting her back to Cian and staring at the wall. She wished she could return to the deep vampire slumber, but she rarely ever did. Oftentimes she just lay in bed reading or listening to music. Her Kindle and iPod sat on the bed stand fully charged and waiting. Yet she didn't feel like doing anything other than staring into the dark.

Sergio's awkward departure weighed on her. His hug had been tight, but it had also been angry. Though Amaliya was certain that Sergio shouldn't be a part of their battle and needed to hide his family just in case they failed, it had hurt to send him away. Sergio and her grandmother were the only two people in her family she felt she could trust and rely on. Now they were both gone, and she felt adrift and alone. Cian loved her for who she was now, but Sergio and Innocente loved her because of who she had once been: a lost child who just wanted to be loved. Though she was now a powerful vampire necromancer who was absolutely loved by Cian, the girl she had once been was still inside her. That girl wanted to run away, hide, and avoid what was coming.

"I wanted to run away," Bianca's voice said with a sigh.

Amaliya sat up, twisted around, and found herself in the coffee shop where she had spent her last few hours of her human life. "I fell back to sleep," she said in awe to the slim blonde girl seated across from her.

"Only for a little bit," Bianca said, shrugging. "The sun will go down soon."

Bianca was just as Amaliya remembered her. Fair hair, big blue eyes, small pink cupid bow mouth, a fashion style that was perfect for the old Nineties grunge scene, and a desperate look on her face for love and approval that reminded Amaliya far too much of herself at eighteen.

"I can't trust you," Amaliya said, sadness filling her. "You might be *him*."

Fingers playing with her coffee mug, Bianca nodded. "That's true. He'll try to fool you. It's what he does."

"I wanted to save you. I had hoped that I wasn't the only one, you know?" It felt foolish to pour out her feelings to a dream phantom, yet Amaliya wanted to say what she'd been keeping hidden away since the night at the graveyard. "I really needed you. I have Cian. I love him. I had my human family, too. I didn't realize how alone I felt until I realized The Summoner had stolen you from me."

Bianca let out a long sigh. "We could've helped each other."

"I'm remembering things now. From when I was a kid and I thought I was making things up. That I had an over-active imagination. But now I know what I saw were ghosts. I just learned to turn it off. Maybe that's why I always felt so removed from everyone and everything. I had to make myself that way to survive, but it robbed me of something important." Amaliya rolled her eyes and laughed. "Gawd, I sound like I'm on *Oprah* or something."

Bianca gave her a wistful smile. "Yeah, you do."

"I'm so sorry you're dead. I'm so sorry that he took your body from you. I'm so sorry that I'm going to have to destroy your body to kill him."

"Amaliya, I'm not dead." Sliding her hands across the table, Bianca's fingers stopped scant centimeters from Amaliya's. With her chin on the table, Bianca stared up at Amaliya. "I need you to find me. I'm still alive."

The atmosphere of the dream instantly darkened as the air grew cold and stale.

"This isn't real." Amaliya hesitated. "Right?"

Bianca closed her eyes, tears sparkling along the edge of her eyelashes. "I'm still here."

"Bianca?" Amaliya lashed out, trying to grab her hands, but darkness flooded over Bianca, consuming her. "Bianca!"

Amaliya awoke again.

Sitting up, she pressed her hands to her face to discover she'd been crying in her sleep.

CHAPTER FOUR

The second Amaliya stepped into the gaming store, every eye in the place turned toward her and all conversations instantly ceased. Benchley rocketed out from behind a long counter toward her while his sister yawned dramatically and continued tapping away on a laptop.

"Hey, Amaliya!"

Benchley's voice filled the store. The noticeable lack of talking was starting to annoy Amaliya, as were the pointed stares in her direction. Wearing black jeans, a Black Sabbath tank top, and high heels, Amaliya knew she looked hot, but the attention she was getting was ridiculous.

"Haven't y'all ever seen a woman before?" Amaliya muttered.

One half of the store was filled with books, collectible dolls, boxes filled with miniature armies, and things Amaliya would label as nerdy. The other half of the store was crammed with long tables covered in small buildings, foliage, and figurines surrounded by human males and only one or two females. The boys and men were of all ages, from a kid who looked around ten to an old wizened man in a wheelchair. Half of them needed a shower desperately.

"Neck beards, return to your games!" Alexia shouted from behind the counter.

The rumble of voices started back up just as Benchley reached her. "I didn't know you were coming to the store tonight."

"Neither did I," Amaliya confessed. Sweeping her hair back from her face, she glowered at a guy who was breathing heavily while staring at her. "But I need to talk to you. It's important."

"Yeah, totally. Let's talk in my office." Taking her arm, Benchley rushed her toward a door that opened to a small office. "Ignore the weird looks. Most of these guys have never seen a girl that looks like you in real life."

Amaliya narrowed her eyes. "So that gives them permission to be totally weird?"

"No, no. It's just..." Benchley shook his head, then ushered her inside the small cramped office.

The walls were covered in posters for a variety of games sporting scary looking men with huge weapons. A few movie posters were thrown into the mix, most of them sporting sexy women in leather. The desk was covered in books, notebooks, paper clutter, a laptop, and then a much bigger desktop computer with a wide screen monitor. On the screen, a spaceship was floating in space. Like the rest of the store, the room smelled like a guy who needed to take a shower and put on fresh clothes. It was the smell that inhabited most of the dorm rooms of the college guys she'd dated.

Sitting down on a folding chair and crossing her legs, Amaliya stared at Benchley. "Well? Why the freakout?"

"Some of the guys out there are totally cool. Good paying jobs, steady relationships, the works. But some of those guys, this is their life. Sitting in this store and playing games. Maybe they lost a job and can't find another. Maybe they had a bad life and gaming is the thing that makes it better. And some of them...some of them have no clue how to interact with another human being because they were never treated like a human being. By anyone. I will talk to them about the staring though. That was totally uncool and creepy." Benchley sat in his battered office chair and scratched at his beard nervously. "Honestly, Amaliya, I'm somewhere down the middle of all those guys. I have a rotten track record with broads."

"Maybe you shouldn't call women 'broads.' That could be your problem." Amaliya folded her arms over her breasts and arched an eyebrow.

"Good point." Benchley's one eye kept twitching, and he kept looking everywhere but at her.

"Are you okay?"

Laughing nervously, Benchley said, "Uh, I'm a little...uh...scared."

"Because I'm a woman and in your office?"

"No. More like because you're a vampire and a necromancer and could kill me with your pinky."

The words stung even though she knew he hadn't meant them to hurt. "You've got a point. But we're friends, so I'm not going to eat you."

Benchley's face turned a shade of red that was pretty impressive. "Cool."

There was a knock on the door, and a second later it opened. Two teenage boys stood in the doorway. One was a chubby Hispanic boy with dark hair and thick glasses that made his dark eyes enormous. The other was a redhead that looked scarily like a short, skinny Napoleon Dynamite.

"Bench, can we set up another table for the card players?" the redhead asked. "The Warhammer dicks claimed all the tables again."

"Sure, sure. You know where they are," Benchley answered in a rush, obviously trying to get rid of them.

"You look like Megan Fox," the boy with the glasses blurted out.

Amaliya scowled.

"No, she doesn't!" the other boy protested. "She totally looks like Eliza Dushku."

"She doesn't look like either one, dumbasses," Benchley said testily. "Now out!"

The boys started to argue, but Benchley pushed them firmly out of the office, shut the door, and locked it. When Benchley looked at her, Amaliya dramatically rolled her eyes.

"Sorry about that. Yeah, so, where were we?"

"I'm not going to eat you."

"Right!"

"And we were about to talk about why I'm here."

Benchley shoved his hands into the pockets of his cargo pants and paced behind his desk. "Look, if you're here to tell me I shouldn't be crushing on Samantha, I know you're right."

"Well, yeah, you shouldn't be, but no, that isn't why I'm here."

"Oh."

"I'm here because I need your skills."

"My skills?"

"Jeff says you're the guy to go to when it comes to researching spirits, ghosts, and that sort of thing."

Benchley visibly puffed up. "Well, yeah. I am. I'm totally that guy."

It was amazing what a little flattery could do to a guy's ego, Amaliya thought. She fished her list out of her pocket. "I need some information about possession. Like...when a person is possessed, how much are they aware of what is going on around them? Can they find a way to communicate past the...uh...entity possessing them."

Benchley sat at his desk, hunched over, and started scribbling on a pad of paper. "Okay. What else?"

"If a dead body gets possessed, is the spirit of the person still attached to it? I did some internet research, but it didn't make sense to me."

"Most of the stuff on the internet is just old wives' tales. The real information is hidden from the general public." Benchley grinned at her. "People get into enough trouble with the occult just screwing around with low-end spells. Can you imagine what would go down if the hardcore real stuff was on the internet?"

"You mean like bring on the end of the world?" Amaliya flipped her hair over one shoulder and winked at him.

Benchley's face reddened again. "Yeah. Something like that. So what else do you need?"

"Everything about Josephine Leduc and her daughter. Everything. Especially details about her powers. I need to know how to do the stuff Bianca's mother did, especially astral projection. I tried looking this up online, but it seemed like bullshit to me."

"Like I said..." Benchley nodded.

"Exactly. I don't have a handbook on how to be what I am, so I need you to help me piece it together the same way you're going to help Sam." Amaliya handed the list over to Benchley. "Here, just take this. I have some more notes on there. Stuff I'm not too keen on Cian or Jeff seeing. It's between you and me."

With quivering fingers, Benchley took the paper and started to read it. "Amaliya, this is some serious shit."

"Yeah." Amaliya shrugged dismissively though she was just as unnerved as Benchley appeared.

"This thing about Bianca…you don't think it was a dream?"

"Maybe. But if Bianca is somewhere trapped inside her own body, I want to find a way to communicate with her."

With a low whistle, Benchley scratched at his beard. "But The Summoner might catch on to what you're doing."

"That's why you're going to find a way for me to do it without alerting him." Amaliya gave him her fiercest glare. She may have overdone it because he visibly flinched. "If I can talk to her, maybe she'll know what he's going to do, where he is, and how I can stop him."

Sagging in his chair, Benchley opened a drawer, pulled out a fresh file folder, and shoved his notes and Amaliya's into it. "Can I say something?"

"Sure."

Benchley's gaze brushed over her, then the cluttered walls, before returning to the folder. "All my life I've been a gamer. I know all the rules. Just like those people out there, I know how to roll the dice, measure the moves, and do all the shit I can see you don't give a fuck about by that look on your face. My point is this. Gaming is neat and tidy. There are rules. But this thing we're facing has no rules. It has no neatness. It's going to be fuckin' chaos, and I hate that. I hate that I can't open up a book and just find the answers. Figure it out. I'll help you with this because it makes me feel like maybe, somehow, you can make all this shit make sense. The rest of the group might not want to admit it, but you're our biggest gun, and maybe our only hope."

Amaliya tried to look as nonchalant as possible. Though she knew he was right, she didn't want to actually admit to it. To do so would be almost too much for her to deal with at the moment. "Fine. But I'm not dressing like that." She pointed to Alice from the *Resident Evil* films glowering out of a poster dressed in a sexy outfit.

"Aw, c'mon. It would be so wicked!"

Amaliya flipped him off.

Benchley grinned. "I'm on this. I'll let you know what I find out."

"Thanks." Sliding to her feet, Amaliya hooked her thumb onto her belt. "Bench, maybe I am the big gun, but you gotta get me my ammo. That makes you important, right?"

The comment brightened his face slightly. "Yeah. Sure."

Amaliya unlocked the door and jerked it open. "See you later."

"Benchley!" a male voice shouted. "We need you. Your sister made a bogus call."

Alexia stood near a table clutching an open book to her chest. She looked as mad as the man glaring at her.

"Alexia knows that rulebook better than me, Jericho! What she says goes!" Benchley called back. To Amaliya he whispered, "I'm not stupid enough to override my sister."

Waving to Alexia, Amaliya swiftly made her exit, ignoring the stares that followed her ass.

The hot, balmy Texas air buffeted her as she strode toward the dark sedan she had driven to the store. Jeff's occult bookstore had lights on even though it was after hours. Samantha's car was in the nearly empty parking lot. Amaliya was glad that Jeff and Samantha seemed to be doing well. Every once in awhile, guilt nibbled on her when she considered how much she had screwed up the blonde's life, but she rationalized it away by concentrating on the fact that Samantha was happy with Jeff.

"He lets you go out alone?"

The dark, rich voice vibrated through her, eliciting an immediate response in her lady parts. Spinning about, she found herself face to face with the coyote.

"What's up, Eduardo?"

It was unnerving how silently he could move. It also bothered her that she had let her guard down and let him get so close.

"Is the old man in the store still? Because there is no way his possessive ass would let you out of his sight," Eduardo said, obviously teasing her.

Amaliya lifted one shoulder. "Maybe I snuck out."

The coyote was dressed in very tight jeans and a white t-shirt that showed off his impressive muscles to full effect. The menace that oozed off of him only added to his sultry sex appeal. He was all bad boy and just the type of guy Amaliya had gone after during her college days. Despite his clean-cut appearance, she sensed the feral aspect of his nature just below the surface.

"So he doesn't totally control you." Eduardo tilted his head, his eyes glinting with dangerous allure.

"No one controls me," Amaliya answered, setting her hands on her hips. He was baiting her and she knew it, yet she couldn't resist playing along just for a little bit.

Eduardo inched deeper into her personal space, sniffing the air. "You always smell of roses."

"And you smell like..." Amaliya hesitated. His usual musky cologne was barely masking the scent of fresh blood.

The grin he flashed her was all sharp teeth.

"Did you eat a bunny rabbit or something?"

"I ate a pussy." The grin widened.

The heavy fragrance of the blood filled her nostrils, and her body responded hungrily. Animal blood held no attraction to her, which meant... "Human blood?

What the fuck did you do?"

"I told you I ate a pussy," Eduardo licked one canine as his other teeth returned to a more human appearance.

Wincing, Amaliya took a sharp step back from him. "Oh, fuckin' gross!"

"Like you never had a period." Eduardo guffawed.

"Not anymore. Thankfully." Amaliya definitely liked that perk of her undead existence. She'd hated the cramps she used to suffer.

Eduardo leaned against her car door, his sexy body carefully posed for her viewing pleasure. "Like you vampires aren't into sick shit. I bet you and Cian are a pretty bloody mess by the time you're done screwing."

Amaliya fished her keys out of her pocket. "My sex life is none of your business."

"I'd like it to be. You and me could tear it up something good, don't you think? I've never had sex with someone I didn't have to worry about breaking. Or ripping." Eduardo's eyes were smoldering.

"Go find yourself another vampire," Amaliya retorted, then shoved him out of her way.

Eduardo swiveled about, his body almost touching her back, his breath hot on her neck and shoulder. "I want *you* though. And I know you want me. So let's do this. Or are you afraid Cian might get jealous?"

"I'll admit that back in the day I would have fucked your brains out. I'll also admit that you're a fine piece of ass, Eduardo." Amaliya cocked her head so she could see his face. "But I'd never fuck you because you just want to hurt the man I love." She elbowed him as hard as she could in the stomach, sending him sprawling. "So fuck off."

Rolling to his feet with predatory agility, Eduardo smirked. "I can smell how much you'd love me to bend you over this car and fuck you."

"Gross, Eduardo." Amaliya hated that to a certain extent he was right. Why did she always have to be attracted to the bad ones?

"It's going to happen. You can't deny it. You and me."

"Fuck off."

Amaliya slid into the car, slammed the door shut, and slid the key into the ignition. She hated the pulse of arousal between her thighs, and her insane desire to do something incredibly stupid with Eduardo. Though Cian and Amaliya were in a committed relationship that was steeped in love, they hadn't agreed to be monogamous. Eduardo wanted Amaliya's body. It was an alpha male thing. Cian loved the essence of who she was. It wasn't too hard to decide how to handle the situation.

When she pulled out of the parking lot, she saw Eduardo slip into the shadows alongside the gaming store, then vanish from sight.

CHAPTER FIVE

Cian sat on the kitchen counter watching Cassandra chopping vegetables with impressive expertise. Aimee had a cauldron bubbling on one burner, while sautéing mushrooms in a skillet on another. Amaliya had rushed off on an errand, so he'd opted to hang out with his daughter and her girlfriend before dealing with any of the problems that had brewed during the daylight hours. He was wearing his favorite Homer Simpson t-shirt and black cargo shorts, which his daughter had found hilarious.

"Oooh, scary vampire," she had joked when she'd seen him.

Scratching his stomach, he tried to ignore the hideous smell of human food. "So you modeled and went to culinary school in Paris."

"Yep. But I had to quit because of Mom." Cassandra's voice took on a guarded tone instantly at the mention of Galina. "She gets confused easily."

"That's what you said," Cian said, lowering his gaze. It was his power that had plunged Galina's mind into constant confusion. He wasn't about to admit that to Cassandra. It had been deliberate. Cian had wanted Galina not to remember the terrible things she had seen. Dr. Summerfield had hid her away and not let Cian know where she was to protect her. Though Cian was still miffed that Dr. Summerfield, who he had considered a friend, had kept Cassandra's existence from him, he had to admit it was a smart move. The man he had once been may have killed his offspring.

Cassandra pinned him with a warning look. Her mother was a topic she did not discuss with him. They had accidently stumbled onto the subject while discussing Cassandra's life before she became a thief and vampire hunter.

"And then you were recruited by this man Scott to be a thief?" Cian asked, prompting her away from the matter of her mother.

"Yep. And I did that while also working as a waitress as my cover story. It was pretty lucrative until I got hired to steal a relic in Vegas."

"Then she ran into me," Aimee grinned. "Literally."

Cassandra bestowed a loving look on the witch. "I got lucky."

"No, I did," Aimee said, smiling affectionately at the dhamphir.

The two women shared a sweet kiss, then returned to their tasks.

"Frank, the asshole who had her enslaved to him, figured out what I was, so he set a trap for me." Cassandra handed off the sliced vegetables to her girlfriend. "Aimee managed to use some of her magic to warn me. So I went in knowing what was up, and we basically rescued each other from the jerk."

"And this is when you broke the blood bond," Cian said, trying to sound nonchalant.

Cassandra narrowed her eyes, while Aimee nodded. "Yes. I cast a spell that broke it."

Busying herself with cleanup, Cassandra pressed her lips together, giving her father speculative looks out of the corner of her eyes, which were green tonight, he noted.

"May I ask how?" Cian tilted his head, his attention squarely on the witch.

Aimee finished whipping the eggs before starting to create the actual omelets. Her long hair was braided around her head, and she wore a simple brown maxi-dress with lots of sparkling necklaces, bracelets, and rings adding color. Cian could see why Cassandra was so drawn to the woman. Not only was she lovely, she exuded intelligence, confidence, and power.

"Cian, I'm a witch. What worked on me won't work on Amaliya," Aimee finally said. "The Summoner's blood made her. His power made her. To completely break the supernatural ties between them may be impossible. Hell, it may kill Amaliya." Aimee didn't look at him while she spoke but concentrated on the egg mixture bubbling in the skillet.

The words she spoke made sense, but Cian couldn't accept them as the complete truth. "Rachoń and I benefited from age and being apart from him for so long. The ties between us wore down and eventually broke. Maybe you could find a way to accelerate that process."

"But you're a regular vampire," Cassandra said over the running water spilling into the sink. Scrubbing the vegetable knife, she finally looked directly at him. "Amaliya is anything but a regular vampire."

"Cass is right. The rules that apply to you don't necessarily apply to her."

"You used Cass's blood, didn't you?" Cian asked, addressing the one point they were all trying to ignore. "Dhamphir blood breaks bonds."

"Yeah, between vampires and humans." Aimee finished one omelet and started on the next.

"And between vampires and witches," Cian added.

"And maybe even vampires and other supernatural creatures. But a vampire and the offspring he or she created with his own blood?" Aimee shook her head. "I doubt it. It would be like trying to remove your genetics from Cass."

The father and daughter exchanged amused looks that perfectly mirrored one another.

Aimee slid a plate over to Cassandra along with a fork. "That just proved my point."

"Can you try to find a way?" Cian tried not to flinch as Cassandra started to eat.

"I'm already on it." Aimee pointed to the small cauldron. "Amaliya gave me some of her blood tonight before she left. Cassandra gave me some of hers, too. I'll need some of yours. Sadly, we don't have any of The Summoner's."

Cian slid off the counter, grabbed a knife from the butcher block, and held out his hand. "Take what you need."

"After I eat, okay?" Aimee laughed.

"Dramatic much, Dad?"

Cian smirked and shoved the knife back into place. Then he realized his daughter had actually addressed him as her father. It hadn't been said scornfully or mockingly. It surprised Cian to realize how much it meant to him.

"And you're not?" Cian raised an eyebrow, and she matched his look.

They both burst out laughing.

Cian left them to their meal and busied himself in his office. Though most of his companies ran themselves, Cian did try to keep abreast of the latest developments. Relief filled him when he saw that Sergio had cashed the check he had given him. If Sergio was wise, he'd have his family safely in hiding within the week. Cian did not want Amaliya to lose any more of her family, and he also did not want The Summoner using them against her. Cian had hired mercenaries to watch over Sergio and his family from afar but hadn't told the man. Sergio was just as prideful as Amaliya.

"Eduardo is an asshole," Amaliya's voice said from the doorway.

"Yeah, I know." Cian glanced toward her. "What happened?"

"I ran into him and he was an ass," Amaliya said dismissively. "He was hitting on me."

"He hits on you because he knows you're attracted to him," Cian said, not with malice. He hated Eduardo, but he wasn't foolish enough to discount the man's appeal to Amaliya. Whenever they hunted together, Amaliya always went after the men who perfectly fit the classification of bad boys. Cian enjoyed watching her feed off of them, her power dwarfing theirs. The sexuality of Amaliya's predatory nature appealed to him, and he enjoyed seeing it in action.

"Yeah, but he's a fuckin' dick. He only wants to sleep with me to put his mark on me or something. He might as well just piss on my leg and get it over with."

Cian burst into laughter. Rocking back in his chair, he swiveled it around so he could see her clearly.

Amaliya leaned against the doorjamb, one hand on her hip. "Honestly, tonight, he kinda freaked me out."

"How?"

"Other than him boasting about eating out some chick out while she's on her period, he was just..." Amaliya hesitated. "I felt he was hunting me."

"Well, Liya, he has been. Since he first saw you." Cian shrugged. "You're beautiful, dangerous, and forbidden. He's going to want you. Plus, he hates me. He probably feels if he can seduce you it's a way of asserting himself over me."

"I'm not property." Amaliya scowled.

"No, but he knows how much I love you." Cian rocked lightly in his chair. "He's figured out that the best way to get to me is through you. Though he's been saying shit to Cass more and more, too."

"Is this going to be an issue? Seriously? Eduardo sniffing around the women in your life?"

"It's just his way. He's a coyote. A trickster. Causing shit is second nature to them. He's going to keep sniffing around you until you give in or he finds another way to annoy me."

"I'm not going to give in." Amaliya sniffed. "His hot factor went down a few notches tonight."

"I'm not threatened by you sleeping with someone," Cian said. "As long as your heart is mine, I don't give a rat's ass."

"Really?"

"Well, we've never agreed to be monogamous."

"No, we haven't." Amaliya tilted her head, her eyes narrowing in thought. "Do you want to be?"

"Throughout my very long life, sex had played many roles in my existence." Cian leaned forward, his elbows on his knees. He felt the past weighing heavily on him. He had lived many lifetimes, and sometimes they blurred together. But there were certain lessons he had learned that had shaped him. The most recent was that he could never be a human man again. During his engagement with Samantha, he'd been very careful with her, trying to hide his vampire nature. It had been difficult, so their sexual relationship had been muted. That was not the case with Amaliya. "My first lover was my wife. I loved her dearly. I somewhat remember our first time together. How awkward it was, but how much it meant. Yet I can't remember her face or voice anymore."

Amaliya's blue-gray eyes took on a sympathetic expression. "I'm sorry. That must hurt."

"It bothers me sometimes that I can't remember her, because I know I loved her with all my heart. We were good Catholics that started having children right away. It was a hard life, yet I was happy. And then...I became a vampire. Nothing was the same afterward. Food and drink had no meaning. Love was replaced with much more base emotions. Sex became part of feeding, power plays, manipulations, and seductions."

Amaliya ventured closer to him. "Are you saying you didn't love anyone all that time?"

Cian settled back in his chair. "Honestly, no. Not like I loved my wife. I lusted. I had feelings for women. I was completely enamored with Etzli. I can't say any of it was actually love. I wanted desperately to love Samantha, but I never really did. Not in the way I should have. I failed her in that regard. I wasn't in love with anyone other than my wife. Not until you."

That brought a smile to Amaliya's face.

"So sex as part of a loving relationship is new to me again. I love you. I also lust you. Sometimes the two intermingle. Other times, they don't. Sometimes I feel completely content just watching you play those damn drums or doing simple mundane things. I feel utterly enthralled with you. Other times I just want to fuck you. And then there are times when sex feels like making love."

Amaliya swept her hair back from her face. "So, basically, what you're saying is that sex isn't love."

"No. Sex with you is intense and exciting, but I don't regard it as the core of our relationship. Do you?"

She wagged her head *no*. "Nah. It's great, but...I agree. Honestly, I was hoping we wouldn't have to stick with the monogamy thing for like...eternity."

Cian laughed. "As long as you and I are committed to being together, united, and in love, I am not worried."

"And we could share," Amaliya said, a teasing smile on her face.

"Exactly." Cian was rather relieved that she was of the same mindset, though he had been certain she would. It was quite liberating to be with someone who wasn't going to try to tie him up in mortal normality. Except for when Eduardo was lurking about. Cian had to admit that he'd been dreading her possibly wanting to invite him into their bed.

Amaliya gave him a sly look. "But admit it. It would bother you if it was Eduardo I messed around with."

Cian had to wonder if maybe she was now able to read his thoughts. "Okay, maybe it would. But you'd still be the love of my life and I'd still be yours." Cian grinned. "Besides, I have a much bigger dick."

"How do you know?"

"I have my sources," Cian said, shrugging.

"In other words, you slept with the same girl and she told you."

"Actually, she told Roberto. He thought that piece of information was amusing." Cian remembered his former minion's delight at the discovery. Roberto had not liked Eduardo.

"No wonder you're so confident."

"It has nothing to do with the size of my cock and everything to do with the fact that I have you in my life."

"Ugh! That's so romantic! Stop!" Amaliya pretended to fan herself.

Cian chuckled.

Amaliya sauntered over to climb onto his lap. Wrapping his arms around her, Cian kissed her lips. They tasted like fresh blood but smelled like cherry lip balm. Caressing her cheek, Cian stared into her blue-gray eyes and saw the deep love they shared reflected in them.

"You hunted already?" he asked.

"I took a sip from a girl at Ross. I stopped to grab some jeans, and we were the only two in the dressing room. I took advantage of the situation." Amaliya snuggled against him. "I want to go hunting with you. Somewhere sexy."

"Then I'll have to change out of my Homer Simpson shirt," Cian complained.

"Oh, boo hoo. What a horrible loss that would be."

Cian pressed a kiss to her full lips, then said, "I love you."

"Sucks to be you," she teased.

Threading his fingers through her hair, he relished the feel of her soft, cool body against his. "Aimee is going to try to see what she can do about your bond to The Summoner."

Amaliya sighed. "Like that's going to happen."

"Maybe she'll find a way, Liya." Cian hated it when Amaliya gave into her fatalistic tendencies. He knew more about what was going on in her head than she realized. Though Amaliya didn't regard herself as a martyr, she often felt she was on a course with certain destruction. Cian would do everything in his power not to allow that to happen.

"Well, I guess it doesn't hurt to try," Amaliya said finally. Sliding off his lap, she grabbed his hand. "Let's go hunt. I'm hungry."

Recognizing her need to change the subject, Cian rose to his feet. "So you want to hunt somewhere sexy, huh? Does that mean you'll dress sexy?"

"If you're lucky," she said in such a way Cian had a feeling that it may be an hour or two before they actually made it out the front door.

CHAPTER SIX

The vegan carrot cake was heavenly, but her cappuccino tasted burned. Yet Samantha wasn't about to say anything after her boyfriend had worked so hard to impress her with his culinary skills. Seated side by side in the back room of his bookstore, they had just finished eating a homemade meal. She was full and she was happy, so that was all that really mattered. It had been a lovely evening. There hadn't been any discussion of any of the supernatural things they were dealing with or the big bad necromancer laying low somewhere out there in the world plotting his next move. Samantha had loved every second of it. She'd almost felt like the world was normal.

"Don't drink that. I burned it," Jeff said, claiming her cup after taking a sip of his own. "Sorry."

"It's fine! It was all good." Smiling at him, she ruffled his floppy brown hair with her fingers. "No one has ever made me dinner before. It's so sweet."

With a pleased smile, Jeff pushed his paper plate away and leaned over the armrest of his chair to rest his hand on her leg. "I wanted to do something special for you."

"Are you going for the sweetest boyfriend in the world award? Because right now, you're totally the frontrunner." Samantha settled her hand on his and pressed it gently.

"Absolutely." Jeff kissed her cheek. "And you get awesome girlfriend points for coming here tonight and roughing it with me."

Originally they'd planned to meet at his place for a romantic candlelight dinner, but then a New Zealand group that was part of The Assembly had contacted Jeff about a conference call. All of his reference books were at the store, where he spent most of his time, so it had made sense to take the call from his work office. Jeff had quickly packed up their meal and brought it to the bookstore so they could relax and not worry about rushing through traffic to make the call in time. They had warmed dinner in the microwave and eaten off of disposable dinnerware.

"It's okay, Jeff. I just like spending time with you."

Jeff gave her his goofiest loving look. "I feel the same way."

"Besides, cleanup is super easy this way!" Samantha picked up the paper plates they had used along with the plastic utensils and dramatically tossed them into the trash bin. "Ta da!"

"Which was all part of my evil plan to begin with. I hate doing dishes!"

Jeff started putting the lids back on the plastic containers that held the leftovers and returned them to the cooler he had transported their dinner in from his house. Samantha wiped off the table with some napkins, then blew out the small tea lights.

"So, Sam, this was our *first* candlelight dinner of many. I think it went okay."

"It was perfect. I loved it."

"No, *you're* perfect. And I love you," Jeff said in such a way it made her heart flutter. His big brown eyes and thick eyebrows gave him such a cute puppy dog expression that Samantha had to snuggle into him. Laughing, he pressed kisses to the top of her head. "Next time we'll have fancier candles if this is the response I get."

"You're on to me! I'm all about the fancy candles." Samantha grinned up at him. "Or maybe I'm just all about the fancy boyfriend who says sweet things."

"I thought I was charmingly dorky, not fancy."

"You're fancily a dork."

Jeff made a big show of considering her words, then slowly grinned. "I can live with that."

"Good! Because you have to!"

His kisses tasted like carrot cake.

Reluctantly, Samantha disengaged herself from his arms. "When's the call?"

Jeff checked the clock on the wall and winced. "In about thirty minutes."

"Want to fool around until then?" Samantha waggled her eyebrows.

"I love the way you think!"

"I just need to freshen up."

Samantha coyly kissed his cheek before slipping down the hall and into the ladies restroom. She had drunk way too much sweet tea, and her bladder was begging for relief.

Washing her hands once she was done, she studied her reflection in the mirror. Even though the world was teetering literally on the edge of eternal darkness, instead of looking haggard with fear, she appeared happy. It was weird to acknowledge the truth that she actually *was* happy. After all the crap that had gone down in her life, losing Cian as her fiancé, turning into a phasmagus, and facing the possible end of the world, she supposed she should be living in despair, yet she wasn't. The cause of her surprising but reassuring peace of mind was her acceptance of her new role in the dangerous world of the supernaturals. It was odd to admit, but once she embraced being a part of the hidden world, her life had somehow started to make sense. Upon reflection of all the choices she had made in her life, it was as if she had been on an inevitable course to this point in her existence.

Turning on the water, she moistened a paper towel and dabbed at face to fix her smudged mascara. Focused on the flecks of makeup and the smear under one eye, she leaned closer to the mirror. Her breath fogged the reflective surface, obscuring her view. Annoyed, she wiped the moisture away.

Behind Samantha stood a woman with her throat and chest torn open. Ropes of dirty, bloody intestines dangled across her pallid, naked thighs, and blood dripped from the edges of her grievous wounds. She'd literally been torn apart. One eye was missing, but the other, pale blue and dead, stared at Samantha.

Frozen in place, Samantha gawked at the ghost in the mirror, absorbing the horrific state of the woman. Tendrils of dark hair were matted with blood to her face and neck. Though Samantha had never seen the dark-haired woman before, there was something vaguely familiar about her. Then it struck her. The apparition was in a similar state to the ghost she had encountered while running one July morning. It had taken a bit of sleuthing to identify the ghost, but Samantha had uncovered she was a missing woman who had vanished while jogging. Her name was Cassidy Longoria. Like the specter reflected in the mirror, Cassidy had been ripped open.

"Who are you?" Samantha whispered.

"He killed me," the ghost answered, though her lips did not move.

Samantha winced when the ghost flickered in the reflection then appeared even closer to her. Frigid air sprouted goose bumps all over Samantha's back and arms. Unlike the movies, she couldn't just close her eyes and banish the ghost. If it touched her, it would gain mass and become solid.

"If you want me to help, tell me who you are and who killed you," Samantha said in an even tone.

"Why did he kill me?" the ghost sobbed. "Why?"

Swiveling about, Samantha braced herself against the sink. The ghost was scant inches from her. Though the wounds were heinous and the ghost had the appearance of a fresh corpse, Samantha couldn't smell anything other than the vanilla air freshener sitting on the back of the toilet.

"I'm sorry he killed you, but you need to tell me who did this to you," Samantha insisted.

The ghost covered her face with her hands, sobbing.

"Hey. Ghost girl." Samantha started to reach for the phantom, then thought better of it. Did she really want the ghost to solidify?

"Why?" the ghost lifted her head and screamed. "Why?"

Samantha flinched, sliding away from the specter. "I don't know, but I'll help you. Just tell me—"

The lights went out, plunging the room into darkness. Dragging in a deep breath of cold air, Samantha waited for the inevitable touch of the ghost.

There was a rap on the door. "Sam? Are you okay? The lights just went out."

"Uh, there's a ghost in here with me," Samantha answered, edging along the sink and toward the door. "She's kinda upset."

There was a long beat, then Jeff said, "Shit."

"He let me die," the ghost said, her mouth so close to Samantha's ear it chilled her flesh.

Samantha's hand found the doorknob, unlocked it, and jerked on it. The door swung open to reveal a gloomy hallway with a dark shape barely illuminated by the street light filtering through the windows. Samantha hoped it was Jeff.

To her relief, the figure said, "Is she still here?" Jeff's warm hand closed on her arm and drew her out of the bathroom.

"I don't know." Samantha shivered, her teeth clacking together. "Maybe. It's so cold."

"Yeah, I feel it. It's isolated to the bathroom." Jeff tugged her from doorway and further up the hall.

"She's just like Cassidy. All torn up." Samantha automatically lowered her voice and wasn't sure if she was doing it because it was dark or because of the ghost.

"You let him do this to me!"

A gush of cold, dank air roared out of the bathroom.

"Okay, I heard that," Jeff gasped.

Placing herself between Jeff and the ghost, Samantha strained to see into the murk. "Hey, ghost girl, no one let anyone hurt you. I promise. We want to help."

Jeff tried to change places with her, but Samantha shoved him back with her elbow.

"Don't let her touch you or we'll have trouble," Jeff muttered, obviously hoping the ghost wouldn't hear.

"Please, we want to help you," Samantha said into the murk filling her vision. Maybe it was her eyes trying to adjust, but she kept catching glimpses of other shapes in the blackness.

There was a low rasp, then the bathroom door violently slammed shut.

"Are you guys naked in here?" Eduardo called out from the front of the store. "What's with the lights?"

As if to answer his question, the lights flicked on. The brightness hurt Samantha's eyes, and she covered her face with her hands.

"We had an outage," Jeff answered. Cautiously, he opened the door to the bathroom and peered in.

Samantha leaned past him, then shook her head. "She's gone."

Eduardo strolled down the hallway, a thermos in one hand. Every night, Eduardo poured Amaliya's blood onto a grave in each cemetery in Austin. It allowed her to call the dead. Tossing it to Jeff, he said, "Did my duty, now I'm off to have some fun."

"What do you do for fun?" Samantha asked, curiosity getting the better of her.

The grin Eduardo gave her was a little disconcerting. "Stuff."

Jeff unscrewed the top of the thermos and looked inside. "Would it kill you to clean it?"

Eduardo turned to go, then hesitated. "Oh, yeah. I don't usually hang with the weres, but I ran into another coyote that does. She had something interesting to say about San Antonio."

Samantha saw the sudden interest bloom in Jeff's gaze.

"Which was?"

"The wolf pack that was on the south side has disappeared. No sign of them. Just gone. But – and this is interesting – some jaguars were spotted lurking around the River Walk. If you want my opinion on what this means, here it is: The Summoner cleaned house across the board and is bringing in his own people."

Samantha frowned at the thought, but they had all known that The Summoner wouldn't just sit by idly. He had definite, terrifying plans for the world. And probably for them.

"Did you tell Cian?" Jeff sounded only a little annoyed at deferring to the vampire.

"Nah. I ran into his woman when she was visiting Benchley's place. I was going to tell her, but she came onto me pretty strong. I got distracted."

"Liar," Samantha said, the word just slipping out. Again it surprised her how easily she defended the woman she had once hated.

"What?" Eduardo held out his arms. "I'm a hot piece of ass. She wants me. You all know it. She's just playing it coy because of her asshole boyfriend."

"She would never leave Cian for you," Samantha declared, setting her hands on her hips and lifting her chin.

"Who said anything about her leaving Cian? Fucking is fucking, and nothing more." Eduardo patted Samantha's head. "You're so innocent."

"Oh, fuck off." Samantha irritably pushed his hand away.

"Eduardo, stop provoking Sam," Jeff said, his annoyance clear.

"But it's so much fun," Eduardo said mockingly, winking.

Samantha narrowed her eyes. Something about Eduardo always had her on edge. It wasn't just the fact he was obscenely good looking and incredibly over-confident but something she couldn't quite put her finger on. Jeff said it was because he was a coyote, a trickster.

"Anyway, I'm out. Tell the asshole vampire what I told you. Let him mull that over." Eduardo strutted toward the front of the store.

"Lock the door," Jeff called out.

Eduardo saluted, then turned the corner. A few seconds later, the front door shut and locked.

"I don't like him. At all."

"I know." Jeff pulled out his phone and checked the time. "I need to get on Skype."

Samantha trailed behind him to his office, her hands still on her hips. "He's such a jerk."

"I know. He's been like that since I met him in college," Jeff said, "but he's a great help." Stopping in the doorway of his office, Samantha's mind switched from pondering how to neuter Eduardo to something the ghost said. "Jeff, she said the same thing Cassidy did."

"Huh?" He redirected his gaze from the computer screen to Samantha. "What do you mean?"

"They both said 'you let him do this to me.' Remember? Cassidy said that."

Jeff winced. "Yeah. I remember."

"Why do you think they said that?"

With a weary exhalation, Jeff stared at the computer screen. "Maybe because I'm the guy who's supposed to keep Austin safe from the supernatural bad guys. And I failed."

"So you think something supernatural killed Cassidy and this other girl?"

Hesitantly, Jeff nodded.

Samantha glanced toward the front of the store, her heartbeat starting to accelerate. "Eduardo. You think it's Eduardo."

Jeff closed his eyes for a second, then again nodded. "I don't have proof."

"Jeff, what the hell? Why didn't you say something?"

"Because I have no evidence at all. I'm looking into it, Sam. I have been since we saw Cassidy. I think the attacks were definitely some sort of supernatural beast. Eduardo is on the list because he's a coyote, but it could have been something else. I can't just accuse him of something when I have zero evidence it's him."

"But you think it might be him!"

"For a really lame reason."

"And what lame reason is that, Jeff?"

"There have been women disappearing around Austin the area for the last few years. All of them have had long dark hair and blue eyes. Like Amaliya. You see how Eduardo is around her."

Samantha pondered this bit of information. It was flimsy, but in a way it made sense. Eduardo was a supernatural beast that was attracted to a certain type. A lot of the supernaturals liked human blood and flesh. "Have you told Cian?"

"No. And I won't. And neither will you. I have no evidence, Sam. None. Just a suspicion."

"If I could get the ghosts to talk..." Samantha bit her bottom lip.

"Well, they're not, so we're stuck." Jeff checked the time again. "And I have a meeting."

"This fuckin' sucks," Samantha decided.

"Yeah. Everything does. Except for you." Jeff wove their fingers together and drew her down for a quick kiss. "I'll get done here then we'll make out. If you want to stick around, that is."

Samantha gave him a wan smile. "I want to be near you tonight. Want to stay over at my place?"

"Okay." Jeff kissed her hand, then moved to answer the incoming call.

Feeling scared and weary, Samantha sat on the floor near his desk, crossed her legs, and wondered why her happy moments always seemed to disappear before she had the chance to truly relish them.

Etzli ran her fingers down the jaguar's back as she rested on a divan in a skimpy white bikini admiring the full moon above. The gentle lapping of the waves in the pool added to the serenity of the scene. The coarse dark hair of the beast was a pleasing sensation. The big cat let out a growling purr, arching against her hand. The jaguar was almost black, with its spots barely discernible on its back and head. She had four of the great cats, and they inhabited the walled-in back yard of the mansion near the downtown area of San Antonio. After she had taken over the city, she had her favorite pets flown in from Mexico City. Along with them had come the were-jaguars and the black magic witches from Etzli's cabal. The mansion was now protected by massive wards and repulsion spells that kept unwanted visitors away.

At the patio table next to her, a thin, pale young man dressed in ratty shorts and a t-shirt with a bizarre yellow creature on it was rattling off the latest information on their endeavors while staring at his iPad.

The waters of the pool twirled into water spouts, sending spirals of mist floating through the air.

"Trish, you're getting me wet!" Etzli shouted at the elemagus standing nearby.

The woman with the wild red hair and bizarre maroon eyes pouted but lowered her hands. The water spouts vanished.

"You're in a bathing suit next to a pool," the boy said, smirking.

Etzli resisted the urge to grab the tablet from his hand and throw it into the water. As annoying as Stark could be, she tolerated him because of his genius. Yet everything about him, from his terrible fashion sense to his ridiculous comic book nickname, aggravated her.

"So the first rings arrive over the next few days. I have definitely tracked down another three. Just like you said, The Assembly is doing most of our work for us. They're in a panic." Stark grinned, flashing his yellowed teeth. He consumed obscene amount of coffee and always smelled like the stale brew. "Collecting the rest of the rings is going to be damn easy if they keep it up."

Etzli supposed he wanted some sort of congratulatory gesture from her. She stared at him through her sunglasses, then reached out and patted his head. Instantly, she regretted doing so. His hair was a greasy mess.

"Gregorio!"

The older mortal man rushed forward with a hot towel already in his hands. Etzli adored the servant because he always anticipated her needs. Gently, he cleaned off her hand, mindful of her sparking diamond rings.

Stark shoved his hair back from his face, frowning. "It's just hair product."

"It's disgusting."

Lowering his head, the boy sulked. He wasn't quite twenty yet, and though arrogant in some ways, he was quite needy in others. Ever since Etzli had recruited him, he'd been eager to please. If she revealed any sign of dissatisfaction with him, he sulked for days.

"I won't use it anymore," he grumbled. Tapping at his screen, he said, "I have more news."

"Go ahead."

"That Benchley guy from the Austin hunter group has been doing research on phasmagi."

"They're extinct." Etzli waved Gregorio away and resumed petting her jaguar.

"Well, I don't think so because he seems real intent on tracking down anything he can on them. He's not as smart as his sister. She always uses a VPN, which makes it way harder on me."

"What is this VPN?" Etzli wasn't particularly keen on any technology, but she understood its usefulness.

"Virtual private network. It's a way to hide what you're doing online. Anyway, he's been doing everything over the public network, so it's been real easy for me to track." Stark's narrow little face took on a smug expression. "Also, he's been researching Josephine Leduc."

When Etzli didn't respond in the way he hoped, his cockiness faded slightly. With a bored sigh, she said, "So?"

"He probably wants to know more about Bianca." Stark's blue eyes flicked toward the French doors that opened into the house.

"Of course he does." Etzli flexed her toes, studying her pedicure. The edge of one red nail was chipped. She frowned, not only at the imperfection of her appearance, but at Stark's discovery. If The Assembly was scrambling to find the rings of Lucifer's Sword, why would they bother to waste valuable time researching an extinct supernatural being? "The phasmagus research is disturbing. I do *not* like this development."

When The Summoner had created Amaliya and Bianca, he had altered the order of things in the supernatural realm. His offspring didn't even abide by the rules of his own power, which made them unpredictable and difficult to deal with. The Summoner would never admit it, but she knew his grip on Bianca's body was not absolute. Every once in awhile, she saw the girl peering out of those big blue eyes.

"Think they found one?" Stark asked.

"Or made one," Etzli murmured. Phasmagi were closely related to necromancers, which was why most had been killed. Etzli wondered if The Summoner's little experiment with Amaliya and Bianca had resulted somehow in creating a phasmagus. "Follow his research carefully. Find out what you can about this possible phasmagus."

"What about a phasmagus?"

Bianca's voice was delicate and sweet, but coupled with the cold, deadly look in her blue eyes, it was a terrifying sound. The Summoner stood in the doorway of the mansion. Bianca's delicate form was dressed in a long black lace dress, and her blonde hair was twisted up onto her head with rhinestone clips securing it.

"Tell him," Etzli ordered Stark.

The young man wilted under the gaze of The Summoner and swallowed several times before recounting what he'd discovered in a raspy, frightened voice. As he spoke, Bianca's pink lips gradually turned upward.

"Well, I guess our friends in Austin aren't so uninteresting after all," The Summoner said with delight. "And here I thought we'd have a dull time of it until I call Amaliya to my side."

"Why don't we just let the mice run on their wheel and ignore them?" Etzli suggested. As the words left her lips, she knew he'd disregard her completely. He loved to play with people's lives. It amused him. Even his plan to rip the veil between the world of the living and the abyss was just one grand game.

"If there is a phasmagus among them, it could prove to be interesting," The Summoner answered, dismissing her outright. "Keep me informed of all you discover."

"We should concentrate on the rings and the temple." Etzli slid off the divan and strode toward The Summoner. "Distractions will slow down our progress."

The smirk on Bianca's face angered Etzli. The Summoner had grandiose ideas but tended to be easily distracted. She supposed it was a product of his ancient age. He constantly complained about boredom. The possibility of a phasmagus coming into existence was irresistible to him.

"We know where the temple is. Many of the rings are already en route. The Assembly continues to uncover the rest for us. And we have a long wait until December." The Summoner tilted Bianca's head and feigned a yawn. "I enjoy my distractions."

Trish, Stark, and Gregorio were perfectly still and quiet, obviously unnerved by the growing tension between Etzli and The Summoner. Etzli believed in The Summoner's quest to plunge the world into darkness, but his methods were infuriating at times. Yet she loved him and his power. She was proud but not foolish enough to defy him. He was a god after all.

Etzli bowed her head, her long dark hair slipping over one shoulder. "Your desires are my desires."

Bianca's hand was soft and gentle against her cheek. "Of course they are."

PART TWO

Hard Lessons

CHAPTER SEVEN

August 2012

S amantha sighed as Jeff finished dressing. She didn't want him to leave but knew he had his duties he needed to fulfill. At least he was trying very hard to make time for her and their relationship. After he'd closed the bookstore, he'd taken her out for hamburgers at Phil's Icehouse, then home for a few hours of cuddles and lovemaking.

With a slight pout, she traced her fingertips over the blue tattoo that adorned his right shoulder blade just before he tugged his t-shirt down.

"You're such a geek," Samantha teased.

"I like Dr. Who," Jeff said, defending his TARDIS tattoo.

"You'd be a sexy Dr. Who."

"He's just the Doctor, remember? That's the joke?" Jeff put on a terrible English accent. "'I'm the Doctor.' 'Doctor who?' 'Just the Doctor.' That's the running joke."

"Whatever. You're like the tenth Doctor with his awesome hair." Samantha ran her fingers through Jeff's brown hair, making it stick up in the way she liked. Samantha watched the show to make Jeff happy, though she did enjoy it more than she had anticipated.

Jeff made a face but endured it. "You only love me because I have great hair."

"I love you because you're adorable." Samantha kissed him lightly on the lips. They were both a little damp from their shower, and he tasted like clean water.

Playing with the blonde tendrils falling over her brow, Jeff sighed. "I wish I didn't have all these Skype calls tonight, but time zones are a bitch. Plus Aimee and Cass are picking up Baptiste and bringing him to the store. I really need to get him up to speed."

"Well, at least he's finally here."

Sharing a few more sweet kisses, the couple ignored the yowling of the cat outside the bedroom door. Beatrice was not pleased at being banned from the room during Jeff's visits. Her small paws slid under the bottom of the door while she continued to protest loudly.

Samantha reluctantly let Jeff slip out of her arms and watched with amusement as he let the cat in. Beatrice haughtily strode past him, flicking her tail with disapproval in his direction.

"Go ahead and stay in here by yourself, bitchy kitty," Samantha said to the cat as Beatrice jumped onto the unmade bed.

Beatrice settled onto one of the pillows, yawned, and turned her face away, as if dismissing the two humans.

"That's why I don't have cats. They're assholes," Jeff said and ducked so he wouldn't get smacked by his girlfriend.

"She's just moody! She doesn't like being excluded."

"Like someone I know," Jeff continued to tease while hurrying down the hallway.

Following Jeff to the kitchen, Samantha couldn't help but admire his rear. She found it insanely sexy in his cargo shorts. Jeff's broad shoulders were also very alluring as far as she was concerned. Beneath his blue shirt which read "The Doctor Will Save Us," Jeff had some very nice muscles. The more she fell for him, the more attractive he became in her eyes. Someone had made a snide comment to her once about him missing one of his legs, and she had torn them a new one. Jeff was all man as far as she was concerned. It didn't diminish him as a person that he had lost a limb. He'd once shown her all the different prosthetic devices he'd worn over the years. The little toddler ones had broken her heart. Today he was wearing a prosthetic leg that looked like it belonged on a robot, but it was the one that gave him the most movement.

"I would totally go sit in on your boring phone calls if I didn't have to study," Samantha answered grumpily. She was still getting used to being a phasmagus and what it meant for her life. At least she had Jeff and the others to help her through.

"You haven't seen any more of the ghostly victims, have you?"

"You mean the women Eduardo is killing?" Samantha answered grumpily.

"We have no proof," Jeff said, sighing.

"I haven't seen any others," Samantha said with a pout. "I still think it's creepy, the one who showed up at the store. Maybe Eduardo killed her there."

Casting a startled look at her, Jeff hesitated in his steps.

"Just a thought," she said.

"A disturbing one."

"That's how our life rolls, huh?" Samantha said.

"Yeah, sadly."

The continuous whir of the air conditioning made Samantha sigh. The hot weather was going to wreck her budget. The electric bill was going to be enormous with the triple-digit weather Austin was experiencing, but the utility bill was the least of her worries with all the bad guys lurking out in the world.

After claiming a bottle of water from the refrigerator, Jeff collected his wallet and keys. "Call me later, okay? I want to make sure everything went okay tonight."

"Don't worry about me. I'm a bad ass," Samantha assured him. Clad in a summer dress adorned with bright red flowers, she didn't look dangerous, but Samantha knew she was more than capable of handling herself.

"Well, you do own a pink Glock."

"Uh huh." She tilted her head to catch his kiss on her lips. "I'm dangerous."

"And I love it," Jeff whispered, his grin affectionate.

Walking with him to the front door, Samantha held onto his hand, reluctant to let him leave. Every day she spent with Jeff was another day of her falling more deeply in love with him. He was funny, smart, and the nicest person she'd ever known. His quiet strength and support of what she was going through only made her love him all the more.

"I'll be the best phasmagus that ever existed in no time at all," she said confidently.

Jeff grinned at her, pressed a kiss to her cheek, and opened the front door.

Benchley and Alexia stood on the stoop ready to knock. The sky was darkening behind the siblings, stars dotting the indigo. The gentle buzz of the cicadas in the trees always made Samantha think of peaceful summer evenings on the porch of her childhood home. She longed to curl up on her porch swing with Jeff and enjoy the last bit of the sunset. However, she knew the night was the most dangerous time now for all of them.

"Hey, Shark Boy!" Samantha waved, trying to keep herself lighthearted despite the fear she felt slowly blooming inside of her. Using her powers was always a bit unnerving. "Hi, Lex."

"Ready to teach my girlfriend how to kick ass and take names?" Jeff asked his friends.

Benchley's round cheeks reddened. "Uh, sure, but only if she wears a super heroine costume."

"Sexist," Alexia growled, shoving her brother into the house. "We've got it covered. No worries, Jeff."

Samantha gently pushed Jeff out the door. "Go do what you have to do. I'll be good and train."

"I just feel like I'm leaving you defenseless," Jeff said, sighing.

"I'm fine," she answered. "The ward is up and holding."

Jeff looked upward, but she knew he couldn't see the transparent dome that encapsulated her house. It resembled a soap bubble, the colors of the rainbow sliding over its surface as the light caught it. Aimee had set a ward over the house right after the battle with The Summoner, and Samantha had worried that the neighbors would freak out at the sight of the magical barrier. It had taken her a few days to realize that regular humans couldn't see it.

"It's been too quiet since that night in the graveyard," Jeff said finally.

"Don't jinx us," Samantha chided.

"Right. I'll shut up now. Love you." Jeff pressed one last kiss to her lips then hurried to his beat-up Land Rover.

Samantha waved until he drove off, then stepped back into the house. Benchley was already rummaging around in her kitchen for snack food while Alexia hooked up a laptop to Samantha's television.

"I got this whole presentation ready for you to watch," the diminutive young woman said from behind the flat screen. "It's going to rock. Benchley figured out some exercises for you to do to develop your abilities."

Flopping onto the sofa, Samantha propped her bare feet on the coffee table. "Teach me, oh wise one."

Benchley appeared with a bag of chips. "It's really cool. We got some scans of an old journal from a hunter in France. Real rare stuff." He shoved some of the crispy snacks into his mouth and settled onto the sofa beside Samantha. "You can do some seriously cool shit."

"Bring it. Let's do this." Samantha really hoped their presentation would help her focus her abilities. She was now acclimated to seeing ghosts around Austin but wasn't too sure what else she could do. Amaliya and Samantha had experimented a bit on their own. They'd figured out that Samantha could definitely enhance Amaliya's abilities, but they weren't too sure if it could work in the reverse.

Alexia finished and sat cross-legged on the floor next to a laptop adorned with stickers of obscure bands and a vampire version of Hello Kitty. "Okay, so being a phasmagus is different from being a medium, because you not only see ghosts and talk to them, but you can make them physical creatures."

"Right," Samantha said, nodding.

"You can get the dead peeps to do your will and help you out. You have an auto-connection to the dead," Alexia continued.

Samantha watched the various sketches and paintings of phasmagi with ghosts swirling around the lone figures. "Hey, those are all dudes."

"Well, you know, if a woman did this kind of thing..." Benchley made motions that took a moment for Samantha to decipher.

"They blew bubbles?"

"They were drowned," Alexia interpreted her brother's very bad pantomime.

"Or burned at the stake," Benchley said around a mouthful of chips.

Alexia scowled. "Because having breasts and a vagina is so scary to certain men."

"Not me! I love them," her brother said defensively.

Samantha raised her eyebrows.

"Well, not Alexia's! Eww."

"But mine are okay?"

Benchley crammed more food into his mouth. He was still smarting over Jeff and her officially being a couple. While Samantha usually found his crush cute and not annoying, if he kept being an idiot, they were going to have words.

"Bench, stop being a wanker and shut up. Giving a lesson here. Stop hitting on Samantha. So...anyway...according to the etchings we acquired, a phasmagus could even use spirits to transport themselves."

Staring at the image on the screen, Samantha widened her eyes. "I can fly?"

"Well, not sure if you can actually fly or if a ghost is carrying the phasmagus and is invisible," Benchley said.

"That painting makes it look like I can totally fly!" The idea definitely had its appeal.

"It kinda does," Benchley agreed. "You could like wear a Supergirl outfit and—"

Samantha hit him. "Shut up."

Alexia tugged on the strings of her hoodie while frowning at them. "C'mon, you two. I worked hard on this!"

Samantha focused on the screen and the image of a phasmagus ordering ghosts into battle. "I'm paying attention."

"So, just like The Summoner, there was a phasmagus who could create entire armies of ghosts and send them against his enemies. If a ghost is angry with the person they're attacking, it makes them stronger and even more effective. That's why the vampires tried to get rid of all the phasmagi. Imagine all the ghosts of your victims going after you." Alexia pulled her hood onto her head, still tugging on the strings. She was obviously nervous.

"Wow." Samantha could easily imagine how terrifying that would be for vampires. Amaliya had told her all about how she'd raised the dead at Santos's mansion. Those were only the victims he'd been dumb enough to bury around his home. Add in hundreds of years of killing, an army of angry, powerful ghosts, and it wasn't hard to see that the vampire would end up so much mush.

"According to the journal of this hunter, the phasmagus could pull ghosts from all over the world," Benchley added. "He could just open portals and suck them through."

"That's hardcore," Samantha said in awe. "So what happened to this phasmagus?"

Alexia's voice was barely audible. "He was killed."

"Who killed this phasmagus?" Samantha asked, dreading the answer.

Alexia lowered her head, her hoodie hiding it entirely.

"Well?" Samantha glowered at Benchley.

"Uh, The Summoner," Benchley muttered.

It made sense. The Summoner wouldn't want a phasmagus that powerful to live. Considering how many people he'd killed, and his abuse of their bodies, it would be his worst enemy. Samantha felt the sick feeling in her stomach intensifying.

Beatrice skidded down the hallway and with a yowl launched herself onto the back of the sofa. Pushing her head through the slit in the curtains, the cat began to angrily meow.

"Uh, that's not good," Benchley muttered.

"He doesn't know about me, right?" Samantha whispered. "Right?" She ransacked her memories of the night in the Fenton graveyard. Had she done anything remarkable? Well, Amaliya had dragged her through the ground to her side, but that wasn't Samantha's powers showing. Or was it?

Back arched, hissing loudly, Beatrice continued to make her unhappiness known.

The three people in the living room were motionless.

"Maybe it's a dog," Samantha said, her voice cracking.

Alexia finally looked up, the lenses on her glasses catching the light from the TV. "Right. Totally."

Benchley let out a nervous laugh. "There's no way he knows about you."

A second later, there was a loud whoosh, and a sound unlike any other Samantha had ever heard filled the house. She clapped her hands over her ears as Beatrice screeched, tore across the back of the sofa, and vanished down the hall. The noise, a cross between rushing water and boulders falling, was deafening.

"What's that?" Samantha cried out.

"What?" Benchley asked. He whipped about, looking frightened as the bag of chips fell from his hands.

"That sound!" Samantha screamed over the din.

Alexia and Benchley stared at her in fear.

"I don't hear anything," Alexia finally said.

"Fuck me! How can't you hear that?"

"You're a supernatural," Benchley said, his voice nearly drowned out by the racket outside. "We're not."

With a sudden surge of anger, Samantha launched herself off the couch and stormed over to where her purse sat on the kitchen table. She jerked her pink Glock out of its hidden holster inside her Betsey Johnson bag and stalked toward the front windows. "Benchley, Alexia, get down. Don't move."

Benchley slid off the couch and crawled to his sister's side. Alexia dug around in a bag she had brought in with her.

The weight of the gun in her hand steadied Samantha's nerves as all the years of lessons at the firing range kicked in. Samantha took several deep breaths, then, careful to keep out of view, she looked out the front window.

Two dark figures stood in the shadows of the pecan trees that bordered the property line between Samantha's small house and the neighbor's two-story. Dark waves of purplish magic flowed out of one of the figures and crashed against the ward. The magical bubble was holding against the torrent of dark magic, but the surface was rippling under the assault. The taller form's eyes were glowing red fire.

"Okay, I got someone hitting the ward with purple magic. Black witch, right?" Samantha asked.

"Yeah, totally," Alexia answered, laying a cross, a dagger, and some spell bags on the floor next to her.

"Second one has red eyes. Vampire?"

"Or demon," Benchley said, shaking his head. "I hate demons."

"Are they eyes like fire or just glowing red?" Alexia asked.

"Fire."

"Demon," Alexia and Benchley said at the same time.

"Shit." Samantha licked her lips. "Can they get through the ward?"

"No one can get in that means you ill will. That's how the ward works," Alexia explained. She crawled over to the front window and set a small camera on the sill before going back to her computer. "Benchley, put these on the back window and side windows."

Benchley vanished into the house with the cameras.

Samantha watched as the purple energy crackled over the ward. It was shot through with arcs of energy that looked like lightning. The dark magic hungrily lapped over the surface, seeking a way in. "Does it hold against bullets?"

"I...think so." Alexia was busy at her laptop. "I'm not sure."

"Can I shoot them through it?"

Alexia shook her head. "I don't know."

"Find out!"

"Cameras are up," Benchley said, huffing back into the living room. He grabbed a small .22 from the bag and stuffed some spells into his pockets.

"I got the feed." Alexia looked up at the television where the views around the house were projected. "Two in the back trying to get through there."

Samantha crouched and stared at the screen. The cameras did not reveal the magic that was pummeling the ward or the ward itself. "Call Aimee and find out what the ward will and won't do."

Searching his pockets for his phone, Benchley gave her a curt nod.

Biting her lip, she tried to sort out what she could do. The sound of the black magic hitting the barrier was making her head hurt, and it was difficult to concentrate through the pain. It amazed her that Benchley and Alexia couldn't hear or see what she was witnessing. Crawling forward, she pushed Alexia away from the laptop and pulled up the presentation they'd been giving her. Scrolling through the pictures, Samantha searched for any clue as to how her magic could help them.

"How did the phasmagus call ghosts?" Samantha asked Alexia.

"He carried dirt from a graveyard and bits of bone," Alexia replied.

"Doesn't help. I'm not going to go dig up Mr. Kibbles. I'd probably only get kitty ghosts." She saw the blank looks and quickly explained. "My other cat that passed away. I buried him in the yard."

"He used corpses as a focus to reach the dead," Benchley explained. "You just need something that will help you contact the spirits. Like a Ouija board or something."

"Hello! Good Baptist here!" Samantha sat back on her heels, her gun still clutched in her hand.

Benchley's thick fingers were trembling as he held his phone to his ear. "No answer. Trying Cass."

Samantha returned to the window and peered out. The assault was growing in intensity. Now there were two more figures joining the first in hurling dark magic at the ward. Beyond them, the neighborhood was peaceful and quiet.

At last, Samantha realized what she needed. "Amaliya."

CHAPTER EIGHT

Amaliya clutched Cian's hand as they strode along the busy sidewalks of downtown Austin. The early evening breeze was heavy with moisture and the threat of late summer storms. The many swanky stores, upscale restaurants, and towering buildings holding luxury apartments were a far cry from the older buildings, dives, and bars that had once inhabited much of this area of Austin. The city was continuing its transformation, and Amaliya missed the old version. She had fit in better with the Austin she had originally fallen in love with.

Most of the people rushing past her were dressed in very expensive clothes, perfectly coiffed, and reeked of money. The two vampires garnered a few curious looks, but Amaliya ignored the people staring at them openly. Cian's chestnut brown hair was long and layered around his face that sported a scruffy goatee. His lean form was in dark jeans, a black shirt with red edging on the collar, and black cowboy boots. Amaliya was in a short black dress with spaghetti straps and a sweetheart neckline. The red-soled platform high heels on her feet were the most expensive pair she'd ever owned. Cian had purchased the Louboutins because the spikes that studded the black leather reminded him of her. She had to admit they looked awesome even if they made her taller than Cian. It was just another sign of how much he adored her.

"Be careful," Cian said, warning her of a crack in the sidewalk.

Pressing closer to him, she felt the coolness of his body through his shirt. "Catch me if I fall?"

"Always." He flashed a grin and kissed her cheek.

Amaliya's long black hair flowed unfettered to her waist, garnering a few admiring looks. She'd considered chopping it off, but it had always been a sort of security blanket throughout her life. One tilt of her head and it formed a shield between her and the world. It was also really good at hiding her face when she was severely pissed off and wanted to rip someone's head off. It had saved her on more than one occasion when it came to her difficult family.

"Where are we going?" she asked.

"I thought we'd wander a bit before we meet Baptiste at the bookstore later," Cian answered.

"I'm still hungry."

"We'll take care of that," he promised.

The taste of blood was still fresh on her tongue, and she was ready for another victim. Cian and she had fed on a few college students earlier, but her hunger was not yet sated. It was more work to find appropriate victims since the vampire couple no longer lived in the high-rise apartment Cian owned where victims had been plentiful and easily accessible. Relocating had been necessary, though disruptive. The Summoner would try to find her and reclaim her.

Amaliya didn't like letting her hunger grow too strong. It made her lose a grip of her humanity as the predator inside took over. She felt close to that edge now. All the pretty people in their impeccable clothes and sweet-smelling perfume were prey in Amaliya's eyes. Delicious, succulent prey.

Cian jerked his head to one side, indicating a group of young women giggling as they prowled up the street toward the swankier pubs. Their glittery high heels and short skirts were awkward on their youthful bodies. Amaliya suspected that the group was carrying fake IDs. Cian drew Amaliya across the street, avoiding the oncoming traffic. Moving as a small herd, the four girls nervously prattled on, briefly glancing at the two vampires dropping in behind them.

Drawing her hand to his lips, Cian kissed Amaliya's fingers lightly. His lips were cold, the need for blood growing in him, too. It would be easy to split the girls apart once Cian made his move and lured them away for a quick bite. Already two of the women were sneaking looks at Cian, their heavily made-up eyes drinking in his vampire allure.

As they crossed an intersection, Amaliya cast a look over her shoulder at the building that had been her home. It rose above her, filling the sky. The automatic lights inside had flicked on, and she could see the balcony where she had often taken a smoke break. She missed the old place, but Cian had been right about relocating for safety reasons. Maybe one day they'd be able to move back.

The explosion that ripped through the apartment shattered the glass windows and plumed into the warm night air. Amaliya gasped, her fingers digging into Cian's hand. Car alarms and screams rent the air. Black smoke poured out of the inferno filling the loft apartment to slither across the sky. A second blast sent people cowering into doorways and behind cars. Amaliya stood transfixed beside Cian watching their former home engulfed in fire.

The braver souls lifted cellphones as they ventured into the middle of the road, recording the disaster unfolding before them. Sirens sounded in the distance. The flames licked along the top of the roof of the building.

Amaliya registered Cian's phone ringing a second before he lifted it to his ear. "Yes? I see it. Is the building being evacuated?" His arm snaked around her waist, holding her close to him as he talked. *Stay close*, she heard his voice in her mind.

Though she wasn't at full strength, Amaliya uncoiled her necromantic power, letting it seep out into the night. It spread out like a net, seeking among the humans watching in awe as the building burned. She didn't sense any dead in the crowds. If The Summoner had sent dead minions to set a bomb, they were long gone. Then it occurred to her that The Summoner could have used human hands to set the charges.

Cian pocketed his cellphone. "We need to go."

"What about the others?" Amaliya asked while he guided her down the street, his arm firmly wrapped around her shoulders.

"I want to get us away from here before we worry about the rest of our cabal."

"I don't sense any vampires or zombies."

"That doesn't discount demons, black witches, or humans, Liya," Cian said in a short tone. "I want to get you somewhere safe."

"I can take care of myself," Amaliya grumbled.

Guiding her through the crowd of people cluttering the sidewalks, Cian shook his head in aggravation. "It's not about you taking care of yourself but me protecting the woman I love."

"Well, as long as you know I can kick your ass..."

With a chuckle, Cian dragged her around a corner. "And if someone was after me?"

"I'd rip their fuckin' head off," Amaliya answered.

"So let me worry about you, okay?"

"Fine!"

Amaliya had to admit he had a point. They were both very protective of one another. It was just that for so long she had floundered through life, constantly scrutinized and mocked by others for her perceived failures, but now that she was powerful she wanted some respect. She had to remember that Cian actually did acknowledge her abilities and not lash out at him for other people diminishing her in the past.

Finally, they reached the parking lot where Cian's new car waited. He had sold all the models he owned earlier and replaced them in an effort to hide from The Summoner. The car beeped as he unlocked it.

"Did you see that?" the parking lot attendant asked from where he sat near the entrance.

"Yeah, we did," Cian answered.

"Was it a plane?" The older man's dark face was creased with worry. "Was it terrorists?"

Shaking his head, Cian opened the door for Amaliya. "I don't think so. Maybe a gas line or something."

"I hope so. Hope it's not getting crazy. It is 2012, you know."

Amaliya slid into the warm interior of the black sedan and pulled her seatbelt on as Cian took his place beside her. The doors shut with a thud.

"Where are we going, Cian?"

"To Jeff's store," the vampire answered. He quickly pulled out of the parking spot, zoomed in front of several cars trying to get out of the lot, and turned out onto the road.

Twisting about in her seat, Amaliya could see their old home still burning. The fire appeared to have skipped to other floors and was consuming the top of the building. She hated to think of the humans affected by the attack on the home she had shared with Cian.

"Do you think The Summoner still thinks we lived there?"

"Possibly. Or it could be a warning shot."

"What do you mean?"

"A clear signal that The Summoner is coming for us. Even if Etzli and The Summoner know we're not living there anymore, what better way to let us know we're being targeted?"

"Do they want us to run away?"

Cian lightly shrugged. "Or they could be trying to get us to go attack them."

"Or it's a distraction," Amaliya suggested.

"To distract us from what?" Cian's brow frowned at the thought. He maneuvered his car swiftly through traffic, scooting around cars with a supernatural agility that was a little exhilarating.

Amaliya.

Samantha's voice filled her mind, afraid and desperate. Fumbling with her phone, Amaliya's hands began to shake.

"Liya?"

"They're after Samantha!" Amaliya's quivering fingers managed to activate her screen just as the phone rang in her hands and flashed an image of Samantha flipping her off on the surface. "Sam!"

"They're trying to get through the ward!" Samantha's voice exclaimed. "I need you to get here right away!"

"Cian, how far away are we from Sam's?"

"Fifteen minutes, or more with traffic," he answered in a tense voice.

"Amaliya, can you do that trick you did in the graveyard?" Samantha sounded scared and impatient.

It took a second for Amaliya to realize what Samantha was asking her to do. "When I dragged you through the ground?"

"Yeah but come here instead?"

Amaliya searched her memory of that night. "I think I need the dead on either side to work." It hurt to think of Samantha crouching next to the dead body of Amaliya's grandmother when Amaliya accidently pulled the blonde to her side using her death magic.

"Think a dead cat will work?"

Amaliya almost laughed.

"I buried my cat in my backyard," Samantha explained.

"Are we near a cemetery, Cian?" Amaliya asked, craning her neck to peer out the window.

"The Texas State Cemetery," Cian replied. He turned the wheel sharply, racing up a one way street, expertly avoiding all oncoming traffic, before taking a hairpin curve that placed them closer to the graveyard.

"Okay, I got the dead on this side, Samantha. Get ready." They were within a block of the entrance to the Texas State Cemetery. Amaliya could easily scale the fence. "Pull over, Cian!"

Cian obeyed immediately. "Be careful, Amaliya!"

"Go to Samantha's! I'll meet you there!"

Amaliya scrambled out of the car and sprinted to the fence. The street was briefly clear of traffic, so she jumped it, landing hard on the other side. She swore as her heels sank into the dirt.

"Amaliya, where are you? You need to come here fast!" Samantha shouted into the phone.

"Little bitch, I need you to call to me when you're near the corpse." Amaliya felt her power sinking into the ground, calling the dead. The dead answered, the necromantic power filling her completely and vanquishing her hunger. Death sated her just as much as blood.

"Fuck! I have to go outside. Benchley, cover me!" Samantha ordered on the other end.

Amaliya could hear the little blonde swearing, a door opening, and a terrifying sound that reminded her of Godzilla dry humping the Empire State building.

"Okay, I'm about to it. Be ready, bitch-face."

"Just do what we did that night. Call to me."

Amaliya crouched down, buried her fingers in the earth, and concentrated on the tendrils of her power reaching out into the night. As always, in her mind she saw them as black glittery ribbons adorned with stars. Within seconds, they intertwined with the wispy white mist of Samantha's magic. Weaving into a thick web, the combined energies grew stronger. Amaliya felt it racing into her, filling her completely.

Come to me, Amaliya, Samantha's voice said in her head, each word throbbing with power.

The earth opened up and dragged Amaliya down.

CHAPTER NINE

Samantha never dreamed she would be so relieved to see Amaliya spew out of the earth like a zombie in a cheesy horror film. The vampire clawed at the ground, attempting to pull her legs out of the dark brown dirt. Samantha grabbed her icy hands and tugged. Meanwhile, Benchley crouched beside them wielding both a gun and spell bags.

"Ugh!" Amaliya grunted, spitting out grass and dirt and kicking away the remains of Mr. Kibbles. "Gross!"

"Poor kitty," Samantha lamented, then noticed Amaliya's shoes. "Louboutins! You have Louboutins! Cian never bought *me* Louboutins!"

"Gawd, they're going to be ruined by the time this night is over," Amaliya complained.

"Could we focus?" Benchley pointed at the dark figures moving along the hurricane fence line. "You know, bad guys!"

Still holding Amaliya's hands, Samantha tugged the vampire to her feet. When she released the other woman, Samantha sensed their combined powers unraveling rapidly and drifting apart. In a panic, the blonde immediately clutched Amaliya's fingers, afraid to lose their connection. Their power again surged between them, bitingly cold and full of death. In her haste, Samantha had unleashed the full force of their magic. Amaliya thrust their clasped hands forward, loosening the excess in a massive wave that swept over the ground and swelled up along the edges of the ward in a torrent of black and white energy.

Samantha gasped.

"Wow!" Amaliya grinned.

Benchley grabbed both of them. "Get inside!"

Samantha stumbled a little, still disoriented, and managed to get a sticker embedded in her big toe, but the three of them made it safely into Samantha's bungalow.

"Did you see that?" Samantha gasped.

"That was crazy!" Amaliya shoved her hair from her face, bits of leaves and grass falling to the clean floor. "I'm buzzing hardcore."

Samantha's hair was standing on end, and her fingers were tingling. "Me too."

"What are you talking about?" Benchley demanded. Frustration reddened his face and made his voice surly.

"Our magic went haywire and did this whole tsunami thing," Samantha explained.

"Did it hit the bad guys?" Benchley's brows knitted into a hard line above his eyes.

Furrowing her brow, mimicking his look, Samantha answered, "I don't think so."

"It bounced off the ward! Dammit!" Amaliya's sour expression matched the one that immediately fastened onto Benchley's face.

"Not a good thing!" Benchley waved the spell bags around. "If we try to use these, we'll have to go outside the ward. Which means we could *die*."

Amaliya wiped her still-dirty hands off on her dress, her dark red lips turned downward. "Fuckin' great."

"Can you astral project yet?" Benchley asked, his brow puckering.

Amaliya shook her head. "No. Not yet. That wasn't your big plan, was it? Me astral projecting and kicking ass?"

"No, no." Samantha grabbed a roll of paper towels off the counter and thrust it at the brunette. "We're kinda stuck. Which is why I summoned you. I can't shoot the bad guys, or the cops are going to show up. And how do I explain the bodies? Unless, of course, they get through the ward and into the house. Then I will shoot the assholes in self-defense. Which will totally be messy, too. Do not want blood all over my house! Plus, what if they end up being demon bodies or something? How do I explain that to the police?"

Pacing, Benchley grumbled to himself. His old leather sandals creaked almost as much as the wood floor.

"I can call the dead," Amaliya offered.

"Zombies invading Hyde Park. So not a good idea. All *Night of the Living Dead* there, bitch-face." Samantha stared at the bits of dirt, grass, and twigs falling onto the floor as Amaliya attempted to clean herself off. "I actually wanted you here because I think maybe your power can help me reach out to the ghosts."

"Eh?" Amaliya squinted at her. "What?"

"You were in a graveyard. You're covered in graveyard stuff. And pieces of Mr. Kibbles. So you're my focus to contact ghosts." Samantha smiled at her sweetly. "Ta da."

"Foci," Benchley corrected.

"Whatever."

Amaliya studied Samantha for a second, then said, "So you don't want me to go beat the hell out of the bad guys?"

"Well, you could try. But there are probably at least two black witches and maybe a demon or two out there along with a few vampires," Samantha said. "Can you take them out?"

"Vampires. Yes. Witches, not too sure. Demons..." Amaliya shuddered. "Cian always told me to stay away from them."

"Right. So I can use invisible ghosts if we can figure out how to reach them."

"What if the ward keeps you from reaching the dead?" Benchley grumbled.

Samantha shushed him so she could listen to the continuing attack on the ward. She was getting used to the heinous sound it was making, but something about it caught her attention. Amaliya had her head tilted, obviously paying attention to the magical assault as well.

"It sounds different," Samantha realized. "It might be weakening."

"Then you two need to figure it out now." Benchley's irritable mood was on Samantha's last nerve.

"We are, Shark Boy! Calm down!"

"Okay, the way my magic usually works is that as long as I'm connected by blood to a graveyard, I can call the dead." Amaliya stopped brushing the dirt off her dress. "So if you can use graveyard dirt, you're now connected to the graveyard I was just at."

"Oh!" Samantha hurried to get a broom and dustpan. "That makes sense. We wouldn't have to worry about the ward because I pulled you through the earth. So there's a...uh...Shark Boy, what's that stupid gaming thingy?"

Benchley stopped pacing. "Portal?"

"Yeah, that!"

"I got a hold of Jeff. He's on his way with Cass, Aimee, and the new guy," Alexia called out from the living room.

"We got Amaliya! They're working on a plan! Right?" Benchley glowered at Samantha.

Wielding the broom, Samantha took a menacing step toward the pudgy guy, but Amaliya stopped her.

Poking her head into the kitchen, Alexia's somber face looked a bit pale. "Well, you better think of something. I have six people near the front yard all clustered together. Seriously, where are the nosey neighbors when you need them? No one's calling the police on the creepy prowlers."

"Should we call the police on them? Before I shoot them?" Samantha glanced at her phone sitting on the kitchen counter as she swept up the dirt. The thought hadn't even occurred to her. She was swiftly adapting to the notion of policing themselves when it came to the supernatural world.

"No! No!" Benchley said adamantly. "We do *not* want to put more people in danger. If the cops show up and the baddies get violent, a lot of people could get hurt."

"He's got a point. Sometimes news stories about explosions or violent gang stuff are really supernatural stuff going down." Alexia checked the television screen. "We need to decide what to do."

Though she hated deferring to the vampire in her own home, Samantha had to admit that Amaliya was the most powerful among them. "Bitch-face, what should we do?"

"Honestly, I don't think The Summoner is going to care much about keeping on the down low if he's planning to rip the veil down. I don't want to risk anyone else. Cian should be here soon, but we need to incapacitate the black witches." Amaliya set her hands on her hips, and her fingers tapped against her hipbones. "Okay, little bitch, try to call the ghosts. I won't call zombies. If you can get the ghosts to attack the witches, I can take down the vampires."

"What can the ghosts do that won't cause a commotion?" Benchley asked.

"The spells!" Samantha pointed at his bulging pockets. "What kind are they?"

"White magic only. Knock out and paralysis spells." Benchley pulled the small cotton bags out. "The red string is knock out. The blue is paralysis."

"Hand them over. I'll give them to the ghosts." Samantha held out one hand.

Benchley obeyed her, but skepticism clouded his face.

Bending down, Amaliya grabbed a handful of the dirt and foliage that Samantha had started to sweep up. She held it out to Samantha, arching an eyebrow. "So, little bitch, let's do this."

Amaliya wasn't one to mince words or waste time, which Samantha somewhat appreciated except for the fact she wasn't sure how to get the ghosts to come to her. Before, the ghosts had always found her and guided her. If only she had a friendly Casper she could depend on.

"How do you call the zombies?"

The dirt in Samantha's hand was buzzing with latent energy. It felt weird yet somehow reassuring. The longer Samantha held it, the more at ease she became. Staring at the tiny bits of grass imbedded in the dirt, she felt her magicks stirring and reaching out. Not for Amaliya, but beyond her, into the night, down into the soil, calling to the dead who sought justice.

"Well, tell her!" Benchley said impatiently.

"She's got it," Amaliya said, pushing Benchley away from Samantha.

Samantha started to raise her head at the sound of their voices, but then Amaliya's hand rested on her wrist and refocused her.

Once more, Samantha experienced the tangible manifestation of her power as it whispered through the world, calling out to the ghostly remains. The kitchen and its inhabitants vanished from her sight as her vision filled with the realm of the dead. The world of the living disappeared until all she saw was an endless darkness spreading around her peppered with tombstones, mausoleums, and other constructs to honor the deceased. Out of the gloom, the dead answered. Their translucent forms drifted closer, drawn by the feather-light touch of her power. The wisps of the spirits solidified, becoming men and women dressed in the clothing of other eras.

What is it you need?

Your help. Come to me.

The ghosts drew closer and were enveloped in the white gossamer threads of her power.

Samantha blinked.

The world of the living returned.

Samantha gasped.

Four beings stood in her kitchen. Two men and two women regarded her with keen interest in their unblinking eyes. They didn't appear quite solid, the edges of their forms blurred and pulsing.

"Whoa," Benchley whispered in awe.

"Tell them what to do," Amaliya urged in a soft voice.

Clearing her throat, Samantha held the spell bags out to the ghosts. "Uh, there are some black witches outside the fence, and they're trying to hurt us. If you hit them with these, it will immobilize them, and then we can take care of the vampires. And demons."

A male ghost tilted his head, curious, but clearly not understanding.

"Samantha, they're figments, not sentient. You need to show them in your mind what to do," Benchley instructed.

Closing her eyes, Samantha imagined the ghosts throwing the bags at the black witches casting the purplish magic. The tiny cotton bags she'd been clutching in her left hand abruptly vanished from her grasp. Eyelids snapping open, she saw that the ghosts were gone. "What the hell?"

"They're obeying you." Amaliya released Samantha's wrist and headed toward the back door. "Which means I'm about to go to work."

Samantha scooted past the vampire, feeling a strange sense of responsibility for the ghosts. "What if the witches hurt them?"

She hurried into the living room and checked the cameras. Alexia sat on the floor staring at the television, chewing on her thumbnail. A stack of spells and her .22 sat next to her. On the screen, the people clustered together under the trees in Samantha's front yard were black blobs. The assault on the ward continued. The sound had altered again, which made Samantha uncomfortable. What if the dome of magic collapsed? She was about to rush for her gun when the people on the screen fell to the ground and the world became eerily silent.

"They did it," she gasped, surprised yet strangely proud.

Alexia tilted her head to regard Samantha with awe. "You totally did it. You *are* a phasmagus."

The air felt like it left her lungs, and Samantha sat down hard on the coffee table. Overcome, she hugged herself, trying to calm her sudden bout of shivers. "Oh, fuck me. The Summoner is going to want me dead in such a bad way."

CHAPTER TEN

Amaliya kicked off her fancy shoes and barreled out of the back door the second the attack on the ward ceased. The neighbor's backyard was blissfully dark, but dogs throughout the neighborhood were barking crazily. Leaping over the hurricane fence that bordered the two properties, Amaliya punched through the ward and landed next to a man clad all in black.

A hiss and a lightning-fast blow aimed at her head immediately identified him as a vampire. Amaliya ducked under his attack and rammed her open hand into his thick neck. Fingers tightening, she pivoted on one foot while she dug into skin and muscle with her sharp nails, then ripped out his throat. Blood splashed over her as she flung the hunk of flesh away. The momentum of her attack completely spun her about. The glint of a sharp silver knife caught her eye. She raised one limb in time to take the blow to her forearm. Seizing the remains of the vampire's ruined neck with both hands, she tore his head off. Dropping it on the crumpled body, she raced toward the front of the house. The dead vampire's blood soaked her dress, but her skin hungrily lapped it up as her body absorbed the energy of his death.

The next attack came from above. A vampire grabbed her by the hair and jerked Amaliya into a tree. Amaliya let out a startled cry that was drowned out by the wild barking of the neighborhood dogs. As she was dragged up through the limbs of the tree, Amaliya floundered, trying to grab onto branches. The vampire, a woman, smashed Amaliya into one of the thicker limbs, pinned her, and attempted to plunge a stake into her heart.

Again, Amaliya took the blow, raising her hand so the stake punched through her palm. The female let out a feral snarl, seized Amaliya by the back of the head, and propelled her face first into the trunk of the tree. Burning blood to immediately heal her broken nose, Amaliya braced her hands against the tree trunk and shoved her body backward into the vampire. Together, they toppled out of the boughs.

Amaliya hit the ward first, her blood sizzling against the shimmering surface. To her surprise, it didn't yield beneath her. She skidded down the invisible dome for a second, then the vampire landed beside her. Screaming in agony, the vampire thrashed around, engulfed by the magical arcs of light emanating from the barrier. Amaliya tried to stop her descent, digging her fingers into the magic. Her necromancy tore into the ward, then the spell gave way with a loud pop, and both vampires plunged onto the roof of Samantha's house.

"Fuck!"

Somehow her blood had eaten through the ward and destroyed it.

The metal ridges of the roofing bit into Amaliya's side as she rolled to her feet. Yanking the blade out of her forearm, Amaliya squeezed her hand around the stake still embedded in her flesh.

The vampire before her rose, dark hair framing a twisted, furious face. For a second, Amaliya thought she was facing Etzli, then realized it was another of Santos's female vampires. Indigenous Mexican in appearance, the tiny woman drew a silver blade and charged Amaliya. Swifter than her now-dead male counterpart, the vampire danced around Amaliya, taking swipes that weren't meant to kill but to draw blood. It was an attempt to weaken Amaliya, but the necromancer-vampire had fed so deeply on death, she was barely affected. The vampire obviously was fighting Amaliya like she would any normal vampire and not taking her necromancy into account.

Attempting to look as pathetic and outmatched as possible, Amaliya lured the vampire closer. Her clumsy attempts to deflect the blade brought a grin to her attacker's face. The silver blade bit cold and hard into Amaliya's skin while she half-heartedly dodged and slashed at the other vampire. A deep cut across her abdomen doubled her over, and her attacker immediately raised her dagger, ready to hack off her head.

With a grin of delight, Amaliya lunged forward and slapped her hand against the woman's chest, the stake impaling her palm stabbing deep into the vampire's chest. Amaliya then rode the woman's body down onto the metal roof, her other hand shoving the stake all the way through her own flesh and into the vampire's heart. The expression of shock and fear on the other woman's face as she died took a bite of Amaliya's conscience, but she dismissed it. She hadn't asked for this war, but she was going to win it.

Leaving the moldering body behind, Amaliya charged across the roof and leaped down just as Cian's car arrived. She landed in shadows of the tall trees bordering the front yard and near the fallen bodies of the witches. Another dark figure was hunched over them, attempting to awaken one of the witches. When it raised its head, Amaliya saw eyes of red fire and a face that wasn't quite human.

"Amaliya, don't attack it!" Aimee's voice shouted.

There was a loud bang, and Amaliya saw another dome of magic ripple over the house just as the demon jumped at Amaliya, its hands exploding into fire. With a cry, she darted out of its way. The demon let out a reptilian hiss and stalked after her.

"Reflection spell is up!" Cassandra yelled, racing toward the house.

"Keep them inside it and kill them!" Cian's voice rang out.

Relief washed over Amaliya now that she didn't have to hide from the view of the neighbors. The reflection spell would give a peaceful appearance to Samantha's house even as they waged battle. Amaliya burned more blood, healing the wounds inflicted on her by her earlier fights as the demon stalked her.

"How do we kill it?" Amaliya called out.

"We vanquish it," the witch answered. "Don't let it close to you!"

"Amaliya, watch out!" It was Cian.

Twisting about, Amaliya was startled to see another demon slink out of the darkness. It had a somewhat human appearance, but its face was somehow wrong. The eyes were too close together, the mouth too flat, the nose ill-defined. Lifting flaming hands, it lurched toward her. Amaliya twisted away, but it managed to briefly touch her arm. Amaliya screamed in agony as flames licked up her arm. Cian vaulted across the front yard, landed, and snatched her away from the demon before hurling her away to safety. She landed with a painful thud, her arm a mass of scorched flesh.

Aimee stood on the front walk hurling white orbs of light at the demons. The creatures dodged her attacks, their lithe bodies more shadow than form. Cassandra tackled a vampire creeping around the corner of the house that Amaliya hadn't even seen, while Cian circled behind the first demon.

"Fuck me," Amaliya gasped. Her arm was useless, dangling at her side. Climbing to her feet, she growled in frustration.

It was difficult not to be distracted by Cian and the first demon squaring off against each other. In Cian's hand was a glowing orb of some kind. Each time he took a swipe, the demon recoiled in horror. Yet it wasn't backing down, its flaming hands casting plumes of fire at Cian, which the vampire deftly avoided. The demon concentrating on Amaliya was thinner, faster, and incredibly tall.

Aimee's orbs of magic smashed into a vampire leaping off the roof, rendering it into a figure of ash that exploded into a gray cloud on impact with the ground. Somewhere nearby Cassandra was swearing in time with the sound of hearty thwacks against flesh.

The demons moved even faster than vampires, skipping out of the range of Aimee's attacks, and easily outmaneuvering Cian and Amaliya. While Cian was on the offensive, Amaliya was definitely on the defensive. Burning as much blood as she could, she tried to heal her arm. The skin and muscle refused to knit together, the pain nearly blinding. The fire erupting from the demon's hand formed into a sword as it flashed a cruel smirk in her direction. It swept the flaming weapon toward her. Amaliya barely dodged out of the way, but the burning blade still left a swath of scorched skin along her back despite the near miss.

Amaliya stumbled, then felt someone grab her about the waist. The smell of Cian's cologne and shampoo filled her nostrils. Arm around her waist, he kept the magical sphere in his hand between them and the two demons.

Chaos filled the world. Aimee battled a black witch that the ghosts had missed, purple and white orbs of magic flashing through the night. Jeff hacked at a vampire with an ax. Samantha stood in the doorway of her house wielding a pink gun and firing at something big and furry charging toward her. Alexia was tossing spell bags at the were and vampires while her brother rushed to help Jeff.

Anger welled up inside of Amaliya. Everything was out of control. Jerking free of Cian, she plunged her necromancy into the ground but immediately felt resistance.

"What the fuck?"

Seconds later, the yard lurched upward as stone spikes burst out of the grass. A stalagmite impaled one of the demons, and Cian took advantage of the moment to ram the glowing orb into its chest. Instantly, the demon was enveloped in white flames, then vanished in an agonized howl. The second demon retreated toward the remaining black witch. Aimee summoned a huge wave of white energy and hurtled it at both of them. The demon grabbed the witch, wrapping her in shadow, and vanished just before the magic hit them. The werecreature finally went down, its claws landing near Samantha's bare feet.

The sudden silence was startling.

"Where's the witch and demon?" Amaliya demanded, clutching her burned arm.

"Gone," Aimee answered, sounding disappointed.

Cian cast a worried look at Amaliya. "Are you okay?"

"Burned, but fine. And pissed. Something blocked my powers. And who the hell made those?" She gestured to the stone spikes.

"How am I going to explain them to the neighbors?" Samantha frowned, kicking the dead were-creature.

"Sorry about that," a voice said from behind Amaliya.

The ground trembled and the stalagmites sank into the lawn, leaving two blemishes of upturned earth.

Amaliya whipped about to see a tall, handsome black man with a clean-shaven head and well-groomed goatee. Wearing black slacks and a maroon shirt that matched his eyes, he looked vaguely familiar.

"The elemagus," she said, narrowing her eyes.

"Baptiste. Rachoń sent me." He extended a hand.

"I couldn't bring my dead because of you," Amaliya said irritably, ignoring his proffered handshake. Her arm was a mass of burned flesh, and the pain was nearly unbearable.

"Sorry about that. I didn't mean to block you," he said apologetically.

Samantha jumped over the dead were-creature and hurried over to Jeff. Meanwhile, Cassandra strolled over to her girlfriend, wincing as she walked with a slight limp.

"Let me see your arm." Cian stepped closer to Amaliya, pocketing the glowing orb. Holding out his hand, he waited.

It bothered her how well he could read her moods. Amaliya had felt ineffectual toward the end of the battle, and it made her angry. Cian seemed to sense it, or maybe he was reading her thoughts. Grumpily, she rested her hand in his. With gentle motions, he moved her arm about, surveying the damage.

"Aimee, how long will it take to heal?" Cian called out.

Aimee and Cassandra looked up from their embrace.

"That's going to take a lot of blood. Demon fire is serious black magic." Disengaging from her girlfriend, Aimee strode over to Amaliya. Leaning forward to examine the scorched skin, she winced. "Maybe two or three days of feeding."

"Great." Amaliya hated being in pain. It made her cranky, and she detested how she kept shifting from one foot to the other in a fruitless effort to somehow diminish it. Cian stood close to her but didn't touch her. Again, she was impressed and annoyed with how well he knew her. She loathed being coddled.

"Is anyone else concerned that the black witches are missing?" Benchley asked. He stood near the spot where the witches had fallen after Samantha's ghosts had pelted them with the spell bags.

"Where the hell is the ward?" Aimee asked, looking more than a little worried. Hands on her hips, she peered upward.

"I kinda broke it," Amaliya confessed.

"You what?" Samantha's eyes widened. "Is that why they got in?"

Amaliya shrugged. "Oops."

"How?" Aimee demanded. "That was a hardcore spell. If you can break it, The Summoner will be able to."

"I don't know! I was trying to stop my fall when I landed on top of it after being ambushed by a stupid vampire."

"You landed on it?" Aimee's eyes narrowed. "You *landed* on it?"

"It's only supposed to keep out the bad guys," Benchley said in a low voice.

"I jumped through it once with no problem," Amaliya said defensively. "And I was bleeding and fighting for my life when I fell on it the second time. I was trying to stop my fall, dug in my fingers, and then it wasn't there and...how the fuck am I supposed to know? *You're* the witch!" Amaliya frowned, irritably staring at her arm. "Fuck, this hurts."

At last, Cian put his arm around her shoulders, and she leaned into him. "It'll heal. Aimee, can you get another ward up?"

Crossing her arms over her breasts, Aimee shook her head. "No, I don't have the stuff for it."

"It was broken anyway," Benchley sniffed. "We couldn't defend ourselves. Sam and Amaliya's magic was deflected off it. We were trapped."

"Dammit," Aimee muttered. "I'll have to come up with a new version of it. That could take a few days."

"You can do it, babe," Cassandra said, giving the witch's shoulder a reassuring squeeze.

"We need to leave now," Jeff decided. "Samantha, get Beatrice. We're going. The ward is down, and I'm not waiting around for a second attack."

"I agree." Baptiste moved toward the were-creature. "But we need to take care of this."

Amaliya sent her power into the earth, felt the dead answer, and asked them to take one of their own. The were-creature vanished into the earth before Baptiste reached it.

Tilting his head in her direction, Baptiste said, "I see."

"You and I have to share territory. We need to work on that." Amaliya tried not to sound as pissed off as she felt.

Samantha and Jeff vanished inside her house while Benchley and Alexia grabbed their stuff from the living room. After pressing a quick kiss to Cian's lips, Amaliya hurried through the house to claim her shoes. Cassandra, Aimee, Baptiste, and Cian kept watch outside. She found the Louboutins in the kitchen where she had left them. They were dirty but not ruined. Leaning over to pick them up, she grunted at the agonizing burning of her arm. No matter how much of her power she directed into her limb, it was healing at a snail's pace.

Straightening, Amaliya was shocked to see Bianca standing before her and took a hard step back, reaching out to brace herself against the counter. The blonde's dark-fringed blue eyes gazed at her with desperation in their depths. It took a second for Amaliya to realize Bianca was translucent. The ghostly aspect of the girl was unexpected and sent her mind whirling.

"Bianca," she whispered.

"I'm not dead," the girl answered, her voice imploring Amaliya to believe her. "I'm not dead. I'm still here."

Beatrice scampered into the kitchen, Samantha right behind her. "Bad kitty, Beatrice!"

Amaliya glanced away from Bianca for a scant moment, but when she looked back, the apparition was gone. With one quick movement, Amaliya snatched up the hissing cat and handed her over to Samantha.

"Little bitch, we need to go now," Amaliya said, grabbing Samantha by the arm and pushing her into the living room.

"I had to get my cat!" Samantha protested but shoved Beatrice into a fancy pink cat carrier.

"Let's go now. We got her," Jeff said, grabbing the carrier. Over his shoulder were two bags. "And I got your overnight stuff."

Samantha held out her hand toward the depths of the house. "I can't just go!"

"Yes, you can," Jeff answered.

Amaliya understood Samantha recognized the truth of the situation but was reluctant to admit that she was about to lose a part of her life. It reminded Amaliya vividly of the moment she had stood in her dorm room and realized her life as she knew it was over. She wrapped her fingers around Samantha's outstretched hand and pulled her out of the house. The blonde phasmagus came willingly, but her sadness was tangible. Cian and Cassandra fell in behind them as they walked to the cars.

"Nothing stirring," Aimee said. Her long bronze-colored hair rippled around her, making her look even witchier.

"Let's get out of here before they regroup," Jeff said.

The group split between Cian, Jeff, and Samantha's vehicles. Amaliya was relieved that she and Cian were riding to Jeff's home alone. She didn't want to tell the others what she had seen. At least, not yet.

Grabbing her unburned hand, Cian kissed it while he drove out of the darkened neighborhood trailing behind the red lights of Jeff's Land Rover. "You did good back there, even if you don't think you did."

"I failed. I could have brought the dead up, but I got blocked. And I ruined the ward."

"Baptiste was just trying to help," Cian said, continuing to hold her hand against his lips.

"Yeah, well, fuck him. I could have taken everything out with a good zombie rising," Amaliya said, scowling.

"But we survived without that happening. You're not always going to be the rescuer of everyone, Amaliya."

Tilting her head, Amaliya gazed at Cian's profile. There was no doubt in her mind that she loved him, but he didn't fully understand yet what she felt inside.

"That you have to win this war alone against him?" Cian said, smirking.

"Oh, fuck you. This mind-reading thing is going to be annoying." Amaliya withdrew her hand from his grip but only to rest on his thigh.

"Yes, you're both very powerful vampires and necromancers, but you have a strong group of people around you. Samantha killed the were-bear—"

"Was that what it was? Gross!"

"—and Baptiste helped vanquish the demon. Aimee and Cassandra killed several vampires. We held our own." Cian slid the small glowing orb out of his pocket and tossed it onto her lap. "One very trapped demon right there. Courtesy of me."

Amaliya picked up the sphere to see it was a crystal that had been shaped into a ball. The heat pulsing inside of it was disconcerting. "Can it get out?"

Cian shook his head. "No. Not on its own. Maybe a black witch could do it but not without a lot of trouble. Aimee gave me that just in case there were demons about."

"We weren't ready, Cian," Amaliya said, her voice barely above a whisper. "We've been talking about this shit for weeks now, and we weren't ready."

"I know."

The sedan sped up to follow the other two vehicles on to Interstate 35. The black smoke from the burning building was a haze against the moon. Sirens still sounded in the distance. Amaliya wondered if the blaze was under control yet.

"He came for Samantha. Not me. Her. She's dangerous to him. She can't go home."

"I agree. She'll stay with Jeff. Next to our house, his place is the most fortified magically and otherwise." Cian reclaimed the orb and shoved it in his pocket. "We'll figure it out."

Amaliya swept her hair back from her face, keeping it off the burns on her arm. What she was about to say was not going to make Cian happy.

"Why not?" Cian asked.

She frowned at him. "Now you're just showing off."

"You're actually projecting your thoughts quite loudly."

Staring out at downtown Austin as they made their way to the Travis Heights area where Jeff lived, Amaliya felt unexpected tears in her eyes. "I saw Bianca."

"The Summoner? At Sam's?"

"No. I saw Bianca. Not The Summoner. I think she was astral projecting. Something I totally need to learn to do, by the way." Amaliya peered up a side road toward her old home. The road was clogged with emergency vehicles. "Anyway, Bianca appeared to me in Sam's kitchen. I know it was Bianca, not The Summoner."

The silence from the vampire beside her lasted much longer than she anticipated. Glancing over at Cian, she saw his eyebrows were drawn downward over his hazel eyes. At last he said, "All right, but what does that mean?"

"I think she's trapped inside her own body. The Summoner may be controlling it, but she's in there. I...uh...have talked to her in my dreams. Each time she begs me to find her. I talked to Benchley about it. About possession. He's doing some research for me. So I can rescue her."

Another long stretch of quiet filled the air between them as Cian switched lanes to follow Jeff's vehicle across the bridge out of the downtown area.

"Cian?"

"Your grandmother saw Bianca and ended up dead. It was a trap, remember?"

The memory of her grandmother's death at the hands of The Summoner hit her like a bullet. It was too fresh, too new, to fully accept as truth. She kept forgetting Innocente was gone. "Right."

"Don't sound pissed, Liya. Your grandmother saw Bianca's spirit several times before she died. She was trying to save Bianca, too. Remember? What's to say that The Summoner isn't once again trying the same ploy as a trap? You know I'm right."

"But what would be the point?" Amaliya asked. "We know it's a ploy, a possible trap, so why try it again?"

"Because you wouldn't believe he would do the same thing twice?" Cian glanced at her briefly, then slowed the car to stop for a red light.

Cian had a point, and Amaliya resented that fact. It hurt deep within her to realize that she had so much in common with the tiny blonde yet had never connected with her, never truly spoken to her. All her life, Amaliya had been adrift, looking for an anchor, trying to understand who she was. As a child, she had told her mother she heard voices and sometimes saw people who weren't really there, but she had been told it was just her imagination. Now, in retrospect, Amaliya knew better. Those old memories were surfacing more and more now that she felt strong enough to actually look into her past for the truth about her existence. The Summoner had killed and transformed Bianca and Amaliya because they were the descendants of powerful mediums. He had managed to make two more of his kind, but Amaliya hadn't known that when she had first risen. By the time it had been revealed, it was too late. Bianca was possessed by The Summoner and Innocente and Pete were dead.

"Pete isn't your fault," Cian assured her, his fingers tracing over her ear lightly.

"He loved me. He wanted me to be human so we could have a life together. He never realized that isn't what I would have chosen for myself. He died for nothing."

The sedan was now making its way up a heavily lined street toward the big Victorian hidden at the top of a hill surrounded by trees. The road wasn't very wide, and cars parked along the road made the passage very narrow. It made Amaliya nervous, wondering if The Summoner would dare attack here. The ward shimmered along the property line, extending far into the sky above. It was huge and beautiful. The sedan slipped through the magic and started up the long drive to the Victorian. The outside motion lights flicked on at the approach of the vehicles, illuminating the dark green house edged in light yellow and red paint. The big house was in quite good condition considering its age.

As Cian parked the car, he finally said the words he'd been holding back but no longer could. "Pete died because he believed that the love he felt for you was worth fighting for, Amaliya. It was his choice."

"Don't say anything more," Amaliya said in a harsh, tight voice. She didn't want to hear the truth coming from Cian's lips.

"But it *is* true," Cian persisted. "If I die, it's because I believe that the love I feel for you is worth fighting and dying for. That's why I'm in this fight against The Summoner."

"Not to save the world?" Amaliya said, trying to sound flippant as she cast a dark look in his direction.

"If I had to choose between you and the world..."

"You'd let it burn," Amaliya finished. "That's really romantic, Cian. Really sick, fucked up, and romantic in a weird way."

"And you?" Cian already knew the answer, but he *wanted* to hear it.

"I'll do anything to save you. Protect you," she answered truthfully.

"Then humanity may be fucked," Cian decided.

CHAPTER ELEVEN

Samantha waited impatiently for Jeff to unlock the door to the massive Victorian, shifting from one foot to the other. She wished she had put on something other than her flip flips. The daisies on the straps kept tickling her toes. Beatrice was surly inside her carrier, letting out annoyed meows every few seconds. Behind her, Benchley and Alexia were arguing as the mysterious Baptiste stood quietly to one side with a heavy leather suitcase in one hand. Amaliya and Cian were still in their car, probably making out.

Every moment she had to stand outside, Samantha felt vulnerable to a possible attack. She hated being in the sights of The Summoner.

Stepping inside the door, Jeff quickly deactivated the alarm system and flipped on the foyer light. The glittering chandelier sprang to life overhead. Samantha darted inside, the rest of the group following. Baptiste craned his head one way then the other, taking in the giant foyer. Benchley and Alexia had been here many times before, so they made themselves at home by heading toward the kitchen.

"Nice," Baptiste said at last.

Jeff smiled proudly. "It's been in my family since the 1800's when we first moved to Austin."

The front entrance wasn't long but wide. It spread halfway across the front of the house. The massive grand staircase wound up to the higher floors to the right of the front doors, while two wood sliding doors led into the library. An arched entrance opened to the dining room that was filled with antique furniture and a curio cabinet filled with porcelain dancing ladies. Another narrower archway revealed the hallway that led to the family room and parlor in the rear of the house, while the last door to the far right was to the hallway that ended in the kitchen. Samantha was forever opening the wrong doors or going down the wrong hallway whenever she visited.

"I'm going to put Beatrice in your room," Samantha said to Jeff, her fingers locked tight around the handle of the cat carrier.

Inside, Beatrice hissed at her new surroundings.

"I'll be up in a second. Let me get Baptiste settled real quick." He kissed her cheek tenderly, his fingers lightly gripping her waist. "I am glad you're here."

Samantha sighed. "I guess I am, too."

The wide staircase wound up to the two floors above. It was a steep climb, and she felt a little winded when she reached the third floor where Jeff's room was located. She could have taken the small elevator that was off the dining room, but it freaked her out because of its size. It wasn't much larger than a broom closet. At least Jeff's room was quite large, consisting of a sitting area and actual bedroom with an attached bathroom.

Once inside the room, she shut the door, set the carrier on the floor, and opened it. Beatrice glared at her, obviously not appreciating the change in location.

"This is our new home," Samantha said, the words filling her with both dread and pleasure. She actually liked the room with its tall windows, large bed, and antique decor. But it wasn't *her* room in *her* house.

Beatrice's eyes narrowed to slits, and she didn't move.

"C'mon, surly kitty. Come out." Samantha bent at the waist to stare at her cat. "It'll be fine. I think."

The bedroom door opened, and Samantha quickly straightened. Jeff slipped inside carrying her two overnight bags. She'd packed them on a lark soon after the events in the graveyard in Fenton. Her father had always taught her to be prepared. One was filled with clothes and toiletries for Samantha; the other was for Beatrice.

"I'm sorry," Jeff said, seeing her expression. "I really am, Sam."

She didn't mean to cry, but tears sprang out before she could shut them down.

Dropping the bags on the floor, Jeff rushed to her, swept her up in his arms, and held her tenderly against his body. "Sam, I will do everything I can to protect you. I swear it."

Samantha snuggled into his chest, her face pressed into the hollow of his throat. "I'm so sorry I'm intruding on your space."

"Sam, you're not!" Cupping her face, he smiled down at her. "I'm actually really happy you're here. I've been wanting you to move in since this all started, but I knew you wouldn't want to give up your place. That's why I asked Aimee to ward your house."

Samantha sniffled. "I'm not a big ol' nuisance?"

"No! Not at all." Jeff gave her an incredulous look. "C'mon, Sam, you know how I feel about you. I love you. Even if The Summoner wasn't breathing down our necks, I'd still hope that you would end up living here with me one day."

"Really?" She felt foolish for asking, but she needed to hear Jeff's answer. Maybe she was still smarting a bit from Cian's betrayal or maybe she just wanted Jeff to remind her how much he loved her. Every time she looked at Jeff, her heart felt so full of love for him, she wanted to know he felt exactly the same way. She'd never felt so completely enamored with anyone before. Not even Cian. The feelings she had for Jeff felt like forever.

"Yes, really, Samantha. This isn't a casual thing for me. I want us to be building a life together that will last."

"Oh, Jeff! Me, too!"

Jeff's kiss was sweet yet searing. It was everything a kiss should be, and she melted into it. Tangling her fingers in his hair, she returned the ardent touch of his lips. When they finally parted, they were both breathless.

"So the world is coming to an end," Jeff started.

"Maybe."

"Maybe. But it might." Jeff stared into her eyes, his fingers gently caressing her flushed cheeks. "I want us to spend every moment we can together."

"Because the world might end?"

"Because I love you," Jeff answered.

A fresh burst of tears, this time happy ones, flooded her eyes. Wrapping her arms around his neck, she pressed kisses to his neck. "I love you!"

There was a loud thump nearby.

Jeff and Samantha separated immediately, both tensing.

Beatrice stared at them from the center of the bed, then began to clean one paw.

They both burst into laughter.

Cassandra watched her girlfriend worriedly all the way to Jeff's house. Aimee kept silent throughout the trip, but Cassandra could tell she was very upset. As soon as Jeff unlocked the front door of the Victorian house and let the group in, the witch immediately headed toward the pantry where the magic supplies were stored. Cassandra followed.

"Aimee?"

"The ward failed," Aimee muttered. Grabbing her long hair, she twisted into a bun on top of her head, then placed her hands on her hips while glaring at the jars and bags lining the shelves.

Leaning against the doorjamb, Cassandra tried to formulate a good reply to Aimee's comment but couldn't come up with anything that didn't sound trite. The ward *had* failed. Epically. Aimee wasn't used to failure, so Cassandra knew she was smarting. After a few tense beats ticked by, she decided to opt for another approach.

"Amaliya landed on the ward and it held her out. I wonder what that means?"

The witch sighed and picked up a jar to study the contents. "It means I should have taken into account that necromancy is dark magic."

"Huh?" Cassandra gave her girlfriend a startled look. "What?"

Aimee sniffed the contents of the jar, looked satisfied, and set it in a wicker basket at her feet. "Cass, we're dealing with vampires, necromancers, and a phasmagus. All creatures of the darkness."

"Like me," Cassandra said, lowering her eyes.

"No, no. Dhamphirs are different. You're more in the gray area of magic."

"I sense the splitting of hairs here." Cassandra frowned.

"Cass, you're half human. The vampire side of your nature is muted by that fact. We've discussed this before." Aimee touched her arm lightly.

"Yeah, I know, but it's still really unnerving to see dear old dad vamp out and..." Cassandra had thought that her daddy issues were put behind her, but she realized that maybe she had been wrong. She was seeing a lot of herself in Cian, and it made her uneasy.

"Yeah, but he's a very old vampire. In that regard you two are very different." Aimee tilted her head, drawing close enough that her warm breath was on Cassandra's cheek. "Do you trust me?"

"Of course!"

"Then trust me when I tell you that you're a fabulous shade of gray."

Cassandra laughed. "Okay. Fine!"

After pressing a kiss to Cassandra's cheek, Aimee resumed searching for ingredients. "Now to answer your question about Amaliya...I think she passed through the ward the first time because she hadn't activated her necromancy yet. She spills blood to make it work, so once she was wounded and bleeding, her magic kicked in..."

"And the ward attempted to kick her out."

"Exactly. Death and blood magic are very dark magicks. The only thing darker is demonic magic, which the black witches use."

Cassandra let out a puff of air. "Yoiks."

"I don't think Amaliya and Samantha are evil, but the magicks they wield can easily cross that line. I'll have to adjust the ward." Aimee selected another jar and placed it in the basket.

"How did Amaliya punch through the ward?"

"Honestly, I think she confused it. When I cast the spell, I infused it with the names of our cabal to allow everyone safe passage. The ward recognized her but was also repulsing her because it read her as a threat." Aimee lifted a shoulder. "I should have thought of that. From now on, everything I do will have to take this into account."

"It makes it harder for you to do your spells, doesn't it? The fact that we have them on our side?" Cassandra fiddled nervously with a nail stuck in the wall used to hang up cotton bags.

"Yes, but I'll deal." Aimee flashed her stunning, confident smile. "Because I'm a badass true witch."

"Damn, I love you." Cassandra couldn't help but return Aimee's smile.

"I know. Shows how smart you are."

"I may be leery about all this other shit going on in our lives, but you're the one thing in my life that I never doubt."

"Aw, babe." Aimee came instantly into her arms and snuggled against her.

Holding her girlfriend close, Cassandra breathed in her sweet scent. It always grounded her when she was feeling agitated. She often wondered if it was the herbs Aimee worked with or the actual fragrance of her magic that always made her smell so delicious.

"Cass, we're going to be okay. I promise."

"You had some sort of vision?"

Aimee wagged her head. "No, no. I don't have those."

"Right. The vampires killed all the oracles." Cassandra rolled her eyes. The vampires had done a lot to make sure the cards were always stacked in their favor.

"Remember that evil tends to get cocky. I was around Frank long enough to see that myself."

Cassandra snarled at the mention of Frank.

Picking up the wicker basket, Aimee motioned for Cassandra to let her out of the pantry. "You're cute when you're growly."

"Then I'm going to be uber-cute when I pull The Summoner's head off."

"That's my girl!"

Aimee carried the basket to the kitchen and Cassandra followed.

CHAPTER TWELVE

Cian stood on the back porch of the Victorian house and surveyed his surroundings with a critical eye. Fireflies darted through the variety of trees that stood sentry around the house, obscuring the view. There was a wrought-iron fence at street level, and a second fence enclosed the rear yard above the greenbelt. The entire lawn sloped downward on all sides.

"It'll be easy to see an attack from up here," Baptiste said, joining him.

"Especially from the higher floors," Cian agreed.

"We could maybe put some spells that work like flash bombs along that fence line. If the enemy breaches the ward, we can at least disorient them as they come over that second fence."

"A very solid idea. Which branch of the military were you in?" Cian asked, watching the other man scrutinizing their surroundings.

"Air Force. But I left after one tour. It was increasingly difficult to hide what I am." Baptiste rested his hands on the rail. A platinum skull ring with ruby eyes glittered on one finger. Cian recognized it as one Prosper had worn.

"Your kind of magus is very rare. Does it run in the family?"

Baptiste nodded. "Those of us with maroon eyes usually have the gift."

"Rachoń?"

"The Summoner killed her and changed her before she manifested any abilities. Maybe the powers would have been latent in her. It's hard to say. The eyes are a good indicator, but the abilities don't always develop. My great-grandfather told me stories about our family in Africa being able to hold off enemy tribes with the power of earth, fire, and air. Sadly, the generation that was conquered and sold into slavery couldn't wield the power." Baptiste shrugged. "So here we are...strange how fate works. We lost our tribal homeland but now control

Louisiana."

The sweet smell of the wildflowers planted in the greenbelt floated on the night breeze. It was a tranquil view considering all that had occurred that night. The shadows shifting through tall grasses and tree trunks were cast by the swaying tree boughs and not the creatures of the night.

"It's beautiful here. Reminds me a little of my home. The big porch, the feel of magic in the air." Baptiste turned around, leaning on the rail, emulating Cian by crossing his arms. "Rachoń told me you were a slave."

"Cromwell sold my family to plantation owners in the West Indies during his purge of Ireland."

"Do you remember Ireland?"

Cian shook his head. "You live as long as I do and you forget so much." He often struggled to remember the names of his wife and children. His wife's face and voice had long faded from his mind, and he feared any recollection of her was false.

"There are members of my family who claim to remember Africa. Of course, they also remember the plantations of the South." Baptiste's maroon eyes were thoughtful. "The Irish used to be considered subhuman. There were even 'scientific' arguments to support that viewpoint."

Unsure of where Baptiste was going with this thread of conversation, Cian just slightly shrugged. "People find reasons to support their hate."

"You see, I find it interesting that you and Rachoń have so much in common. You were both slaves, spat upon by others, and then turned by The Summoner, yet none of that seems to bind you together. I know she respects you, but she doesn't like you."

"The feeling is a bit mutual," Cian admitted.

Baptiste gave Cian a slow, lopsided smile. "Well, just so you know, I am a man who makes up my own mind. I came here to fight against The Summoner because he killed the man who was my father figure throughout my life. I'm not here to undermine you or spy for her. I am aware of your pasts, but I'm more concerned about the future. My future and that of my family."

"I am sorry about Prosper. I had very little interaction with him, but I remember him as someone who was loyal."

Tilting his head, Baptiste's gaze settled on the view within the windows. The people in their cadre were settling into the back room. "I just want you to know who I am and where I stand. It's important for us to trust one another. Tonight proves that The Summoner has his sights on Amaliya."

"And Samantha. He somehow knows she's a phasmagus."

The flash of headlights down the hill made Cian a little uneasy. The street was closer than he'd like.

"A phasmagus. Unbelievable." Baptiste grinned.

"An elemagus. That's unbelievable."

"There are a few of us left in the world."

"Thanks for the help with the demon, by the way."

"Glad to help."

Cian rather liked the man's measured way of speaking. It was obvious that Baptiste was not one to mince words. He respected that. "I hope you don't mind staying with Jeff."

"It makes sense. The witch and dhamphir are staying with you. I should be here with the phasmagus and human. It evens it out a bit. I do appreciate the hospitality."

Glancing over his shoulder, Cian saw Aimee tending to Amaliya's scorched arm while Cassandra watched with a worried expression. Alexia and Benchley were still arguing about matters that Cian didn't really care about. Sometimes he found the siblings to be insufferable.

"The demons are a concern." Baptiste was also watching the people within the house.

"Aimee will be preparing weapons against them."

"It's good to have a witch on our side."

"That it is."

While the vampire was observing the scene inside the house, Samantha and Jeff reappeared. It bothered Cian to see she'd been crying. The guilt he felt for dragging her into his dark world still ate at him. He still loved Samantha but not in a romantic way, and he'd always want her to be safe and happy.

Spotting Baptiste and Cian through the window, Jeff hurried over to the exit that led to the porch. The hunter stepped out to join them, the door clicking shut behind him.

"Are we going to talk about what went down?" Jeff asked, his heavy brows angled in such a way that revealed his nervousness.

"In a moment," Cian answered.

Jeff shifted around nervously. "Should we be out here?"

"The ward is in place," Baptiste assured him, lifting his eyes toward the glimmering dome that Jeff couldn't see.

"This place is actually very defensible," Cian added. "I'm going to speak to Aimee about adding spells around the property to slow down any possible attacks."

Jeff stared out into the darkness engulfing the trees. "And if they try to burn us out like they did your apartment?"

With a swipe of his hand, Baptiste expended a pulse of magic that flashed bright blue. A moment later, globs of water floated into the light of the porch to swirl around him. The levitating water balls sparkled in the light. "I could summon more if you like."

"Wow. No, no. That's...good. Where'd you get the water?"

"The dew has fallen," Baptiste answered.

Cian chuckled. "Impressive, huh?"

"Yeah!" The look on the human's face was one of total astonishment.

Baptiste flicked his hand, and the orbs of water splashed onto the flowers below the porch. "Now, if you're concerned about fire, don't be." Baptiste withdrew a lighter from his pocket. Flicking the flame into existence, he cupped his hand over it. The fire burned brighter and hotter beneath his palm. Baptiste withdrew the lighter and flipped his hand over. A ball of fire hovered above his hand. "I can deal with fire."

"Okay. I'm feeling a lot better about this," Jeff admitted.

Cian clapped the human on the shoulder. "You should."

With a grin, Baptiste closed his hand and the flame vanished.

"Now I wish you had gotten here earlier," Jeff confessed. "I wasn't too sure what to expect."

"I had to put my personal matters in order. If we win, but I die, I want to make sure that my family is taken care of," Baptiste answered. "Besides, Rachoń assured me that The Summoner was too busy setting his plans in motion to attack you right away."

"I wish she had told us that," Cian said, trying to keep a snarl out of his voice.

"Family first with Rachoń. Remember? Anyway, I had my will drawn up and that sort of thing."

"You have kids?" Jeff queried.

"No. No. It will all go to my siblings and my mother." Baptiste tucked his hands into his trouser pockets. "At least I can rest easy in the here and now as I do my duty. Of course, if we fail, it won't matter."

"Rachoń doesn't believe we can defeat him." Cian lifted an eyebrow. "Does she?"

"She's preparing a second front but hopes it won't be needed," Baptiste said. "Family first."

It angered Cian that Rachoń wouldn't support the endeavor he was leading. Yet it made sense that she'd be implementing her own plans. She didn't control such a large territory without reason. Rachoń was intelligent and strong-willed. It pained him to admit that she had succeeded where Cian had failed. She'd built up a vampire and supernatural presence that was impressive and strong enough to hold an entire state. If Cian's small cabal didn't succeed in stopping The Summoner, Rachoń and her group would be a formidable opposition to The Summoner.

Without another word, Cian entered the house to face the group of people that would stand with him against his creator. The family room was filled with large comfortable red sofas and chairs and heavy tables emblazoned with the Lone Star. The conversation fell silent the moment he stepped into view. Baptiste and Jeff scooted around him to find a place to sit. Arms still folded across his chest, Cian stood with his legs apart.

"We knew this night was coming. It was a matter of time," he started. "We learned a few things tonight. The Summoner knows that Samantha is a phasmagus. Also, he's building an army of supernaturals just as we are. The were-bear, witches, and demons are all evidence of this."

"Fuck my timing," Eduardo said, coming in from the hallway and joining the group. "I would be just in time for the long-winded speech."

"Took you long enough to get here," Jeff muttered.

"I was eating."

Cian saw Samantha start in her chair and give Eduardo a very pensive look.

"Can anyone just walk in here?" Baptiste asked with concern.

"My crew members all have keys and the alarm codes." Jeff was snuggled on a loveseat with Samantha, his fingers gently stroking her hair, obviously soothing her. "I'll get you one, too."

Baptiste nodded, his eyes watching Eduardo thoughtfully.

"Who's the guy that smells like fire?" Eduardo stopped to eye Baptiste suspiciously.

"Baptiste. I'm the elemagus Rachoń sent."

"Huh," was all Eduardo said.

Much to Cian's annoyance, the were-coyote took his sweet time deciding where to sit, finally scooting in between Alexia and Benchley. Putting his feet on the coffee table, he motioned to Cian to continue.

Cian pinned the coyote with a hard stare, then continued. "According to Rachoń, he's been ignoring us to set his plans in motion. This is most likely true. She had a very different relationship with him than I did."

Eduardo rolled his eyes.

Cian had the desire to pluck them out. "She fought alongside him. She knows his tactics. I, unfortunately, bore the brunt of them. I know from my own experiences that he likes to play games. He likes to keep his victims off-balance. Honestly, I think he fully expected to kill Samantha tonight. We surprised him. He'll regroup, reconsider his methods, then try again. We have a little time."

Amaliya sighed from where she sat. With her legs crossed, she looked wickedly sexy. "He never fuckin' changes."

"Which is a good thing," Baptiste pointed out. "It means he'll keep the same pattern."

Benchley chuckled darkly. "Does that mean we'll keep our pattern of barely surviving?"

"Hey, we kicked ass," Samantha protested.

Though Cian was inclined to actually chastise the group for everything they'd done wrong tonight, he'd learned enough over his long years of life that this would be the wrong tactic. Swallowing his annoyance, he said, "Cassandra, you did a good job in arming everyone. Samantha was able to kill the were-bear because of the silver bullets."

"It's still not good enough. We were too scattered. We need to train together." Cassandra looked remarkably like her mother in that moment, and it made Cian love her just that much more. His daughter was a reminder that there had been good in his life at one point. "I suggest we start training together so we don't accidently shoot each other."

"Sorry," Samantha said, wincing.

"I ducked," Cassandra said.

Aimee clutched Cassandra's hand gently and squeezed it.

"Can you take care of that training, Cassandra?" Cian lifted an eyebrow at the dhamphir. "You have a very good idea what all our strengths and weaknesses are. Make us all into a better fighting unit?"

"Yeah, yeah. I can handle it." Cassandra grinned, tilting her head to gaze at him with something akin to affection.

"Aimee, your ward was very effective. Maybe too effective." Cian gestured toward Amaliya. "It complicated matters a bit."

"I'm already working on a new ward," the witch said, her expression pensive. She sat cross-legged on the sofa between Cassandra and Baptiste, her bare feet sticking out from the folds of her flowing, embroidered skirt. "I'm sure I can adjust the wards. I'll need to borrow Amaliya a few times to make sure it holds up against necromancy."

"Can do," Amaliya said.

Cian could tell she was bored. He wanted nothing more than to go home and crawl into bed with her, but there was much to discuss.

"Also," Aimee continued in such a way Cian knew her next phrase may upset a few people, "Amaliya and Samantha both practice forms of death magic. It's technically dark magic. That may make it a bit difficult to tune the ward."

"Dark magic?" Samantha's brow furrowed. "Jeff, it's dark magic?"

"Yeah, but not black magic. It's because it involves dead things, not living things like white magic. Don't panic." Jeff cuddled her up tighter.

"Who fuckin' cares what kind of magic it is as long as it kicks The Summoner's ass?" Amaliya said. "C'mon. That's what really matters."

Aimee nodded somberly. "Exactly."

Cian didn't want to get into a discussion about magic, so he plunged onward. "Honestly, I think the most positive outcome of the night is that we now have everyone gathered under two roofs. As far as we know, Aimee's spell to hide the location of my house has worked. Sadly, it won't take too much to find Jeff's, but it is the best fortified of both houses. The old wards that Dr. Summerfield placed on the house are still holding according to Aimee. I think a few additions will make it even safer."

"Plus, this house is built on a positive energy nexus. I need it to renew my energy and so does Baptiste," Aimee pointed out. "I also have another idea."

"Go on," Cian urged.

"I think I can create a magical grid that will allow us to know when supernaturals enter the city. Like an early warning system."

"Awesome idea, babe!" Cassandra flashed a prideful look at her girlfriend.

"It may take a little bit of work, but once I'm done with the wards, I'm sure I can come up with something really effective."

Benchley loudly cleared his throat. "Okay, you supes are all in the same spot, but Alexia and I are not so safe, right? The Summoner is probably going to figure out who the hell we are, right?"

Jeff winced. "Yeah. You're on my website."

"The website!" Alexia groaned, covering her face.

"So we should move into one of the two houses, too." Benchley looked between Cian and Jeff. "Right?"

Amaliya gave Cian a significant look at the same time Samantha did the same to Jeff. Cian knew neither woman would prefer to take Benchley into their abodes. The man was helpful, but he'd been increasingly on their nerves with his pessimism during his training sessions with the women.

"We'll take Alexia," Cian decided. "She's building a command center in my basement, so it makes sense."

Amaliya instantly looked relieved.

"I think that makes sense. Besides, Bench has been helping Samantha with her training," Jeff agreed.

Benchley looked pleased.

Eduardo cleared his throat loudly.

"You're not moving in with us," Cian said swiftly.

"Ah, c'mon. I could curl up on the end of the bed." Eduardo smirked. "I can keep Amaliya's toes warm."

Cian glowered.

"I have room," Jeff said, raising one hand. "You can stay here."

Samantha gave Jeff a sharp, startled look.

"Nah, I don't have any desire to crash at either place. I'm fine on my own. I need my space." Eduardo ruffled Alexia's hair, much to her annoyance.

Baptiste looked amused by the exchange but remained silent.

"Why don't we all move in together?" Samantha asked. "Isn't there strength in numbers?"

Cian and Jeff glanced at each other uneasily.

Cian answered the question. "If he successfully attacks one safe haven with all of us in it, we lose. If we're split between two, if one haven falls, we still have the second to take up the fight."

"Well, that doesn't make me feel too good," Benchley decided grumpily.

Samantha let out a little startled sound, jerking away from Jeff. "What the hell?"

"Phone." Jeff shifted his weight so he could yank his cellphone out. Frowning, Jeff stared at the screen. "It's been acting up a little, and it does this thing where it sends all my emails at once and it makes it vibrate like a...a..."

"Vibrator?" Amaliya asked, her gaze teasing.

Alexia snorted. "That was funny."

The growing look of horror on Jeff's face killed any joviality in the room.

Cian stepped closer to the hunter. "What is it?"

"Oh, hell." The color drained out of Jeff's face. "We weren't the only ones hit. London, New York, Boston, Seattle, and Rome were all attacked tonight. London thought they were close to finding one of the rings. Rome reported that they had found one of them still in the Vatican. I was going to tell you tonight, but..."

"Let me guess," Eduardo said in a flat tone. "The Summoner has them."

"The Vatican is on fire," Alexia said, looking up from her own phone. "It's on Yahoo news."

"The Assembly group in Bristol is reporting the destruction of the group in London. Portland has taken in one survivor of the group in Seattle. Boston..." Jeff faltered.

"Another fire there," Alexia said, staring at her phone.

"New York managed to fight off the attack with no losses, but they're heading underground," Jeff finished.

Cian gave the group a sharp nod. "So he's on the move."

"We're losing," Samantha murmured.

"Fuck." Cassandra frowned, shaking her head.

"That's four possible rings he has," Amaliya said, then ticked them off on her fingers. "He has one. Etzli has one. The one in the Vatican. Maybe one in London."

"But he doesn't have all of them," Baptiste pointed out. "We are still ahead in the game."

Cian appreciated the reminder. "Very true."

Jeff stood and continued to scroll through his phone. "Don't you get it? He's just not going after the rings. He's killing our allies. The Assembly. The Vatican even."

"Cian," Samantha asked, lifting her eyes to gaze at him, "how many of The Summoner's children are still alive? What if they have the other rings?"

"Rachoń doesn't have one," Baptiste pointed out.

"Yeah, but he didn't trust her." Amaliya lowered her head so that her dark hair shielded her face. "Or Cian. That's why they don't have rings. But Etzli has one. What if he has favorite kids out there?"

The thought of The Summoner's surviving children assisting him was uncomfortable for Cian. He'd not met the survivors of The Summoner's games. "I'm uncertain how many might be alive."

"But Rachoń might. Until their falling out, she did know more about him than you did." Baptiste shifted in his seat, clearly uncomfortable with the topic. Cian supposed it might be difficult to accept how close Rachoń had been to the man who wanted to destroy the world. "But Samantha is right. What if his other children have the other rings already?"

"Then we might possess the last one." Cassandra widened her eyes dramatically. "Great."

To his surprise, Cian was hit with the impulse to comfort her. Yet another indication of his growing attachment to the daughter he didn't raise or even know about until recently. "Baptiste, see what you can get out of Rachoń."

"I'll speak to her tonight."

"So now what?" Benchley asked, his voice a bit higher than usual.

"We keep focused," Cian said. "Same as before. And we learn, adapt, and try to beat him at this game."

"Do you really think we can win?" Eduardo's inquiry was laced with sarcasm.

Cian pondered the question, then answered truthfully. "Yes."

CHAPTER THIRTEEN

"You really think we can win?" Amaliya asked, staring at Cian skeptically. Standing at the end of their bed in only his pajama bottoms, Cian gave her a short nod.

"You're fuckin' nuts." Perched at the top of the bed with the pillows piled behind her, she cradled her bandaged arm against her.

Her lover gave her the slow, wicked smile she loved so much. "Well, I'm with you."

She hurled a pillow at him, which he easily dodged.

She loved him, but after the events of the night, she had to wonder if he was a bit crazy. So much had gone wrong she was still amazed that they had won. Yet she had to admit that she and Samantha had worked well together as a team. That had to be a good sign.

Returning his gaze to the screen of his phone, Cian frowned. Since the gathering at Jeff's broke up, the vampire had been fielding phone calls from his human contacts in regards to the fire at the apartment building, which one of Cian's companies owned. The investigation into the fire was being dealt with, but the apartment building had taken major damage. Fortunately, no one had died, though a few people had been hospitalized.

Before their return home, he'd taken the time to feed, but she wondered if it had been enough. The death she had absorbed earlier had filled her, but Cian was dependent on blood.

"It was enough. Though I could always take a sip from you," Cian answered her thoughts, his Irish brogue sending shivers over her skin.

"Stop reading my mind."

He grinned roguishly at her.

At this point in all her previous relationships, Amaliya was already gone or about to leave. Easily bored, she was usually annoyed and out of love with her partners after just a few months. Yet with Cian, she fell more deeply in love with him every night. Even just watching him dress for bed elicited feelings of happiness and desire inside her. Years of slave labor had hewn his body into lean muscle, and she found him immensely sexy. Happily, he found the few extra pounds on her hips alluring.

"Insanely so," he said, obviously reading her mind.

She narrowed her eyes at him, then lifted them to the heavens. "Fuck me."

"In a moment." Cian finished texting someone, then set the phone on the charger.

"So why do you think we'll win?" Amaliya extended her good arm outward as he climbed onto the bed. He slid under it, snuggling into her side, one arm over her waist.

"Because we can't lose," he said simply and kissed her.

"You're argument is flawed."

Careful of her wounded arm, he nuzzled her neck. "I outwitted him. You killed him. My daughter has one of his rings hidden. We're ahead in the game. I promise."

"Well, those are all valid points." Turning her head, she caught his lower lip with her teeth. Immediately, their kiss grew a little more feral.

As the heavy metal shutters descended over the windows, Cian moved to straddle her.

"We don't have much time until the sun is up," Amaliya whispered against his lips.

"Then no more talking," he answered, sliding down her body.

Twisting her fingers into his hair, Amaliya closed her eyes with pleasure and forgot about everything else but Cian's tongue, lips, and sharp teeth.

The Summoner, tucked into the delicate body of Bianca Leduc, listened to all the reports streaming in from all over the world. With only a short time before sunrise, he sat in the elegant opulence of the house Etzli had secured for them near downtown San Antonio in the King William Historic District. The old ballroom was still decorated in the elegant style of the turn of the former century, but modern contrivances like computers, phones, and work stations had been added. Etzli and her cabal were scattered about the room, helping closely monitor the events of the night. Stark sat nearby, face tense, staring at his monitors. The hacker cast uneasy looks in The Summoner's direction. The boy was wise to be afraid. His usefulness was short term, and The Summoner just didn't see him as worthy of the new world.

Years of preparation were producing positive results, but he had still been thwarted on several fronts. Again, Cian and his little cabal had repulsed The Summoner's plans for Samantha.

This did not please him.

The Summoner had left Cian and his group to scramble about like rats on a sinking ship. He hadn't been too concerned with them or the threat they posed to his plans. The discovery of the phasmagus had been unsettling, but The Summoner had found it intriguing that Cian's old fiancée could wield an ancient power considered long extinct. He had to wonder if she'd always been a phasmagus or if his beloved Amaliya had somehow transformed her. The attack on the phasmagus had been a test to see what she was capable of, and if she had been captured or killed, that would have been fine. The Summoner had never imagined that the assault would be rebuffed. This meant that Cian's little group was much more powerful than he'd anticipated. It made the situation far more dangerous. Far more intriguing.

That *did* please him.

Etzli sat at a nearby desk, her tiny frame outfitted in a white pantsuit. Her dark hair was drawn into a chignon, and diamond earrings sparkled in her ears as she spoke on her cellphone. The Summoner was quite pleased with his adopted daughter. She was efficient, trustworthy, and ruthless. Yet The Summoner felt some dissatisfaction because Etzli was not Amaliya. His flesh, blood, and bones yearned for his lost child. His desire for Amaliya was now magnified by the need Bianca's body felt for the lost necromancer. It was a bitter reality that he had been killed and forced to take residence within Bianca. If he could have had both of his beautiful fledgling necromancer vampires at his side during his conquest of the world, it would have been perfect. To see the blood of their enemies dripping off their flesh as they crushed their opposition would have been exquisite.

Instead, Amaliya was playing house with his wayward son, Cian, and The Summoner inhabited Bianca. Sometimes he felt the young medium stirring deep within him, but he kept her firmly under control. Her powers magnified his own magic. Until he could determine how to transfer himself into another host body and retain his full power, he would remain within her slender frame.

The Summoner found the female body intriguing. The smaller build and the way the body naturally moved were so much different from his old one. Sex was very, very different, though he was bored with it now. He missed the act of penetrating his lovers.

Maybe he could find a way to possess Cian's body so he could claim Amaliya as a man. The thought appealed to him.

A tiny flutter within him indicated that Bianca was awake. Closing his eyes, he concentrated on the tender wisp of her consciousness and subsumed it into the deeper reaches of his mind.

"We have the ring from the Vatican en route," Etzli said.

Opening his eyes, he saw the vampire learning over him. "Very good. You please me."

Preening under his praise, she returned to her phone call.

Within The Summoner, Bianca was still.

PART THREE

Ghosts, Blood, and Death

CHAPTER FOURTEEN

September 2012

S amantha could hear Jeff and Benchley speaking in the kitchen in strained
voices. Pausing in the long hallway, she considered going back to bed.
It was almost one in the afternoon, but she spent a good portion of her
nights learning to use her powers and often slept in. Barefoot and wearing a pink
sundress, she stood in silence trying to decide if she wanted to deal with the day
just yet. The sunlight spilling into the darkened hallway from the kitchen was a
welcomed sight, but she was still exhausted.

Beatrice purred past her on the way to her breakfast, tail flicking back and
forth.

The rattle of glass jars emanating from the large pantry off the hallway was
a good indicator that Aimee was collecting more items for her spells. Dr. Summerfield, Jeff's deceased father and mentor, had collected a massive collection
of magical ingredients. Samantha couldn't step into the pantry without feeling a
bit giddy. Aimee explained it was normal reaction for a magus until they learned
to properly block out energies. Samantha was getting better, but she still felt like
she was struggling to get a solid grip on her powers.

Taking a few more steps toward the kitchen, the words being spoken became
more distinct.

"Nothing is going right," Benchley's voice complained.

"We're still alive," Jeff answered.

"Amaliya is still struggling with her powers, and Samantha isn't doing much
better."

Samantha frowned at this truthful assessment.

Aimee emerged from the pantry with her arms full of jars and a few cotton bags dangling over one arm. Her bronze hair and multi-colored, earth-toned maxi-dress rippled around her like silk in a breeze. Samantha liked Aimee, but the ethereal quality of the witch intimidated her. The witch cast a sweet smile over her shoulder at Samantha, then disappeared into the kitchen.

At last Samantha's growling stomach compelled her into action. Following in the witch's sweet-smelling wake (must be the herbs), Samantha entered the brightly lit kitchen.

A cauldron sat on the massive cast iron stove with steam and bits of sparkly magic floating above it. Next to it was a much more modern one where another pot was filled with something that smelled spicy and delicious. The kitchen was long and narrow with very high pressed-tin ceilings and big windows that opened to the side yard. It didn't resemble the concept of a modern kitchen at all. There wasn't one bit of stainless steel, granite, or modern cabinets anywhere. There was just one counter with a deep sink, and the rest of the surface space came from tables and china cabinets set along the walls. A huge refrigerator was shoved into an alcove and covered in what Samantha considered the ultimate nerd clippings which included superhero pictures, cartoons, and bumper stickers. It looked like multiple eras of the house collided in the kitchen making it a bit funky, yet inviting. The oddest part of the decor was the huge whiteboard fixed to one wall filled with information in various colors of markers.

"How many does he have now?" Benchley asked. He was seated at the kitchen table, arms folded on the table, and looking very grumpy. Sadly, grumpy seemed to be his default emotion of late.

"Eight," Jeff answered in a grim voice from where he leaned against the wall near the doorway into the family room.

"He has eight rings?" Samantha gasped.

"That's our estimate." Jeff leaned over to pet Beatrice as she made her way to her food bowl.

Surprisingly, the cat allowed it.

Samantha yanked open the refrigerator and pulled out the jug of sweet tea with lemon slices swimming at the top of it. She needed caffeine and sugar. "How do we know he got more rings?"

"The Swedes reported a break in at the palace. Apparently, the royal family had one of the rings." Jeff opened one of the china cabinets and pulled out three glasses. After setting them on the kitchen island that was actually an antique table, he rubbed his bottom lip nervously.

"And?" Samantha prompted while pouring the tea.

"Part of The Assembly in Sweden is actually palace guards. They tried to stop The Summoner's people but failed. The rest of the group is still in hiding." Jeff claimed the glass with Superman on it and handed the one with Batman to Benchley.

"The Assembly is falling apart." Benchley stared into his tea, then poked the ice with one finger. "It's all going to hell."

Returning the jug of tea to the fridge, Samantha sighed. Austin felt like an enclave surrounded by chaos. They weren't foolish enough to believe The Summoner would not come for them. He was taking his time for his own nefarious reasons. That truth made Samantha very scared.

"The Assembly was never that strong to begin with," Aimee chimed in. She was adding pinches of various herbs to her cauldron. "Most of them were having fun playing researcher and historian. There weren't that many real warriors in the mix. Cass and I figured that out right away."

"There are a few teams of actual fighters that are in hiding." Jeff sounded annoyed. Samantha knew he was a huge supporter of The Assembly, but she didn't think they had done much to help other than to constantly report bad news.

"Waiting for the last big battle to help?" Aimee rolled her eyes. "Lovely."

"We'll need them." Benchley sipped his ice tea. His big shoulders sagged, and he looked depressed. Samantha hadn't heard him rattle on about gaming in weeks. She supposed imagining fighting bad guys was very different from actually doing it.

Picking up the Wonder Woman glass, Samantha sipped the sweet liquid, then wandered over to the bubbling food. The spicy food made her stomach rumble. "Chili?"

"My own recipe." Baptiste sauntered into the kitchen dressed in jeans and a black t-shirt. Not only was he a powerful magus, he was the most amazing cook.

"Not as good as Texas chili," Samantha said, lifting her chin haughtily, teasing him.

"Oh, I'm sure it is," Baptiste answered with absolute confidence. "It's ready. Take a bowl. Fresh cornbread is in the covered pan."

"It really is good," Aimee said to Samantha. "It's scary good. I think he's cheating and using magic."

"Ha, ha." Baptiste walked over to the white board and started making a notation. "I just heard from my cousin. We have a confirmation on another child of The Summoner."

"Let me guess. No one has seen them since July?" Benchley shook his head. "Same old story."

In the last few weeks, it had been confirmed that three of The Summoner's children had still been alive but had disappeared soon after The Summoner had revealed himself at the graveyard in Fenton.

"That makes four, but there is serious doubt there are any more surviving. He did tend to kill them after all." Baptiste finished writing down the information.

"So why are these four alive?" Aimee asked.

Samantha spooned some chili into a bowl. "I betcha they got the rings for him." Lifting the cover on the cornbread, she felt her mouth start to water. The coarse yellow bread was already dripping with melted butter.

"That would explain how they got favor with him," Baptiste said, sounding impressed.

Jeff gave her a proud smile. She beamed back at him. "That's my girlfriend. Always seeing the obvious stuff we miss. Those four get him his rings, then go to him when he summons them."

Samantha slid into a chair at the table and set her meal in front of her. "I bet they're not alive anymore."

Benchley raised his head. "Why would you say that?"

"Because he's a dick?" Samantha said. "Just a thought, that's all."

"Why keep them alive? They're not necromancers." Baptiste folded his arms over his chest and shrugged. "It sorta makes sense. He was ready to kill Rachoń."

"But he has Etzli on his side," Benchley said, pointing at the chart on the white board. "She's not even his creation."

"But she's a vampire with unique abilities." Aimee continued to measure herbs just by pinching a bit with her fingers or piling them on her palm. Samantha wasn't too sure how accurate that method was compared to measuring cups and spoons. "She can call blood out of people once she wounds them with her daggers."

Jeff rocked back and forth on the back two legs of his chair. "Well, if you think about it, he'll want to have a lot of minions but very few top dogs. He'll want to sit on the top tier but have someone that can keep the others in line. I've been reading up on what we know about his history, and that's his pattern."

"And he's so old he's going to stick with what he knows," Samantha agreed. "Hell, my grandma can barely use her iPhone, and he's way older than her."

"You're missing something very important," Benchley said. He picked up a napkin and blotted his sweaty forehead. "If those four vampires all had a ring, that means he has nine rings. Meanwhile, we're just sitting here like a bunch of morons guessing what he's up to with our thumbs stuck up our asses..." Benchley's voice trailed off.

"We still have one," Samantha said. That was their mantra now. It was the only real solace they had as the situation became increasingly dire.

Jeff leaned toward his friend and gave him a direct look. Samantha recognized it as Jeff's serious business face. "This is the deal, Bench. In the end, we don't know what the hell The Summoner is doing other than gathering the rings and wiping out The Assembly. All we can do is depend on our connections to give us an idea of what is going on with The Summoner and prepare."

"In other words, what we're already doing." Benchley's frustration was very evident in the way he ground his teeth together and hunched over his tea.

Aimee brandished the spoon she was using to stir the contents of her cauldron in Benchley's direction. "This is the reality of the situation. You have to accept it, Benchley."

"I'm tired of us not doing anything, Aimee! We just sit around and collect all this useless information. We don't do anything but wait to die!"

"Actually, I work all damn day preparing spells," Aimee retorted. "While you're sulking, *I'm* doing something."

The witch rarely raised her voice, but the steel in it now silenced the entire room. The only sound was Samantha's spoon scraping against the edge of her bowl as she ate.

"Well at least you have something to do while you're waiting for the end of the world," Benchley spat out.

Samantha plopped some of the warm chili in her mouth and chewed. It killed her to admit it, but it was better than any she'd had at a chili cook-off. Baptiste gave her a knowing smile and a wink. She stuck her chili-laden tongue out at him.

There was a loud pop and a wash of glowing white energy flowed through the kitchen, pierced the walls, and vanished into the backyard.

Samantha twisted about in her chair. "What was that?"

"I just reinforced the ward," Aimee answered.

"How are the perimeter alarms working?" Jeff asked.

He appeared just a tad grumpy. Samantha knew he hated that he couldn't see the magic taking place around him. Samantha had to admit it looked really neat and wished she could share it with him. Instead, she tried to describe what she saw to him when he asked.

"Any supernatural crossing Austin's city limits will trigger the alarm and a tracking spell attaches to them immediately. Cass took out two vampires last night in Oak Hill. We think they were a scouting team."

"Why didn't anyone say that before?" Benchley exclaimed.

"I was waiting to report it to Cian," Aimee answered.

"Jeff's the one in charge!" Benchley glowered.

"Cian's the master of the city," Aimee stated calmly and started to eat, not looking directly at Jeff.

"But Jeff's the leader of our hunting group!"

"That consists of you, your sister, Eduardo and Jeff."

"And Samantha!" Benchley thrust a finger in her direction, and Samantha batted it away. "Right, Samantha?"

"Why can't we all be one big group?" Samantha asked.

Her boyfriend was slowly ruffling his hair, his expression tense. Jeff and Cian did work together, but Jeff was bullheaded about acknowledging Cian as their official leader.

"We are one big group consisting of two factions," Baptiste said calmly. "And we answer to Cian. Even Jeff. Because in the end, Cian has hundreds of years of experience and knows The Summoner better than we do. He also knows all our strengths, our weaknesses, and how to utilize us. Jeff, you lead our research, but you're not the military leader of this outfit."

"True," Jeff admitted, though his expression was sour.

Under the table, Samantha propped her bare feet on his leg and caressed his knee with her toes. She smiled when his hand settled over her ankle and squeezed it lightly.

"This is bullshit," Benchley growled and stormed out of the kitchen.

Silence fell over the remaining group. After a few seconds, Jeff started to get up to follow.

"I need to discuss something with you, Jeff," Samantha said, her tone quite serious. "I came up with an idea on how I can gain more control over the ghosts."

"Oh?" Jeff sat back down. "What did you come up with?"

While Amaliya continued to grow in power, Samantha was feeling stuck of late. Though she constantly saw ghosts, she found it difficult to control them the way she was supposed to be able to. Only when Amaliya was with her was she able to get the ghosts to do her bidding. Alexia and Benchley had provided a lot of information for her to read, and she was sure she had finally found a way to get her abilities firmly under her dominion.

"I want to go find Roberto in Fenton."

"Roberto?" Baptiste cocked his head. "Who's Roberto?"

Samantha saw Jeff flinch. Taking a deep breath, Samantha said in a rush of words, "He was Cian's bitchy human right-hand dude that drove me fuckin' crazy until he betrayed Cian and Amaliya to The Summoner. He became a vampire and betrayed them again, then got himself staked by a zombie under Amaliya's control. Then he survived this epic ghost apocalypse when The Summoner basically used all the ghosts in the graveyard in Fenton to infuse himself into Bianca all the way over in Louisiana. So he's still out there and cranky."

"And you want to go talk to him and then what?" Baptiste looked skeptical.

"Get him to come with me," Samantha said, avoiding Jeff's look of disbelief.

"You hate Roberto," Jeff said.

"Well, yeah. He's a snarky bitch," Samantha said, "but he's the only ghost I know really well. We kinda have a connection. He'll totally want out of that town, and I can offer him a way out. Aimee is going to make me a foci."

"It'll tether him to Samantha," Aimee explained.

"Can you do that with another ghost?" Jeff leaned toward Aimee to emphasize his next words. "Because *any* other ghost may be a much better option."

"Well, yeah," Aimee said, "but then she'd be stuck with a ghost who may not be sentient or cooperative."

"Jeff, Roberto knows me. He knows our situation. He'll be on board." Samantha tried to sound more confident than she felt.

"He tried to *kill* Cian and Amaliya. How do you think they'll feel about this?" Jeff stared at Samantha with an incredulous look upon his face.

"They'll deal. Because I need him. I know him. He knows how to fight. He knows what's up. He's a fuckin' jerk and a half, but he knows what's up. The Summoner would have eaten him up like all the other ghosts and he knows that. He'll want payback. Plus, Jeff, he did try to warn us something was up in the graveyard the night it all went to hell." The thought of Innocente's tiny broken body brought tears to Samantha's eyes. Using a napkin, she dabbed at her eyes. "He tried to warn us."

Jeff exhaled and flopped forward, his head in his hands. "Shit."

"If this can help her..." Baptiste said, then fell silent.

"You need to do it." Aimee's voice was firm. "You need to be at full strength. If you need a ghost to help you channel your power, then go get him. Cian will understand." A slight smirk appeared on the witch's lips. "Maybe Amaliya won't, but Cian will."

"How can we chance this?" Jeff asked. "If she leaves the city, it's a big risk."

"I can go during the day," Samantha suggested. "I thought Benchley and Alexia could take me."

"You need another supernatural with you." Jeff looked toward Baptiste. "Are you game?"

"I'll go where needed." Baptiste sat back in his chair, his usually placid face slightly tense. "This is the graveyard where Prosper died, isn't it?" His long fingers played with the edge of a napkin.

"Yeah." Samantha squirmed in her seat. She often thought of the graveyard as the place where Innocente had died, but Rachoń had lost Prosper and Amaliya had lost her childhood friend, Pete, that very same night.

"I'll go," Baptiste said. "I want to pay my respects." The solemn pain dwelling in his eyes spoke of how much he had loved his fallen father-figure.

"Oh...kay." Jeff tapped his fingers on the table. "Aimee, could you—"

"I can get them set up." Aimee gave him a reassuring smile. "Don't worry."

Samantha met the concerned gazed of her boyfriend with a wide grin. "It's okay. Really."

"Uh huh," Jeff said, not sounding confident. "When should we do this?"

"Tomorrow. I need time to prep." Aimee grabbed her empty bowl and spoon.

"And we need to talk to Cian," Baptiste added. "Our fearless leader."

A snort from the hallway gave away Benchley's eavesdropping.

Samantha arched an eyebrow at Baptiste. He returned the gesture, then grinned.

"Ready to go ghost wrangling?" she asked.

"I thought you'd never ask," Baptiste answered with a wink.

Jeff's head hit the table with a clunk, and he moaned. "Could this get any worse?"

"Bench, we need to talk."

Jeff watched his friend shift his weight on the sofa as he paused the game he was playing on Jeff's old Xbox console. Benchley set the controller on his lap, folded his arms over his hefty chest, and gazed at Jeff. "Okay, talk."

Taking a seat opposite Benchley, Jeff rubbed his hands together nervously. He hated dealing with the interpersonal dynamics of the group, and it was worse when he had to give a talk to his best friend. Maybe this was why Cian was the one to lead. Cian could be an asshole. "It's about earlier."

"Yeah. So? I already said I'll go to Fenton. It will at least give me something to do," Benchley said moodily.

"I meant about the situation with Cian being in charge."

"Does it bother you that we're trusting a bloodsucking vampire?" Benchley's glower intensified. "I mean, I kinda like Cian, but he's a vampire. So is Amaliya. I kinda like her, too. But they're shifty as fuck."

Jeff narrowed his gaze, studying Benchley thoughtfully, then had an inkling that something was up that his friend had yet to tell him about. "What's going on?"

"Are you my leader or not?" Benchley demanded.

"Uh, is this a research scenario?"

"Yeah."

"Then I'm your leader."

"Good!" Benchley hurled the controller aside and leaned forward. "Amaliya came to me a while back and asked me to research possession. She gave me notes about this freaky dream she had. She didn't want me to tell Cian about it. Which is very shifty."

"Okay, I'm lost."

"It's about Bianca. Amaliya thinks Bianca is still alive and trapped in her own body by The Summoner. Amaliya believes that Bianca is communicating with her and asking to be rescued." Benchley widened his eyes. "And we all know what happened when Innocente tried to rescue Bianca."

Jeff flopped back in the chair and stared at the ceiling. "Okay, so Amaliya came to you about possession, told you to keep it on the lowdown, and you're in a bad mood because she told you not to tell Cian?"

"No, I'm in a bad mood because I discovered something." Benchley covered his face with his hands. "She might be right."

Jeff gawked at him. "Bianca's alive?"

"Yeah, I think so. Our original assumption after the events in Fenton was that Bianca never rose as a vampire. That it didn't take. Remember?"

"Yeah..."

"And that The Summoner used all those ghosts to infuse himself into her body. So basically he rose from her grave, not Bianca."

"Yeah..." The whole conversation was starting to make Jeff's head hurt.

"I've been searching through some really old cases. Most vampires rise from their graves within three days of their deaths. Three days is the established cut off. Bianca rose four days after." Benchley pulled out his cellphone and opened an app that he used to take notes. "So...the assumption was that Bianca really, really died. Gone. Moved on. But I don't think so anymore. There are a few rare cases of other supernatural beings becoming vampires."

Now Jeff knew he was getting a migraine. Resting his hand on the top of his head, he stared at Benchley in disbelief. "Are you shitting me?"

"No, dude. I'm totally serious here. Those supernatural beings took longer to rise. A vampire back in the day made vampires out of an elemagus, were, and true witch. They all took much longer to rise as vampires. And they were scary, because they retained their old powers plus gained their new vampire powers. The three went on a rampage and were put down finally by the Russian army back in the late 1700's. An *army*, Jeff." Benchley lifted his head and gave Jeff his most worried look. "See what I'm getting at?"

"Bianca is still alive and retained all her powers."

"Which means The Summoner has all her powers, plus his own. And Amaliya is totally going to want to rescue her."

"Fuck me." Jeff exhaled long and slow. "Fuck me!"

"Amaliya has been badgering me for this information. I gave her all the details on Josephine Leduc like she wanted. All the stuff on astral projection. But I held this back because once she knows about it..."

"I getcha. Totally. She'll take off to San Antonio to save her." Jeff folded his arms over his chest and glowered at nothing in particular. "Go ahead and tell Amaliya before she does something crazy anyway. But I'm going to tell Cian, too. We can't have her going off without us. He can keep her from doing something nuts."

"We are talking about the same Amaliya, right?"

"Point." Jeff sighed.

"Look, I hate all this sitting around bullshit, but I also don't want us to lose Amaliya on some crazy rescue mission. She is our big gun. We don't even know where The Summoner is located."

"That won't stop Amaliya. She'll tear San Antonio apart."

"Exactly. And drag Samantha with her."

Outside the tall windows, the summer sun was busy scorching Texas. The bright light washed over the tall trees, which in turn cast long shadows over the backyard that appeared to reach toward the house like inky claws. Jeff couldn't help but take it as a sign. Darkness was coming.

"You have a point," Jeff said at last. "We'll hold it back from Amaliya, but I'm going to tell Cian tonight."

Benchley made a scoffing noise as he slumped on the sofa and picked up his controller.

"Bench, seriously, the others were right about Cian. He's the guy we've got to trust."

"Even though he has been a self-serving prick in the past?"

"Yeah." Jeff shrugged. "Because the truth is that we're doomed without that self-serving prick and his girlfriend."

Turning his game back on, Benchley's fingers flew over the controller. "Life was so much easier when I thought the monsters were only make believe."

Jeff had to agree.

Slumping onto the computer chair next to Alexia, Cassandra peered at the array of monitors. "What's up, Lex?"

The younger woman sighed. "Same bullshit as always."

Alexia spent most of her days in Cian's basement hub doing research and chatting with the remnants of The Assembly. Since the area was remodeled to look like just another swanky floor in the vampire's home, it wasn't like she was situated in a musty, ratty basement. Yet it was still cooler than the floors above, so Alexia was wearing two hoodies instead of one. Her fingers fidgeted with both sets of strings.

"No one knows anything and they wish us good luck?" Cassandra rolled her eyes.

"I hate people."

"Well, a lot of them suck." Tapping in a lascivious message to Aimee on her phone, Cassandra grinned with pleasure. "Some better than others."

"You're so lewd," Alexia said with the wrinkle of her nose, but she looked amused.

"I have it on good authority that you spend quite a bit of time flirting with some Russian guy online."

"Aimee is a snitch." Alexia stuck out her tongue as she opened a message box on one screen and typed a quick line before closing it again.

An alarm beeped on Cassandra's phone just as Aimee sent a message back. Blushing slightly, Cassandra killed the alarm before she opened her contacts list. "Time to behave and call my mom."

"Oh, tell her hi for me. I miss her. She's so sweet."

Galina's photo filled the screen. She greatly resembled Cassandra but with much longer hair and a few more lines. Due to the blood she had imbibed while part of the Austin cabal in the seventies and the drops of Cassandra's blood she took every day (thinking the bottle in the refrigerator contained B-12), she appeared to be in her early forties and not at the tail end of her sixties. The photo had been snapped while Galina had been in a very happy mood one day, and her smile was radiant. A pang of homesickness resounded through Cassandra. She missed her mother so much. Calling the number, she listened to the phone ringing.

"Hello?" her mother's voice said, the slight Russian accent a welcoming sound.

"Hey, Mom. It's me."

"Cass! How are you? How's camp?"

With a slight wince, Cassandra answered, "Mom, I'm grown up now. Check the back pages of your notebook."

"Grown up?" Galina sounded flustered. "Are you calling from Paris? Are you getting a lot of modeling jobs?"

"That's the wrong notebook, Mom. Look for the one with the pink leopard print cover."

"Okay." The sounds of shuffling filtered through the connection. Galina must have set the phone down because Cassandra could clearly hear her flipping pages. There was quite a racket when her mother picked up the phone again. "Oh! You're so beautiful! You look like your father!"

"I look like you." Cassandra smiled as she plucked at the frayed cuff of her jeans. It was an old argument that they repeated in every conversation. Though, now that Cassandra knew Cian better, she could see that they greatly resembled each other in appearance and manner.

"You're with Aimee in Austin," Galina read. She said Aimee's name with great fondness. "I remember now. You're visiting your father." There was a long pause, then Galina asked the questions Cassandra dreaded. "Does he miss me? Does he want me to come back now?"

"Mom, he's really busy right now." Cassandra flinched. She had yet to tell her mother about Amaliya. "You know, with vampire stuff."

Alexia tossed a worried look over her shoulder at Cassandra.

Galina was very quiet, but Cassandra could hear her breathing. "Does he still love me?"

"I love you. That's what matters."

"Always! Oh...Delta came today and we made tacos because I miss Texas," Galina said, obviously recounting her latest entry in the notebooks that substituted for her memory. The vampires had left her mind riddled with massive holes.

"How is Delta?" Cassandra asked, glad to change the topic.

For the next few minutes, she listened to Galina prattle on about the caretaker Cassandra had employed to drop in every other day and check on her mother. Galina was fine with performing simple things around the house and was getting much better with recalling her daily schedule, but she would often forget to take her pills and vitamins. Sometimes she would not remember Cassandra was an adult and panic when she couldn't find her daughter. There were framed reminders throughout her house, but sometimes Galina had severe episodes. Cassandra felt guilty for not being with her, but she consoled herself with the thought she was doing the right thing by being in Austin.

When she finally closed the call, she flung her arms into the air and let out an exaggerated, "Ugh!"

"She's not okay today, huh?" Alexia gave her a sympathetic look.

"She's a little more off than usual, but she's okay. I just miss her and I feel guilty for not being with her." Cassandra slouched in the chair, frowning. "I miss her. A lot."

Alexia, who had no living parents, gave her a sad smile. "I know how that feels."

Cassandra gave her friend a tight hug. "I know, Lex. Ignore me being stupid."

"You're never stupid," Alexia said, squirming out of the hug. "Just way too huggy."

"Ha! I'm giving you lezzy cooties! It's already working on your butch hair!" Cassandra playfully ruffled Alexia's short locks.

"I hate doing my hair! It takes up too much time! And I like penises!" Alexia protested but giggled while smacking Cassandra's hands away.

They teased each other for a bit longer, then settled in to watch movies on Netflix while Alexia continued to keep an eye on her emails and the websites she frequented for information. Cassandra couldn't wait until Aimee got home. She needed to snuggle with her girlfriend and forget that the world was slowly going to hell.

As Alexia discreetly kept typing to her online boyfriend, Cassandra was glad to see that people didn't stop falling in love and living their lives. She wondered if they would continue to after the earth was plunged into the abyss.

CHAPTER FIFTEEN

Sitting across from Samantha on the ground in the yard behind Jeff's house, Amaliya tapped her fingers on her knees. She could tell the blonde was nervous about something from the way she kept glancing toward the house. Amaliya flexed her toes in her boots and wiggled about, trying to get comfortable. Her jeans were a little snug, and the waistband was biting into her midsection. She lamented her inability to lose weight, but it was her own fault for buying clothes without trying them on. Samantha, meanwhile, was dressed comfortably in black yoga pants and a pink tank top with an adorable chainsaw-wielding bunny on it. The vampire reluctantly admitted the blonde looked cute.

"Are you going to concentrate at all, little bitch?" The affection in her tone still surprised her. Though Samantha could annoy her to no end, she did really care about the phasmagus.

Samantha scrunched her face. "I'm trying."

"No, you're staring at the house out of the corner of your eye." Amaliya poked the center of Samantha's forehead with one finger. "C'mon. Pay attention."

"Ugh! It's hard." Samantha's frown deepened.

In spite of all their practice, in the end, they hadn't branched out their abilities but only enhanced what they already had. It was frustrating. Amaliya had religiously studied all the notes Benchley had given her, but she still couldn't astral project. Samantha still struggled to call ghosts on her own without Amaliya's help. Their powers were best when they were together, which could work against them if they were separated in battle.

The back door creaked opened, and a female silhouette appeared framed in the doorway. The witch's long white skirt fluttered around her legs and her tank top covered in silver sequins sparkled in the moonlight as she hurried off the back porch. Amaliya admired the long bronze hair that rippled on the breeze like a cloak. The witch carried a large wicker basket in her arms as she strode down to where the two women were sitting.

"Care if I join you?" she asked.

Amaliya shrugged. "Samantha's concentration is shot, so sure."

"Hey!"

"It is!"

Samantha pouted. "Fine."

Sitting cross-legged on the ground beside them, Aimee set the basket aside. "I know you two are struggling, and I think I can help. If that's okay?"

"Anything to help Samantha concentrate is appreciated."

Samantha rolled her eyes. "Seriously, it's like studying for math. Annoying."

Aimee withdrew a very old tome from the basket. It was bound with strips of leather, and most of the pages were frayed. "This is my Book of Shadows. It came through my mother's line. It has this special little quirk where it adds information when I need it. It's been a little reluctant to help me sort you two out but—"

"It can *think*?" Samantha asked, bending toward the book.

"Leave it alone," Amaliya said, pushing her upright. "She just said it's been reluctant to help us. Don't freak it out."

"So it's alive?" Samantha persisted, eyes wide.

Aimee gave a slight nod. "Well, in a way it is. It's not flesh and blood like we are but a different sort of energy. Anyway, it was not very happy about the whole dark magic aspect of what you two do. It took some cajoling on my part to finally get it to talk to me."

"It *talks*?" Samantha's eyes grew wider.

Amaliya smacked her lightly. "Sam! Listen." The blonde was off her game and it was annoying Amaliya to no end. Samantha was obviously distracted.

Scowling at Amaliya, Samantha made a point of clamping her lips together.

Looking amused, Aimee continued, "Your magicks resemble the necromancers and phasmagi of the past, but the reality is that it's something uniquely yours. I had my *a-ha* moment earlier today when listening to Samantha's plan to recruit Roberto to be her ghost minion."

"*What?*" Amaliya gasped. She was climbing to her feet before she realized what she was doing. Aimee grabbed her hand and yanked her down to the ground, surprising Amaliya with her strength.

"Samantha, you didn't tell Amaliya, I see."

"Oops." Samantha gave Amaliya a wide-eyed innocent look.

"What the fuck are you talking about, little bitch?"

"I need a minion! A ghost to give me the inside scoop on the ghost shit, bitch-face," Samantha answered.

"And you picked Roberto? Are you fuckin' kidding me? He tried to kill me and Cian!"

"And he also tried to warn us about The Summoner! Remember? The Summoner was going to obliterate him, too, to infuse himself into Bianca's body. He's going to want payback!" Samantha scowled at Amaliya defiantly.

Leaning toward the blonde, Amaliya stared into her friend's eyes, trying to gauge if she believed the bullshit she was spewing. To her surprise, she saw that Samantha didn't flinch.

"Look, bitch-face, I'm right on this. Okay? Trust me."

"Fine," Amaliya grunted. "But I'm so not happy with this. The first time he does anything that I think even hints at betrayal, I will find a way to banish him."

"Agreed!"

The witch looked back and forth between them. "Are we done?"

Amaliya curtly nodded her head while Samantha rolled her eyes.

"As I was saying, you two are unique. The Summoner created a new type of necro-vamp when he made you, Amaliya. You created a new type of phasmagus when you gave Samantha your blood. The old rules aren't going to apply. That's why you have to shed blood to raise the dead and Samantha is struggling to reach the dead. There's an imbalance going on." Aimee flipped through the pages of her book. "I think we've been looking at this the wrong way."

"I'm listening," Amaliya said, attempting to not sound bitchy.

"It's all about the blood. You're still a vampire at the core of all your power. When vampires feed off each other, they are infused with the other vampire's blood. Sometimes they can use the other vampire's power to enhance their own."

"Cian doesn't get my necromancy from drinking from me," Amaliya observed.

"That's because you're not a normal vampire. But you're stronger when you feed from him, right?"

Amaliya considered this, then nodded. "Yeah. I get the ability to fly after feeding from him a lot."

Aimee set her hands on the open pages, bright specks of magic stirring under her palms. "Therefore, I'm going to ask a simple question." She looked first to Amaliya and then to Samantha. "Amaliya, have you drunk from Samantha since her transformation?"

"Eww, no." Samantha flinched at the idea.

The question surprised Amaliya, but it also made an immense amount of sense all at once. "No, I haven't."

"I think you need to drink her blood. And she probably needs more of yours. I have a feeling Samantha is in mid-transition. Not fully a phasmagus. Also, you two are connected. Once Samantha has all her abilities, she will be able to instantly attune to the dead." Aimee's gaze shifted back and forth between them. "I think once Samantha is at full power, it will allow you to be at full power, too."

That surprised Amaliya. "You don't think I'm at full power?"

Aimee shook her head. "Not yet. Maybe if The Summoner had kept giving you his blood you would be, but he abandoned you, and your connection with him dimmed. When you accidently made Samantha into a phasmagus, I think your connection with her kinda took his place. Your powers feed each other. They're complimentary. I've been doing a bit of experimentation with the blood both of you gave me. When used together, the results are always much stronger."

"So I have to drink her blood. And she has to drink mine?" Samantha gave Amaliya a revolted expression. "That's all sorts of *gross*."

"Maybe," Aimee said. "But once at full power, Amaliya may be able to summon the dead without spilling her blood on cemetery graves. She may be able to pull them straight out of the earth like The Summoner."

Falling onto her back, Amaliya stared up at the night sky. "Fuck me. That would be brilliant."

"That would be...good." Samantha's voice was hesitant.

Amaliya felt a little overwhelmed. Aimee's words rang true. Her magic was always lashing out, trying to find stability. With Samantha, she felt more focused and powerful. Whenever she was around The Summoner, she felt her magic responding to his, which was quite dangerous.

The witch sat in silence, waiting for one of them to say something more.

Amaliya rolled over to face her, one hand cupping her head. "Will this help with the blood bond?"

With a sad look, Aimee gave her head a little shake. "He'll still be a huge magnet to you, but it may help lessen his hold a little. All my experiments failed. You're infused with his power and blood. I can't remove that without killing you."

"We should do it," Samantha said abruptly. "We need to do it. There's no room for discussion. I need my powers. You need yours."

Amaliya observed the blonde's pensive face and sympathized. They had started off as adversaries and were now friends. Their magic demanded even more of them now, and it was a little frightening. It was another form of commitment. Up until recently, Amaliya had run away at the mere hint of committing to anything.

"It might get all sexy," Amaliya teased.

Samantha's face paled a little. "Eww."

"Aw, it's fun getting all sexy with another girl," Aimee said with a sly look.

The phasmagus's pallid pallor was abruptly altered to bright red.

"She's giving you a hard time," Amaliya assured Samantha.

"I just like my sexy times to be with only Jeff," Samantha muttered.

"It'll be fine." Amaliya sat up, crossed her legs, and took Samantha's hand.

Instantly, their magic intermingled, darkness and light. Both women promptly relaxed, their earlier prickliness dissipating.

"See," Aimee said triumphantly. "Complimentary."

"What's in the basket?" Amaliya asked.

"Things to make it less sexy," Aimee said, her gaze amused, her tone mocking.

"I'm all for that." Samantha perked up significantly.

When the witch withdrew a dagger and chalice, Samantha deflated. Amaliya didn't care how they exchanged blood. She could quickly heal. It would be more painful for the human with the dagger than with Amaliya's sharp teeth.

"I'll leave it up to you, Samantha." Amaliya offered her an encouraging smile.

Closing her eyes and thrusting out her arm, Samantha said, "Bite me, bitch."

The kitchen smelled of magic and some awful human food. Cian tried to block out the stench and concentrate on the human seated across from him at the kitchen table. Jeff's nervousness was obvious. He kept running his hands through his hair and avoiding direct eye contact with Cian. To unnerve the mortal further, the vampire sat with his arms folded across his chest, head slightly tilted, and his legs stretched out in front of him and crossed at the ankles. Cian was feeling agitated, and Jeff's hem-hawing around the topic he wanted to discuss wasn't helping his mood.

"...so I'm trying to keep focused on keeping the group unified, you know?" Jeff was saying.

Cian inclined his head.

The house was empty. Cassandra, Baptiste, and Eduardo were patrolling the city, checking all the perimeter spells, while Benchley was visiting Alexia at the electronic command center at Cian's home. Cian could clearly see Amaliya, Samantha, and Aimee through the windows. The three women were seated on the lawn and having an animated conversation. He'd rather be hunting than dealing with Jeff, but the man was anxious to talk to him.

"...and so that's why Samantha needs Roberto."

"What?" Cian's attention snapped back to Jeff.

"Samantha needs a ghostly minion," Jeff said, obviously repeating himself. "Because she needs someone to help her with the ghosts."

"And she wants to recruit Roberto's ghost?" Cian's emotions were immediately mixed. Roberto had been a close companion for years and someone he had relied upon until Roberto had betrayed him to The Summoner. He did miss the old camaraderie he shared with Roberto for many years, but the anger he felt over his betrayal could not be so easily assuaged in the glow of fond memories.

"Well, she knows him. And Roberto will most likely want revenge on The Summoner. The Summoner did almost obliterate his ghost to infuse himself into Bianca's body." Jeff finally looked Cian directly in the eyes. The earnestness in his gaze did little to soften Cian's reluctance.

"Did you consider, Jeff, that he may also want revenge on Amaliya for killing him?"

Wincing, Jeff inclined his head. "Yeah...maybe. But if he agrees to help, Samantha will hold authority over him. He'll be totally dependent on her."

Cian didn't blink as he continued to stare at Jeff. "And you think this is a wise idea?"

"Samantha is a phasmagus who has yet to totally manifest her powers. She needs this help. We need her at full power." Jeff waved his hand at the white-board. "The Summoner has anywhere from nine to eleven of the rings. It's almost October. We're running out of time, Cian."

Returning his attention to the women outside, Cian saw Amaliya resting on the ground gazing up at the stars. A pang of sorrow surprised him. For a moment, he wanted to rush outside and lay next to her. It had been so long since they'd had a quiet moment to just enjoy the night. For a short period of time after they had first gotten together, they'd spent hours sitting outside on the balcony of their penthouse apartment, smoking cigarettes and talking. It had been incred-ibly peaceful. He longed for those nights again. Perhaps it was inevitable that to return to a more halcyon existence he would have to make deals with devils.

"You're not asking my permission to do this, are you?" Cian shifted in his chair. He was amused when Jeff started.

Jeff wagged his head. "No. Not really. It's Samantha's choice, you know. In the end. It's her power. Her life. We won't even see him unless she decides to let him manifest. His entire existence will be tied to her." Once the words left Jeff's mouth, his demeanor significantly altered. Cian recognized his look im-mediately. It was of a man who realized he didn't have control over the situation either.

"Point well made. I will support Samantha's decision then." Cian cleared his throat. "Is that all?"

Jeff winced. "No. One more thing." The human clasped his hands together in front of him and took a deep breath. "Benchley uncovered some information about Bianca that complicates everything."

"Enlighten me."

As Cian listened to Jeff explain all that Benchley had unearthed, a feeling of dread washed over him. It was vividly clear to him what Amaliya's reaction to the news would be. She would want to immediately launch a rescue. Cian had enough insight into her mind to know that Amaliya would not be able to abide Bianca being held captive by The Summoner. What his beloved hadn't shared in actual conversation he had already glimpsed in her mind. Amaliya was adrift. As a vampire fledgling, the first years of her undead existence would have been under the guidance of her creator, but The Summoner had abandoned her. The power within her sought out vital connection. Coupled with the loss of her grandmother, Amaliya was craving familial bonds that were denied to her throughout her life. If Bianca was alive, she was in essence what was left of Amaliya's vampire family. The Summoner, Bianca, and Amaliya would have created a troika of power unlike any other if The Summoner had not been so set in his ways.

"Blood calls to blood," Cian said at last.

"What does that mean?"

"Vampires that are created by the same vampire have a strong attachment to one another. Though Rachoń and I have a very adversarial relationship, when I'm near her I feel the connection between us. That is what initially drew me to Amaliya. I still feel a pull to The Summoner after all this time, though it has diminished with time. I suspect that the link between Amaliya and Bianca is even more intense. They are the only two of their kind." Cian finally relaxed his posture. He rested his elbows on the table and cupped his chin in his hands.

"So this is bad," Jeff decided.

"Possibly. Depending on how I deal with it. And you must let me deal with telling her. Understood?"

"Yes, absolutely!" The young man was clearly uneasy with the entire situation. "Benchley calls Amaliya our big gun, and she really is. If she goes off after The Summoner on her own, we're fucked."

"I almost think I preferred it when she ran away from danger, not toward it." Cian gave Jeff a slim smile.

"A nice middle ground between the two would be good."

The massive pulse of power almost knocked Cian off his chair. It thrummed through the room like a cello playing low notes.

"Cian?" Jeff rose to his feet in alarm.

Scrambling to his feet, Cian stared out the window. "Shit."

"What is it?"

A thick wall of risen corpses stood in a tight cluster around the area where the women had been seated. Completely immobile, the zombies gave the impression of being sentinels. As Cian watched, the decayed and desiccated forms gradually flushed with life until they resembled living, breathing humans. What was most disturbing was that from the center of the beings a thick, roiling, ghostly mist tumbled upward into the sky. Sparks of light and vague flashes of wraithlike bodies and faces filled the miasma.

"What the fuck is that?" Jeff gasped.

"I have no idea," Cian answered.

The two men rushed to the back door.

Samantha kept her eyes firmly closed, anticipating the bite of the vampire. The first and last time Amaliya had drunk from Samantha, she had drawn blood from a stab wound inflicted by a sword-wielding zombie controlled by The Summoner. It had been the only way to save Samantha's life. Therefore, Samantha had never experienced a vampire's actual bite. In some movies and books, the bite was sensual and pleasurable, but in others it was agonizing. As she waited in dreaded anticipation, Samantha wasn't sure which would be worse.

Flinching when Amaliya's cool lips closed over her wrist, Samantha balled her free hand into a fist. The razor-sharp teeth punched through her skin, a flash of pain popping her eyes open. Instinctively, Samantha started to jerk her arm away, but Amaliya had a vice grip on her forearm and didn't relent. Within a few short seconds, the agony of the vampire bite vanished to be replaced by sublime bliss.

"Oh, wow," Samantha panted, swooning despite her resolve not to do any such thing. It was as if she was submerged in a cloud of pleasure that left her reeling with an intoxicating rush. Eyes fluttering closed, she let the waves of ecstasy close over her and sweep her way. She didn't even realize she had slumped onto her side until Amaliya leaned over her and gave her a firm shake.

"Samantha, you need to drink from me," Amaliya said, sounding as though she was speaking from far away.

Opening her eyelids just a slit, Samantha stared at the vampire. "Oh, wow. You're so pretty...and scary."

Amaliya's power was coursing out of her like great majestic wings that trembled above her shoulders. Eyes glowing like white fire and her long black hair twisting about her head in inky tendrils, Amaliya looked like a death goddess.

"Drink, Samantha, while the magic is strong," Aimee's voice ordered from nearby.

When her gaze drifted to the witch, Samantha drew in a sharp breath of surprise. Aimee's figure was outlined in the glowing colors of the rainbow with orbs of light drifting around her head like a halo.

"Drink," Amaliya insisted, holding out her arm.

The liquid dripping from the vampire's pale flesh was black and filled with stars. Samantha drunkenly tried to sit up, and Amaliya rapidly slid her other arm around the blonde to support her.

"It's full of stars," Samantha whispered, then her lips clamped over the wound and she drank in the darkness of the eternal night. It was cold, rich, and coppery.

The world transformed around her instantaneously, taking on the appearance of the negative of a black and white photograph, the dark and light hues transposed. Only Amaliya in her dark goddess mode and Aimee glowing like a rainbow remained the same. A thick mist roiled around Samantha, full of whispering voices and soothing caresses. A small part of Samantha's mind thought that maybe she should be afraid, yet the altered world was comforting. The more of Amaliya's dark blood she drank, the clearer the ghostly realm became. She could see for hundreds of miles in all directions. Brightly glowing patches of land called to her, whispering her name, and she discerned these were graveyards. Ghosts drifted through the trees, coming to greet her and welcome her home.

The coppery taste of the night filled with stars stained her tongue and lips when Amaliya drew her wrist away.

"It's so beautiful," Samantha breathed.

Amaliya was stunning, yet terrible. Her eyes smoldered with white fire, and her immense black wings filled the air. "I see it."

The vampire drew Samantha to her feet, her hands cold, yet burning with power. Their combined magicks writhed around them like great snakes made of the glittering darkness and luminescent mist.

"You freed us, Samantha," Amaliya whispered, looking downward.

Samantha followed the vampire's gaze and was stunned to see their bodies lying side by side on the ground, their fingers intertwined. "We're astral projecting!"

With a triumphant, gleeful grin, Amaliya's power lashed out, and the dead rose out of the ground around them. Tendrils of their ghostly memories sifted among the decayed bodies, murmuring in hushed voices to the phasmagus. Samantha watched transfixed as Amaliya's power restored the broken bodies of the dead. Samantha sensed the fine strands of her own magic throbbing with energy, waiting for her command. Concentrating on the wisps floating among the dead, she called the ghosts forward. To her amazement, they answered, taking on form.

"You are completely The Phasmagus now." Amaliya's voice pulsed with power.

"And you are The Necromancer," Samantha answered.

"Let's find out just what we can do," Amaliya said, obviously enthralled.

Still holding Amaliya's hand, Samantha rotated about so she was facing the west. "Let's go find Roberto."

Not certain of what exactly she should do and acting purely on impulse, Samantha concentrated on the nearest phosphorescent nodule resting in the hills outside Austin. Instantly, there was a dizzying rush around them, then they stood in the center of a graveyard.

"Whoa," Samantha breathed.

Amaliya gripped Samantha's hand ever tighter. "Do that again!"

Nodding, Samantha stared across the strangely illuminated terrain and concentrated on the brightest spot in the west. Again, there was an exhilarating whoosh, then they stood among the gravestones of yet another cemetery. Before Amaliya could say a word, Samantha looked toward the next spot. This time they appeared among a grove of trees, with no graves to be seen. Yet the ghostly dead were nearby, watching curiously.

"Wherever there are bodies..." Amaliya said in awe.

Again and again, they moved through the world at an exhilarating pace until they stood in an eerily dark and dreary cemetery. The only glow came from a single figure sitting in the center of it. The beautiful luminance of the other graveyards was absent here. The graves were black, hollow holes.

"He took them all," Samantha wailed. "He took them all and burned them up like candles." The horror of The Summoner's act washed over her. All the fragments of memories of lives lived and lost were gone. Only one ghost remained. He wasn't a memory but sentient and weeping.

"Roberto," Amaliya said, pointing.

"Have you come to finish his work?" Roberto asked, his voice raw. He sat upon a grave, his body hunched over with his arms hugging his upper body.

Holding hands, Amaliya and Samantha approached him. The dark necromancer power slithered over the ground, seeking the dead but finding none. Samantha's own magic twisted and twirled about her in wispy ribbons, cautiously approaching Roberto but not touching him.

"We did come to find you but not to do The Summoner's bidding," Samantha answered.

"You're more powerful than before. Isn't this his work?" Roberto's form looked like the cutout of a black and white photo. It crackled and speckled as he moved.

"No, it's ours," Amaliya said.

"Plus, he's the bad guy. We're the good guys."

"Are you?" Roberto looked doubtful.

"We are." Amaliya's power receded to pool around her, covering her like a great cloak.

Roberto stared at them fearfully. "Are you here for revenge? For what I did?"

"Actually, we're here to make you an offer." Samantha wondered briefly what she looked like. Amaliya looked like a death goddess, so did Samantha look like some sort of ghost goddess? Was there such a thing?

"So what *is* this offer?" Roberto lowered his arms slowly. The lost expression on his face was slowly fading into a hopeful one.

"I need a ghost minion. Someone who can help me."

"You don't look like you need help."

Samantha studied the bleak world around her. Maybe Roberto was right. Now that she was at full power, did she need him? It wasn't doubt, but her own instincts born of her magic that whispered in her soul that she did. "Yeah, true. But I thought you might want to get out of your limbo and get some revenge on The Summoner."

A subtle smile crept onto the ghost's lips. "I would like that."

"But not against her," Samantha said, pointing to Amaliya. "She killed you because you were a dick."

The ghost's body sputtered as he slid off the tombstone, his black eyes boring into the vampire. "I thought you would be Cian's death, you know."

"Yet you were willing to betray him and torture him to get what you wanted, weren't you?" Amaliya retorted.

Roberto chuckled, a dark sound in the barren world. "Love and hate are close siblings."

"If you're a psychopath maybe," Samantha sniffed.

"I will help you, Samantha, but only if the past can be laid aside and forgotten." Roberto was staring squarely at Amaliya.

A delicate thread of Samantha's power curled around his head, not quite touching him but close enough that she could detect the tumult of emotions and thoughts filling him. "He means it, Amaliya."

The vampire's glowing white eyes studied the radiant halo of Samantha's power pulsating around the ghost's head. "I will leave the past behind if you don't do anything to fuck us over. Understood?"

Fear, loneliness, and desperation vibrated through the faint connection between Samantha and Roberto. Roberto was half-mad from the isolation of this terrible limbo. Unable to leave the graveyard, he was in his own hell.

"I understand," Roberto said, not a hint of malice or cockiness in his voice or manner. "And I accept."

Samantha plunged her magic into the ghost, the threads of her power weaving around him. Resting her hand on his shoulder, she faced toward Austin. "Let's go home."

CHAPTER SIXTEEN

Jeff pushed at the zombies, but they wouldn't relent. They stood in such a dense formation that he couldn't squeeze through. If not for their glowing eyes, they would have resembled living humans wearing zombie costumes for Halloween.

"You cannot pass," the zombies spoke as one.

"They're talking!" Jeff gasped.

From amidst the throng, Aimee's voice rose. "It's okay, Jeff. Amaliya and Samantha are fine. I'm with their bodies."

"Their bodies!" Panic filled Jeff, and again he tried to plunge into the undead horde. The zombies did not budge.

Cian's cold fingers gripped Jeff's shoulder and dragged him backward.

"The Summoner—" Jeff gasped.

"They're fine!" Aimee called out again. "Samantha and Amaliya finally tapped into their full power. They're alive but spirit walking. Astral projection, Jeff. Amaliya raised the dead to protect them. There are ghosts, too. I'm sitting with their bodies. It's okay."

Frustrated at not being able to see Samantha, Jeff paced before the zombies. Cian stood in silence, arms folded over his chest, watching both Jeff and the protective circle of the undead.

"I don't like this," Jeff muttered.

"It's fine," Cian said with annoying confidence. "I can see their power rising above the zombies."

"You know what? I'm so sick of that!" Jeff whirled about on Cian. "I can't see any of this magic! It's supposed to be all around me, and I can't see it at all! You and the other supes can see all the shit I can't! I'm just supposed to trust you that it's there!"

Cian grabbed Jeff so fast he didn't even have a chance to cry out. The vampire banged him onto the ground, straddled him, tore his wrist open, then blood was filling Jeff's mouth. The vampire hunter fought back, fists smashing into Cian's body, but it was ineffectual. As quickly as Cian had attacked, he released Jeff. In a flash of motion, Cian stood calmly nearby, licking the wound on his wrist.

Spitting, Jeff rolled onto his side. The taste of the cold blood caused him to heave, yet the little he threw up did not stop the icy burn filling his veins. As Jeff raised his eyes, he saw the shimmering dome of the ward, the writhing pillar of black shadows, and the ghostly glowing swirls of power.

"Oh my God," he whispered.

Magic was everywhere. Pulsing in spells set along the perimeter. Glistening over the windows and doors of his house. Writhing in black tentacles among the zombies. The world was filled with magicks of the supernaturals he called family and friends. It was so overwhelming, Jeff lay on the ground enraptured, yet terrified. On delicate little paws, Beatrice sidled up to him and sat at his side. She let out one soft meow, then begin to clean one of her back legs.

"The infusion will last a few more hours, then will dissipate," Cian said in a matter-of-fact tone.

"You could have asked," Jeff grunted, climbing to his feet.

"I was tired of your complaining."

"Infused humans see like this all the time?"

"Yes, when they wish to."

Beatrice twined between Jeff's legs, her tail wrapping around the prosthetic one. To Jeff's surprise, he could feel it. Looking down, he saw the ghostly outline of his phantom limb superimposed over his prosthetic. "This is freaky."

Like the Red Sea parting, the mass of zombies split apart, revealing Aimee kneeling between the vampire and the phasmagus. Bright, glowing colors flowed around her, and orbs of light twirled around her body. Amaliya and Samantha were gradually stirring. Cian moved so fast he was a mere blur, then he was cradling Amaliya as she opened her glowing white eyes.

Samantha sat up, her blonde curls falling into her face, then lifted her hands to her head. "Ow."

Rushing to his girlfriend's side, Jeff knelt before her. "Sam, are you okay?"

"I think I gave myself a headache." Samantha lifted her eyes.

Jeff recoiled for a second, then gasped, "Oh, shit."

"What?" Samantha's eyes glowed white like Amaliya's, but there were specks of black swirling in their depths.

"We match," Amaliya said, pointing to her eyes.

"Fuck me, bitch." Samantha's expression was unreadable, but her hold on Jeff stiffened.

The dry, leathery smell of the zombies was cloying, and Jeff wanted to get Samantha back into the house. Regardless of the shimmering dome overhead, he felt vulnerable in the night. Beatrice crawled onto Samantha's lap, purring loudly.

"Are you okay?" Cian's concern for his girlfriend was stamped all over his face. It almost made him look nice.

Amaliya rubbed her temples with the tips of her fingers. "A headache, that's all."

Jeff helped Samantha to her feet.

"They're at full power now," Aimee said, a triumphant smile on her face.

The witch clutched an old book to her chest as she stood to one side. Jeff noted that it was her Book of Shadows. It cast light like a prism, illuminating the witch's face in a glow of bright hues.

Amaliya also appeared wobbly on her feet, leaning heavily against Cian. "That was a rush." The zombies stretched out their hands to help keep Amaliya steady. "I'm okay," she assured them, and the undead fell still again.

The glow in Samantha's eyes slowly abated.

Amaliya's eyes faded into their regular blue-gray color. "I can raise the dead without spilling blood in cemeteries now."

Jeff and Cian both looked around at the zombies maintaining their watch.

"And apparently keep the dead under your power without..."Jeff pointed to her eyes.

Amaliya nodded her head, then flinched in pain. "Yeah."

"Also, I brought back Roberto." Samantha forced a smile onto her face. "He's right there." She pointed to a spot just outside the ring of zombies.

"I can't see him." Jeff squinted.

"Neither can I." Cian's accented voice was clipped.

"You won't unless I want you to," Samantha said. "It's probably better if I deal with him on my own until everyone calms the fuck down about me recruiting him to our cause." She nailed Cian with a glower.

The vampire turned away, shaking his head. "You can't trust him."

"Yeah, well..." Samantha trailed off.

"I feel deliciously drunk and hung-over at the same time." Amaliya touched one of her zombies gently on the shoulder. The male creature turned toward her, waiting. "Keep watch for me. Let me know if you sense any dangers." The zombies nodded, then as one they sank into the earth.

Jeff gawked at the spot where the zombies had stood. "Things are different now, aren't they?"

"My zombies can help us keep watch. Samantha's ghosts can, too." Amaliya gave Samantha an affectionate squeeze.

Samantha's fingers in his hand felt strange. Almost as if she wasn't completely in this world. Gazing at her, she looked like her same normal self, but he sensed a difference.

"Are you okay?" Jeff asked.

Samantha tilted her head to smile at him. "Oh, yeah. Just...freaked a little."

Jeff sighed with relief when she came into his arms, snuggling into his chest. Closing his eyes, he rested his cheek on her soft hair. Jeff hated to admit it, but for a second he had feared he had somehow lost her. As her warm lips touched his, those fears were vanquished.

The music in the small club pounded with violence and anger. Most of the audience gathered around the narrow stage was long haired, drunk, and thrusting their fists into the air while whipping their heads back and forth. The smoking ban was in full effect, but plenty of people were puffing away on electric cigarettes. Fragrant mist floated through the air, mixing with the stench of sweating bodies, cologne, weed, and alcohol.

Amaliya pinned the beautiful brunette with vibrant green eyes to the wall, her body stretched out over the other woman's. Her victim's fingers stroked Amaliya's waist as they chatted and flirted. The vampire and mortal were dressed very similarly in black jeans, tank tops with metal band album art printed on the front, deep red lips, and leather bracers. The metalheads brushed past them on the way to the bathrooms and bar, a few casting admiring looks, but kept walking when Amaliya gave them her piercing glare.

"My boyfriend would totally be into you," the human purred against Amaliya's ear. "You really should come home with me. He likes it when I bring pretty girls home."

Amaliya grinned, tilting her head seductively. She was famished instead of revitalized from the events earlier in the evening. After three feedings, she was still hungry. "I want to have fun *now*," Amaliya said seductively.

The other woman giggled as Amaliya's fingers gently tugged on a loop on the waistband of her jeans. Acquiescing, the mortal let Amaliya escort her down the narrow dingy hallway covered in flyers and graffiti to a small bathroom with a female devil painted on the battered door. Since it was a weekday and the band performing was local, the crowd was small so the bathroom was empty. Pushing her beautiful victim inside, Amaliya ignored the repugnant odors of mildew, shit, urine, and a whiff of vanilla from an air freshener listing on the badly battered sink. There was only one stall, and the door was ajar. They were alone. With a grin, Amaliya shut and locked the door. A brief glimpse of a shadow out of the corner of her eye betrayed Cian's presence.

The dark-haired beauty pulled Amaliya close, and her lush red mouth pressed against the vampire's lips. She tasted of cigarettes, liquor, and mint. Amaliya appreciated the woman's desire to get right to business. Pressing the mortal against the sink, Amaliya kissed her fervently, the hunger inside her building. Lightly sucking on the tip of her victim's succulent pink tongue, Amaliya slid her hands into the woman's dark hair that was damp with sweat. Sliding her mouth along the curve of her cheek, Amaliya relished the taste and smell of makeup and salty flesh. Unable to wait anymore, she bared her elongating teeth and slid them into the woman's neck. Feeding thoughts of pleasure into her victim's mind, Amaliya drank deeply. The warm liquid rushed through her undead body, restoring her, giving her life, and replenishing her power.

The woman in her embrace gasped loudly, her breasts rubbing against Amaliya's as she locked her legs around Amaliya's waist. The human and vampire were lost in the ecstasy of the feeding.

"Enough," Cian's voice said sharply.

Amaliya ignored him, wanting more. The blood was so rich, so delicious. The soft body of the woman in her arms elicited the desire for so much more. The more the girl writhed, the more Amaliya wanted to take her fully.

"Enough!"

To her dismay, Cian's fingers pried her teeth out of the girl's flesh, and he shoved Amaliya into the wall. Clutching her shirt, he scowled at her.

"I'm hungry," Amaliya moaned, licking her lips.

"I know. But we do *not* kill."

"I wasn't going to..." Amaliya's voice trailed off as she saw the girl slumped over on the sink. "Is she...?"

"No. She's not." Cian licked the bloody wound on the woman's throat closed and grabbed the few paper towels left in the dispenser. Running some water over them, he cleaned the streaks of blood from the woman's neck and breasts.

Hugging herself, Amaliya watched, dismay replacing her feeding fervor. Her victim was sluggishly rousing, but she was a bit more pallid than she should have been. Amaliya felt a twinge of guilt as she realized she had taken a little too much.

"Look at me," Cian said to the human, his hands cradling her face.

Slowly, the woman's eyelids opened.

Cian's hazel eyes peered into the human's, and Amaliya felt his power, red and vibrant, twisting about the woman's mind. A delighted smile flitted over the mortal's smeared red lips. The false memories that Cian was pressing into her mind were obviously very erotic from the way the human was writhing under his touch. When he finished, the girl's eyes closed.

"She'll awaken in around ten minutes," Cian said, his Irish brogue a bit thicker than normal, revealing his agitation.

"I am just so hungry," Amaliya said, lowering her eyes. "I usually feel high and totally full after being with the dead, but not tonight."

"Tonight you served as a battery for Samantha." Cian rubbed his eyes, then sighed. "You will need to find a balance between you."

Amaliya hated letting Cian down. The trust they shared was important to her. He trusted her not to bring the attention of the authorities down on them by killing her victims. Though it was embarrassing to admit, she had almost drained the girl completely dry.

"But you didn't." Cian took her in his arms, the hardness of his body and the coolness of his touch a familiar comfort.

For once, she didn't complain about him reading her mind. Instead, she rested her head on his shoulder. The hunger inside of her was still gnawing at her gut.

"Feed from me. I fed well earlier. You need to regain control of yourself," Cian whispered in her ear.

A smile crept onto her lips. "I remember the first time I fed from you."

Cian's mouth was cold and soft against hers. "I remember, too."

Sliding her fingers through his chestnut locks, she bent her head to his throat. From the very beginning, they had been drawn to each other in a terrifying and dynamic way. It had been lust in the beginning but had quickly evolved into something much deeper and more frightening.

When Amaliya sank her fangs into his throat, Cian trembled, and one hand settled underneath the mantle of her hair to rest against her neck. There was still a hint of warmth in the blood. The life threaded through it seeped into the marrow of her very being. With a low growl, Amaliya's hands strayed downward, but her hands paused on his belt. She needed to regain control, not encourage him to lose his own, so she snaked her arms around him and held him close.

Every time she fed from Cian, she was bound more intricately to the vampire on a supernatural level. There was a time when such knowledge would have sent her fleeing, but now she embraced it. All her life she had failed the expectations of others. Before her mother, Marlena, had died, she had shared her hopes and dreams for her daughter's future. College, a career, a family: all the trappings of a good life in her mother's eyes. After Marlena's death, Amaliya had been type-cast as the family failure, the black sheep, and the unredeemable troublemaker. Her father's looks of disappointment haunted her throughout her childhood. Nothing she had ever said, or done, had satisfied him. Amaliya had careened through her life with no sense of real purpose until she had woken up in a forest grave with a new, terrible hunger. It was then she had found her purpose in life: to survive.

Though that goal remained at the core of her being, she had also evolved into a fighter, a protector, a lover, and a true friend. She was definitely not the same girl she had been before, yet she was still a rebel who did not like to be told what to do or constrained in anyway. Maybe that was what made her and Cian work so well. Neither one of them had any real interest in adhering to any particular societal rules.

Cian's hand stiffened in her hair and drew her away from his throat. Her tongue flicked over the tiny wounds she had inflicted and the last few precious drops of blood. Pressing her against the grimy wall, Cian's lips covered hers and overwhelmed her mouth. The kiss was full of everything that throbbed between them: love, lust, blood, and power.

Finally, they parted.

"Almost out of time," he whispered against her lips. His eyes darted toward the young woman still held in his thrall. "Meet me outside."

"Okay," Amaliya breathed, trying to keep herself from crawling on top of him.

The human began to stir, the embedded suggestion that Cian had planted in her mind taking hold. Fading into shadows, Cian waited by the door. Amaliya licked her lips and stepped closer to woman. Sliding her hands over the mortal's hips, Amaliya waited.

Several seconds later, the other woman flashed into awareness as a massive orgasm seized her. Clutching Amaliya close, the girl writhed with pleasure. Amaliya couldn't help but grin. Cian must have given her victim one hell of an implanted memory.

"You're amazing," the girl gasped, then kissed Amaliya ravenously.

Amaliya lost herself for a few minutes in the afterglow of her feeding, relishing the softness of the other woman's body and her full lips. Giggling, they finally parted, flushed and sated. Stepping back, Amaliya helped the pretty brunette off the sink.

"Are you sure you won't come home with me?"

Amaliya lightly ran her hand down the girl's arm. "I wish I could, but my husband's a real tyrant. He doesn't get my needs."

Pouting, the mortal nodded her head. "I used to have one of those. I ditched him."

"He's rich and has a big cock. It's hard to give up," Amaliya said. She sensed Cian's amusement but didn't look toward the place where he was hidden by his power.

"I hear ya," the other woman sighed.

Slipping out into the club, she gave the girl one last peck on the lips before weaving her way through the tight cluster of people near the bar. The harsh music thrummed through her body, and she wanted to lose herself in it. It made her a bit grumpy to know that any fun nights out would have to wait until after she ripped The Summoner's head off his shoulders and finished him for good.

There weren't a lot of people on the sidewalk, so Amaliya spotted Cian right away. He was leaning against a lamppost waiting for her. Strolling up to him, she put her hands on her hips.

"Did you get her number?" Cian asked.

"Nah."

"She was very pretty," Cian said, his tone teasing.

"Well, yeah. I know how to pick 'em." Amaliya slanted her body toward him, giving him a sly smile. "So did you give her a really awesome memory of me?"

"You were amazing. The best ever. You've ruined her for all other women. And probably men."

"Yes!" Amaliya high-fived him.

"You could probably still go get her number. For after the apocalypse." Cian caught her about the waist with one arm and guided her down the sidewalk.

"Oh, *you* liked her!" Amaliya had to admit the girl had been delicious. "I can go back."

"Nah." Cian kissed her temple. "I just thought she might be a nice meal and a bit more sometime in the future."

Snuggling into his side, Amaliya felt content despite the cloud of impending doom hovering over their heads. This is the life she wanted. Freedom to be with Cian. Freedom to hunt. Freedom to feed from and flirt with pretty young things or dangerously hot metalheads. Blood, sex, magic, metal, and Cian were all the things that made her happy. She still felt guilt that Pete had died trying to save her from the life she loved. Pete had dreamed of a life with her filled with sunlight, a perfect home, marriage, and children. She was grateful that he didn't know that those were the things she had never really imagined for herself. The thought of marriage made her skin crawl, and she could never imagine herself being pregnant.

"You, pregnant." Cian chuckled.

"Fuck you."

"I can't imagine that either. Or the marriage thing. Though you would be a lovely bride. All dressed in white." He was mocking her.

"Fuck you again." Amaliya shook her head.

A slight smile graced Cian's lips. He was being the mysterious, moody vampire tonight. She wondered if it was because of what had occurred between her and Samantha.

"No, no. It needed to happen. You both needed to rise to full power. It's something else."

"You're not freaked out because I now have this deep connection to your ex-fiancée?" Amaliya had actually wondered if it would bother him. Though both of them had a big disconnect between sex and love, the emotional bond between them was very real and even sacred.

"Do I suddenly fear you're madly in love with Samantha and want to leave me for her?" Cian smirked. "Why, yes I am."

"You're such a dick," Amaliya exclaimed.

"I'm not worried about that. I'm concerned about something else altogether." Cian drew her around a corner, and they walked up a darkened side street toward the parking lot.

"What is it?"

Cian stopped in mid-stride, turned toward her, and took her hands gently in his own. "Bianca."

"What about Bianca?" Amaliya knew before he even answered. The vision she'd had and the dreams had already told her the truth, but now she was going to hear it from Cian's lips, and her emotions began to harshly bubble in her chest.

"Benchley discovered that there's a good chance she's still alive," Cian answered, then poured out the rest of what he had been told by Jeff.

Standing in the shadows of an old vacant bar, Amaliya fought against the urge to be furious at all three men. She balled her hands into fists and struggled with the impulse to storm off.

"Benchley had no fuckin' right to tell Jeff. And Jeff had no fuckin' right to tell you! Behind my back," Amaliya wanted to scream with her frustration.

Cian folded his arms across his chest and gave her his most intense look. "Do you want to know what scares me, Liya? Bianca. Because I know you will do everything in your fuckin' power to save her."

"She's like me!" Amaliya cried out. "I can't abandon her! Our roles could have been so easily reversed. Why did I rise in three nights when she didn't?"

"Jeff thinks it's because you suppressed all your magical abilities and were living as a human. All accounts about Bianca are that she was struggling constantly with what she was, Liya. She was severely haunted by her power."

A vivid memory of Bianca stepping out in front of her on the last day of her life sprang into her mind. The hesitant nervousness of the other girl had been off-putting. Bianca had tried to talk to her. She had said something, then The Summoner had come out of the building.

"I think she tried to save me," Amaliya said, her voice catching.

"What?"

Though her death was shrouded in a haze, Amaliya had distorted dreams of dying. Sometimes, she saw flashes of Bianca's face. "I think Bianca tried to warn me about The Summoner. I think she may have tried to save me but failed."

"You never said this before." Cian's brow furrowed beneath the fringe of his hair.

"It's always been a really messed-up memory. More a dream than anything, but I think it's real." Running her trembling fingers through her hair, Amaliya held her long tresses back from her face. "Shit, Cian. I can't just abandon her!"

"But you also can't go off half-assed," Cian retorted. "You can't go running off to rescue her when we don't even know where she is. And how are you going to remove The Summoner from her body?"

With a cry of anger, Amaliya slammed the side of her fist against the building next to her. There was a loud crack as a spider web of fissures formed in the bricks. He was right, and it infuriated her. Her inclination was to commandeer his car and drive immediately to San Antonio. But she knew that was foolhardy.

"We'll sort this out together," Cian said calmly but with steel in his tone.

With an exasperated sigh, Amaliya stared past him, her vision blurred by the tears in her eyes. "I'm not going to kill him if she's still trapped inside her own body."

"Okay."

"I mean it. I won't kill her, Cian. I won't sacrifice her for him." Too many people had already died trying to save Amaliya's life. She wasn't about to let Bianca die a second time.

"I understand. We'll find a way." He met her glare with a steady gaze. "I promise you."

The fight left her at his vow. The one thing Cian never did was let her down. Once he committed to doing something, he did it. He wasn't lying to get her to not do something foolish.

"I won't bullshit you on this." Cian gave her a weary smile. "I know that if I did, it would backfire immediately."

"I'd go to San Antonio and find a way to save her."

"Or die trying."

"Yeah."

"You're incredibly, annoyingly stubborn."

"Fucking-A."

Cian dragged her into his arms, his lips pressed to her forehead. Wrapping her in his embrace, he rocked her gently. "I love you for it even if it scares me to death."

"Sucks to be you." Amaliya twined her arms around his neck and allowed herself to calm down. If she wanted to, she could keep her anger going for hours, but it wasn't worth it. In the end, Cian would help her disengage The Summoner from Bianca's body and she would save the world.

"It's as simple as that," Cian agreed.

"Exactly."

CHAPTER SEVENTEEN

Roberto prowled around the bedroom Samantha shared with Jeff, ignoring the cat sitting in the middle of the bed hissing at him. The ghost's body was frayed around the edges and his face tended to be out of focus, but it was almost like the old days when Roberto and Samantha had given each other hell. Though she was grateful he had agreed to help her, he was already on her nerves.

Throwing out his arms, he declared, "It's so...plebian."

"Fuck you," Samantha automatically answered.

"Though the antiques have potential. If they were properly restored." Roberto sniffed.

"You're not here to snark on the house's decor."

"I wouldn't call this decor. I would call it a...catastrophe. This is far worse than Cian's IKEA obsession."

"Yeah. What's up with that?" Samantha shook her head and returned to her task. Scrounging around in her large purse for her iPad, Samantha wondered how something so big could get lost. Pulling a stack of bills, a couple of fashion magazines, and her makeup bag out of the purse, she finally spotted the tablet. Jerking it out, she flipped open the case.

"What's that?" Roberto asked, drifting closer.

"My notes on how to deal with you, dickface." Samantha drew up the information she had collected from Benchley and Alexia's research.

The ghost smirked.

"What?"

"Your power is wasted on you."

Samantha raised one finger, ignoring him. "First off, you can't leave the property without my permission."

The moment she said the words, she felt her magic surge out in a big wave. She was peculiarly aware of it building a perimeter around the house. It was as if she had some sort of supernatural radar that pinged back information to her. Maybe she did. Tilting her head, she let her new powers decipher what she was feeling. It was a bizarre sensation, but she could feel, see, and almost taste the ward she had placed to keep Roberto in check.

Roberto narrowed his eyes. They looked more like smudges of black in his slightly blurred face. "Hmm..."

Giving him a victorious look, Samantha said, "See. My powers aren't wasted. I can do this."

"Apparently," the ghost answered with a hint of grudging respect.

"Where was I? Oh, yeah. You're not allowed to enter any of the bedrooms without permission. Especially this one. We don't need you spying on us having...you know...relations." Another ripple of her magic flowed out, creating new wards within the house.

The ghost winced, then began to slide along the floor as misty tentacles of her magic gripped him and dragged him toward the door. Pinwheeling his arms, he tried to grab onto something.

"Samantha!"

"Oh, you have permission to be here right now!"

Roberto's skid stopped just before the door. He glared at her.

"Oops." Samantha made a mental note to remember that her magic took her words literally.

"What *is* my job exactly?" Roberto's voice was cold, angry, and stubborn.

"You're going to be the general of my ghost army," Samantha answered. "Cool, huh?"

"Possibly," Roberto replied noncommittally but appeared intrigued.

"Also, play nice with the others. Cian's in charge. Don't piss him off."

His hazy form slightly drooping, Roberto averted his face.

"Are you listening to me?"

"Yes. I am. Unfortunately."

"Be nice, Roberto. I saved you." Samantha frowned, worried that maybe this had been a bad idea after all.

"I am grateful for that, but a ghost can have many regrets once their life is over. I know I do."

"Feeling bad for betraying Cian?" Samantha sat on the edge of her bed, setting her iPad on her lap.

The ghost flicked in and out of reality as he moved toward her. With a sigh, he sat next to her. "I should have killed Amaliya right away. Then you'd be married to Cian right now, and none of this would be happening."

Samantha was surprised by his words and also a little unnerved. "Don't say that."

"I brought The Summoner down on all of us by not doing my duty to Cian.

When I recognized Amaliya as a threat, I should have handled it. If I had, you and I wouldn't be in this position right now."

"A phasmagus and a ghost," Samantha said.

"Exactly."

"But you forget, I'd be married to Cian, who is a bit of a cheating bastard, you'd still hate my guts, The Summoner would take over the world, and we'd all die." Samantha lifted her shoulders. "You may be worse off, but I'm better off. Jeff is a sweetie, and I love him. Plus I'm a phasmagus and I will kick some serious butt. I'm scared but happy here. Plus, bitch-face and I have a truce now. We're even...kinda...sorta...friends. Honestly, Roberto, you fucked yourself over by betraying your friend. If you hadn't been a jerkwad, you'd still be alive."

The ghost whipped his head toward her, his features smearing together, his eyes holes of darkness, then his face returned to some semblance of normalcy. "Maybe Cian betrayed me! Just as he betrayed you!"

A year ago, Samantha would have been terrified; now she was just slightly unnerved. She exhaled, her fingers fidgeting with the cover on her iPad. Even though she was the aggrieved party in their past drama, she had forgiven Cian and resolved a lot of her issues with Amaliya. She was also relieved that the romantic fantasy that she and Cian had created had fallen apart. There was no way Amaliya could have come between them so easily if they had truly been in love.

"I can tell by your expression that you know what I'm saying is true," Roberto said after her silence had dragged on a little too long.

"I don't think Cian betrayed you at all. Yeah, he didn't listen to you about Amaliya, and he didn't listen to me either, but that's because he was lying to himself. I'm not saying he was right to ignore us. I'm saying that in the grand scheme of things, him being a bullheaded dick is a lot different from you going off and siding with The Summoner." Samantha fastened a steady glare on the ghost.

"I was angry," Roberto said with what could have been a slight pout.

"Yeah, so? I was furious. But I didn't go siding with the enemy. I tried to *save* Cian from Amaliya. I didn't *betray* him."

"After so long together, I could see that Cian was going to move on without me."

"Oh, God. Were you two boning?"

Roberto bestowed her with a sardonic smile. "And if we were?"

Scrunching up her face, Samantha said, "Eh, whatever. I'm over Cian. I'm with Jeff. You're dead and a ghost. Fuck the past."

Visibly deflating over not being able to rile her up, Roberto sighed. "Though we have shared many women over the years, and endured much together, we were not 'boning.' We were like brothers, or so I thought. I knew Cian was unhappy when he started trying to be human again. You were bad enough. But Amaliya...when he wouldn't send her away even when he knew The Summoner might descend on all of us, I knew my time with him was at an end."

"So why didn't you just go off and find your own life?"

"Without a vampire's blood, I would grow old and die. I wanted neither of those things."

"Well, at least you won't grow old now."

Roberto's grimace deepened.

"I was trying to look at the bright side." Samantha hesitated, then asked, "Why didn't you just ask him to make you into a vampire?"

"I was angry, impatient, and wanted to hurt him for destroying the life we had built. I also knew he was opposed to making fledglings. Maybe Cian wouldn't have completely abandoned me. I don't know. But I also didn't want to depend on him to make the choice for me."

"So you betrayed him even though you had a super-long friendship."

"There is only so long you can cling to the past."

"And now you're dead."

"And I won't grow old," Roberto said with a sardonic smile.

The door opened. The light spilled in from the hallway to illuminate Jeff's startled look.

"It's not what you think," Roberto said swiftly.

"My girlfriend is laying down the law on your ghostly ass?"

Roberto frowned. "An automatic response from my...living days."

"You were such a whore, weren't you?" Samantha rolled her eyes. It felt strange to be locking horns with Roberto again, but in a weird way she had missed him. He had been a part of her life for nearly a year, then had suddenly been gone.

"Yes, yes, I was," Roberto said, his voice filled with longing.

"Eww."

"Do you mind taking your ghostly ass out of my bedroom?" Jeff pointed at the doorway.

Roberto's hollow eyes menacingly darkened.

"Go patrol, Roberto," Samantha said, waving her hand at the apparition. "You're not welcome in the bedroom anymore."

One second the ghost was beside her, the next he was in the hallway. With a grunt, Roberto blurred into a smear of darkness and was gone.

"Can everyone else see him, too?" Jeff asked, entering and shutting the door behind him. "Or is Cian's blood still affecting me?"

"Oops. Pulling the plug," Samantha answered, internally disconnecting her thread of magic from Roberto so he would fade. "He's invisible again."

Sitting next to her, Jeff fastened one of his sweet looks on her, his hand sliding over her fingers. "I wanted to talk to you about something. It's serious."

Samantha set her iPad aside with her other hand. "Those words make me a little scared."

"Well, I'm a little scared, too, but I really need to talk to you about this. Especially after tonight, seeing you like that. It was amazing but scary."

"Are you sure this isn't a bad talk?" Samantha's stomach coiled into a tight knot. If Jeff was going to dump her, she didn't know how she'd deal with it. She really loved him, but she was evolving into something that even scared her a little. Maybe he couldn't hack the change.

"I don't think it's a bad talk. Of course, you might think it is." Jeff sighed.

"Jeff, just tell me what is going on."

With a sigh, Jeff nodded his head. "Okay. Here we go."

When her boyfriend drew out a small platinum ring with a single diamond, Samantha literally stopped breathing.

"This is my mom's. It's been in my family a long time. Before my dad died, he said to give it to the woman I loved. That's you." Jeff held out the ring.

"You're just going to give me a diamond ring? As a gift?" Samantha was dizzy not only with the whirl of emotions inside of her but because she couldn't seem to catch her breath.

Jeff's eyebrows drew together. "No, no. It's not a gift. I'm asking you to marry me."

"But you didn't really ask," Samantha pointed out.

"Oh, yeah." Jeff hesitated, then lifted the ring. "Sam, will you marry me?"

"No! Wait! Is this because we're going to die?" Samantha had already made a mistake once when answering "yes" to a marriage proposal, and she wasn't about to get married for the wrong reason.

"Not the answer I hoped for."

"Is it?" Samantha pressed one hand to her wildly beating heart. "Because we're going to die?"

Jeff adamantly shook his head, his floppy hair getting messier. "No! No. Well, sort of. Not really."

"Well?"

"Look, Sam. This is the thing. I love you. I love you being in my house with me. It feels right. I want this to be our home together. And, yes, the thought that we might die in a few months scares me enough to compel me to say things that I might have talked myself into waiting on. You know, waiting for the perfect moment. Yet there might not be one. A perfect moment." Jeff was flummoxed. "I'm doing this all wrong. I'm sorry. I'm sure Cian did this much better."

Samantha stared at the ring in his hand and watched it gradually go out of focus as tears welled. Cian had done it perfectly with a carriage ride, tons of red roses, champagne, a proposal on one knee, and a whopper of a ring. It had all been a charade. Jeff's floundering proposal had her breathless, speechless, and stunned.

"I forgot to get down on one knee," Jeff muttered. "Okay, this was probably a bad idea. I'm doing this all wrong. Maybe I should try again later?"

Wagging her head, Samantha managed to say, "No."

"No?" Jeff visibly deflated.

"I mean, no, don't ask me later." Samantha grabbed his wrist before he could draw away. "Not don't ask me. I mean. Yes."

Jeff squinted at her. "Okay. Lost."

"Yes. Let's get married." The second the words left her lips, Samantha burst into tears.

"I didn't mean to make you cry!" Jeff reached out to draw her close.

Behind them, Beatrice meowed with irritation, trying to sleep.

"I'm crying because I'm happy."

Despite all the insanity in her life, Samantha was sure that she wanted to be with Jeff. No matter what supernatural weirdness was occurring within her or around them, Jeff was her stalwart supporter. He believed so entirely in her, loved her so completely, that she couldn't imagine not having him at her side. She loved him in a way that brought her an incredible amount of peace. She wasn't afraid of sharing her future with him, even if it did end disastrously for both of them. As long as she was with him, whatever was left of her life would be worth living.

"Oh, thank God. I know I'm doing this all wrong, but I'm a little frazzled." Jeff pressed his lips to her hands, then slipped the ring on the wrong finger.

With a little smile, Samantha switched the ring to the proper one. "Engagement finger," she explained, wiggling her digits. "Marriage finger is the opposite hand."

"Oh." Jeff grinned. "I've never been engaged before."

Samantha clutched his trembling hands tightly. "I was, but it was totally not with the right guy."

To her surprise, Jeff's eyes were wet with unshed tears. "Samantha, I'm so glad you found me that day at the Spiderhouse. Life has been so incredible since that day. Just being around you makes me so happy. I love you so much, honey."

Wiping away his tears, then her own, Samantha pressed a tender kiss to his lips. "I love you. You make me happy."

"I'm doing this because I love you. Yeah, the whole end of the world thing speeded it up a little, but I would have done it anyway."

Samantha snuggled into him as they fell back on the mattress together. Beatrice hissed and haughtily hopped down off the bed.

"I would have said yes anyway." Samantha held up her hand so the lamplight could catch the sparkle of the diamond.

"It's curse free, by the way. Aimee checked it."

"Then it's perfect," Samantha said, grinning. "Like you."

Combing his fingers through her blonde hair, Jeff grinned. "No, you're perfect. And a little scary. When I was high on Cian's blood, I could see your new nature. It was...intense."

"Did I look supercool? Because Amaliya totally looked supercool."

"You were beautiful. It was like you had ghostly wings and a halo around your head. Like a goddess."

Samantha liked that description. It made her feel even more confident in her new abilities.

"So even though Cian was being a total dick when he force-fed me his blood, I'm kinda glad he did." Jeff's lips lightly brushed over hers.

"It was mean." Samantha had been pissed off when Jeff had told her what had happened. Cian had quickly received an earful, though she could tell he wasn't really listening to her at all. He'd been worried about Amaliya, who had looked somewhat pale and a little sickly after all was said and done. They'd left soon after to go hunt.

"Yeah, but I think I may ask him to do it again in the future. It was reassuring to actually be able to see the magic going on around me. Seeing the ward and your powers made it more tangible." Jeff exhaled. "I just don't like the whole blood thing."

"It's pretty gross," Samantha agreed.

"Well..." Jeff rubbed his face. "It's more than that. Don't tell anyone this, but Cass nearly killed me when she hit puberty. One of the side effects of being a dhamphir is bloodlust. We didn't know that though. We were young, foolish, and thirteen. I had the biggest crush on Cass. She was so beautiful, and I was a hormonal teen. One day, I grabbed her and kissed her."

Samantha immediately knew what had happened next. "She bit you."

"Actually, she shoved me off her, tackled me, beat me up a little bit, then bit me."

"I can see why you didn't want this story getting out," Samantha said, patting his arm.

"My dad found us and saved my life. It was not a good moment for any of us. Cass and I have never even talked about it. We just pretend it never happened."

"It must have been really hard for you to let Amaliya feed off you when we were trapped in that farmhouse."

"Well, it was hard for me to ask her to save you because of what had happened with Cass. Yet it saved your life."

"And changed me into a phasmagus."

"I didn't see that coming!"

"None of us did." Samantha laid her head on his chest, listening to his heart beating.

"If I decide to become an infused human, I'll have to let Cian drink from me and then drink his blood to allow his blood to imbue me for much longer than a few hours."

"You don't have to, Jeff."

"No, but I may need to."

Jeff's warm embrace, the rise and fall of his chest, and his heartbeat were quite soothing. "Let's not think about it for now."

"Right. We're engaged. We should celebrate it." Jeff grinned at her. "Have any ideas?"

With a wicked smile, Samantha lifted her head and kissed him.

PART FOUR

Interlude

CHAPTER EIGHTEEN

September gave way to October. October faded into November.

The heat of the summer gradually faded away as cold fronts slithered across Texas, dropping the temperature in Austin to a much more palatable degree. Austinites started to don their sweaters, hoodies, and boots, leaving their shorts, tank tops, and flip-flops in their closets. The leaves of several species of trees turned dull orange and yellow, while others shed their coats completely. The chaotic energy of summer gave way to a more relaxed atmosphere as the holiday season loomed on the horizon.

The transformation of the city around the small cabal was barely noted as they fought their battles against the growing tidal wave of darkness threatening to devour the world.

It became increasingly evident that while Cian did not want to make vampires as cannon fodder, The Summoner was perfectly willing to do so. As the reports of missing people in San Antonio and the surroundings towns escalated, fledgling vampires crazed in the madness of bloodlust began to invade Austin on an almost nightly basis. Aimee's perimeter spells instantly alerted the witch to any incursions. Tracking spells immediately went into effect, allowing Cian's cabal to chase down the intruders and eliminate them. Most of the trespassing into Cian's territory took place in less populated areas, which the vampire master regarded as The Summoner's attempt to observe either Samantha or Amaliya's powers from afar.

With that in mind, Cian deliberately kept Amaliya and Samantha back from the front lines. Cassandra, Aimee, Baptiste, Eduardo, Cian, Jeff, and Benchley managed quite well against the intruders with the invisible assistance of Roberto and his growing army of sentient ghosts under Samantha's remote control. Amaliya, though frustrated, raised her zombies and sent them out to patrol nightly while remaining behind. She no longer had to have her blood spilled in the cemeteries around Austin to raise the dead, though she still had to shed her own blood to activate her magic. It was obvious by the startling human appearance of her zombies and their super-human strength that she was growing in her power. She could now observe through the eyes of her raised zombies, something she could never do before.

Even as the cabal grew in strength, they were aware of the dwindling number of days until the inevitable battle against The Summoner.

Cassandra vaulted through the air and landed behind the rabid vampire. The creature twisted about, baring long fangs. The dhamphir barely registered the woman's youthful appearance before slamming the stake through her heart and barreling toward the next vampire.

White flashes of light zipped through the night as Aimee tossed orbs of magic at the rush of vampires descending on the old neighborhood on the east side of Austin. Bronze hair flying about her face, she levitated off the ground, her magic swirling around her like a rainbow.

Meanwhile, Baptiste cast conflagrations at the vampires, setting them aflame. Before the dying vampires could set the dry foliage about them on fire, the elemagus wrapped them in swirling winds and lifted them into the air to let them burn to ash.

Cian slashed his way through the vampires, decapitating them with a swipe of his obsidian blade. Around five of the blood-crazed fledglings leaped onto him trying to take him down, but he easily flung them off before dispatching them.

Benchley hurled spell bags at the assaulting forces. On impact, magical vines of power wrapped around the vampires and dragged them down to the ground where it was easier for Jeff to plunge stakes into them.

In his beast form, Eduardo gleefully tore limbs from the vampires. Chunks of flesh and blood spray followed in his wake.

"How many left?" Cassandra gasped.

"Maybe twenty!" Aimee shouted back.

The neighborhood street glowed with suppression spells keeping the humans inside their homes and out of danger. Red-eyed, fearsome vampires ripped through the shadows. Crazed with the bloodlust, the feral creatures hurtled themselves at Cian's cabal. Nearly fifty were scattered across the ground or burning to ash in fiery whirlwinds spinning above the ground. It was the biggest incursion yet.

Cassandra slashed at a vampire with her silver-bladed daggers, taking it to the ground where she could lop off his head. After burning so much of her blood power, she was starting to tire. Nearby, a vampire tackled Benchley from behind. Cassandra started toward him when she saw Cian materialize next to the fallen man and jerk the vampire off him and toss it into an oncoming group about to tackle them.

Aimee and Baptiste set the attackers on fire with a combination of magicks. The cool damp air filled with ash while steam rose into the night.

The Summoner's vampires were relentless in their madness. Cassandra swept her blade through the neck of one vampire, then seconds later felt fangs clamp down on her shoulder. With a scream of pain, she grabbed the attacker's thick dark hair and wrenched them from her flesh. The vampire's teeth rent a hole in her sweater and skin. Cassandra tossed the growling creature to the ground with an angry grunt. Before she could move in to kill it, Aimee hit it with an orb of light that set it on fire.

Blood, hot and coppery, pumped from the wound, and Cassandra pressed her hand against it to staunch the bleeding. The vampire had hit something major. She had to burn even more of her blood power to heal, making her dizzy. Cian abruptly landed before her and grabbed her hand away from the wound. Without hesitation, he clamped his mouth over it, and she felt his cold tongue probe the wound. Aimee slid through the air toward them, bolts of magic erupting from her hands as she kept the vampires at bay. Removing his mouth, Cian tore open his wrist. Already, Cassandra's wound was starting to heal as his saliva worked on it.

"Drink."

Cassandra hesitated, then grabbed her father's wrist and took three big draughts of his blood. Instantly, she felt a rush of power hit her like a sledgehammer. It felt great. "Thanks, Dad," she muttered, wiping the last of his blood from her lips.

Cian nodded and rushed back into the thick of the battle.

"Where are the ghosts?" Benchley exclaimed.

Jeff pounded another stake into a vampire, then scuttled toward another one. "No clue!"

"Keep fighting," Cian ordered.

With a grin, Cassandra dove into a cluster of the vampires, fighting with renewed vigor. Her blades flashed in the streetlight as she slashed, feinted, twisted, and fought her way through them. Eduardo battled near her, his claws covered in blood and flesh. It was a deadly tango they danced through the vampires. The fledglings' only advantages were their insanity and numbers. With many of their comrades moldering on the street, The Summoner's forces were rapidly falling into disarray.

As the head of the vampire in front of her flew off into an overgrown yard, Cassandra was startled to see a very handsome, pale man standing in the center of the street watching her. White-blond hair fell to his shoulders, and his fine-featured face was both handsome and cruel. Because he was clad completely in black, it was as if he was clothed in the very night. When his cold blue eyes met hers, Cassandra's gut contracted painfully. Fear ripped through her, paralyzing her in place.

"He's here," she rasped.

The sound of the blood dripping from her blades filled the night as the world was plunged into silence.

"He's here!" she screamed, her gaze not wavering from the necromancer. "Dad!"

The Summoner granted her a slight smile as he nodded his head. "The dhamphir is Cian's daughter. I see."

"Dad! Aimee! Jeff!" Struggling to move, to breathe, to even think straight, Cassandra was utterly trapped in the power of The Summoner's gaze. Her daggers fell from her fingers as they grew slack. The numbness that was spreading through her limbs sent her to her knees.

"This will be so much more interesting than I anticipated," The Summoner said with delight.

Then he was gone.

"Babe!" Aimee gathered Cassandra into her arms. "What happened? Are you okay?"

Gasping, Cassandra saw that the battle was over. The street was littered in the decaying bodies of the fledglings. The suppression spells cast flickering light over the dead.

"Did anyone else see him?" Cassandra let Aimee help her to her feet. "Dad, did you see him?"

"Who, Cassandra?" Cian strode toward her, wiping his blades off on his jeans.

"The Summoner. He was right there. Watching us." Cassandra pointed to the spot where the necromancer had stood.

"I didn't see Bianca," Jeff said, his face somber.

"It wasn't Bianca. It was *him*. I saw The Summoner as himself." Cassandra ran shaking fingers through her hair. "He looked at me, and I was paralyzed. His power was overwhelming."

Cian and Aimee glanced at each other, both appearing unsure.

"I saw him! I swear to God, Goddess, and all that is holy that he was standing right fucking there." It still hurt to breathe even though she was released from his power. "He said something about me being your daughter, Dad."

With a somber look, Cian sheathed his weapons as Baptiste and the others gathered behind him. "How did he know you're my daughter?"

"I called for you." Cassandra winced, realizing her folly. "Sorry."

It was shocking how much older her father suddenly appeared. Cian's expression projected clearly what he was thinking. Cassandra had just granted The Summoner yet another pawn to play against Cian. "It's fine. He would have figured it out eventually. We do look a bit alike."

"But how could he be here? Isn't he in Bianca's body?" Baptiste asked. He smelled of smoke and rain, a strange combination.

"Astral projection," Aimee said in a glum voice.

"But wouldn't that let Bianca free?" Benchley looked at Jeff. "If she's possessed by him and he left her body, she'd be free to escape."

"Unless she's not in the body, and it's just an empty shell," Jeff answered.

"Or they tied her up." Eduardo was naked, human, and slathered in blood. The grin on his face was a little disconcerting, as was his big erection.

Cassandra and Aimee both made a point of looking away from it.

"Tied her up?" Cian mulled this over. "A possibility."

There was a shimmer in the air then Roberto appeared. The ghost looked almost human, his edges solid. Only his strange hollow eyes spoke of his true nature. "You need to get back to the house. There was an attack."

"Is Samantha okay?" Jeff and Benchley asked in chorus.

"They couldn't breach the wards, but there was a skirmish in the street," Roberto answered. "It was over almost as fast as it started. I took care of it along with Amaliya's zombies. But that's not what has them spooked."

"Did you see The Summoner?" Cian asked pointedly.

Roberto looked at his former friend in surprise. "Yes, we did."

"In his old form?" Aimee's fingers were trembling in Cassandra's grip.

"Yes, but then Amaliya saw Bianca. Inside the house." The ghost flickered. "Samantha is calling me back."

"This just keeps getting more and more fun," Eduardo decided.

"Put some clothes on, Eduardo, and stop showing off," Cian said, then motioned to the bodies. "Baptiste?"

"On it." The elemagus set the last of the vampire bodies on fire, burning them embers in seconds. A strong wind followed, scattering the remains along the road.

Aimee flicked one hand, and the suppression spells fell.

"Let's head back." Cian slid his arm around Cassandra's shoulders and guided her toward his car.

"Dad," she said in a lowered voice, "I'm really sorry."

To her surprise, he kissed her temple. "Never say you're sorry for something that isn't your fault. You were immediately a target once you joined my cabal. Now you're just a little more interesting to him."

Suppressing a shiver, Cassandra glanced toward her girlfriend. The witch gave her a worried look along with a faint smile. Tightening her grip on Aimee's hand, Cassandra wondered just how much worse things could get.

She was afraid they were going to find out.

"It was a flicker," Amaliya explained. "I saw Bianca for just an instant. She looked like she was in distress."

Cian rubbed the whiskers of his goatee between his fingers as he listened to Amaliya speaking. They were in Jeff's kitchen, the crew scattered across the room. Some were eating peanut butter and jelly sandwiches, while others were sipping hot chocolate. His daughter kept giving him apologetic looks that didn't help his mood. He wished adamantly that she hadn't slipped and revealed who she was to The Summoner, but he also knew it was only a matter of time before their enemy would have sorted it out. He was hungry and tired. The attack had come early enough in the evening that he hadn't been able to feed yet. It had been a deliberate ploy and a smart one to catch him when he was weak.

"Did she look tied up?" Eduardo asked, then shoved an entire sandwich in his mouth.

Amaliya gave the coyote a disgusted look.

"Eduardo thought maybe The Summoner had Bianca tied up so she couldn't escape while he astral projected," Jeff explained.

"Oh. No, she didn't. But would she? If she was out of her body, too?" Amaliya gave Benchley a quizzical look.

"Well, probably not. It would have been a projection of her body but not her actual state," Benchley decided. He was busy helping his sister make an obscene amount of sandwiches. The battle had exhausted everyone, and they were cramming calories to recover the energy they had burned.

Cian wished he could eat a sandwich and replenish himself. He craved blood, and his veins were starting to burn.

"Anyway, she appeared just for a second. Right there." Amaliya pointed to a spot near the back door. "Then I heard Samantha screaming outside."

"That's when they were assaulting the ward." Samantha was peeling the crust off her sandwich like one long ribbon. "Alexia and I were going over all the emails from the stupid Assembly when they started hitting the ward. It was really loud. We rushed outside to make sure it was holding, and that's when we both saw him down in the street. I'd recognize that asshole anywhere."

"He was scary and creepy in a handsome way," Alexia added. She licked the peanut butter off the butter knife before tossing it in the sink. It clattered loudly.

Benchley did a little hop, startled.

"Shark Boy, you okay?" Samantha asked.

"A little rattled about the big bad showing himself," Benchley admitted.

"Why do you call him Shark Boy?" Baptiste leaned one elbow on the kitchen table and slanted toward Samantha. "I've been meaning to ask you."

"Peter Benchley wrote *Jaws*." Samantha shrugged her shoulders. "I'm random like that."

"Ah," Baptiste said, though he sounded a little mystified.

Cian listened to the people around him prattling on, but his thoughts were concentrated on the trouble at hand. The incursions into his city were growing more numerous. Cian was certain that The Summoner was trying to ascertain exactly how much firepower Cian had on his side.

"There were a lot of vampires tonight," Benchley continued, his attention on Samantha. "They were really young, hungry, and out of their heads."

"It explains all the missing people, doesn't it?" Alexia took a seat at the table and tapped on the map she had laid out. Red dots showed the locations of all the people who had gone missing in the last few weeks. There was no real pattern to discern.

Cian knew that the human girl had been working on trying to locate The Summoner's haven in San Antonio using police reports and news articles. Aimee couldn't penetrate the massive black magic spells coating the city. San Antonio was in chaos. The crime rate was escalating while earth tremors made the authorities and inhabitants nervous. Though the media joked about the ground shaking was a sign of the coming 2012 apocalypse, Alexia took it very seriously. Earthquakes were not common in the region.

The cabal chattered on, but Cian didn't pay them any heed. The night's events had revealed something very important, and he wanted to use it to his advantage. Raising his eyes, he saw Amaliya staring at him with curiosity. They were more connected than ever, intertwined in a way that was thrilling and comforting. She settled back in her seat, flashed a grin, and played with her pack of cigarettes on the table. Apparently, she had overheard his thoughts.

"It's time to make a move," Cian said at last, and the conversations around him fell silent.

PART FIVE

Trap

CHAPTER NINETEEN

November, 2012

Amaliya watched Samantha eating the hamburger and fries with a look of utter distaste on her face. It had been eight months since the vampire had eaten actual food, and staring at it now did not make her miss it. It looked disgusting and smelled even worse. Yet Samantha happily dunked the potato spears into ketchup and wolfed down the juicy burger.

"That's so fuckin' gross," Amaliya said at last, her lip curling with distaste.

"Look, bitch-face, you dragged me all the way to Waco, so the least you can do is let me eat my supper in peace, okay?" Samantha gave Amaliya a wide, fake smile, then took an obscenely large bite of her burger.

"Do you have to eat it so...messily?"

Rolling her eyes, Samantha shoved another fry in her mouth.

Seated inside the Denny's on the outskirts of Waco, Texas, the two women were awaiting the arrival of two emissaries from the vampires who ruled over Dallas and Houston. The restaurant was attached to a big truck stop that catered to the long distance drivers. A few weary-looking families were clustered around tables, and a young teenage couple flirted outrageously in one corner. Two truckers sat at a corner table, nursing cup after cup of steaming coffee.

Though it was Thanksgiving Day, there were already Christmas decorations on the walls. A year ago, Amaliya would have been sitting in her father's living room watching TV while recovering from a massive feast of fried turkey and all the traditional side dishes. This year, she was steeped in the middle of vampire politics, a supernatural war, and considered dead to her family.

Tilting the brim of her black straw cowboy hat, Amaliya glanced out into the darkness filling the world beyond the windows of the restaurant. Her necromantic power slithered out of her, tasting the night. The dead tucked into the graveyards in the town stirred in their graves, but Amaliya left them to their rest. She didn't sense any vampires lurking, but in the last few months she had learned that she wasn't always able to detect supernatural creatures.

"Roberto says it's all clear," Samantha informed her. She dabbed the remains of her burger into a blob of ketchup before shoving it into her mouth.

The mere mention of the ghost Samantha used as her personal assistant brought a frown to Amaliya's face. She didn't like Roberto in life and definitely not in death.

Folding her arms on the table, the heavy studded leather bracers on Amaliya's wrists clunked against the surface. "Tell him he better keep an eye out for black witches. We don't need to get jumped by them again."

"He heard you. He's not deaf," Samantha reminded Amaliya. "You know, I can make it so you can see him."

"I have an idea. Why don't you touch him and make him solid so I can punch him in the face a few times?" Amaliya flashed a wide smile.

The blonde flinched a few seconds after Amaliya's comment.

"Did he just say something?" Amaliya demanded.

"Kinda." Samantha made a big show of drinking her soda.

"What did he say?" Amaliya leaned forward, her blue-gray eyes raking over the area surrounding their table. The arrogant ghost was probably being a dick again. They had not liked each other when he'd been alive, and that animosity had not diminished with his death.

The phasmagus continued to gulp down her drink, making sure she couldn't answer right away. Maybe she was right to avoid answering. The atmosphere was tense enough as it was without adding to it.

"I need a cigarette," Amaliya groused.

"You're a vampire and still addicted. So sad," Samantha shook her head. She was teasing Amaliya, trying to alleviate her anxiety.

Amaliya snarled, but it was playful. Her long black hair spilled over her shoulders to her waist, covering her tank top. Her rebellious streak had hit her at the last minute before their departure from Austin, and she'd shed her plain black shirt for one that read, "Jesus was a long-haired rebel against the establishment." Waco was the home of Baylor University, a very conservative Baptist enclave, and during her mortal life Amaliya had been the brunt of some nasty comments when in the area. She had to admit she had dressed to provoke. Already she had garnered a lot of uneasy looks due to her skin-tight black skinny jeans, her high-heeled platform sandals with studded heels, her tank, leather bracers, and her straw cowboy hat adorned with raven feathers and a bird skull on the brim.

Samantha, meanwhile, was in blue jeans, a pale pink sweater, boots, and a dark-rose leather blazer. It was bitingly cold outside, but Amaliya was immune to it.

The waitress set down a refill for Samantha's drink and stared at Amaliya's arm for a long moment. "What happened to the middle of your tattoo?"

A scar adorned the spot where a rosary had been etched into her skin. When she had transformed, the image had burned away. "God doesn't like vampires," Amaliya said. "The cross went bye-bye."

"Austin freaks." The waitress rolled her eyes and stalked off, her full hips swaying.

"Could you be nice?" Samantha hissed, leaning forward, blue eyes narrowing.

"We're in fuckin' Waco." Amaliya shuddered. "Why the fuck did we have to meet them here?"

"Because this is where they said to meet, bitch-face. Be nice." Frowning, Samantha sat back, shoving her empty plate aside. "It took Cian a long time to get them to agree to this meeting. Besides, it's all part of the big plan, remember?"

Exhaling, Amaliya tapped her black nails against the table. "I just hate Waco."

"Yeah, I got that. You know, since you said that a billion times on our way here."

Amaliya sighed. "It just makes me cranky to be here."

Samantha checked her pink iPhone. The case sparkled with rhinestones. A small smile touched her lips.

"Jeff?" Amaliya asked.

The vampire hunter was cute in a geeky sort of away. He and Samantha made an adorable couple. The diamond sparkling on her ring finger said all that was needed about their relationship. It had appeared without fanfare. Amaliya had taken note but hadn't asked. If the couple didn't want to talk about their engagement, there was probably a reason for it. Well, that reason was probably that they were probably all going to die very soon. The fact that the usually bubbly, over-the-top blonde had remained mum about it had even kept Amaliya from questioning her.

"He just wanted to make sure we're okay," Samantha answered. "You know how men are."

Amaliya's own battered iPhone kept flashing messages from Cian. He was worse than Jeff. It made her boyfriend nuts that he couldn't leave the Austin city limits without risk of a serious incursion the moment he left.

The vampire stared at her cooling coffee. She couldn't bring herself to drink it. Basically, she stirred the brew and pretended to sip it. "I don't know how the fuck we're going to keep The Summoner from ripping down the veil."

"We still have one of the rings. He needs all thirteen. Right there, we're far ahead of him." Samantha flashed an encouraging smile at Amaliya. "And he doesn't have *you*. It must make him nuts."

Amaliya rolled her eyes. "It's like having the worst ex-boyfriend in the world."

"Or is it girlfriend? I mean, since he's in Bianca."

"Either way, it's annoying as hell. So sick of this bullshit. Is it wrong to just want it all to blow up so we can get it over with?"

Samantha cast a leery look. "Even if we all die?"

Shifting uncomfortably, Amaliya wondered if she should confide in Samantha about what she'd been experiencing since July when she had first seen Bianca and known The Summoner was embedded in her body. Their small group was counting on Amaliya in a way that made her very uncomfortable. As the only other necromancer-vampire, she was the only one who could truly fight back against The Summoner. She couldn't fail them. Yet every night she struggled with the invisible ties that tethered her to The Summoner encapsulated in Bianca's tiny body. There were days when she woke up with her body on fire with the lust for the one who had created her. It went beyond sex to something darker, more powerful, dripping in death and evil. She wondered if Cian suspected. Sometimes she'd catch him worriedly watching her with his beautiful hazel eyes.

Tonight, her necromantic power was buzzing around her, craving release. Just like she desired blood, she desired to raise the dead. Each time she brought them forth from their graves, they fed her with death and power.

"Well?" Samantha was demanding an answer.

Sliding her hands across the table, she lightly touched Samantha's fingertips. Their power flared between them, spinning around in a whirlwind of ebony streaked with glowing white luminescence. They alone could see it, but it was reassuring. "I'm not going to let you die, Samantha. Or anyone else if I can help it. I just want to kill *him*."

Samantha grinned. "Me, too. So bad." Tilting her head, she said, "Shut up, Roberto."

Amaliya was always surprised with how much Samantha's touch grounded her. Their abilities meshed perfectly, bringing balance.

"You better let go of me. The ghost isn't the only one thinking we're lezzing out," Samantha said, gently squeezing Amaliya's hands. Her eyes slide to one side, indicating a table filled with people staring at them openly.

Releasing Samantha, Amaliya immediately felt the churning sensation return. Her cellphone buzzed again. Picking it up, she saw the message she'd been waiting for. "They're here."

"Time to be bad asses," Samantha said, grinning.

Amaliya smirked. "Totally."

"Just don't scare them off. No, snarling, threats, or bad attitude, okay?"

Amaliya rolled her eyes. "Fine. Whatever. Is it wrong to wish they'd be assholes so we could have a fight?"

"Yeah. Very wrong! Now behave," Samantha chided her.

With a weary sigh, Amaliya nodded. "Gotcha." She'd do her best, but she couldn't promise anything.

Samantha was seriously worried about Amaliya. Everyone was under a lot of duress, and so everyone just assumed Amaliya was showing signs of the strain they all felt. In theory it made sense, but Samantha could *feel* something was wrong. As much as it pained her to admit it, there was a link between the two women. Sometimes it flared to life, giving Samantha a glimpse into Amaliya's internal struggles.

With so much on the line, she had expected more people to step up to the plate and join them in Austin to hold off The Summoner's minions. Jeff kept pointing out that the Assembly had actively tried to stop The Summoner from acquiring the rest of the rings, but entire factions had been wiped out by The Summoner's forces. Samantha didn't understand why they couldn't get anyone to actually volunteer to move to Austin to help hold back The Summoner. It pissed her off.

Jeff's last estimate on how many of the rings The Summoner had acquired was between ten and twelve. The only reassurance was the fact that Cassandra and Aimee had hidden the last one. None of the experts on the occult were certain how much damage could be caused without the complete set. Some were estimating that only sections of the world would be permanently opened to the abyss, which, of course, included Texas.

Now seated across from Amaliya in a Denny's waiting on the emissaries from two of the most powerful vampires in Texas, Samantha wondered if they were doomed to fail. She didn't want to be negative, but it seemed like they were constantly scrambling to anticipate what would come next.

"They're here. Both are human. Both are infused with vampire blood. They obeyed the negotiations for the temporary peace pact and brought one guard each," Roberto's voice said. "Which you broke by bringing more."

Samantha didn't dare answer the ghost. She didn't want to be overheard. There was no way the emissaries could detect Roberto, so technically Amaliya was Samantha's only visible guard. She never dreamed being Cian's right-hand would be so terrifying, but she didn't have a choice anymore. There was no going back to a nice normal life now that The Summoner was close to destroying the world.

"Here they are," Amaliya said, slouching into the corner of the booth.

Samantha swiftly switched sides, sliding in beside Amaliya. The vampire beside her always smelled like cigarette smoke and roses. The scent used to annoy Samantha, but now she found it reassuring.

The two mortal right-hands of the vampire masters of Houston and Dallas avoided the hostess and headed straight for their table. Their two guards slid into a booth near the doorway to the convenience store part of the building. Jeb was all blond curls and cowboy charm in tight jeans, a light blue button-down shirt, and white Stetson. Varra was clad in an elegant navy pantsuit with a pale pink silk blouse shimmering against her very dark skin. Her hair was skimmed back into a high bun on her head, and delicate diamond and pearl earrings glittered in her earlobes. Everything about her screamed sophistication and money. Samantha eyed the red-soled Louboutins on the other woman's feet with admiration. The unlikely pair slid onto the bench across from them, Varra pushing

Samantha's soiled plate further away with distaste.

Jeb flashed a wide, good ol' boy grin at them, his blue eyes sparkling. "Hey, ladies. Nice to see ya."

"Hi, Jeb. Nice to see you, too." Samantha tried to look lighthearted and enthusiastic. Instead, she was sure she came across as a bit spastic.

Amaliya made a noise that sounded like a cross between a snort and "hello."

Varra opened her purse and took out a small packet of hand wipes. Her brow furrowed, she cleaned the table surface. Samantha caught herself before she rolled her eyes. Finishing, Varra tossed the wipe onto the discarded plate and set her Coach bag on the area she had washed.

"I'm not pleased to see anyone," Varra said. "I think this meeting is a waste of everyone's time."

Silence ruled the table.

Amaliya appeared to be so mad she couldn't find her voice, while Samantha was too stunned to come up with a retort.

Thankfully, the waitress appeared to take Samantha's dishes and listen to any potential orders from the newcomers. Jeb requested a Coke while Varra asked for a coffee. Samantha was glad for the few minutes to collect her thoughts. She wasn't sure if Jeb's friendly demeanor was a good sign or not, but it was clear that Varra was bad news.

The waitress collected the dirty dishes, then sauntered away.

"So..." Jeb set his hands on the table, interlocking his fingers. "What do you ladies want to talk about? My mistress, Courtney, is very anxious to hear any additional news about you know who."

Varra lifted her eyes, shaking her head.

"Nicole isn't interested?" Samantha asked her.

"Nicole sent me to hear what you have to say. That's all." The right-hand of the master of Houston didn't smile in the least.

"Well, Cian wants to extend his friendship to both Courtney and Nicole. This is a difficult time—"

"For you," Varra said cutting off Samantha. "We're fine in Houston."

"Yeah, we're sitting pretty in Dallas, too." Jeb winked.

"You won't be though," Samantha said swiftly. "The Summoner is planning to claim the whole world."

"I thought he was planning on tearing the veil," Varra said, her dark eyes boring into Samantha.

"Well, yeah! But so he can take over the world! World domination!"

Varra laughed.

Samantha stared at the other woman in disbelief. "That's all kinds of bad."

"See, this is where Courtney isn't too sure why Cian is upset. The veil tears and eternal night comes. That's really good for vampires and supernaturals," Jeb pointed out. "Not so great for humans, but it's not like they're much more than cattle."

"You're human." Amaliya's voice was clipped with annoyance.

"For now." Jeb grinned. "Once the veil rips, Courtney will bring me over."

"We're looking at an extinction event for all of us," Samantha argued. "Without the sun, humanity will die. Vegetation is a goner. Animals will follow. Humans starve."

Varra wagged her head. "There are plenty of technologies to keep humans alive. Many of the vampire masters across the world have been preparing for the coming night."

Jeb nodded in agreement. "Except for Cian, of course. He should be creating vampires to police the humans in Austin, hoarding food, setting up hydroponic gardens, moving cattle to secure locations...but instead, he has you two sitting in a fuckin' Denny's in Waco flappin' your jaws with old information."

"They're *mocking* you," Roberto's disembodied voice whispered to Samantha, both annoyed and amused.

Amaliya muttered, "Assholes."

The waitress appeared long enough to set down a glass of soda and a steaming cup of coffee. She gave them all a curious, yet disdainful, look before moving on to another table.

Varra leaned over her purse and stared into Samantha's eyes. "Do you really believe the supernaturals will help you? They're going to finally be able to come out of the darkness and live freely once The Summoner succeeds."

Samantha pounded her fist on the table, rattling the coffee cups and glasses. "The creatures of the abyss will come through. You do realize that, right? Demons!" she hissed. She felt the other customers looking her way but didn't care.

Jeb laughed. "It'll be great. The humans will need vampires to hold back the demons. Vampires will be their saviors. They'll open their veins willingly for protection against the creatures of the abyss."

Nodding in agreement, Varra said, "Governments will plead with the supernaturals for assistance once they realize their militaries are useless. Science will be obsolete as magic takes its place."

"You do realize that if your masters don't change you, you're fucked?" Amaliya glared at the two human minions. "Who's to say they won't fuck you over?"

Jeb and Varra exchanged glances. They both chuckled.

"We threw our lots in with vampires who understand how this world works," Varra said, her voice dripping with scorn. "Nicole suspected you'd have nothing new to say. I see she was right. This has been a waste of time."

"Cian's playing hero when he should be doing exactly what Courtney has been since he first told her about The Summoner's plan." Jeb shrugged his wide shoulders. "Maybe you two should tell him that. You're wasting time spinning your wheels against something you can't stop."

"We *are* going to stop him one way or the other," Samantha hissed. She was furious at how easily they were being dismissed.

"After The Summoner is dead, I'll be the only necro-vampire left," Amaliya said in a low voice. "And I'll fuckin' remember this night."

Samantha visibly shivered as Amaliya's power rippled outward. It was cold, full of fury, and ready to strike. Nervously, she set her hand on Amaliya's forearm. Their connection flared to life. Amaliya's anger licked along the connection, pulling on Samantha's own high emotions. Instead of steadying Amaliya, Samantha felt sucked into the vampire's vortex of rage.

The two humans across from the table were very still. Samantha was happy to see fear registering on their faces. Instead of being dismissive, they looked uncomfortable.

"Yeah, you heard me, shit-stains. I'll remember what you said tonight and the fuckin' bitches you serve. When The Summoner is gone, I will still be here and you'll have to deal with me." Amaliya glowered at the two humans.

"You can't do jack shit to us. We're under a peace pact," Jeb said, trying to sound calm but failing.

"Maybe not tonight, but some night." Amaliya pointed at him. "Trust me on this."

Samantha willed Roberto to smack Jeb in the back of the head. She was still working on her telepathic links, but when Jeb exclaimed out loud, jerked, and twisted about in his seat, Samantha grinned.

"What was that?" Jeb gasped.

"What?" Samantha asked innocently.

Varra slid to her feet. "We're leaving."

Amaliya virtually shoved Samantha out of the booth, moving swiftly to confront Varra. Samantha frowned but quickly stepped to Amaliya's side, trying to be supportive.

"You might think you have the upper hand and that we're doomed, but keep this in mind. Even if we fail, even if the veil drops, I will come for you. I don't give a rat's ass who your masters are. You're turning your backs on humanity." Amaliya's voice was low, clipped, and dangerous.

Everyone in the restaurant was watching now. Jeb's jaw was dropped, his white teeth gleaming in the fluorescent light.

Varra's cool exterior started to crumble, her jaw tightening. "I'm doing what I have to in order to survive. You should understand that."

"I understand that you're traitors. That's what I'm hearing."

Stepping closer, Varra whispered, "Do you really think you can defeat him?" Her dark eyes searched Amaliya's for the truth.

Amaliya didn't answer immediately, which made Samantha very nervous.

"I'll die trying," Amaliya said at last.

Varra's scornful look returned. "I thought so."

"I can trip her," Roberto's voice suggested to Samantha.

Narrowing her eyes, Samantha said, "*Fine.* Be a total moron. Just remember we warned you."

Twirling about, Varra stormed toward the exit, her guard rising to follow. She stumbled, nearly falling into him. Catching her, the guard looked around nervously, then they both hurried out the exit.

Amaliya glanced at Samantha, lifting an eyebrow.

Samantha smiled innocently.

Jeb scooted out of the booth. Hesitantly, he set his hands on his belt and stared at the two women. "I can try talking to Courtney, but she thinks this game is over. Honestly, so do I."

"If she'd stand with us, we'd have a better shot," Samantha said swiftly, hoping he was swaying to their side.

Lifting his shoulders, Jeb said, "Maybe. Or it would be a fast way to die. Courtney wants to survive. She's not going to sacrifice herself for humanity. Like all the other vampires, she's aiming to be ready for when the veil falls and not get on The Summoner's bad side."

"Well, you tell her she's now on Amaliya's bad side." Samantha set her hands on her hips. "And Amaliya is a total bitch. I mean, like a total raging bitch."

Tilting her head, Amaliya said, "She's right."

Swallowing visibly, Jeb said, "I'll talk to Courtney..."

"Yeah, do that." Samantha tried to look as threatening as Amaliya and wondered if she was doing it right.

Jeb twisted about and stalked toward the door. His guard slid out of his booth and followed. Amaliya stormed toward the cash register, fishing her wallet out of her jean pocket. She never carried a purse. Samantha remembered her own and hurried to yank it off the floor beneath the table. While Amaliya paid, Samantha kept an eye on the entrance. Just a few months before, she would have been scared out of her mind doing something like this, but now she was much more confident.

Amaliya checked her iPhone after paying the surly waitress and quickly tapped in a message. Samantha scanned her own messages. It was like Cian and Jeff were tag-teaming her phone.

"What did you tell him?" Samantha asked when they headed toward the exit.

"That I'm going to kill Courtney and Nicole and their cabals," Amaliya answered tersely.

"Cool." Samantha shoved open the door. "After you."

CHAPTER TWENTY

Amaliya didn't feel like talking on the return trip to Austin, but the perky blonde driving wouldn't shut up. Maybe it was her nerves getting the best of her, but Samantha rambling on endlessly was making her feel twitchy. Feet propped on the dashboard, Amaliya scrutinized her chipped toenail polish. She was still pissed off. It was nauseating how easily the supernatural world capitulated to The Summoner. She wasn't naive. The only reason they were afraid of her was because she was a necro-vampire made in The Summoner's image.

"I'm so sick of this shit," Amaliya said, interrupting Samantha. She realized after she spoke that she hadn't even registered what Samantha had been talking about.

There was a beat, then Samantha said, "Yeah. Me, too."

"You know, my kind really sucks it."

"Well, you *are* blood-sucking vampires. You're not supposed to be the good guys." Samantha flashed a teasing smile, then sobered when she saw Amaliya's expression. "I'm kidding."

"But you're right. We're not supposed to be the good guys. I hated hearing them mock Cian. He's the only one with the freakin' balls to stand up to The Summoner, and they're making fun of him." Twisting the ends of her hair with her fingers, Amaliya gazed into the night slipping past the car.

"Cian's a good guy. I always knew that. That's why I loved him. That's why I'm still his friend." Samantha's voice didn't hold a hint of malice.

It was a relief that they had put animosity behind them. Of course, Amaliya still felt guilt over the chaos she had brought to the lives of the people she now stood on the front lines with in the battle against The Summoner. Bringing him into their lives was much worse than sleeping with Cian when he was still with

Samantha. Sometimes she wondered how any of them forgave her.

"Maybe I'm too new at this vampire thing to understand their thinking. Or maybe I'm just damn naive, but I thought some of them would step up and defend humanity. Rachoń and Cian are doing what they can."

"Amaliya, you have to remember they're both attached to humans. That's the big difference. Courtney and Nicole use their dickwad human minions. They don't love them." Samantha switched lanes, scooting the car out of the wake of a big semi-truck, the wind shear buffeting the car briefly. "Cian and Rachoń have more invested in this than the other vampires. Don't you think Cian is thinking about his daughter? Cass is a dhamphir, but she lives as a human. If she's going to survive once the veil drops, she's going to have to go full vampire. What about me? If the abyss swallows the world, am I even going to be human anymore? I hardly feel human now at times."

"I'm so sorry about that." Amaliya sighed, guilt clawing at her gut.

"Stop apologizing! Fuck me! We had no clue it would happen. You did save my life. Plus, I'm adjusting." A smile crept onto Samantha's face. "I kinda like it, honestly. It makes me feel like a bad ass."

That elicited a laugh from Amaliya. "Well, yeah. You even have Roberto being your minion. And he's a total bitch."

"Oh, yeah. Totally."

"We have a few weeks. Just a few more weeks." Amaliya hated that fact. Biting at a hangnail on her thumb, she wondered if they'd find the location where The Summoner planned to tear down the veil in time to stop him. They were assuming it would be in San Antonio, but that wasn't necessarily the case.

"We can do it. Somehow. We have to." Samantha glanced significantly at her diamond ring. "I mean...c'mon. I have so much to live for. Besides, I'll look like shit without a tan."

"You could always try spray-on tanner," Amaliya suggested with a smirk.

"And be orange? Gross!"

Samantha urged her little car past yet another semi-truck. Interstate 35 was crammed with long haul vehicles. The highway narrowed when they entered a construction zone, the sides hemmed in by concrete dividers. Amaliya exchanged glances with Samantha.

"This is it," Samantha said.

"Yeah," Amaliya whispered through still lips.

Setting her arm on the console between them, the vampire opened her hand. Samantha wove her fingers around Amaliya's. Instantly, their magicks tangled together. The two women steeled themselves for the attack they knew was coming. There was no chance The Summoner wouldn't attack when both of them were together and outside of Austin.

The rending of metal, squeal of tires, and screech of air brakes tore through the night. Amaliya whipped about in her seat to see out the rear window. One of the big trucks traveling behind Samantha's car was jackknifing across the two lanes. The fender of the cab slid along the concrete barricade, sparks cascading into the air. The squeal of brakes was followed by the crash of vehicles colliding. The trailer flipped onto its side, blocking the entire road behind them.

Samantha pressed her foot down on the accelerator, keeping her little car ahead of the epic collision. The two lanes ahead were strangely clear of traffic. There was an absence of red brake lights in the all-encompassing darkness before Samantha's car. On the other side of the construction barricades, oncoming traffic continued to roll past, the headlights blazing in the absolute darkness. They were miles between towns, hemmed in by overgrown fields, trees, and silent construction vehicles.

"This is it," Samantha muttered again.

Amaliya observed that the semi-truck had finally come to a standstill. "We're cut off."

The spell exploded seconds later. The purple haze shimmered in the air, arcing over the area. A second spell popped into action, encompassing the car in a protective shell of blue power that would block any spell attempting to render the occupants unconscious. Samantha shoved her foot onto the brake, her fingers tightening on Amaliya's hand. Their seatbelts caught across their chests as the car squealed to a sharp stop. The dome of purple black magic spread out overhead, glittering menacingly. It appeared to be a repulsion spell, one that would keep humans out of the area until the ambush was over.

"You're on, little bitch!" Amaliya tensed her hand around Samantha's.

Samantha closed her eyes, her ghostly magic shimmering around her, sucking Amaliya's necromantic energy into its swirling mist. "Roberto!"

The handsome Mexican man flashed into existence in the back seat of the car. His hands became solid, cupping the intertwined fingers of the two women. Amaliya bit her bottom lip, allowing Samantha to drag deep on her power and pump it into the ghost.

"Do what I told you," Samantha ordered. "No fucking around, or else."

Roberto scowled. "Of course."

A dark shape leaped over the concrete barricade and hurtled toward the car. Amaliya freed herself from her seatbelt just as the werewolf hit the car, flipping it over onto the passenger side. The window shattered. Amaliya didn't pay the bits of glass any heed as she kicked out the windshield and jumped out. The werewolf rushed her. It was massive, well over six feet tall and covered in a dark black pelt. Long claws swiped through the air, aiming for her chest. Amaliya ducked under its attack and slammed her fist into the taut muscles of his stomach, sending the wolfman sprawling.

Amaliya unfurled her necromantic power, feeding it into the darkness to summon the dead. "Come to me," she ordered. She felt the dead stirring, but something was wrong. They couldn't come to her.

"Amaliya?" Samantha called out.

"They're blocking me! Fuck! The spell they cast is blocking me! I need bodies!"

"Bodies? Gotcha!" Samantha shouted back.

The patter of feet in the darkness announced the arrival of more attackers. The sound of gunshots echoed through the air.

Amaliya rushed the werewolf as it sprang to its feet. When it straightened to its full height, it was even taller than she realized. The half-man, half-wolf creature growled, revealing all its gruesome fangs. Amaliya bared her own sharp teeth and attacked. It caught her about the waist as she jumped at it, trying to kick it in the groin. Sharp claws raked her skin, drawing blood. Amaliya grabbed its snout with her hands in an attempt to keep it from biting her. The pointed teeth ripped at her hands.

Amaliya hissed with frustration, determined to take the werewolf down. Its massive head whipped back and forth, trying to break her hold. She managed to brace one of her heels against its leg, gaining some traction. Her long black nails dug into its face, drawing thick, dark blood.

To her surprise, it fell forward onto its knees, releasing her from its grip. Amaliya fell onto her backside and hands. Behind the werewolf, Roberto glee-fully plunged a silver dagger into the back of the great beast. Whipping about, the werewolf knocked Roberto into the concrete divider, but the ghost only laughed, winking out of sight. The wolf howled in frustration. Roberto reappeared on the other side of the creature and, silver blade flashing, kept up his assault.

Amaliya climbed to her feet just in time to deflect the oncoming blow from a vampire. Shoving him off his feet, she followed him to the ground, and her hand punched into his chest. One hard tug and his heart was in her hand. Tossing the crumbling organ away, she surveyed the battle scene.

Samantha sat on the driver's door of her lopsided car, wielding her pink Glock. The werewolf continued to try to attack Roberto, but the ghost was slip-ping in and out of the physical plane, eluding its swipes. At least six vampires and vampire-infused minions were circling, trying to get to both Amaliya and Samantha. It was Samantha's blessed bullets that were slowing them down. The low number of vampires was a very good sign. It meant that a powerful being was among the attackers and that they were over-confident in their ability to seize Amaliya and Samantha.

"I need bodies!" Amaliya screamed again.

"Working on it!" Aiming at the werewolf, the blonde unleashed a volley of bullets.

Dark blood pumped onto the cold asphalt from the many wounds inflicted upon the wolfman. The red liquid steamed in the frigid air. The beast twisted away, trying to avoid the silver dagger and bullets. Amaliya darted after him. She jumped onto its furry back, arms wrapping around its thick neck. It thrashed beneath her body as the spikes from her shoes dug into its sides. Amaliya sensed, more than saw Etzli descending on her and thrust her long nails into the wolf-man's fur and flesh. Rolling off his back, she dug in, ripping out his throat as she fell. The creature crashed to the ground beside her seconds before Etzli was on her.

Flying dark hair, blazing eyes, and a feral snarl was all Amaliya saw seconds before the bone knife thumped into her ribcage, ripping through her flesh and shattering bone. Amaliya screeched in pain. The Aztec was clad in a black dress slashed to her thighs. She appeared every inch of the blood goddess she claimed to be. Etzli jerked the blade out, twisting it as she did so to cause even more damage. An arc of blood flowed from the wound to form a red aura around Etzli. The vampire could draw blood from wounds, living up to her name perfectly.

Roberto fought against the vampires savagely, slipping in out of the night, stabbing and slashing with his silver dagger. Samantha reloaded and opened fire again on the vampires trying to close in on her. The smell of vampire blood filled the night. The blessed bullets exploded in their bodies, slowing their healing while also crippling them.

Amaliya grinned at the vampire. "Hey, cunt, what's up?"

Etzli started, obviously surprised by her flippancy. Spinning her daggers in her hands, she brought them downward, intending to stab Amaliya again.

A burst of sharp, cold wind knocked the Aztec vampire off her feet. Landing on the road, she skidded into the darkness with a cry of anger.

Amaliya scrambled to her feet. Blood was still flowing from her wound, streaming through the night like a red ribbon. "Fuckin' bitch!"

Baptiste, clad in a leather jacket, stepped out from behind Samantha's car. "Amaliya, you okay?"

"No!" she shouted, then felt the touch of death slither through her. "Wait, no! I'm good!" With a grunt, she gestured toward the werewolf with her bloody, mangled hand. "Up!"

The dead wolfman rose in obedience.

A vampire darted past her toward the car, heading toward Samantha. The blonde was reloading her Glock.

"Baptiste!" Amaliya shouted.

"Got him!" The black man raced forward, his hand lifting. In his palm, a fire orb formed.

The vampire in the black jumpsuit skidded to a stop. He looked like one of Santos's henchmen that had abducted Amaliya earlier in the year.

"Catch," Baptiste said, grinning, and tossed the ball of flame.

The night lit up with an orange glow as the vampire was transformed into a torch.

Amaliya sent the werewolf after the nearest human infused with vampire blood. She needed more bodies. Etzli would be coming back to finish the battle at any second. They had managed to surprise her by hiding Baptiste in the trunk of Samantha's car. Now The Summoner's ally would be much more careful.

The zombie-werewolf killed the human minion with a powerful blow to her chest. Amaliya immediately snatched the dead woman with her power. Another fell dead under the onslaught of Samantha's bullets, and Amaliya gripped that one in the web of her necromancy as well. Casting a quick look behind her, she saw Baptiste helping Samantha off the car and setting her on the ground. Meanwhile, two vampires had retreated into the night with Etzli. Roberto hacked at the last infused human, and soon Amaliya had four zombies at her call.

The phasmagus, elemagus, ghost, and vampire-necromancer gathered in the center of the interstate in front of Samantha's car. Shielded from human eyes by the spell, they knew no one would be coming into the battle arena.

"We have at least one witch, two vampires, and Etzli," Baptiste said, rubbing his hands together. His multi-colored magicks swirled around them. With a clean-shaven head, trimmed goatee, and maroon-colored eyes, he was both handsome and imposing.

Roberto reached out to touch Samantha, drawing more energy from her. "I'll find them." The ghost dashed into the gloom.

"I know where Etzli is," Amaliya said in a grim tone. "Just follow the blood. Stay here. Cover me."

Samantha gave a curt nod.

Baptiste hurled balls of fire into the darkness, attempting to illuminate the hiding vampires. Dark magic filled the air with an impenetrable gloom. The fiery orbs simply vanished into the blackness.

Stalking forward, Amaliya summoned her zombies to follow. The massive werewolf walked just in front of her. Smearing her blood over the zombies, she imbued them with more power. The blood from her wound slithered through the air, leading deeper into the darkness. She followed the trail more by smell than by sight. The dome of magic shimmered overhead, but the preternatural darkness made it nearly impossible to see.

Roberto flickered in and out of view as he searched the edges of the magical dome. The zombies were the freshest she'd ever controlled. It felt odd having so much life left in them. Little sparks of who they were remained. Amaliya picked up tiny flashes of their memories. The werewolf had been from Mexico. The woman had been afraid of Bianca. One of the two men had wanted to run away. The last had been in love with Etzli. Even as she grasped those remnants of the people they had been, those aspects of the zombies were already slipping away beneath the cloak of death.

"You can't win," Etzli's voice taunted.

"Wanna bet?" Amaliya answered.

Though Etzli was pulling her blood, Amaliya wasn't weakening. The deaths of the werewolf and humans had filled her with necromantic power.

The Aztec whirled through Amaliya's zombies, slashing, hacking, and ripping with her bone knives. Body parts fell to the ground, then the vampire was gone.

"Fuck!" Amaliya exclaimed as the head of the werewolf landed at her feet.

The remaining vampires rushed Baptiste and Samantha. Etzli appeared above

Amaliya, grabbed her by the hair, and tossed her into the air. Limbs flailing, Amaliya sent her death magic into the broken bodies of her zombies. It was difficult to control her necromancy and her vampire abilities at the same time, but Amaliya managed to catch herself in the wind. Hovering, she spun about, ready for Etzli's next attack. The werewolf rose, pieces held together by the tendrils of her magic, and charged after the attacking vampires.

Floating, Amaliya traced the blood trail into the night sky. Etzli liked to fight in the air. It allowed her to sweep in and out of the battle. The vampire was still drawing Amaliya's blood. Amaliya felt her vampire abilities diminishing, but her necromancy was still strong. Her long black hair whipping about her face, Amaliya gave up depending on her vampire nature. She released the zombies to true death, reclaiming her power. Despite recalling her necromancy, she still felt a long tendril of her power spiraling into the night. It took her a few seconds to realize the source of the pull on her magic. The blood Etzli was stealing was Amaliya's, and it was dead just like her. With a triumph smile, Amaliya summoned it back to her. The blood returned to her in a gush.

Etzli spiraled out of the night, caught in the aura of blood. Wailing in surprise, she slashed her bone knives uselessly through the air. Like most of her abilities, Amaliya had to learn them by trial and error. Concentrating on the writhing tentacle of her blood that effectively wove a net around Etzli, she raised her hands in an attempt to keep the other vampire trapped. Etzli writhed in the mass of blood, her knives continuing the rip at it. Bobbing in the air a few feet from the Aztec princess, Amaliya unleashed more of her power. It spread out around her like great wings.

"I found the witch!" Roberto's voice called out from below. Once the witch died, the spell hiding the supernatural battle would collapse, revealing them to the humans.

"Don't kill her yet!" Amaliya struggled to contain the struggling vampire in her power. "I almost have this bitch under control."

Swearing, Etzli fought even harder, trying to pull Amaliya's blood from her control and into her own. Amaliya felt the leash on her power slip and cursed. Drifting closer to Etzli, Amaliya watched the vampire thrashing in the blood cloud. Etzli's dark eyes blazed with fury. Battling against the necromantic power holding her hostage, she bared her fangs.

Again, her power slipped. Etzli was older and more in control of her abilities than Amaliya. Most of the time, Amaliya just winged it, learning as she went. This time, she couldn't depend on chance.

"Kill the witch!" Amaliya ordered.

Etzli's eyes flashed with fear.

The magical dome vanished a second later.

The fresh death flared through Amaliya like cold fire, filling her completely and imbuing her with the power she needed. With a cry of triumph, she sent Etzli crashing into the ground. Amaliya landed beside her, straddled the vampire, and pinned her arms to the road as the bloody vapor swirled around them. Digging her nails into Etzli's wrists, she destroyed tendons and bone. The bone blades fell from Etzli's hands.

Roberto emerged from the darkness and pounded his silver blade through Etzli's chest, impaling her heart, instantly paralyzing her.

Samantha's battered car pulled up next to them. The passenger side was a mess, but it was drivable. Baptiste jumped out and jerked Etzli into his arms.

"Make sure the knife stays in her heart," Amaliya said.

Baptiste nodded, sliding into the backseat with her.

Amaliya once more cast out her necromancy, snagging all the dead bodies scattered across the roadway. She willed them to rest in peace. The corpses sank through the road and into the earth. Climbing into the passenger seat, Amaliya dragged the warped door shut.

"You're scary," Samantha informed her.

Amaliya shivered, nodding. "Yeah. I am."

The sirens of the emergency vehicles sounded in the distance as the small car sped on toward Austin.

CHAPTER TWENTY-ONE

Cian stroked his goatee with his long fingers while watching the array of monitors sprawled across several desks lined against the wall in his home. Slouched in an office chair, he watched the progress of Samantha's vehicle on a map displayed on one of the screens. He was grateful that the GPS signal of the vehicle could be tracked. It was reassuring to see the car on the outskirts of Georgetown. Amaliya and Samantha were almost home.

Checking his phone again, he saw Amaliya's latest message. The autocorrect was having a lot of fun with her swearing, and it brought a small smile to his worried face.

Alexia sat next to him, occasionally tapping away on the keyboard. Cassandra was perched beside him on a stool she had dragged over from the bar. Elbows on her knees, she studied the banks of monitors that displayed the latest information on the battle against The Summoner.

The basement game room looked like something out of a science fiction movie. Most of the gaming equipment Cian had bought for the room was in storage. In its place were the state-of-the-art machines that Alexia had purchased to create an information hub. The young hunter was incredibly resourceful. Whereas the supernaturals of the cabal were dependent on their otherworldly abilities to fight The Summoner, Alexia used her intelligence and tech skills to keep track of every facet of the battle against the ancient vampire across the world. Sadly, most of the recent activity was in their area.

"Aimee, any sign of trouble?" Cian called out.

The true witch leaned over the old billiard table that was now covered in maps, spell materials, and crystals. "Nothing. None of the detection spells have activated." Her long hair was drawn into a ponytail and fell over one shoulder.

Clad in a sequined multi-colored skirt and lightweight blue sweater, she gave off an aura of softness and femininity. Yet Aimee was probably one the most dangerous of all his cabal.

Cian had been skeptical of Aimee's detection spells at first, but after witnessing their effectiveness in alerting them to their enemies, he trusted her completely. Cassandra and Aimee had buried spells along every possible route into Austin. Aimee then activated all of the spells, creating a net that activated an alarm if any supernatural creature entered the city.

"I still can't believe we got Etzli," Cassandra said in awe.

"The Summoner must want Amaliya really bad to send her," Alexia agreed.

"The Summoner is running out of time," Cian said somberly. "He'll get a lot more aggressive now. He wants the last of Lucifer's rings."

"I'm going to have to come up with a counter-spell to make sure they don't block Amaliya's power again," Aimee said, annoyance in her voice. "I should have anticipated their black witches trying something like that."

"You can't think of everything, babe," Cassandra said, giving her girlfriend an encouraging smile.

Aimee wagged her head, disagreeing. "I should have thought of it. They could have ended up prisoners, then The Summoner would have Amaliya."

"Amaliya did what she always does when backed into a corner. She found a way to fight back." The pride Cian felt in his lover helped balance the fear he felt at the thought of Amaliya not returning safely. The GPS signal was proceeding without interruption, much to his frayed nerves' relief.

Cian's plan to set a trap for Etzli had been helped by The Summoner making a move of his own. Cian had known immediately when Nicole and Courtney had abruptly agreed to send emissaries to meet with Cian's representatives after months of refusing that The Summoner had decided to take Amaliya. In the last few months, it had become increasingly evident that the vampire powers of the world were not going to defy The Summoner, so the offer of a meeting had been questionable to begin with. The insistence of the two vampire masters that Amaliya be in attendance at the meeting outside of Austin had only confirmed his suspicion. For once, the plotting of The Summoner had worked in Cian's favor. If he had sent Amaliya and Samantha out of town on a random errand, The Summoner would have been suspicious. The meeting in Waco had been perfect.

Now, they would hopefully discover where Bianca was located and rescue her while The Summoner was out of her body.

It felt good to finally be able to win against The Summoner after months of fending him off. He could see it in the eyes of those around him that they were relieved to finally have a win in their column. They had all lost much in the last few months. Alexia and her brother Benchley had been forced to abandon their regular lives and go underground. Benchley's gaming store had been sold to his business partner while Alexia took a leave from attending St. Edward's University. Jeff had closed his occult bookstore, moving all his files and books home. Samantha no longer worked a regular job in one of Cian's companies. Instead, she was his human right-hand and spent all her time helping in the efforts against The Summoner. All of the members of the makeshift cabal split their time between Jeff's Victorian and Cian's mansion. Except for Eduardo. The coyote came and went as he pleased, but no one knew where he lived anyway. The coyote always showed up when needed but tended to keep to himself.

Cian's phone buzzed again, and he checked the incoming message. It was Amaliya. He grinned as he read.

"What'd she say?" Cassandra asked, leaning over his shoulder in an attempt to take a peek.

"In Round Rock. Almost home." Cian answered, hiding the rest of the message. It was rather pornographic. Amaliya tended to be horny after a big fight.

"Uh huh," Cassandra said, obviously not believing that was the cause for his grin.

Cian winked at her.

Cassandra rolled her eyes. "Gross."

He chuckled in response.

Cian adored his daughter. Every time he looked at her, he only loved her more. She looked so much like her mother, Galina, that it was a bit startling. Yet he could clearly see himself stamped in her features and especially her attitude. Even though he hadn't raised her, she definitely had inherited some of his personality traits. He was also very fond of her girlfriend and was glad to see his daughter in a solid relationship. In spite of the high state of anxiety they all lived with, he did find happiness in the small moments he spent with Cassandra. Their relationship was still evolving, but it was good.

Jeff emerged from the stairwell with his brown hair a bit messy from him running his fingers through it. Cian noted the slight limp the man walked with. He knew Jeff suffered phantom pains. Yet the hunter never let his disability slow him down. "Rachoń called. After she heard we got Etzli, she was more than a little ecstatic." Jeff strode over to study the bank of monitors.

Aimee face was somber as she watched the bits of magic floating across the map of Austin on the table before her. "They're still in the clear."

"If we can get Etzli to tell us where The Summoner is located, that will be a big plus on our side." Jeff took a seat nearby, his phone still in his hands.

"If The Summoner doesn't immediately relocate once he...or is it she?...realizes we have Etzli," Aimee pointed out.

"It sucks that we can't go to the government to help us." Alexia swiveled her chair back and forth while typing on her keyboard.

"We all know how that worked out for the Washington group that tried to get help," Cassandra said sadly.

"Guantanamo." Jeff sighed. "I can't believe they got pegged as terrorists. Or maybe the government knows. Maybe they don't care. Maybe they're in on it. Maybe they want The Summoner to win. Who knows?" Jeff ran his hands through his hair again, exhaling loudly.

"What does it matter? We're on our own. We already know that. When it comes to dealing with The Summoner directly, we're it. There's no point lamenting that fact anymore." Aimee folded her arms over her breasts.

"The hot witch has a point," Cassandra agreed.

"We'll deal with Etzli, get the information we need, and go from there," Cian said in a firm voice.

There was a long beat of silence, then Jeff said, "Holy shit, we got *Etzli*! Does that blow anyone else's mind?"

"I won't believe it until I see it," Cassandra admitted.

Cian checked his phone again when he felt it buzz. "They'll be here soon. We do have the cell prepped, right?"

"Benchley is putting the finishing touches on it," Jeff answered.

"Cian, how are we going to keep her from pulling her slick assassin moves?" Cassandra tilted her head, curiosity in her eyes.

"Silver chains. And if that doesn't work, I'll chop off her arms and legs," Cian answered simply.

"For real?" Cassandra's eyes widened.

"Of course." Cian stood, stretched, and lightly stroked his daughter's hair with one hand. "If she attempts to break free, I'll do it."

Cassandra opened her mouth, then shut it abruptly.

"This is a war, Cass," Cian reminded her.

"No mercy," Aimee agreed. "Etzli would never show it to us."

"And when we get the information we need?" Alexia asked.

"We kill her," Jeff said, also standing.

The thought of destroying a woman he had once cared about should have bothered him, Cian thought, but it didn't. Etzli would kill all of them and take Amaliya to The Summoner if she could.

Cian and Jeff exited the room together, walking down the narrow hallway to another room. It was actually another one of Cian's resting places, but they had altered it to hold whomever they managed to snatch. That it was Etzli made Cian especially nervous.

"Do you think she'll talk?" Jeff asked in a lowered voice.

"Honestly, no. But we'll find a way to get the information out of her. We have to."

Jeff stopped in mid-stride and turned to face Cian. Arms folded, the human looked dour. "If we find out where The Summoner is from Etzli, we'll have to attack soon."

Cian nodded. "As soon as possible."

"Which means we should get the information out of her tonight. If we don't, there's a chance The Summoner will move locations." Jeff fidgeted a little. "Do you think we can do it?"

"We don't have a choice, Jeff. This is our best break so far."

"Is Amaliya sure she can actually carry out her plan?"

"She's certain of it. If we can rescue Bianca, we will have The Summoner at a great disadvantage. If she can untether The Summoner from Bianca's body, he'll be a ghost again, and Samantha thinks she can possibly banish him." Cian knew it was all conjecture, but it was all they had. There was really no way to plan in certainties. They'd have to wing it. He didn't like it any more than Jeff did but didn't see where they had a choice.

"I hate this," Jeff sighed, rubbing his face with his hands. "If The Assembly hadn't fallen apart, they might have been able to figure out how to eliminate him."

"I know you trusted your vampire hunting buddies, but they were ill-prepared for all of this in the end. How many groups have simply gone quiet?"

"Too many. They're out of the game now. We're it."

Resting his hand on Jeff's shoulder, Cian looked him in the eye. "The best people to deal with what is happening are already here in Austin. I do believe that."

"I still wish we could get help from the government, the military, the cops." Jeff leaned against the wall, appearing exhausted. "I didn't tell the others, but one of the groups in England also tried to raise the alarm with the government. No one has heard from them since. After what happened to the group in Washington and now the English one, I'm really starting to wonder if the vampires have some of the governments in their back pockets."

Cian knew it was a distinct possibility. "So if the veil falls...?"

"Some of the people in power will end up vampires and continue to be in power. That's what I'm guessing. Or am I just paranoid?"

"You might be right. We've been a bit naive about things since the beginning. Remember when we thought it was a fluke that The Summoner had made Amaliya? Now we know better. When he set her free after she rose, it was all a test. To see if he had accomplished what he set out to do." Cian mirrored Jeff's posture by leaning against the opposite wall. "Maybe he's had this planned much longer than we think. Consider the abduction of Etzli over a hundred years ago. The rings of Lucifer are worn by his followers. His exclusion of me and Rachoń, the most 'human' of his offspring."

"Yeah, yeah." Jeff let out a harsh exhalation. "It's just he's had how long to prepare compared to our measly four months?"

"You think we're going to fail, don't you?" Cian wasn't surprised. Jeff was pragmatic and intelligent. It didn't take much thought to come to that conclusion. Yet Cian believed they would somehow beat The Summoner. So much had changed since Amaliya had come into his life. She was a catalyst for so much that he believed she would continue to play a valuable part of what would happen next.

"I won't lie. I wish I could take Sam and run. But there is nowhere to go, is there? The veil falls and hell comes to earth. I just wish my dad was here. I feel like he'd figure all this out. He'd know what we need to do."

"Did you ask Sam if he's around?"

"Yeah. No sign of him or Innocente." Jeff's thick brows drew into a hard line over his eyes. "I sometimes feel like we're abandoned by the whole damn world."

Cian grinned. "But we'll save it anyway, right?

"Because we're the good guys?"

"Because we love two amazing women that we want to have futures with."

Jeff chuckled. "So you're saying we're being selfish bastards and not actually noble."

Cian shrugged. "I have Amaliya and Cass to think about. I don't want to see them altered by the veil falling."

"I'd like to have a family with Sam," Jeff confessed. "Be a dad. Have a regular life."

"Sometimes people do the right thing for selfish reasons," Cian said.

Jeff was silent for a beat, then said, "No, no. I want to save the world and all the people in it. I want them to be safe from the monsters in the abyss. I don't want to just stop The Summoner for me and Sam but for everyone."

Cian wished he could say the same, but he really couldn't. A world filled with darkness would actually benefit him in many ways, but he feared what the veil falling would do to Amaliya and Cassandra. A world ruled by The Summoner would be an incredibly dangerous place for them.

"You're a better man than me, Jeff," Cian said at last.

That brought a smile to Jeff's face.

"Will you two hurry up and kiss?" Benchley poked his head out of the room. "Seriously. Gay. Sam and Frodo gay."

"You do realize Sam wanted to go home and marry a girl," Jeff responded, smirking. "The girl with ribbons in her hair."

"Whatever. I got the silver-coated shackles secured in here. Are you sure it will hold her?"

"If she tries to escape, she's not going to have arms and legs," Jeff replied.

Benchley looked at Cian, frowning. "Seriously?"

"I'll chop them off," Cian answered.

"Fuck, dude. Okay, well, I can rig a harness if I need to. Very *Boxing Helena*, Cian." Benchley disappeared back into the room. "You guys aren't playing around."

"Actually," Cian responded, "we're playing to win."

CHAPTER TWENTY-TWO

Keeping close to Baptiste as he carried Etzli into Cian's modern multi-level house through the door exiting the garage, Amaliya didn't dare remove her eyes from the paralyzed vampire. She knew their prisoner was unable to move as long as she was impaled by silver, but it didn't keep Amaliya from experiencing the irrational fear that the Aztec vampire might somehow escape.

"I keep waiting for her to twitch," Samantha muttered behind Amaliya.

"Glad I'm not the only paranoid one." Amaliya dared to look at Samantha for a split second. She registered the blonde's worried frown.

"Just when you think the monster is whipped, it jumps up and starts killing," Samantha said somberly. "That's how horror movies always work."

A shiver slid up and down Amaliya's spine at the thought. But the small woman in Baptiste's arms didn't even appear alive. Her arms dangled at her sides, head tipped back, her eyes empty.

"Tasty. For me?" Eduardo slid out of the shadows of the short hallway leading past the kitchen.

As always, Amaliya's body throbbed with heat at the sight of the coyote. Smirking, he winked at her.

"Really, you shouldn't have. How could you know what I wanted for my birthday?" Eduardo continued, falling into step beside Amaliya.

"Your birthday isn't until January," Samantha said crossly. "It's on Jeff's birthday calendar."

It touched Amaliya that Samantha was so protective of her, but Amaliya could handle Eduardo just fine. Despite his raw sexuality and the carnal lust he inspired between her thighs, she kept him firmly at arm's length.

"True, besides I have my eye on something much more delectable." Eduardo's eyes swept over Amaliya, his gaze lingering on her breasts.

"Fuck off," Amaliya said, roughly pushing him through a doorway into the dining room.

The coyote growled.

Amaliya ignored the delectable shiver that raced through her at the sound. She hated how much he turned her on.

When she followed Baptiste down the stairs into the basement, the first person she saw was Cian. The somber look on his handsome face was expected, but the sword in his hand gave her pause. She wasn't looking forward to what was coming next.

"Put her in the cell," Cian instructed Baptiste.

"You got it." The tall man cautiously carried the small woman along the narrow hallway and past the rest of the cabal gathered to gawk at their captive.

"Wow, it's really her." Benchley sucked in a deep breath. "Wow!"

"Anyone else really, really nervous?" Alexia asked.

When Cian pressed a kiss to her lips, Amaliya lightly touched his cheek. She sensed the violence stirring beneath his calm veneer. He was already mentally preparing himself for what he had to do.

"Do you think she'll tell us where The Summoner is?" Amaliya dared to ask.

Cian's frown only deepened. "I don't know, but what other choice do we have? She's our best chance."

Biting her bottom lip, Amaliya matched his dour expression.

Tenderly touching her arm, Cian said, "We're running out of time. Even if The Summoner can only partially open the veil, it will cause severe damage to this world. We have to do this."

Aimee and Cassandra stood nearby, matching looks of concern on their faces. Etzli being in their haven was unnerving, but what Cian planned to do made everyone uneasy. Amaliya trailed behind Cian to the small room they had made into a prison cell. Etzli was sprawled on the floor with her eyes wide and staring while Baptiste and Benchley secured her arms and legs. As the silver shackles closed over her wrists and ankles, Etzli's skin sizzled. Around the silver dagger plunged into her chest, the flesh was charred. The sight of the weapon sticking out from between the woman's breasts disturbed Amaliya more than she would have thought possible. No matter how monstrous Etzli could be, she was also a woman just like Amaliya. Though her instinct was to hate the other vampire, Amaliya recognized that in some ways they were quite similar. They were both doing exactly what they thought was right.

Stepping away from Etzli, Baptiste surveyed the somber vampires standing in the doorway. "I can use fire on her if you need me to."

"I'll keep that in mind," Cian said, grim-faced. He motioned to the men with the sword in his hand. "I'll call you if I need you."

With bleak looks upon their faces, Baptiste and Benchley slipped past Amaliya into the hallway where the others stood clustered. Cian glanced at

Amaliya and she deliberately leaned against the cell wall, obviously refusing to budge. Acquiescing to her wishes, Cian shut the door. Without any fanfare, Cian leaned over, jerked the dagger out of Etzli, and stood back.

Etzli immediately began to laugh.

This wasn't what Amaliya expected.

Cian folded his arms, staring down at Etzli. He didn't speak but waited.

"You make it all so easy," Etzli said at last.

"Cian," Amaliya whispered.

Etzli spoke in a posh accent that was distinctly not her own.

The woman chained to the floor opened her mouth, and darkness bellowed out in a thick cloud. It struck Amaliya and Cian like a mighty fist. With a painful whack, Amaliya's head impacted with the wall. Black magic filled the room completely, drowning out all light, sound, and sensation. The oily miasma writhed over her skin attempting to slide into her mouth. Stunned, Amaliya clamped her lips together. The Summoner's presence dwelled in the blackness. Or maybe he was the essence of it.

"You disappoint me," The Summoner's voice whispered in her ear.

Struggling to shove herself off the wall to confront him, Amaliya concentrated on drawing upon her own magic to protect her. It was a mistake. The Summoner had created her, and his magic had birthed hers. Instantly, her power was wound around his, drawing her deeper under his spell. The darkness enshrouding her obliterated every sensation except for his fingers lightly stroking her throat. Even the wall she was pinned against sifted away until she was left with the impression of floating in deep, dark, frigid water. She was trapped in the heart of the absolute evil, feeling weightless, empty, and afraid.

"Again, you disappoint me. How easily you stumble into my traps."

Deep within the gloom was another presence. It wasn't Cian or Etzli. They were lost to her in the ocean of the necromancer's magic. It was the other one. The blood sister she had failed to rescue. Now they were both trapped in the majestic deathly power of The Summoner.

"Bianca," Amaliya uttered.

The spell slithered across her lips, seeking entry. She clamped her mouth shut, fearful of what may happen should the magic manage to infect her.

"She's here with us. My little necromancers are united at last."

Amaliya sensed movement within the murk and lashed out, trying to capture The Summoner in her grip. She didn't know how to fight him, but she had to try. The sensation of being adrift in the deepest waters of the ocean continued, her arms and legs flailing as she tried to find purchase. Soft, cold fingers gripped her hand. They were slim and delicate.

Bianca, Amaliya thought.

"I'm sorry," Bianca said from the black stillness.

The low, terrifying voice of The Summoner spoke in Amaliya's ear. "We are all three together once again. It's been so long since the night I killed both of you."

A small, delicate female body mostly made of darkness and cold drifted into Amaliya's embrace. At first she feared it was Etzli but realized it was Bianca when the tendrils of powers instantly wove together, uniting them. Feeling more like a shadow than flesh and bone, Bianca clung to Amaliya. Tears welling in her eyes, Amaliya clutched the other necromancer to her quaking body. Fear ravaged her thoughts.

"Submit to me and I won't kill those you love," The Summoner's voice murmured, the timber of his voice rushing over her flesh like the icy prick of a needle.

In a panic and desperate to escape, Amaliya unfurled her power, the dark wings of her magic reaching out to find those who loved her and grounded her. Instead, she found the welcoming power of her creator and her sister in blood.

The Summoner's long body pressed against her back. Though she knew it wasn't possible, she could feel the hardness of his chest. Amaliya had destroyed him with her zombies. She had seen the horde tear him apart. Yet here he was, tangible and terrible.

When The Summoner wrapped his arms around both of them, Amaliya shivered. There was completion in his touch. It was impossible to deny they were a triad of immense power. Amaliya felt it to her marrow, and it terrified her. Cian, Austin, the house, and all her friends felt like wispy dreams of another life. The darkness felt eerily like home.

"Submit to me and I will spare all those you love. Name them and they will survive when the abyss swallows the world."

"You're lying," Amaliya hissed. The spell again attempted to plunge into her mouth, but she managed to spit it out. There were still parts of her magic that were not intertwined with The Summoner's.

"He's lying," Bianca's voice said at the same time.

"No, no. I'm not," The Summoner answered. "I am willing to allow your family and friends to live if you will willingly come to my side. Submit to me. Be mine. We will rule the new world together. In exchange, I will grant your loved ones immunity."

"They'll try to kill you," Amaliya responded to the darkness.

"Yes, but they won't be able to with you at my side."

"And if I say no?"

"I will kill them tonight. Sergio and his family in Wyoming. The Vezoraks in Spooner, Texas. Cian's cabal in Austin."

Raw rage coursed through Amaliya. How casually he threatened all those she loved. Releasing Bianca, she managed to spin about, gripping The Summoner's neck in her hands. She could barely see him now, his eyes glowing in the blackness engulfing her. He wasn't flesh and bone but something else that was nearly as tangible. The glow of his eyes barely illuminated his face, but she could make out his sensuous lips, strong nose, and elegant brow. A sharp pang of need punctured her soul. No matter how evil and cruel he was, a piece of her always yearned for him. She tried to speak, but the torrent of conflicting emotions stilled her tongue.

"Etzli awaits your answer. By taking her into your home, you opened a pathway to my power. Already her witches, demons, and jaguars are waiting to enter the house through the portal and slaughter them all."

Bianca's presence lingered at her side but was silent. The great wings of Amaliya's power sought solace in the darkness. If only she could feel the touch of Cian's mind or Samantha's power. Instead, there was a small spark of familiarity.

Do as he says, Innocente's voice whispered through her mind.

Amaliya's fingers tightened against The Summoner's throat but had no effect. She wanted to rip his head from his shoulders so that she wouldn't submit to him and give into the throbbing need she felt for him.

"Well? Shall I kill all you love? Shall I drag you back with me and tie you in silver chains? Or will you come willingly with me to rule at my side when the abyss consumes the world?" His fingertips slid over her body seductively.

Quivering, Amaliya cursed him, herself, and the world as a whole. A feral, wicked part of her wanted to plunge into his power. It angered and disgusted her.

"Do you love me?" Amaliya asked, the question coming unexpected from her lips. The spell played along the corners of her mouth, retreating while The Summoner waited.

"More than any other," The Summoner answered.

Somewhere in the absolute dark, Bianca wept.

"You will let the others go. You will *not* hurt them."

"As long as you are by my side, I will not hurt them."

"Why do you want me?" This time the question was one she had been craving to ask for months. Ever since the night he had taken her out for coffee, then fucked and killed her.

"Because you're chaos personified. Pure power. Dark and beautiful. You are perfectly destructive."

The Summoner meant every word he said. She felt the truth resonating deep within her.

Do not run away, Amal.

Again, her grandmother's voice, but no one else trapped in the icy dark heard it but her.

Unable to utter the words he wanted to hear, Amaliya seized upon the alternative. Releasing the dam that held back her deepest, most terrifying desires for The Summoner, the darkness, and death, she pressed her mouth against his. He wasn't quite flesh, but he was corporeal enough to touch. The necromancer's kiss was bitter ashes and blood. His tongue was cold and demanding. She attempted to slide her mouth from his when it became too much to endure, but he held her captive. Within her, the last bit of resistance broke apart, and the magicks of both

The Summoner and Bianca flooded into her. Weeping, she clung to The Summoner, her mouth devouring his hungrily.

This was what she had always feared in the recesses of her broken soul. That only in the absence of all that was light and good would she find the place where she belonged.

The people gathered in the narrow hallway flinched when Cian slammed the door shut, cutting them off from the view of Etzli bound in silver and splayed out on the floor.

The ugly knot in Cassandra's stomach had her on edge. Though a part of her was thrilled to see Etzli subdued and at their mercy, she was well aware of just how dangerous the situation actually was. Cassandra lightly touched her girlfriend's hand, seeking solace, but Aimee didn't even look her way. The witch's forehead was furrowed and her lips pressed into a tight line.

They weren't the only ones ill at ease. Baptiste slid his hands slowly over his bald head, exhaling slowly. Benchley nervously scratched his nose, while his sister frowned at the tips of her battered sneakers. Jeff rubbed Samantha's back gently, trying to soothe her, but the ugly scowl on her face did not disappear. Only Eduardo didn't seem affected to what was about to occur. He leaned against the wall, tapping his fingers against it.

"Something's gone wrong," Aimee whispered.

"Yeah, we're going all Guantanamo on Etzli," Benchley answered.

Baptiste grimly dipped his head. "Not a good feeling."

"Kinda like we're the bad guys now," Benchley agreed.

"No, that's not it!" Aimee lifted her blue eyes, and Cassandra saw stark fear in them. "Something is here!"

"Oh, God! I feel it!" Samantha took a step away from the door, visibly shivering as revulsion poured into her expression. "It's full of death and...and..."

"Evil," Aimee finished for her.

"Well, it *is* Etzli," Alexia pointed out, but she also retreated down the hall.

"Maybe you're feeling Cian...you know...torturing her." The suggestion obviously made Jeff very uncomfortable, but he, too, took a few cautious steps backward.

"It's not Etzli. It's *him*!" Samantha started toward the door. Jeff futilely tried to tug her back, but Samantha twisted away from him. "Let go! He's here!"

Aimee fell in behind Samantha, magic beginning to spark around her fingertips.

"How can you be sure?" Cassandra took a step toward the door and froze.

"Uh...that?" Benchley nearly stumbled in his haste to get away from the cell.

Black magic coursed out around the edges of the door, giving it a dark, wispy aura. Ribbons of frosty energy lashed out, Aimee and Samantha both flinching under the assault. Cassandra cried out as she was whipped by the magic, welts appearing on her flesh where they struck.

"I can see that!" Jeff exclaimed.

"Dude, we all can!" Benchley grabbed Alexia's arm and shoved her behind him as he backed in the direction of the stairwell.

Baptiste surged forward. "We need to get them out of there!"

Cassandra was a few steps in front of him. Raising her arms to protect her face, she plunged past Samantha and Aimee. She pivoted on one foot and kicked out with the other, the heel of her boot striking the door. It took three more kicks to knock it entirely off its hinges. Baptiste thrust out his hands, a gust of warm air shoving the falling door out of their way so it spun across the cell floor.

"Oh, hell!" Samantha gasped.

A massive hole spread along the wall directly across from the doorway. It was filled with darkness, and inky threads crawled along the floor, ceiling, and walls like swiftly growing vines. Cian lay close to the door, his sword at his side. There was no sign of Amaliya or Etzli. The shackles that had bound Etzli were empty.

"It's a portal!" Benchley waved at the maw of shadows. "It's a portal!"

Tendrils of shadow lashed out toward the doorway. The floor beneath Cian shuddered, cracked, and started to give way. Cassandra grabbed her father under the armpits and dragged him out of the room seconds before the floor broke apart and fell into a pit opening up beneath the foundation of the house.

"This isn't good!" Samantha cried out.

"Everyone out!" Jeff ordered.

There was a mad scramble to the stairs. Aimee tossed a few orbs of energy at the spreading darkness. Small explosions of energy filled the air with an acrid smell but did not deter the black magic. The pitch-black filaments snaked past the threshold and spread into the hallway, forcing the witch to retreat.

"Well, that didn't work," Aimee muttered, then turned and fled.

Cassandra heaved her unconscious father over her shoulders and raced behind Aimee and the others toward the stairs to the main floor. Behind them, the ceiling broke apart with a mighty crack, and cement dust filled the air. Choking on the mix of chilly air and smut, Cassandra clambered up the stairs. Violent coughing drew her attention downward. Alexia was at the base of the stairs, doubled over and trying to catch her breath. Clutched in her hands were several external hard drives.

"Baptiste," Cassandra managed to force out of her clogged throat. "Alexia's in trouble!"

The elemagus's tall frame pressed past the witch and dhamphir to the tiny woman below. His sweater was pulled over his mouth to keep the dusty air out of his airways. Once Cassandra saw he had Alexia, she continued her ascent, following in Aimee's wake.

Out of the corner of her eye, Cassandra saw the black tendrils rapidly crawling along the walls, flanking their ascent. With a burst of speed, the dhamphir scrambled upward under her heavy burden, her hand grabbing Aimee's. Dragging her girlfriend along, Cassandra trailed behind the others in a desperate dash to get out of the house. The shadowy serpents of black magic slithered over the floor and walls and wove through the building, ripping it apart.

The house gave out a loud moan before the ground floor began to buckle and cave in.

"Hurry, hurry!" voices rang out through the haze.

Cassandra stumbled a few times, but Aimee helped her along. Cian started to rouse, moaning against her back. She didn't dare set him down until they escaped. The outside lights were a cloudy blur in the thick, choking air. Cassandra aimed for the illumination, banging into furniture as she fled. There was a loud whoosh then a tunnel of clear air formed before her. Baptiste's magic sizzled along their escape route, holding back the thick haze.

They reached the front door just as the house shuddered violently. The sound of concrete cracking, girders bending, and glass shattering was a terrifying dissonance. Dodging chunks of the house as it toppled, the witch, dhamphir, elemagus, and the people they had rescued scurried toward the street.

Benchley's van backfired loudly as he started it. The side door was open. Jeff, Samantha, and Eduardo were already inside on the rear seat, all three covered in a thick layer of dust and trying to clear out their throats and lungs. Cassandra helped Aimee inside just as the house gave another loud groan before breaking apart and disappearing into the gaping sinkhole opening beneath it.

"What the hell..." Cian muttered, finally coming to as Cassandra shoved him onto the middle bench.

"You missed some stuff," Cassandra said, sliding in beside him.

Baptiste tucked Alexia into the front seat before jumping into the back, crouching on the floor and sliding the side door shut.

"Go! Go! Go!" Jeff shouted.

Cassandra glanced toward the house to see the sinkhole spreading outward. The van's tires squealed as the vehicle raced up the street, Benchley honking the horn wildly as he drove.

"What are you doing?" Alexia panted.

"Trying to warn the neighbors," Benchley answered.

Joining the others in looking out the back window to watch the destruction, Cassandra wrapped an arm around Cian in an attempt to console him.

"It's not spreading past the property line," Aimee observed, relief in her voice.

"He took her." There was deadness in the words.

"Yeah, Dad. I'm so sorry." Cassandra hugged him, not sure if he would accept her sympathy.

To her surprise, he lifted one arm, draped it over her shoulders, and held her close. "It was inevitable."

CHAPTER TWENTY-TWO

The van swerved around a corner and sped along a dimly lit street.

"Benchley, slow down! It's not following!" Jeff ordered. "We don't need to crash!"

Benchley obeyed but was still driving far too fast.

"What the hell happened back there?" Samantha demanded.

"The Summoner found a way into our haven through Etzli. Then he took Amaliya," Cian answered. Everything about him was grim, from his words to his face.

"Fuck! Fuck! Fuck!" Samantha slammed her fist against the back of the seat for emphasis.

Baptiste let out a long breath, cupping his head with his hands. "Dammit. We shouldn't have brought Etzli back."

"I can't believe our plan failed," Alexia said through her coughing fit.

"We're dealing with The Summoner," Cian said simply.

"You're taking this pretty well considering that he just stole the hottest piece of ass in Austin," Eduardo said, a smirk twisting his lips.

Cian moved so swiftly Cassandra didn't even realize what was happening until Cian hurled Eduardo through the back window. Glass exploded outward, then the coyote's body hit the street and rolled away into the night.

"Whoa," Baptiste said, his maroon eyes widening.

"Did you just bust out my rear window?" Benchley howled in distress.

"I'll pay to repair it. " Returning to his seat next to Cassandra, Cian stared straight ahead.

"Dad?" Cassandra said softly, wrapping her arms around one of his. "Dad, we'll get her back."

Aimee started to rest her hand on Cian's other arm but thought better of it and set it on her lap instead. "Samantha may be able to track her. We'll find Amaliya and rescue her."

"No," Cian said, shaking his head. "No."

"Dad, don't say that," Cassandra protested. She wasn't sure how they hell they could rescue Amaliya, but she knew they had to try.

"You don't understand," Cian said, pain in his voice. "Amaliya and I discussed something like this happening. We agreed that if he came for her, she would go with him. We have to know how to stop him, and by being close to him she can figure it out. Like Benchley likes to say so often, she's our big gun. If anyone can find a way to stop him, she will."

Samantha smacked Cian. "Asshole! You can't just let her do that!"

Though Cassandra could tell Samantha was upsetting Cian even more, the vampire didn't lash out. He opted to let her yell at him for a few more minutes before lifting a hand and stopping her from hitting him again. No one else had tried to stop her, so it was quite clear that Cian was not very popular at the moment.

"Amaliya is resourceful. She'll find a way to let us know how to help her when the time is right. I trust her," Cian said fiercely. "She's more powerful than all of us. She went with him willingly to *help* us."

"She's sacrificing herself," Aimee protested.

"Yes, she is." Cian focused on the road ahead as Benchley drove toward Jeff's Victorian. "But that's what people do for those they love. Let's not diminish what she's doing."

"This is bullshit," Samantha muttered but sounded like she grasped what he was saying and maybe agreed.

Leaning toward the vampire, Cassandra sought out his gaze. He finally looked at her, and the depth of his despair ate at her. "Dad, what if she can't do it?"

"She will." There was no doubt in his inflection. He absolutely believed his words.

Cassandra's gaze drifted toward Aimee. She understood where Cian's strength came from in that moment. Cassandra trusted Aimee completely. She didn't doubt Aimee's abilities or strength. She also knew that Aimee would sacrifice herself in a heartbeat to save Cassandra, and Cassandra would do the same for her.

"Okay, Dad. I believe you." She snuggled into his shoulder, attempting to give him some solace and a bit of the love that was growing in her heart for the man that was her father.

To her surprise, he slanted his head so his brow touched hers. "And I believe in you, Cass."

PART SIX

Amaliya, Bianca, and The Devil

CHAPTER TWENTY-THREE

The freezing vacuum expelled Amaliya from its grip and deposited her in a large room lit by candles. Ornate designs drawn with dark red paint covered the white marble floor. The scent of wax, ashes, blood, and sweat drifted through the murk and smoke filling the grand room. With hands raised and oily black tentacles springing from their palms, thirteen black witches stood in a circle around the portal, feeding it with their magic.

In the void, The Summoner and Bianca had been tangible presences, but as Amaliya observed the scene, she realized she had exited alone. Disoriented, she raised a hand to her head, straining to adapt to the physical world. It was unsettling to feel the weight of gravity upon her body. How long had she been trapped within the conjured doorway?

She attempted to take a step but fell to the floor. The impact was jarring and painful. Her teeth clanked together, biting her inner cheek and drawing blood.

"It will take you a moment to adjust," Bianca's voice said with The Summoner's accent.

Lifting her eyes, Amaliya observed that just beyond the circle of black witches, the slim girl was secured to an ornate wood chair with heavy silver chains. Two people, a redhead woman with maroon eyes and a nervous young man clutching a tablet, stood on either side of diminutive blonde.

The black witches around Amaliya continued to feed the portal, their dark magic twisting and wiggling through the air. There was a heavy thump beside Amaliya. She tilted her head to see Etzli lying on the floor next to her. The smaller woman gagged, then threw up foul-smelling blood. Cursing impressively in Spanish, Etzli tried to push herself upright but obviously had great difficulty doing so. Hastily, an older mortal man rushed over to help her to her feet. Amaliya was glad to see she wasn't the only one suffering the aftereffects of the portal. Though Amaliya was close to vomiting, she fought the urge. She refused to show any weakness. The two women exchanged fierce glowers, then Etzli was guided to a chair set near the wall. As Etzli was helped away, Amaliya gingerly balanced herself on her feet and sluggishly straightened.

"Gregorio, I need a blood minion," Etzli snarled.

After making sure his mistress was settled, Gregorio rushed through an arched doorway into the main part of the house.

Gesturing toward Bianca, Etzli said, "He's returned. Release him, Trish."

The slim woman with wild red hair and eyes the same color as Baptiste yanked a ring of keys from her jeans and set about unlocking the padlocks.

"Come on," the young man with the iPad urged Amaliya, waving her toward him. "Don't step on the markings."

Narrowing her eyes, Amaliya ambled on unsteady feet away from the portal. She could hear the thrum of its power and feel the artic coldness that dwelled within it. The black witches were completely silent, their eyes riveted to the gateway. Dressed either in a black shirt and jeans or a black dress, the thirteen people were of various ages and ethnicities and split almost evenly between the sexes, with women having just one more of their number. Their eyes were utterly black. Amaliya carefully edged between two of the witches and approached The Summoner.

There was no mistaking he was control of Bianca's body. Cold blue eyes watched Amaliya approach as he was released from his bindings. Lifting his charred wrists, he smiled with Bianca's sweet cupid mouth as they healed.

"So this is how you keep her from escaping," Amaliya said, folding her arms over her breasts and cocking her hip. Eduardo had been right.

"It's effective," The Summoner said simply.

Glancing over her shoulder, Amaliya saw that the black miasma hovering in the air was now churning violently. Thick bubbles ran along the tendrils connecting it to the witches. Amaliya could feel the power escalating, becoming more dangerous.

"You said you would spare them!"

"They're closing the portal," The Summoner answered with a dismissive shrug.

"I don't believe you!"

"Watch. It's closing. I can't have your friends coming through to disrupt our time together."

One by one, the witches dropped to the floor with loud, painful sounding smacks. The portal swelled outward once, like a large bladder filling with liquid, then it crumpled in on itself, vanishing with a fleshy pop.

"What the hell?" Amaliya stared at the spot where the portal had floated, then at the witches. Blood oozed from their mouths, noses, and ears. "Are they dead?"

"No, no. They'll recover," the young man answered, nervously fidgeting with his tablet. He was wearing clothes that looked like something out of an anime film.

Out of the darkness that bordered the room, tall beings emerged to bend over the fallen black witches. Their eyes glowed like red fires in odd faces that were not quite human. Amaliya recoiled, realizing they were demons. The creatures claimed the witches and carried them out of the room. As they filed past the candles, the flames expired one by one, smoke curling upward toward the high ceiling.

"Stark, the lights," The Summoner said crisply.

The young man nodded, slid his finger over the iPad screen, and the three large chandeliers suspended above their heads came to life. "There you go."

The Summoner stood. Bianca's body was clad in a long white dress and white lace-up boots. Her blonde hair was brushed into soft waves around her delicate face. Though the face of the younger woman was youthful and lovely with big blue eyes, sweet pink lips, and rosy cheeks, cruelty lingered just beneath the surface. Bianca had never appeared this way in life. Amaliya stared into the blueness of the other woman's gaze, seeking out any sign of the other medium.

There was none.

"Your plan succeeded," Etzli said, her voice raspy. "Now we should move to crush Cian's cabal."

Amaliya glared at Etzli. "As if you could."

"That wasn't the agreement between me and my prodigal daughter. I have agreed to allow them to live since she has so graciously returned to the fold. It spared me having to bring her back unconscious and bind her in chains."

Bianca's fingers were cold, yet enticing against her cheek.

"What if they try to stop us?" Etzli glowered at Amaliya, obviously not trusting her. "What if *she* tries to stop us?"

"Cian's cabal is inconsequential. They were amusing pawns in my game to acquire Amaliya, but we are done with it now. All is as it should be." The exultant smile on Bianca's lips was cruel in its certainty.

Gregorio returned to the room, dragging a young dark-haired woman with him. She was already covered in bloody bites. Sobbing, Etzli's prey futilely attempted to break free, but the man ignored her clawing fingers. Gruffly, he thrust her into Etzli's arms. With a loud, hungry hiss, Etzli sank her sharp teeth into the girl's throat. The fragrance of warm, fresh blood filled the room.

Slipping his arm around Amaliya's waist, The Summoner escorted her past the feeding vampire and out into a long hallway with an arched ceiling. "Stark, monitor the unrest in San Antonio. We may need to release more of the black magic spells to incite more violence. Trish, make sure to dispose of the body once Etzli is done feeding."

Amaliya shivered involuntarily as The Summoner escorted her through his haven. The dark power dwelling in the house was heavy and foreboding. The air itself was so thick with black magic it was like walking through a fog. It dampened the light spilling from the wall sconces and overhead chandeliers. Death magic was intertwined with a much blacker, scarier power. Amaliya had to fight not to let it sink into her.

The house was old but beautifully preserved. Arched doorways, red-tiled floors, and white walls spoke of a Spanish influence, yet it didn't resemble Santos's old haven. There was a hint of Victorian opulence in the design.

As they walked, she kept her head slanted downward, her hair sliding forward to shield her features from The Summoner's gaze. It was difficult to hide her anger, contempt, and frustration. She supposed she should be pretending to be much more subservient, but it wasn't in her nature. With a growing sense of foreboding, she realized that she may have to give in to her darker nature to actually succeed.

"I knew you would come once I threatened your loved ones," The Summoner said, his arrogance antagonizing her. He was very good at reading her, which pissed her off.

"Whatever."

The Summoner was mocking her. "You are a strangely loyal person when it comes to your family. Even after you were transformed, your first instinct was to run home to your father even though you knew he would most likely reject you. And then there was your delightful grandmother. You ran to her immediately after your father's rejection. She really was a strong soul, wasn't she? May she rest in peace."

"Don't you dare bring her up," Amaliya said tersely. "Don't you fuckin' dare!"

"Oh, my. Still a sore spot?" Bianca's blue eyes widened. "What else did you expect me to do after she helped *kill* me?"

"I *did* kill you."

The Summoner's expression darkened. "True. But I *want* you."

Amaliya frowned at the words. "I thought you ditched Rachoń because she put family first. Why do I get a pass?"

"Because I've *always* wanted you. Even before I took on the persona of that unfortunate professor, I knew I wanted you. The history of your family is fascinating. Do you even know that every firstborn daughter of your family is a powerful medium?"

"My mother wasn't," Amaliya said with defiance.

"Yes, she was. They all were. But they all started hiding from the truth of their natures much like you did when you were a little girl."

"You know nothing about me!" The denial flew from her before she could swallow it down. Even as she said the words, she knew it wasn't the truth. She actually feared he knew too much about her. He'd spent a lot of time observing her while she sat in his class, and he had probably watched her from afar when she hadn't even been aware of his presence. Obviously, he had also known about her grandmother and Bianca's mother, which meant he had researched their families.

The Summoner chuckled. "I know much more than you know."

Amaliya dared to give him a sharp look. For a brief second, she thought she saw Bianca lingering in the shadow of her own body. "What do you know then?"

Drawing close, The Summoner said, "You're afraid that you really do belong with me."

"Fuck you." Amaliya tried to pull away, but the grip on her body did not relent. She hated how easily he could read her.

"Rachoń is merely a vampire. You are much more than that, and you know it. Once you fully embrace your new, true nature, your pathetic attachments will dissolve. You will soon understand your rightful place."

Amaliya certainly did not like being told who she was or where she belonged. It hadn't worked when her family, society, and religion had tried to do that. It wasn't about to work now, but she kept silent.

The Summoner directed her up a winding staircase with an ornate wrought-iron railing. Their footfalls on the marble steps echoed through a large foyer. Somewhere, deep in the house, someone screamed in pain.

"You were inside Etzli," Amaliya said as they climbed. Her mind was still piecing the events of the night together.

"Yes. Hidden inside, waiting."

"You knew we were hoping to ambush your people."

"Yes. Of course. It was obvious. I laid out a trap for you that would be very apparent, so you would lay a trap for me."

"Which was the *real* trap." Amaliya realized how foolish they had been. The Summoner loved to play games with people's lives. He had easily maneuvered them into delivering him straight into their haven. "How did you open the portal? Oh, wait. Of course. The portal spell was inside Etzli, too."

"See. You're clever." Bianca's face proudly beamed at her.

"And somehow you were able to connect the portal here..." Amaliya pondered what she had seen when she had arrived. The dark red designs were significant. "Blood?"

"Santos and Etzli are related by blood."

"So you formed a bridge through their blood." Amaliya pressed a hand to her forehead. Of course. She had smelled blood when she exited the portal. It was Santos' blood that had created the portal. "We were so stupid."

"You're children," The Summoner said with a sigh. "Mere children."

Guiding her through a set of doors, they entered into an enormous bedroom. It wasn't furnished except for a massive bed covered in ivory silk bedding and an antique table in one corner. As soon as they stepped over the threshold, Amaliya's head swam and her body sagged. The air throbbed with malevolent energy. The pulse of the magic surged against her body in potent waves. Feeling disoriented, she staggered as The Summoner drew her to the table. Resting on the surface was a length of red velvet with twelve gold rings sitting upon it in a glittering row.

"Oh, God," Amaliya gasped.

"There is no god here other than you, me, and Bianca." The Summoner's voice was male, strong, and exactly like her nightmares.

Daring to look at him, she saw his true form transposed over Bianca's. The double image wavered but maintained itself. The doors to the room thumped shut as the light overhead fell dark.

The rings on the velvet glowed with hellfire. The illumination formed a sword with one piece of the hilt missing.

"Isn't it lovely? The instrument that will bring this world to an end and begin a new one?" The Summoner stepped out of Bianca. The younger woman instantly slumped against Amaliya.

Catching the blonde girl, Amaliya supported her weight while she fought against the growing malaise in her limbs. The viscous atmosphere in the room was making it difficult to focus on anything other than the vibrating power of the rings. The phantasmal sword repulsed her.

The apparition of The Summoner approached the rings and held his ghostly hands over it. Gradually, his form grew in density until he appeared to once more be made of flesh and blood. With a sly smile, he turned toward Amaliya.

"This can't be happening," Amaliya said with disbelief.

The Summoner stood before the two women completely nude. He was breathtakingly handsome with his fair hair, blue eyes, finely etched features, and sculpted physique. Amaliya vividly remembered what his body had felt like when he'd fucked her in the blood of her first victims. It had been one of those most fulfilling and erotic experiences of her life. It disturbed her to no end that she had lost herself in blood and sex with the man who had killed her.

Amaliya dared to stretch out her hand and touch his chest. It didn't quite feel like flesh, but it was solid. The sensation left her fingertips buzzing, and the tingle spread through her limbs until it settled between her legs. He appeared to read her mind for he smiled lasciviously at her.

"It took some time to harness all the ectoplasm needed to form this temporary shell, but it suffices when I need it." The Summoner rested his hands against her cheek and Bianca's. "Doesn't it, Bianca?"

The girl had tears in her eyes, but she nodded mutely.

Amaliya's fingers closed over his wrist, and she could feel the fine hairs on his skin tickling her palm. "How?"

"Do you think me weak?" The Summoner inclined his head near hers, his eyes narrowing. "Do you really believe you could keep me from returning?"

"Yes," she answered truthfully. "I did."

Chuckling, he shook his head with amusement.

Bianca's slim body pressed tighter against Amaliya's as the younger woman clung to her.

CHAPTER TWENTY-THREE

"Bianca has been witness to my greatness. You have much to learn."

"Maybe I do. I have like a bazillion questions to ask you. But let's start with this one. If you want to fuck your pretty little things, why don't you just take over someone else's body? Why the big show?" She gestured toward his erection.

Her mockery clearly amused him. "I know from our history that you prefer my true form."

Bianca squeezed Amaliya's side as a warning. Amaliya ignored her. She rather enjoyed provoking The Summoner.

"It was okay. But maybe I'd rather you possessed Santos. He's pretty hot."

The Summoner arched an eyebrow. "Oh?" He ran his hand through the radiance of the rings. "It requires a completely subservient person and then I am trapped by their *limitations*. I don't like to be limited." His eyes shifted downward to his cock.

"Men! Why is it always about the size of your dicks?" Amaliya rolled her eyes.

Again, Bianca's fingers dug into Amaliya's waist. The fear in her eyes was growing.

Amaliya didn't give a rat's ass. There was the distinct possibility she was going to die, and if she was going to meet her end, she was going to enjoy herself on the way out. That meant annoying the hell out of The Summoner.

"So why possess Bianca on a regular basis? She's got tits and a pussy. Obviously, you're limited there." She pointedly looked at his penis before raising her eyes to stare at him definitely.

The Summoner tilted his head and bestowed her with a bemused look. "Because I am connected to her. She's my creation like you are. It's easier for me to tuck myself inside her." His smile broadened. "In more than one way."

Amaliya dug her cigarette case out of her back pocket. It had a devil woman embossed on the lid, a gift from Cian. The thought of him hurt, so she pressed it away. Popping open the case, Amaliya drew a cigarette out. "So basically, this is all about you getting laid."

"Do you think me so crass?" The Summoner asked, surprised.

"Fuckin' absolutely." Lighting her cigarette with the electric lighter she kept in the case, she inhaled the smoke, then slowly blew it in his direction. "You're the one who flicked my bean as you killed me. You're all sorts of kink. So is your reason for wanting me here so we can do the nasty?"

Bianca flinched.

"I want you here because you belong here with me," The Summoner said calmly.

"Which is why you're doing the big show?" Again she gestured at his fake physical form. Despite her bravado, she continued to struggle against the stupor threatening to drag her down into its embrace.

"He's limited in this form, too," Bianca dared to say. "And he can't maintain it for long periods of time."

"Ah, there you go. Telling secrets, Bianca." The Summoner gave the blonde a sharp look. "What did I tell you about that?"

"She's one of us," Bianca answered, defiance in her eyes. "Isn't she? So why not tell her?"

Stepping closer to the women, The Summoner towered over them, forcing them to look upward to meet his gaze. The penetrating blue eyes slid from one face then the other. "Yes, she is. Aren't you, Amaliya?"

The lethargy slipping into her bones and muddling her mind frustrated her. It reminded of her being drunk or feverish. The world was hazy and didn't feel quite real.

"Amaliya, aren't you?"

The sharpness of his question focused her. The answer she wanted to say was not the one she actually uttered. Blowing out a plume of smoke in his direction, she said, "Yes. I am."

The Summoner plucked the cigarette from her trembling fingers and extinguished it by crushing against the tiled floor. "Your defiance always intoxicates me."

"I never wanted to destroy the world," Amaliya retorted. "That's your dream. I just want to live my own life."

"You're my dream," The Summoner answered. "My death goddess."

The kiss he pressed to her mouth was hungry, demanding, passionate, and full of lust. Again, he didn't feel quite like flesh, but she could feel his tongue darting into her mouth, claiming hers. Sharp teeth grazed her lips, and she tasted blood. His elegant fingers wound into her hair, pulling her tighter to him. Amaliya attempted to keep her necromancy tightly bound inside of her, but it began to unfurl as the pleasure in her body began to build. Cold tears seeped from her clenched eyelids as she recognized that a part of her never stopped craving him. She had been created to stand at his side and rule a dark world.

But so had Bianca...

The Summoner's lips abandoned Amaliya's to kiss his other progeny. His fingers continued to caress Amaliya's neck, pulling her against his naked form.

A vivid vision filled her mind's eye. The Summoner stood between Bianca and Amaliya as their army of zombies ravaged a darkened world, blood spilling onto the ground. Among those dying were all the people who had ever hurt her, mocked her, and dismissed her as nothing more than a failure. A terrible delight filled her.

"They never knew what you were." The Summoner gripped both women by their hair, pulling their heads back so he could gaze into their faces. "But I did. I saw what you both were and I took you. You are mine."

Dizzy with the low humming power of the rings, Amaliya struggled to regain control of her magic. But death called to death, blood to blood, and it was entangled in the magic of the other two beings.

"Do you feel it?" The Summoner demanded, his gaze capturing hers. "Do you feel it, Amaliya?"

With a shuddering sob, Amaliya nodded, then met his hungry kiss with her own. She had always felt that she belonged with him. That was why she'd destroyed him before and would again.

CHAPTER TWENTY-FOUR

Samantha stared at the air mattress on the floor of the attic. The battery for the air pump was dying, so it had taken her forever to blow it up. It was a twin size, so she'd folded some of the king-sized blankets Jeff owned and tried to make a decent bed for Cian. It was a far departure from his usual sleeping chambers.

The sound of the hammer striking the nails being pounded through boards and into the window frame gave her a headache. Jeff and Cian were almost done with covering the small windows of the long narrow space filled with boxes of holiday decorations and old family heirlooms. Samantha had tucked the small bed into an area behind a huge stack of boxes. Though she was still peeved at Cian, she didn't necessarily want him bursting into flames if sunlight somehow found its way into the attic.

"This should be sufficient," Cian said finally.

"I've never had a vampire stay over before." Jeff cast nervous look in Cian's direction. "I'm sorry about the loss of..." Faltering, Jeff closed his mouth. There was really nothing to say that could possibly offer Cian a bit of comfort.

Cian strode away from the human, his fingers raking through his long hair. His goatee was now more of a beard. The vampire looked tired and a bit lost.

"Here's your bed," Samantha said, pointing to the air mattress. "It's not much."

"It'll do." Cian gave her a slight hug. The distracted air about him was disconcerting. He'd never seemed so lost before.

"Cian, I'm really, really sorry I yelled at you earlier. And hit you." She attempted to look as apologetic as possible but wondered if she was successful because she was actually still peeved at him.

"It's all right."

"Bitch-face is going to be fine, you know. She's such a total pain in the ass. He'll not be able to stand her and will send her back." Samantha gave him a fake perky smile.

When Cian actually cracked a slight grin, she felt a surge of satisfaction. "She is a bit of a handful." The vampire sat on an old chair and clasped his hands together as he leaned forward. "Samantha, I need you to do something for me."

"Whatever you need, Cian."

Jeff finished putting away his tools and joined them. His hands settled on Samantha's shoulders, and his thumbs gently circled against her tense muscles.

Raising his hazel eyes, Cian said, "I need you to find a way to reach her through your magic. You're connected. She told me so. She was counting on that if The Summoner took her."

"But what if *he* does something?" Samantha felt stark terror at the thought of The Summoner somehow reaching through their connection.

"Your magic is linked to her, not him. I believe it's set apart from her bond to him." Cian stared at her steadily and she sensed his desperation.

"What if you're wrong?" Jeff asked.

"Aimee can help protect Samantha. I know Amaliya will be waiting for us to contact her so she'll be able to feed us the information she's gathering."

Cian sounded completely confident that this was the case, but Samantha experienced a small twinge of doubt. What if the bond between Amaliya and The Summoner was brainwashing her? Samantha wasn't about to express that thought to Cian, but it did bother her.

"It wouldn't hurt to try," Jeff admitted.

"I would have to do it before the sun goes down when vampires are the weakest." Samantha scratched her temple and pondered the situation. "I suppose her necromancy might be a little stronger during the day when vampires are usually asleep. I could try to reach her and find out where she is."

"That sounds good." The sadness in Cian's eyes tempered his smile.

"Then we can plan our rescue mission." Jeff sounded tired and a little scared, but she could hear the resolve in his voice.

"We're not going to rescue her," Cian said softly. "We're going to stop her and The Summoner from tearing the veil."

"What?" Samantha gawked at him. "Are you saying she's on his side?"

"No, I'm not saying that. We can't waste our miniscule resources on trying to rescue her. We need to focus on stopping whatever he's planning." The vampire stood and folded his arms over his chest. "Trust me. My instinct is to find her and rescue her, but that's not what she'll want. She wants to stop him. She wants him dead. Permanently."

"He'll expect us to launch a rescue, won't he?" Jeff asked.

Cian concurred. "We'd be playing into his hands. I don't think he considers us a true threat now that she is with him, but he'd also expect me to rush to her rescue. It's what I've done in the past."

"Like when you tried to rescue Roberto," Samantha said, understanding. "And what I did for you. And what we tried to do for Bianca, Sergio, and Innocente. We have a history of rushing in to do big rescues."

"Exactly."

"So he'll be waiting." Jeff rubbed his eyes wearily. "Definitely. He'll be waiting."

"So we need to concentrate on reaching her and finding out what he's planning and where we need to go to stop him." Cian glanced at the makeshift bed.

Again, Samantha was struck with the utter loneliness that filled his gaze. He loved Amaliya in a way he had never loved her, and though it should have pissed her off, it made her heart bleed for him. Without thinking, she threw her arms about him and hugged him. To her surprise, he clung to her, burying his face in her hair.

"Cian, I'm so sorry about bitch-face," Samantha whispered.

The vampire was silent, but she felt his shoulders quaking. His remote behavior and eerie calm made sense in that moment. He was barely keeping himself together.

"I would rip the world apart to save her," Cian said, a quaver in his voice. "But I can't. It's not what she'd want, and I can't risk falling into another trap."

"If you die, he wins," Jeff agreed.

Slipping from her embrace, Cian retreated to the bed. The sun was close to rising, and he looked exhausted. "Yes. He'll win."

"I'll see what I can do. I promise." Taking Jeff's hand, Samantha moved toward the attic door. "When you wake up, I'll let you know what I figured out."

"Thank you," Cian said, a grateful look in his eyes.

When Samantha closed the door, the last thing she saw was Cian wipe a tear away.

Amaliya stirred, her eyelids gradually peeling open as she awakened. She'd been dreaming of her grandmother but lost the old woman's urgently whispered message when she woke. The cloying scent of blood, incense, sex, and black magic hung in the air, reminding her of where she was and all that had occurred the night before. The emptiness within her was agonizing, and she fought back the sudden desire to cry.

Cian wasn't at her side slumbering through the daylight hours. He was in Austin sleeping alone. She craved his touch, his kiss, and the sound of his voice whispering her name.

Last night, it was not Cian's kiss or touch that had brought her exquisite pleasure but the one who had created her. It had actually been a relief that The Summoner had wanted sex and hadn't tried to force her into some bizarre black magic ritual. After witnessing the twisted manifestation of the black witches' magic, she was afraid of what he might force her to do. Sex was something she could handle without many qualms. She'd just turned off her emotions and enjoyed the physicality of it.

Stretching out her legs, she ignored the pleasant soreness between her thighs. Whatever The Summoner was now, he had been just as ravenous and passionate as the first time he'd tried to claim her. Unable to bite and drink her blood, he'd been especially rough. It had frightened her a bit to realize just how much he wanted to make her his own. How far would he go to try to secure her loyalty?

Rubbing her face, she tried not to think too much about what had occurred. She had no regrets, but she hated to admit that it had been a bit more than just casual sex. It was undeniable that the power that existed among the three of them was terrifying in its intensity, but it also bound them together with a strength and fervor that was difficult to process. Whereas Cian's touch made her feel safe and loved, The Summoner and Bianca awoke the darker aspects of her nature in a frightening yet enthralling rush. Locked in their embrace, she'd felt like a goddess ready to demand blood, death, and darkness. In the aftermath, she was shaken by how alluring the promise of the new world was when she was drunk on the potency of their combined power.

A tender touch on her shoulder drew her out of her dark reverie. Rolling over, she saw Bianca was already awake, one hand tucked beneath her cheek. She wasn't staring at Amaliya but past the end of the bed. Moving her fingertips away from Amaliya's skin, she pointed toward the far side of the dimly lit room. Still nude, the necromancer was on his knees before the glowing rings, his hands held aloft over the illusion of a sword. Eyes closed in rapture, he was chanting in a language Amaliya had never heard before.

"He does this every day," Bianca whispered. "It's what helps him gain a corporeal form when he's in this room and only in the room."

"Is that why he possesses you outside of it?" Amaliya inched closer to Bianca, the silky sheets brushing over her naked flesh.

Pressing her lips together, Bianca nodded sadly.

The Summoner appeared lost in his meditation.

"Is he aware of us right now?"

"No. Not right now." Bianca sighed and curled into a little ball. The room was incredibly cold, and the silk comforter was not very warm.

Pulling another blanket that had been shoved to the end of the bed over them, Amaliya tucked it in around their bodies. It was strange that they were actually feeling the low temperature in the room. Usually, cold didn't affect vampires. With dread, Amaliya realized that the icy air was supernatural.

Snuggling under the covers, Bianca said, "Thank you."

"Have you tried to escape while he's doing that?"

"Yes." Bianca's gaze slid away from The Summoner to Amaliya's face. "I can only make it a few steps before it stops me."

"What does?"

"The sword."

Propping a few pillows under her throbbing head, Amaliya wished she could get away from the hellish sword. The energy flowing in waves from Lucifer's weapon made her feel oddly disconnected from herself and the world. The sensation was not entirely unpleasant, which worried her.

"How does it stop you?" Amaliya concentrated her attention on Bianca and ignored The Summoner's chanting and the pull of the horrible rings.

"I get confused. Muddled. I can't remember what I'm doing. Or why I'm trying to leave. Once, I stood in the same spot in front of the doors for hours until The Summoner came out of his trance. He was very upset." Bianca returned to watching the man that had brutally killed her but was now her captor and lover.

"I'm so sorry," Amaliya said and meant it. Despite all she had been through, Bianca gave off an aura of innocence. It made Amaliya want to protect her. "I wanted to save you once I knew you were still alive in your body. I just didn't know how."

"I know. I shouldn't have tried to reach you. I was just so scared and desperate." Bianca nervously bit her bottom lip. "I should have known he would find a way to bring you here. He always wanted you so much more than he wanted me."

Bits of memory sifted through Amaliya's mind. "You were there the night I died, weren't you?"

A slight shudder slipped through Bianca's body. "I tried to save you. I failed. You died. He killed me."

"I think I remember," Amaliya frowned as she tried to recall the night The Summoner had murdered her. Their date had been so wonderful until the moment he had torn out her throat. Maybe it was a false memory, but she had a recollection of Bianca trying to touch her hand as she died. "You whispered something to me."

"I told you to find me," Bianca said. "I thought we'd rise together and that we could find a way to defeat him together."

"But I rose before you."

"And he possessed me as soon as I awakened."

"I'm so sorry." She laid her hand on Bianca's cheek. "I failed you."

Edging closer, Bianca rested her fingers over Amaliya's. "Don't say that. You didn't know. It took me a long time to fight through the possession. It was like I was in a very deep sleep and caught in a nightmare I couldn't escape. Once I managed to slip past his power, it took a long time to find your grandmother. I'm so sorry about her dying. I never dreamed he would kill her."

"So you did try to reach my grandmama?"

"I thought she would be like my mother and be able to fight him."

Amaliya tried to banish the image in her mind of her grandmother's tiny broken form. "Your mother fought The Summoner?"

"He tried to claim her. She fought him and won. I was very little when it happened. When he couldn't reach her inside the house, he burned it to the ground. She died saving me. I didn't see him again until he arrived at the college. I recognized him but thought he didn't know who I was. I was wrong."

"Fuck me. He's been watching us for a very long time then?"

"We are his grand experiment." Bianca peered at Amaliya over the edge of the blanket. "We're his chosen."

Flopping onto her back, Amaliya slid her hands through her messy black hair and tried to wrap her mind around what Bianca had said. "So, you reached out to my grandmama..."

"Yeah, but he caught on. I should have learned then, but I wanted to escape..." Bianca faltered.

Amaliya understood very well the desperation that must have been ripping through Bianca. How many times had Amaliya tried to escape from the troubles of her life? Now, instead of running, she was facing the evil that haunted her existence. "I get it. Trust me. I would have been doing the same thing."

"Then he started to astral project, leaving me alone in my body. It was the first bit of real freedom I'd had in so long that I didn't really think about the consequences of reaching out to you. It was so freeing to see glimpses of your life." A slight smile touched Bianca's lips.

Amaliya couldn't help but to return it. "I can imagine."

"It was so wonderful. Those little peeks. I thought maybe I could find a way to escape, but then..." Bianca's gaze briefly shifted to view The Summoner. "Once the twelve rings were here, he harnessed the power to shape himself into a tangible being, and our relationship changed."

It had been clear the night before that Bianca had become well-versed in the art of sex, but Amaliya suspected that had not been the case before her transformation. The Summoner had made her his lover, his slave, and his vessel. "Did he force you?"

Bianca sadly shook her head. "I wish I could say he did, but I gave into his seduction almost immediately. You felt it. Didn't you? That power..." The rapture of the memory caught her for a moment, altering her innocent beauty into something more seductive. "He terrifies me, and I know he's evil, but..."

"It's like we belong with him."

"Yeah. It's so delicious and terrifying because if I were to totally let go... completely give in..."

It disturbed Amaliya that she did understand. It was as if she were standing on a precipice and if she were just let go of her humanity and attachment to the mortal world she would become untethered and fly through the abyss as a risen death goddess.

Gathering Bianca close, Amaliya rested her cheek against her fair tresses. Bianca snuggled into her, seeking solace and maybe strength. Sadly, Amaliya knew it was a mistake to try to comfort each other, because instantly their magicks mingled and grew in magnitude. It fed into the energy in the room, making the atmosphere thick with magic.

"He couldn't wait until you were here. I'm a poor substitution for you, Amaliya."

Amaliya felt a flash of sadness, realizing that Bianca felt like the lesser of them. The Summoner had paid more attention to Amaliya during their night of sex, but she thought it was because it had been so long since he had touched her.

"You're a powerful necromancer, too, Bianca. I think you're more powerful than I am. There's a reason he created both of us."

"Because of what we were as humans," Bianca agreed. "But you're the one he wants at his side. He killed me out of malice. He admitted he thought I was too far gone, driven crazy by my powers, to bring over safely. I've been his unexpected consolation prize in all of this. It's you he really wants. It's you he may even love. You're everything I'm not. Everything I can't be."

"A fucked up metalhead with attitude?"

Bianca giggled. "Actually, yeah. It's your rebelliousness that sucked him in. I'm sure of it. It always fascinated the hell out of me."

"Yeah? Cian says it's part of my charm." Wincing, Amaliya wished she hadn't uttered her love's name. It hurt to be without him, to not have him at her side.

"You love Cian, don't you?"

"Completely."

"He's very handsome," Bianca said. There was a hint of jealousy in her voice.

"He's amazing," Amaliya admitted, trying to be truthful but careful. "When we get out of here, you'll get to know him and see for yourself."

Bianca's eyes lit up. "You still want to escape?"

"Of course." Amaliya gave her an incredulous look.

"I was wondering because..." Bianca faltered. "The way you were with *him.*"

Amaliya snorted. "Sex is just sex." Thousands of years of practice made The Summoner one intense lay, but her feelings for him were decidedly not romantic.

Bianca's eyes widened. "But it was so...so..."

"You had sex with him. Do you love him?" Amaliya pointed to the still form of The Summoner.

Shaking her head adamantly, Bianca said, "No, but it feels like *something* important."

"Only if you have feelings for the other person and you want it to *be* important."

"So with Cian it's different?"

"With Cian, everything is perfect," Amaliya said, the pang in her heart almost too poignant to endure for a moment.

The thought of Cian brought some clarity to her mind, and she clung to it. Slipping away from Bianca, she swung her legs over the edge of the bed. The air was a fine cold mist on her skin, and when she stood, it weighed upon her like a blanket of snow. Amaliya didn't know how to kill The Summoner, but that didn't mean she couldn't try. Taking a step toward his kneeling figure, she felt the rushing frigid waves of Lucifer's sword buffeting her. Maybe if she scattered the rings it would make The Summoner dissipate.

"Don't," Bianca called out to her. "Don't step closer. You'll get caught in its power, and then you'll be lost until he snaps out of the trance. He'll be angry. He'll see it as betrayal."

Amaliya wanted to ignore Bianca, but already she felt as though her feet were turning into lead. A steady weight was pressing on her mind, forcing her to lose focus. Bianca's hand gripped hers and dragged her back onto the bed. Immediately, she was released from the power of the rings.

"I fuckin' hate those things," she grunted, annoyed.

"When the thirteenth gets here, I can't imagine what it's going to be like." Bianca shivered beneath the covers. "When he tears apart the veil and the abyss swallows the world, he won't need to possess me or anyone else."

"He won't get the thirteenth. It's hidden," Amaliya assured Bianca.

"No, it's already on its way."

"What do you mean?" Amaliya twisted about to face the other woman.

"They already cast the spell this morning to compel it to return. With the arrival of the twelfth ring, they were able to finally call it here. It'll possess the closest person to it and have them come here."

Dread filling her, Amaliya stared at Bianca. "Are you sure?"

Bianca nodded.

"But we have until December 21st, right? The end of the Mayan calendar?"

Bianca sadly shook her head. "No, no. Once the sword is whole, he can slice the veil apart. To allow the abyss to consume the world, he'll have to perform a ritual. For the ritual to work, he'll need to feed off the fear of thousands. The hysteria over 2012 is helping him."

"So it has nothing to do with the end of the Mayan calendar?" Amaliya stared at Bianca in disbelief.

"Other than he's going to use the fear over the possible end of the world to actually end the world? No. Not really." Bianca's hand gingerly touched Amaliya's. "He loves his games though. He's going to make the end of our world and the beginning of his spectacular." Leaning toward Amaliya, she cast a wary look at The Summoner. Satisfied that he was still in a trance, she whispered, "He doesn't know that I saw some of what he was doing while he possessed me. I know the location of where he is going to rip the veil."

Amaliya angled face closer to Bianca. "Tell me."

When Bianca did, Amaliya just stared at her for a second, then said, "Fuck me."

CHAPTER TWENTY-FIVE

Cassandra stared at her cellphone with trepidation. Seated at Jeff's kitchen table, she was trying to call her mother and check in with her as she did every day. They had spoken the day before, and everything had seemed fine. Today there was no answer.

The muted winter sunlight filtered through the curtains and cast a reflection over the display, mirroring her face in the dark glass. Cassandra glanced toward the stove where Aimee was putting the finishing touches on a spell.

"Mom's not answering," she said at last.

"Maybe she's taking a nap," Aimee answered, casting a reassuring look at her girlfriend.

Setting the phone down, Cassandra stared at it. "Maybe. But it feels weird."

"It's because we got hardly any sleep and everything that happened last night was..." Aimee hesitated, searching for the right word.

"Insane."

"Exactly."

Cassandra gestured toward the concoction on the stove that was tossing flecks of magic into the air. "Is that going to work?"

"We'll see. It's hard working around the dark magic, but I believe I figured something out."

Aimee shoved her long hair back from her face and peered into the cauldron. The true witch had faced some difficult challenges when it came to magic in the last few months but had adapted. Cassandra was immensely proud of her girl-friend. She loved Aimee with all her heart and soul for a myriad of reasons. Her feelings crawled out of her heart and choked her with emotion. Sliding out of the chair, Cassandra drifted to Aimee's side.

As always, the magic smelled like all the delicious things in life, and it permeated Aimee's skin and hair. Sidling up behind the witch, she wrapped an arm about Aimee's waist and rested her chin against her girlfriend's shoulder.

"It's all going to be okay, Cass," Aimee assured her, leaning back into the embrace.

"My father looked so sad." Cassandra sighed wistfully. "I wanted to make him feel better, but I didn't know what to do."

"You showed him that you love him. It meant a lot to him. I could tell." Aimee's lips were soft against Cassandra's cheek.

"You're so much more perceptive than I am. I always feel so weird around him. Like I don't know how to act." Cassandra hadn't been raised to hate Cian, but his absence in her life was felt throughout her childhood. Finally having a father in her life was odd and sometimes a little overwhelming.

"Cian adores you. I don't think you could do anything to make him not like you." Aimee dipped a heavy pewter cup into the magical potion and set it on the counter to cool.

"Oh, I'm sure I could think of something," Cassandra joked with a playful grin. Immediately, the notion that if she ever wanted him to hate her all she'd have to do was stake Amaliya shot through her mind. It was a cruel and bothered her that she'd even think of such a thing. At times like this, she wondered if she was more like her vampire parent than she'd like to admit.

"You're not evil," Aimee said, poking Cassandra's stomach. "Stop that."

"Stop being insightful," Cassandra said with a pout.

Aimee lovingly kissed the frown away. "None of that."

Cassandra seductively slid her hands around Aimee's hips. "How long before you have to do the magic stuff? Because...I was thinking maybe we could do a little magic of our own."

Lightly tracing her fingers across Cassandra's collarbone, Aimee sighed. "In like five minutes."

The pout returned to Cassandra's lips. "I need longer than five minutes."

With a sultry smile, Aimee said, "That's why you're a good girlfriend."

"Fuck my life. Where's the caffeine?" Samantha grunted, stumbling into the kitchen.

With great reluctance, Cassandra let go of Aimee and returned to her seat at the table while Samantha fumbled around with the coffee cups, coffeemaker, and sugar. Aimee helpfully got out the creamer while Samantha let out an epic yawn.

Cassandra once again called her mother's number and listened to the rings on the other end. Baptiste shuffled into the kitchen and headed toward the coffeemaker. It was evident the cabal was up and moving about except for the vampire in the attic. Raising her eyes, Cassandra left yet another message for her mother.

"C'mon, Mom. Call me back."

Samantha nervously stepped into the circle of salt that Aimee had carefully poured out on the floor of the library in Jeff's Victorian. The witch already sat inside the circle, the skirt of her green velvet dress splayed out around her. Sitting across from the witch, Samantha nervously wiped her hands on her jeans and took a deep breath.

Baptiste was seated in a chair outside the circle, concern etched on his handsome face. He would be observing and at the first sign of trouble would intervene following the directions Aimee had given him. He was the only other person Aimee had allowed into the room.

Aimee picked up a small bowl of salt, poured out the white grains, and carefully closed the circle. A dome of iridescent magic formed over them, shimmering and humming. It was a reassuring sign. Samantha had come to depend on the wards for protection. She tried not to think about the fact that The Summoner had found a way through the one over Cian's house.

"Okay, remember what I told you, Sam. I have separated us from the rest of the house, so you can utilize your magic without interference. You need to concentrate on finding that thread of magic that connects you to Amaliya. You've used it before, and you need to do it again. Once you've found her, send Roberto. Got it?"

Samantha nodded mutely.

"Okay, now drink this. I used what little blood I had left from Amaliya to create it. It's not going to have the same kick as fresh, but I've enhanced it a bit with other magical ingredients." Aimee gently set a pewter mug in Samantha's hands.

"What if he tries to come through?" Samantha said worriedly.

"We'll cut the connection and break the circle so we'll be back in the protection of the house." Aimee gave her knee a gentle squeeze. "You can do this."

Saying a prayer that she hoped Jesus would be cool with, Samantha bravely swallowed the concoction Aimee had conjured. It was both bitter and sweet, with a faint coppery taste. Closing her eyes, she fretfully tried to concentrate on the task at hand without becoming overwhelmed with her own fears.

It took several minutes and Aimee's gentle reassurances, but Samantha finally felt the root of her power respond to her summons. It sprung up from deep within her and fanned out in a beautiful sparkling mist that filled the circle. Samantha's vision altered to allow her to see into the world of the dead. The black and white world wavered around her, and she saw Roberto waiting for her patiently in a cemetery just outside of San Antonio. The city itself was shrouded completely in a thick blanket of darkness. She couldn't see beyond the black magic boundary.

Standing in the world of the dead, she looked down at her body. It was shrouded in the white-gray glistening mist that was the manifestation of her power. It took some concentration, but she finally found the fine black tendril of power that connected her to Amaliya. It was glossy and filled with stars.

"I found it," Samantha said aloud.

"Do you feel her?" Aimee's voice asked.

In the ghostly world, Samantha's fingers slid gently along the thread. It both frightened and thrilled her that she could faintly sense Amaliya's presence.

"Yes. I do feel her, but it's really scary over near San Antonio. It's black and blobby."

"Like before?"

"I think it's worse. A lot worse."

Ghostly figures drifted through her vision, curious about her presence in their world. Roberto waited in the distance, and she sensed his growing agitation. She was impressed by his fearlessness, but it wasn't like The Summoner could kill him again. Or at least Samantha didn't think he could.

Focusing her magic, Samantha took a deep breath, then willed herself to where Roberto waited. When she arrived, she found the graveyard eerily vacant except for him.

"What the hell?" she exclaimed, confused by the emptiness that filled the cemetery. Not one fragment of a memory remained. The graves were black hollows.

"He's done the same thing here as he did in Fenton. Burned up the ghosts to feed his power." Roberto jerked his head in the direction of San Antonio. "Whatever is going down is going to happen soon. Look at that."

"Fuck my life," Samantha muttered.

The miasma of black magic encircling San Antonio greatly resembled the grotesque portal that had opened in Cian's mansion. Fingering the fine thread of Amaliya's connection to her, Samantha wondered if they should dare to follow through. Already The Summoner had fooled them into losing their most valuable warrior.

"I'm ready," Roberto said, staring at her with his hollow eyes.

"Are you sure?" Samantha stared at the churning cloud of darkness.

"I'm dead, Samantha. The worst he can do now is banish me to the abyss, which will soon take over this world, so what's the difference?" Roberto shrugged. "At least I'll be doing something other than waiting."

Resting her hand on the ghost, Samantha lifted her fingers, the fine tendril of necromantic power humming in her grip. "Follow this to her. Find out what you can. Let her know we're not giving up on her or the fight."

The energy of her command flowed out of her and trembled in a visible cloud around Roberto. It sank into his being and he nodded.

"I will."

Samantha carefully laid the thread in his hand. As soon as his fingers wrapped around it, his body was swept away along the link.

Returning to her body in Austin, Samantha opened her eyes. "He's gone."

Aimee nodded somberly. "Now we wait."

The tension in the Victorian mansion could have been cut with a knife. Jeff sat next to Alexia on the couch in the family room as she worked on her laptop, her face scrunched with concentration. Benchley was playing a video game on the Xbox, while Cassandra spent half the time glowering at the television and the other half trying to reach her mother. Eduardo wandered into the house close to sunset and served himself some leftovers from the refrigerator before settling on the loveseat to watch Benchley's game play. It could have been just another day around the house if not for the major magic going on in the library.

Brushing his fingers through his hair, Jeff cast a longing look toward the hallway. He kept hoping Samantha would appear with some good news.

"Everything is fucked," Alexia muttered.

Jeff completely agreed. In the beginning of all of this, they had all believed they could somehow build an army to fight The Summoner. Instead, they were on their own, abandoned by everyone. The Assembly was in shambles, the vampires were waiting for the eternal night, and the human world was obsessed with the possible end of the world when the Mayan calendar ended.

"Did you find anything?" Jeff asked Alexia, leaning over to observe her screen.

"More missing people in the San Antonio area. Escalation of violence. Those weird tremors are continuing, and scientists can't figure out why. And the Christmas shopping season is in full swing. It's Black Friday." Alexia's head flopped back against the sofa as she gave Jeff a tired frown. "Christmas is coming. Maybe. Ugh. Stupid shopping crowds. As if things weren't bad enough."

"You went the wrong way," Eduardo said to Benchley, gesturing at the screen between bites of food.

"Yeah, dude. I know," Benchley growled, his fingers nimbly punching away at his controller.

Alexia pointed at the computer screen. "I've been tracking the violent crimes in Austin like you asked, and it's actually holding steady. But...more missing women. Another one last night."

"Where?"

"Well, weirdly, Cian's old neighborhood. About two streets over. Speculation is that she's in the sink hole. Which is all over the news, by the way." Alexia pointed to the picture of the missing dark-haired beauty with blue eyes in the news report

Jeff's shifted his gaze to Eduardo, who was eating leftover jambalaya and not paying attention to anything other than the video game Benchley was playing. "Thanks, Alexia. It's good work."

"I emailed all the people who are still active in The Assembly this morning to give them an update and in hopes of someone coming to join us."

"And?"

"No one answered." Alexia showed Jeff her inbox. "More than half bounced back because the email addresses don't exist anymore."

"So it's just us." Jeff regarded the people in the room thoughtfully.

"Yep."

"Dude, you keep going the wrong way," Eduardo complained from across the room.

"I got turned around. I'm nervous!" Benchley wiped at the beads of sweat dotting his brow. "I'm almost to the big boss fight."

"Heh. Aren't we all?" Eduardo continued eating.

Scrutinizing Eduardo, Jeff pondered the options before him. The sun was sinking below the horizon, and Cian would be up soon. Hopefully, Aimee and Samantha would emerge from the library with some good news. Baptiste had been on the phone with his relatives in Louisiana earlier in the day, but Jeff hadn't had a chance to discuss with him what he had learned.

Scratching at his knee, Jeff decided that none of the options before them seemed particularly good. In fact, he wasn't too sure how they could possibly live through what was coming, but he wasn't willing to just give up.

Footsteps in the hall drew their attention and compelled them to sit bolt upright in anticipation. Benchley paused his game, and Eduardo shoved his empty plate onto the coffee table.

Baptiste entered first, followed by Aimee. The witch immediately joined Cassandra, wrapping her arms around the dhamphir. The looks on their faces made Jeff very uneasy.

"Where's Sam?" he asked.

"Here," Samantha answered, stepping into the room with Roberto close behind. The ghost looked entirely solid and almost alive. Samantha had infused him with a lot of her magic. Jeff's fiancée came to him immediately, sliding into the spot between him and Alexia.

"I take it the news isn't good?" Benchley remarked.

"Did you reach Amaliya?" Jeff's gaze darted to the four people who could give him an answer.

Roberto took up the spot before the television and clasped his hands behind his back. "I was able to."

"And?" Alexia prompted.

"We should wait for Cian," Samantha said, chewing on her thumbnail. She rarely bit her nails.

"I'm here," the vampire said from the hallway. He sounded groggy, and a quick glance out the window revealed that the sun was still setting. Lingering in the shadows of the hallway, Cian was barely visible. "I woke early. For once."

Roberto stared at his old friend and the man he had betrayed with a strangely compassionate expression. It unnerved Jeff.

"Tell them," Samantha instructed the ghost. It was more of a command. She was trembling in Jeff's arms. Obviously, she knew what Roberto was about to say and was terrified. Jeff felt his heartbeat accelerate, and his stomach clenched in apprehension.

Roberto didn't raise his eyes as he spoke. It was evident to Jeff that the ghost was frightened, too. "The haven of The Summoner is near the downtown area of San Antonio. It has many spells cast on it to hide it from not only from supernaturals but from humans. The only reason I was able to see it and slip inside was because of the connection between Amaliya and Samantha. The thread between them cut right through the wards like a knife, and I was able to travel along the connection through the barriers."

"How bad is San Antonio on the magical end of things? The crime reports today are off the charts," Alexia said.

Jeff knew the coming answer was going to be bad when the Roberto actually shuddered. "The Summoner's witches are casting powerful spells that are infecting the entire city. I've never seen anything like it. There are enormous pockets of negative energy all over the city that are ready to erupt. He's going to plunge the city into chaos."

"Why?" Baptiste asked. "A diversion?"

"The violence and blood will feed his spells," Roberto grimly answered.

"If the energy build up is as bad as you say, then that's a whole lot of violence and blood," Alexia pointed out, then her eyes opened wider. "Shit."

"And it's going to get worse," Samantha said sourly.

Aimee shifted in her seat next to Cassandra, her arms tucked around her girlfriend. The witch appeared close to crying, which frightened Jeff even more.

"Eh, it always gets worse," Eduardo said nonchalantly.

"But you saw Amaliya, right?" Cian sounded like he was half-asleep, but his tone was commanding and laced with anxiety.

"Yes. I saw both Amaliya and Bianca. They're trapped in a room with The Summoner. When I arrived, they were confined to the bed in the room, unable to leave. The Summoner was in a trance. Preparing."

"He's not possessing Bianca?" Benchley squinted. "Huh?"

Roberto nodded. "Amaliya says he's found a way to create a corporeal body, at least as long as he's in the presence of the Sword of Lucifer."

"What?" Cassandra's eyes flashed open. "What? It's formed?"

The ghost shifted on his feet, the edges of his body blurring. He appeared reluctant to answer. "Not yet. Almost. The black witches summoned the last ring this morning once The Summoner had Amaliya. It'll possess the person closest to it and force them to bring it to The Summoner."

"Mom!" Cassandra lurched out of her chair, her phone clutched in her hand.

In a panic, she tried to pull up her mother's number on the screen.

Aimee clutched Cassandra's arms and forced her to sit down. Holding her close, Aimee said, "Cass, we'll find her. We can find her."

Silence filled the room as Cassandra sobbed. "He has her, Aimee! He has my mom!"

Cian dared to enter the room, keeping to the shadows. He embraced his daughter from behind. "Cassandra, we'll find her."

"Galina had the ring," Alexia said, stricken at the realization of what must be happening.

Aimee nodded sorrowfully. "We hid it in a box under her house. We thought it would be safe."

"So when they called the ring, she was the closest one to it." Benchley covered his face with his hands. "Oh, shit."

"Where was she?" Cian asked, his hand gently rubbing his daughter's back as he tried to console her.

"Tennessee. Near Nashville," Aimee answered.

"Did you know about this?" Jeff asked Samantha.

"I knew they were calling the ring, but I didn't realize Cass's mom had it."

Baptiste leaned forward to pat Cassandra's leg gently. "Cass, I'm sorry. I know how it is about family."

Alexia was typing away on her keyboard and scrolling through information. "It's about a fourteen-hour drive to San Antonio. Maybe fifteen with stops for the restroom, food, and gas. If they called the ring today, then she's probably still on her way."

"Assuming she drove," Benchley said, wincing.

"I can check flights." Alexia started typing again.

Cassandra clung to her girlfriend, sobbing. "We need to find her, Aimee."

"Cass, baby, I need to start working on a tracking spell right away." The witch carefully disengaged herself from Cassandra's grip. Giving Cian a significant look, she kissed Cassandra then ran out of the room.

Cian climbed over the back of the loveseat and drew his daughter into his arms. Holding her lovingly, he stroked her hair as she wept. "What else did you find out, Roberto?"

The sun was below the trees now, and the vampire was more lucid and appeared much more dangerous.

Roberto rocked back and forth, heel to toe, his gaze on the floor in front of him. "Amaliya told me that The Summoner can tear down the veil at any time once the sword is restored. There is a ritual to maintain the tear and allow the abyss to consume the world. They've been preparing for it for months."

"You know where his haven is, so we'll go there immediately," Cian said.

"The ritual won't take place there. It will take place in a Mayan temple." Roberto raised his eyes, and Jeff wished he could read the expression in them.

"We have to go to Mexico?" Benchley gasped.

CHAPTER TWENTY-FIVE

"No." Roberto shook his head.

"It's under San Antonio," Samantha spoke up. "The Mayans had a temple in the area of San Antonio, and it is still there. Buried underneath the fuckin' junction of Highway 1604 and Interstate I-35. Bianca told Amaliya about it."

"Holy shit," Benchley said. "Holy shit!"

"He's going to bring it forth," Roberto continued. "And then tear the veil. He doesn't have to wait for December 21, 2012, to do it either. He can do it as soon as the sword is formed."

"And with the ring on its way..." Baptiste rubbed his hands over his bald head. "Shit."

"It'll happen tonight," Alexia breathed.

"Yeah." Samantha raised her eyes, tears filling them.

"So it's time to save the world," Jeff said, finding it hard to take a breath. "Tonight."

CHAPTER TWENTY-SIX

The ambience of the room continued to weigh on Amaliya's mind and body as she lay on the bed waiting for the night to come. She had tried several times to walk across the room to the door only to feel an intense lethargy that started to paralyze her limbs. Each time, Bianca had pulled her back to the bed. At last, she had relented to the reality that she was trapped as surely as Bianca was. Pulling on her discarded tank top and panties, she'd lit another cigarette and contemplated the situation while Bianca drifted back to sleep curled into Amaliya's side.

When Roberto had slipped into the room, hesitant and fearful, she'd been startled at his sudden appearance but in retrospect wasn't really surprised. Samantha had been diligently working on her abilities. Though it was difficult to feel it through the layers of mind-numbing energy filling the room, Amaliya was grateful for the fine thread of magic that connected her to Samantha. She was even more grateful for Roberto's bravery at breaching The Summoner's defenses.

Their conversation had been quick, thorough, and anxiety-inducing. Amaliya had watched the silent, kneeling form of The Summoner while Roberto had hid in the shadows. She'd told him everything she had discovered, then watched him vanish.

Now, she was on her last cigarette and feeling more hopeful than she had earlier when Bianca had revealed that much of what she, Cian, and the others had believed to be true was actually wrong. Exhaling, Amaliya ruffled Bianca's wavy hair with her fingers. The stillness of the other vampire's form was strangely comforting. She could almost pretend it was Cian next to her, but the illusion was broken by the feminine softness of Bianca's body. No matter what happened next, Amaliya vowed to not abandon Bianca. She could find a place in her home and heart for the girl. Bianca had tried to save her once and failed. Now Amaliya was determined to find a way to save Bianca. She was sick and tired of people dying for her.

It was difficult to maintain her focus in the presence of the nearly reconstructed sword, but her stubbornness was benefitting her. Every time her mind would begin to drift to The Summoner's promise of the new world and her role in it, she would force herself to remember her grandmother. It helped fight off the mind-altering power of her bond to The Summoner and the black magic writhing in the air about the nearly completed sword.

"It's close now." The sound of The Summoner speaking broke her out of her reverie.

"The other ring?" She dragged heavily on her cigarette.

"Yes."

Amaliya watched the muscles beneath his skin ripple as he stood. It was difficult to believe it was not a true body that was standing before her. Brushing his blond hair back from his face, The Summoner turned to gaze at her. In another time, in another place, she could have fallen hard for him and kicked her humanity away to be with him. Maybe if he hadn't abandoned her in the beginning, he could have won her love. Amaliya was aware of her weaknesses. Bad boys, sex, alcohol, cigarettes, and loud music were all she had really enjoyed for a long time. Now she enjoyed those same things but also had the added pleasures of Cian's love, friendships, and a place that felt like home.

"Our time is soon," The Summoner said with delight. "Tonight we ascend as gods over the new world."

Crawling onto the bed, he sprawled out alongside her, his long muscular frame alluring in the dim light. His hand slid over her legs to cup her hip. Ignoring him, Amaliya continued to smoke and stroke Bianca's hair. The Summoner desired her, and she was keen to use that to her advantage. Confidence filled her as she realized just how much power she actually had in the situation. When he kissed her, she passionately responded, her tongue dominating his. With a little growl, he pulled her closer, consuming her mouth. When he finally released her lips to tease her neck with his teeth, she took another long drag on her cigarette.

"So...tonight you get your body back, huh?" Amaliya hated how quickly her last smoke was turning to ash. She wondered if one of The Summoner's minions would go get her more.

Biting her earlobe, The Summoner growled, "Yes."

"Will you be a vampire again?" Ignoring the hands wandering over her body, she slung her arm over his shoulders.

"No, something more. A god."

"And Bianca? Me?" Amaliya tilted her head to gaze at him.

"What you are now." The Summoner laid his hand gently on Bianca's head. "Alas, our little one will have served her purpose."

Amaliya narrowed her eyes. "What?"

"Are you fond of her?" The unemotional blue eyes revealed nothing of his thoughts.

"She's part of us," Amaliya answered.

"My blood is the key to ushering in the new world. I have no blood. It's in your veins and hers."

"What are you talking about?" Amaliya flicked the butt of her cigarette at the table with the rings.

The Summoner's face showed his disapproval of her disrespect. "The spell to bring forth the new world demands the sacrifice of the necromancer's blood that casts it. All of it."

"So you have to kill yourself?" Amaliya looked at him with disbelief. "There's no fuckin' way you'd do that."

"The reward is becoming a god once the abyss has consumed the world."

"Oh, that you *would* do." Looking down at the sleeping girl beside her, Amaliya tried to fit the pieces together. "If you use her blood, won't she become the god?"

"It's my blood in her veins. I'm doing the spell. I will be the god. She will merely...die." The Summoner twisted his fingers in Amaliya's hair and drew her into his arms.

"And what are you going to do with me?" Dread filled her.

The Summoner's long fingers stroked her cheek and played along her full lips. "Keep you at my side. You are my most wondrous of all my creations. I want you with me."

"Enough to let my family and friends live. Which I know is tough for you because you really like to get your killing on." Amaliya wished she could read him, but it was difficult.

"Yes. Though my hope is that once you feel the death of millions imbuing you with power you will finally realize the folly of keeping them alive. They're your weakness. Eventually, you will have to eliminate those weaknesses."

Laughing, Amaliya shook her head. "God, you're such a fuckin' asshole in every single damn way."

The Summoner moved over her before slipping between her thighs. Bianca didn't stir, which made Amaliya suspicious of what he was doing to her. As his weight settled on her, Amaliya stared into the eyes of the man who had been her ruin and salvation.

She really, really wanted another cigarette.

"I may be an asshole, but you're drawn to me, aren't you?"

"I'm going to kill you," Amaliya said, smiling.

"I know you'll try. I also know you'll fail." His kiss was searing, demanding, and full of need.

Amaliya bit his lip hard, and he jerked his head back. He felt pain in his new form. That was interesting. "So, since I'm going to make you kill me later, why don't you kill me instead of Bianca?"

"Self-sacrifice really doesn't suit you," The Summoner chided her. "Besides, I have no intention of killing you. You *are* mine. My dark bride." As if to prove a point, he shoved Bianca's prone, unconscious form away. "Our time has come. You must accept it."

With a grin, Amaliya shook her head. "No, I don't."

"But you will." The hunger in his kiss was intoxicating.

Even as she succumbed to his seduction and the dark, twisted power of the sword flowed through the room, Amaliya knew she would never allow him to rule the world. Somehow, she would stop him.

Aimee set stones and crystals in a distinct pattern over the large map she had spread out on the dining room table. Candles burned in a circle on the floor and the scent of Cassandra's blood wafted with the fragrance of magic. Cian and Jeff stood just inside the doorway observing the preparations. Cassandra sat at the table within the circle, her eyes red and swollen.

"This will work," Jeff muttered, sounding like he was trying to convince himself.

Deeper in the house, the cabal was preparing to leave. They hoped to intercept Galina before she reached San Antonio. If they were lucky, she was driving to meet The Summoner. Her route would take her through the Austin area.

The longing for Amaliya filling Cian mingled with his fears of losing her. She was strong, and he knew she'd find a way to manipulate, then kill The Summoner. The necromancer's obsession with Amaliya was something Cian knew she could use to good effect if she was clever. It wasn't difficult for Cian to understand why The Summoner desired her at his side. Amaliya was powerful, beautiful, and possessed a wild energy that was very seductive. Cian loved Amaliya for many reasons, but she was the catalyst that made him feel alive. He could easily see her doing the same for The Summoner, which would be a heady experience for a vampire who was so old he was far removed from his humanity.

"This *will* work, right?" Jeff whispered, now sounding doubtful.

"Yes. Of course." Cian gave the man a pat on the shoulder.

Nodding his head, Jeff edged closer to Cian. "I need to talk to you about something before we go."

"Now?"

The witch continued to lay out the small stones and crystals, her long bronze hair catching the light of the chandelier overhead.

Jeff winced, then nodded.

Cian stepped into the main foyer of the house. It was empty except for them. Drawing a little too close for Cian's comfort, Jeff leaned in to Cian.

"It's about Eduardo."

"Oh?" Cian said inquisitively.

Jeff swallowed hard, then said in an ever quieter voice, "He's a serial killer."

Cian lifted both of his eyebrows.

"Girls that look a lot like Amaliya have been disappearing. Samantha has seen two of their ghosts. They were ripped apart, ravaged by a were-creature. The last girl to vanish was near your old place after you tossed Eduardo out of the van. Both ghosts were angry at me for not stopping the person who killed them." Jeff sighed. "I know it's flimsy evidence, but..."

Cian gave a shake of his head. "No, I believe you. Though I'm not sure you can call him a serial killer. He's a coyote. His nature is to hunt."

"Yeah, but he's not supposed to kill humans, right? That's your rule over your city."

"True." Cian reflected on the things Amaliya had told her about Eduardo. "He did say something once to Amaliya about wanting to have sex with her because he could rip her up and she'd survive."

Jeff winced. "He thought that was a come on?"

Cian lifted a shoulder dismissively. "He's an idiot."

"What should we do?"

The human was obviously worried and unnerved by the situation on top of everything else they were experiencing. "We need him tonight."

"Yeah."

"Then we tell him to leave the city or die."

The spot between Jeff's eyebrows furrowed. "Okay. I guess."

"It's working!" Cassandra's voice called out excitedly.

Cian moved faster than the human could follow to the table and leaned over the map. A single drop of Cassandra's blood was slowly sliding along the surface of the map just over the I-35 corridor. From what Aimee had explained earlier, Cian knew the red globule indicated Galina's location. Her daughter's blood was the best way to find and track her.

"She's just past Austin," Cassandra exclaimed. "We can catch her!"

"Grab everyone," Cian said to Jeff. "We go now."

The long black dress fluttered around Amaliya's legs as she walked behind the possessed Bianca. The other necromancer was dressed in a white lace dress, and her blonde hair was twisted up onto her head and held in place with diamanté hair clips. The Summoner had insisted on them looking "proper," and Amaliya had reluctantly complied. The gauzy silk material of her gown whispered against her skin, and the fishnet insets in the arms and torso were a nice nod to her usual fashion choices. Her dyed black hair flowed unfettered to her waist, and she wore her regular heels. On those two points, she'd refused to capitulate to The Summoner. He'd been amused.

Before them, hovering in the air, were the twelve rings. The pulsing light emanating from the jewelry formed an ethereal sword. Only a section of the hilt was missing. It was nearly complete.

Striding down the stairs behind the glowing sword and The Summoner/ Bianca, Amaliya saw Etzli and the thirteen black witches waiting in the foyer. Vampires, infused humans, were-jaguars, and demons stood behind them. All were garbed in dark colors, even Stark and Trish. The levitating sword swept downstairs to the floor below, and the crowd bowed their heads. The Summoner/ Bianca smiled triumphantly at the sight. Amaliya supposed it was a small taste of what was to come once he conquered the sun and plunged humanity into the abyss.

Amaliya expected some sort of arch-villain speech about the end of the world, but instead The Summoner regally strolled through the gathering and out the front door. The cold, moist air and dark, low clouds over the San Antonio sky-line threatened a winter storm. Sirens tore through the night from all directions. An orange glow illuminated the sky over the south side of the city. It was a little after seven in the evening, but already the city was in chaos. The black witches had unleashed the volcanoes of negative energy, and violence ruled the city.

A black Navigator waited on the driveway, Gregorio holding open the back door. The Summoner waited for the sword to slip inside, then followed. A quick gesture from Bianca's hand indicated that Amaliya was to sit next to The Sum-moner. She slid inside just as Etzli climbed into the front seat.

In eerie silence, Amaliya watched the big house slide out of view as the SUV turned out the front gates and drove toward their destination.

Grabbing his coat out of the hall closet, Jeff bumped into Eduardo when he took a step back to shut the door. The coyote was as quiet as ever. Jeff started, not having heard him approach.

Tilting his head, Eduardo regarded Jeff with the eyes of a coyote, not a man. "I heard you and Alexia talking," Eduardo said after a long, unnerving moment of silence between them.

"Yeah?" Jeff shrugged on his coat.

"And I saw you talking to Cian," Eduardo continued. His teeth were sharp behind his lips.

"Okay. Your point?" Jeff fought to maintain a calm exterior.

"Stay out of my business."

"Your business?"

The cabal was scattered through the house and the front drive as they rushed about in preparation. Cian was gone, having departed to hunt for blood in the neighborhood. The vampire had promised to catch up with them on the road.

Eduardo smirked, leaning his beefy shoulder against the wall. "Yeah. My business. And yes, our friends are too far away to stop me if I decide to rip out your throat."

"Why would you do that?" Jeff slung his winter scarf about his threatened throat.

Chuckling, Eduardo wagged his head. "Don't play innocent, Jeff. We're old friends. I know when you're trying to bullshit your way out of something."

"Really? Well, I know you well enough to know you're worried about the fact I figured out your secret."

"You don't know anything," Eduardo said gruffly, his look predatory.

"Then why are you worried?"

"You have no idea what it's like to be two-natured. The needs I struggle with." Eduardo shrugged his shoulders, flexing his muscles.

"Yeah, I don't. But you know the rules of the city. Cian's rules and my rules. No killing. And you've killed close to twenty women this year."

"There's no proof of that. The cops haven't found anything – not even bodies – and neither have you."

"I haven't started to look yet," Jeff answered. His hands plunged into his coat, and he found his pockets empty. He was unarmed, yet he met Eduardo's gaze steadily. There was nothing he could do about his accelerated heartbeat, but he sure as hell wasn't going to back down in his own house. Sadly, he realized that Aimee's wards were not going to work against Eduardo. All the cabal members had their name engraved into the wards that protected their homes. Jeff maybe should have changed that fact when it had come to Eduardo, but he hadn't wanted to believe the worst of his college buddy.

"I'm helping you tonight. I'm going to go fuck this asshole up and save the fuckin' world. That has to count for something."

"So I should just look the other way as you kill Amaliya lookalikes?"

Eduardo snarled. "Amaliya just looks like the girls I like to play with."

"You mean kill."

"I like to play with my food, okay?" Eduardo gave another dismissive shrug, but from the way his head was tilted, Jeff suspected he was listening to keep track of the cabal.

"That's sick, Eduardo. You do realize that?"

"If Amaliya would come play with me, maybe that would take the edge off my needs." Eduardo didn't seem aware of how ridiculous his words actually were, for he wore a completely sincere expression.

"You want Cian to let you fuck his girlfriend and do who knows to her what so you won't kill in his city?" Jeff shook his head in disbelief.

"I'm helping to *save* her."

"Right," Jeff intoned sarcastically. "Well, Eduardo, this is what's going to happen. You're going to help us tonight then stop killing."

Laughing, Eduardo drew closer to Jeff, his face increasingly feral. "Yeah, sure. What's in it for me? Maybe I should step back and watch the world go to hell so I can kill whenever I want to."

"You and I both know that weres are going to be stuck in their animal form *forever* once the abyss takes the world. Some might like that, but I don't think you will."

"What?" Eduardo flinched. "No one told me that!"

"Well, it's the truth. You'll be in your were form all the time. An animal. And you know how demons and vampires treat weres. You'll end up some vampire's lap dog. Do you really think you're going to make it out of this on top?" Jeff skewered Eduardo with his most forceful stare.

Eduardo sniffed at Jeff. "You're telling the truth?"

"This is how it's going to go down. We save the world. You stop killing."

"I could just kill you."

"And that solves what? You don't think Cian won't find you and kill you even if the world goes to hell tonight? You think he'll forgive you for not helping him save Amaliya?"

Shifting on his feet anxiously, Eduardo finally looked away from Jeff.

"What makes you think you are in control of your life right now? How do you know that the wards Aimee set up in this house won't fry your ass the second you sink your teeth into me? This is *my* house." Jeff stepped closer to the coyote. "My house. My rules. My wards."

Eduardo's jaw flexed, his throat moving as he swallowed angry words.

"Are you with us? Or not?"

Eduardo nodded curtly, stepping back.

"Right. This conversation is done." Jeff strode past the coyote toward the front door just as Cassandra walked through the dining room with bags of weapons, Aimee hot on her heels.

Jeff motioned toward the door with his head. "We roll now."

Eduardo stalked out of the house. If he had been in his were form, he would have had his tail between his legs.

"What's that all about?" Cassandra asked.

"Nothing. It's taken care of," Jeff assured her and hoped it was true. Looking toward the kitchen, Jeff shouted, "Sam!"

Samantha finished pouring extra food for Beatrice, then picked up the annoyed cat to press kisses to the top of her head. Even if she died tonight, she'd find a way to have her cat taken care of from beyond the grave.

"Love you, snookum," she said.

The cat endured it all, one eye on the food.

Setting Beatrice on the kitchen floor, Samantha grabbed her big Betsey Johnson purse and ran through the house as Jeff called her name yet again. The rest of the cabal was already packed into Benchley's passenger van. The engine was running, and Benchley couldn't keep his hand off the horn.

"Sam!"

"I'm here!"

She ran past her boyfriend onto the front porch, then down the walkway to the drive. The air was freezing and damp. She had wanted to wear something dramatic for the epic final battle but ended up grabbing whatever was first in her drawers and closet, which was jeans, cowboy boots, a long-sleeved t-shirt, and her leather coat. Jeff's reassuring footfalls revealed he was close behind her.

As soon as she and Jeff clambered into the van, Benchley punched his foot down on the pedal, and the vehicle roared downhill to the opening gates. Samantha flopped onto the middle bench between Jeff and Alexia. The tech girl was busy on her smart phone. Behind them were Cassandra, Baptiste, and a very sulky Eduardo. Samantha wondered what was up with the coyote but didn't bother to ask.

Aimee sat in the front seat with a map on her lap. The magical glow emanating from the paper was comforting, as was the tiny red dot that was making its way toward San Antonio. It gave Samantha the impression things were looking up for their ragtag cabal. Nestling her hand in Jeff's palm, she glanced at her fiancée. He looked more imposing and tougher than she'd ever seen him before, yet the sweetness was still there. Heart swelling with love for him, she laid her head against his shoulder.

"We'll be okay," Jeff said quietly.

"Of course." She tilted her head to give him an encouraging smile.

Benchley shoved a CD into the old battered player in the dashboard, blasting "*We Are the Champions*" by the epic rock band Queen.

"Really?" Aimee said, glancing at Benchley and arching an eyebrow.

Benchley's response was to start singing.

Alexia enthusiastically chimed in, though her eyes never left the glowing screen, then surprisingly Jeff joined in, too. Samantha glanced over her shoulder at Cassandra's somber face. The dhamphir's lips were moving along with Freddie Mercury. Baptiste's deep baritone was added in the next verse. Aimee raised her hand in a fist, singing in a lovely soprano voice.

Benchley turned the music up, then pounded on the steering wheel as he sang. Samantha giggled at the lunacy of it all. At last, she joined in, singing at the top of her lungs and slightly off key.

The van sped down the road toward Interstate 35 and the final battle.

PART SEVEN

The End of The World

CHAPTER TWENTY-SEVEN

The Summoner's cavalcade of black Navigators sped along I-35 toward State Highway 1604. The evening traffic was brisk and heavy on both sides of the interstate. The lights of the neighborhoods and business streamed past Amaliya's window as lightning slithered in the dark clouds above. The heavy atmosphere outside was reflected within the SUV. Above their heads, the rings glowed in the shape of the sword that would rent the veil and usher in the abyss.

"So, Etzli," Amaliya said into the eerie silence.

"What?" The Aztec's voice was clipped.

"Where's your brother?"

"Dead. His usefulness ended when we used his blood for the portal."

"You're a real fuckin' bitch."

The sharp edges of Etzli's profile were outlined by the flashing lights outside. Another emergency vehicle roared through the traffic on the way to yet another fire, accident, or crime.

"Don't pretend you're going to miss him." Etzli's dark eyes gleamed dangerously.

"I thought you two had a thing."

"We did," Etzli said. "Then The Summoner came to me."

"So...you two?" Amaliya tilted her head to regard the silent form of Bianca beside her.

"Jealous?" The Summoner asked.

"No, no. The more the merrier I say."

This comment drew an angry look from Etzli and a smirk from The Summoner.

"I noticed last night," The Summoner said.

"Guess you weren't invited," Amaliya said to Etzli with a bright smile.

The Aztec woman pointedly glared out the passenger window.

Amaliya poked the driver, Gregorio. "Do you have a cigarette?"

As an answer, Gregorio pulled a pack out of his pocket and handed it to her.

"Don't smoke in the car," Etzli ordered.

"It's not like it's going to give you lung cancer. Sheesh, chill out."

Amaliya loved needling Etzli. It was very evident that the blood goddess was lower down on the totem pole than Amaliya, and Amaliya had every intention of rubbing that fact in. Lighting her cigarette, she glanced out the window to see a family car whiz by, the back filled with kids. It sickened her to think of what would happen to them if The Summoner succeeded. The upcoming battle was for people like them. Amaliya wanted to survive but wasn't certain she would. Since she'd awakened, she'd been pondering everything she had learned about the powers at play. She had an idea of what she might be able to do to throw a wrench in The Summoner's plans, but she'd have to wait for the perfect moment to strike.

The incandescence of the rings increased overhead. Amaliya puffed harder on her cigarette and ignored the trembling of her fingers. The magic around the sword writhed like snakes within the vehicle, and she kept her own powers tightly wound inside of her. Using her necromancy would backfire since she was so closely bound to The Summoner. With him using both his powers and Bianca's, it would be easy for him to snare Amaliya. It pissed her off that she had to abandon her death magic for this fight.

A light rain started to patter against the windshield. Ahead were signs announcing the 1604 exits. The area had three sharp loops and several flyovers that split off in various directions. 1604 encircled San Antonio, and Interstate 35 was a major thoroughfare. The area was very busy due to holiday travelers and shoppers. All the cars sliding past the SUV were packed with people who had no idea that the sweet, innocent girl sitting next to Amaliya was possessed by one of the most evil creatures to ever walk the earth.

"It's time," Etzli said.

Gregorio rolled down his window, the cold wind blasting into the interior. Pulling out a pistol, he locked his grip on the steering wheel.

"What are you doing?" Amaliya demanded, surging forward.

The Summoner slammed her back into her seat, cracking her ribs from the force. Gasping in agony, Amaliya watched the next events in dismay.

Gregorio started to fire at the passing vehicles. Windows shattered, tires popped, and the cars began a crazed dance across the lanes as drivers panicked. Aiming at the oncoming traffic, Gregorio shot the gun multiple times. Chaos erupted on the other side of highway divider.

The Navigator swung onto the shoulder of the road as the 1604 junction loomed ahead. Amaliya fought against The Summoner, but he was much stronger than she was and easily pinned her to the seat. He had the combined powers of both him and Bianca at his call.

The SUV veered onto the hard-packed earth encapsulated by one of the loops of the highway. The rest of The Summoner's vehicles swerved off the road and parked in a circle.

Gripping Amaliya's arm tightly, The Summoner pulled her from the vehicle and into the freezing drizzle.

"Why are you shooting innocent people? Isn't it enough that you're going to destroy their world?" Amaliya cried out.

"Observe," The Summoner said, sweeping Bianca's arm out dramatically.

All lanes of the interstate were clogged with crashed vehicles. The entire area had been brought to a halt. People were rushing to rescue the accident victims, darting around the battered cars. One car was on fire, and some men fought the flames in an attempt to rescue the people inside. Panicked screams sounded above the wild honking of the piled-up traffic.

The Sword of Lucifer floated out of the vehicle and grew brighter in the presence of the despair, fear, and death.

Choking back a sob, Amaliya unexpectedly felt powerless in the face of such destruction. People were dying, and she wasn't sure any more if she could save them. The rings pulsed with radiant golden power, and it spread out over The Summoner's group, creating a protective bubble.

"Trish," Etzli called out. "It's time."

The woman with the masses of red curls stepped forward. Her maroon eyes flicked toward Amaliya, a sneer upon her lips.

"Don't," Amaliya begged, afraid of what came next.

The Summoner's grip on her arm tightened to the point of crushing bone. The nearly complete Sword of Lucifer rotated above their heads, then pointed its tip at Amaliya, freezing her in place.

Trish cupped her hands, one over the other, then began to rotate them in opposite directions. The night breeze started to swirl about in front of her, the dead grass flattening into a circle. Moving her hands faster and faster, the elemagus called the winds. Above their heads, the storm clouds stretched downward, answering her call. The funnel formed with a terrifying roar. Only the power of the sword kept The Summoner and his people safe from the fury of the winds. The screams of the people clustered around the accident site were lost in the terrifying bluster of the tornado.

Amaliya watched in terror as the overpasses trembled under the onslaught. Cars hurled over the rail to the ground far below while the tornado continued to grow and consume the center of the junction of 1604. Concrete crumbled and disintegrated. Long-haul trucks arched through the air like toy vehicles to crash onto the crowded interstate below, crushing onlookers and cars.

Fighting against the power holding her captive, Amaliya screamed at the elemagus to stop, but the redhead barely acknowledged her cries.

The young man named Stark stepped next to Amaliya and grinned. "Wow.

Talk about 3D end of the world epics."

Benchley drove on the shoulder half of the way to San Antonio, the van speeds far exceeding the posted limit. Aimee continued to track Galina's progress as the van barreled down I-35.

Samantha observed the red illumination of the rear car lights through the windshield, wincing when they kept flashing as the drivers braked. The traffic was slowing the closer they got to San Antonio. Emergency vehicle sirens sounded in the distance, and she caught sight of a few speeding along the frontage roads.

The van left New Braunfels behind and charged toward San Antonio. Away from the town lights, the night was more ominous. The steady growl of the road and the loud rush of the wind weren't very comforting.

"There's a ton of fires in San Antonio," Alexia said somberly, scrutinizing her smart phone screen. "A lot of gang violence. Domestic disturbances."

"All good news on a holiday weekend," Baptiste muttered.

Samantha knew the elemagus was in a bad mood after failing to reach Rachoń. One of his cousins had admitted to Baptiste that there was a possibility that Rachoń had entered an agreement with The Summoner to protect Louisiana. Baptiste had been furious but had no way of confirming the rumor since Rachoń wouldn't answer his calls. Samantha thought that fact pretty much confirmed there was a deal between Rachoń and The Summoner. Maybe Baptiste had come to the same conclusion.

There had been no time to repair Benchley's back window, so the plastic attached to it with duct tape flapped loudly in the wind as the van barreled along the asphalt. Cassandra kept checking out the windows, searching for her father. The vampire had needed to feed to be at full strength. Cian had yet to make an appearance, but Samantha knew he'd show up. There was no way he wouldn't fight to save Amaliya.

Eduardo was a dark cloud and Samantha was ignoring him. She didn't like him anyway. She was still convinced that he was a serial killer. The way Jeff had been looking at his old friend all evening had her wondering if he may finally have found proof and believed it, too.

Closing her physical eyes, Samantha opened her other set to the world of ghosts. The Summoner had wiped out all the cemeteries around San Antonio, but Austin's graveyards were heavily populated. Looking toward her home city, she saw the bright illumination of the apparitions. Roberto was gathering the specters into an army.

For months, Samantha and Roberto had been cultivating a strong relationship with the sentient ghosts of the city. Though Roberto was an asshole, he'd actually done a very good job explaining to some very old, confused ghosts what was happening with The Summoner. Though Samantha could force the ghosts to obey, she'd rather they understood what they were getting into. Of course, the memory wisps would never understand since they weren't sentient, but they, too, would come at her beckoning and fight.

"Everything okay?" Jeff asked, stroking her clammy fingers tenderly.

"Yeah, they're on their way." Samantha's eyelids slid open, and she smiled at Jeff. "I'm a bad ass, you know."

Jeff kissed her gently. "I know."

A sharp tearing sound startled Samantha, and she whipped about in her seat to see Cian peeling back the plastic. He clung to the back of the van, his long hair whipping about his face. Cassandra helped him inside, then pressed the tape back into place.

"Hi," Samantha said, waving to him.

Cian gave her a short nod, ignored Eduardo completely, hugged his daughter and kissed her cheek. Looking flush with life, the vampire shook out his wind-blown hair, leaned forward, and rested his hand on the back of Samantha's seat. "How's it going?"

"She's a few miles ahead, but we're gaining," Aimee answered.

"Jeff, do you want to be infused?" Cian asked. He was all business, his hazel eyes hard as stone.

Jeff glanced at Samantha, obviously seeking her opinion.

"Do it," Samantha said. "You need to be able to see everything that is going on."

"Me, too." Alexia cast a look over her shoulder at Cian. "That cool?"

"Absolutely." Cian lightly ruffled her short hair, showing rare affection to the human.

Alexia grudgingly allowed it.

Benchley tossed a stainless steel coffee mug over his shoulder. Cian snatched it out of the air before it hit Samantha.

"Hey!"

"I knew he'd get it," Benchley answered. "Hit me up with some of that blood, too."

"Is that clean?" Alexia asked worriedly.

"Does it matter?" Cian unscrewed the top before slicing his wrist open with his thumbnail.

"I guess this isn't the time to worry about being hygienic," Cassandra said thoughtfully.

The sound of the thick vampire blood spilling into the canister grossed out Samantha. Trying to ignore it, she leaned forward to view the map with the tiny red drop sliding over its surface.

Jeff was the first to sip the blood.

"Take three drinks," Cian instructed, raising his wrist to lick the wound closed.

Samantha deliberately looked away when Jeff drank. He handed the canister across Samantha's lap to Alexia. As calmly as if she was swigging a soda, Alexia took three drinks.

"Yuck," was all she said before leaning forward to give it to her brother.

"Like communion, huh?" Benchley joked, then swigged from the canister.

Samantha frowned. "So sacrilegious."

The van swung onto the shoulder again, scooting around a thick gnarl of big rig trucks rushing along the interstate.

"Watch it, Shark Boy!"

"It's slowing again," Benchley responded, then thrust the canister toward Jeff. "Put the lid on. There's some left. I don't need it on my floor."

Cassandra darted around Jeff, grabbed the canister, and gulped what was left. When she finished, Cian handed her the lid. Screwing it on, Cassandra returned to her seat.

Samantha reached back to touch her hand. "We're almost there. We'll save her."

The dhamphir gave her a slight smile. "I know."

Again, Cian showed a softness that was rare as he gathered Cassandra in his arms and held her close. His daughter laid her head on his chest, obviously comforted by his affection.

"Shit! Shit! Shit!" Alexia cried out. "A tornado just set down at the 1604 junction!"

"What?" Samantha slanted over to see the smart phone. On Twitter, there was a picture someone had snapped with their phone of a massive tornado tearing apart the overpass. Trucks and cars hurtled through the air.

"That's where the temple is!" Benchley shoved his foot harder on the accelerator, the van sliding onto the grass bordering the shoulder. The van sped past the slowing traffic.

"It's starting." Aimee checked the map again. "Galina's almost to the 1604!"

"The good news is so are we, and the traffic is going to slow her down, too!" Benchley swerved briefly onto the shoulder. His big arms were tense, and his jaw was set.

Cold wind filled the vehicle with a loud roar. Samantha twisted around in her seat to see Cassandra and Cian were gone.

"Oh, shit."

Cassandra clung to her father as he swooped over the traffic below them. She had never doubted that he could fly, but to see it in action was electrifying. They hadn't even exchanged words before he'd torn them out of the van. It was a relief to have him so likeminded. They were definitely on the same page. Like father, like daughter.

"It's a blue Mini Cooper, white roof!" Cassandra shouted into the gust.

The long lines of vehicles stretched toward the violently swirling winds of the tornado ripping apart the 1604 junction. From their vantage point, the dhamphir and vampire could see the chaos clearly. The van would have difficulty getting through unless Benchley got very creative. As the drivers of the cars spotted the massive tornado consuming everything ahead, they were futilely attempting to get off the interstate and escape. Metal crunched and tires squealed as the cars collided. The frontage, shoulder, and the swatch of land between them were cluttered with cars and people. Some people simply abandoned their vehicles and ran.

Shrouded in shadows, no one saw the two people flying low overhead, seeking out one car among many. Cassandra didn't have time to enjoy the thrill of the flight since she was so anxious to spot her mother. The cold rush of air tore at her hair and clothes as their speed increased.

When she spotted the familiar car attempting to edge around a massive snarl of vehicles, relief flooded her. "There, Dad! There!"

Cian swooped lower, and then they both dropped to the ground right behind the rear bumper of the car. Cassandra darted around to the driver's door, and Cian took the passenger side. A strange glow was emanating from within the car.

"Mom!" Cassandra dragged the door open, breaking the lock in her haste.

Galina stared straight ahead, her hands gripping the steering wheel tightly. Foot still pressed on the accelerator, she urged her car forward, trying to push the big SUV in front of her out of her path.

"Mom!" Cassandra snatched the keys out of the ignition. "Mom!"

Staring straight ahead, Galina calmly unbuckled her seatbelt and shoved Cassandra violently out of her way. Cian made a grab for her, but Galina moved with preternatural swiftness to avoid him.

"She's under its control!" Cian darted in front of Galina, raising his hands to stop her.

"Where is it?" Cassandra clutched her mother's shoulders and twisted her about.

Galina struck her across the cheek with a closed fist. Cassandra staggered backward, shocked, hurt, and angry. "Stop it, Mom!" Her mother was still beautiful, but her sweetness was gone, replaced with a zombie-like stillness that terrified Cassandra.

The eerie illumination that Cassandra had witnessed before caught her eye again. It was emanating from Galina's coat pocket. Cian saw it at the same time. Taking hold of the front of the coat, Cassandra ripped it open, the buttons bouncing off the asphalt as Cian yanked it off Galina's arms.

Galina blinked her eyes, tilted her head, then a befuddled look came into her blue eyes. "Cass?"

The dhamphir had only a second to relish the return of her mother when she saw her father swarmed by people from all sides. Men, women, and children attacked him with nails, teeth, and hard punches. Surprised, Cian staggered backward, falling under the torrent of attackers.

"Dad!"

Cassandra began dragging people off of him, startled by their strength and determination. They struck out at her, and she shoved them away. She didn't want to hurt them, but she didn't know what else to do. The mob of bodies thrashed about, then a small child broke free and ran toward the stationary tornado that continued to rip apart the area.

"He has the ring!" Cian shouted at Cassandra, pushing people off him.

The spell to bring the ring to The Summoner was in full effect, influencing all the humans around it. They rushed alongside the boy, guarding him as he ran toward the tornado.

"Cass, what's happening?" Galina asked, tears in her eyes. Shivering in the cold, she looked around in confusion.

"Mom, I have to go," Cassandra said, kissing her cheek.

Cian gave up on trying to not hurt the humans and hurled the last few away before taking flight.

"Why? What's happening?"

"I'm saving the world," Cassandra answered.

There was a rush of cold air, then Aimee stood next to them. "The others are almost here. They're on foot."

"Aimee?" Galina smiled with relief at the sight of the witch. "You're here!"

"Galina, sit in the car until our friends get you. Okay?" Aimee touched Galina's shoulder gently, magic slipping from her fingertips into the confused woman.

A tranquil smile flitted over Galina's lips. "Of course."

After one last loving look at her mother, Cassandra grabbed her girlfriend's hand, and they ran after Cian.

CHAPTER TWENTY-EIGHT

The tornado dissipated with much less drama than it had appeared. One moment it was tearing apart the highway and interstate, and the next it was gone.

What remained were the jagged remains of a once-great structure. Like broken bones, the remaining cement pillars raised skeletal fingers made of rebar toward the dark and threatening sky.

Death surrounded Amaliya. Broken, shattered, and burned bodies called to her. Confusion ruled the living, but the dead cried out for justice. It was difficult for her not to reach out to them with her necromancy, but she kept it wound tightly inside of her, refusing to unleash it.

A crowd of people ran in the direction of The Summoner. A small boy led them, clutching a winter coat to his chest. The little Hispanic boy's big dark eyes didn't blink as he darted around dead bodies, battered cars, and the concrete and asphalt chunks that had peppered the area.

"Well done," Etzli said to Trish.

The redhead looked unsteady after the use of so much of her power, but she grinned.

The Summoner wearing Bianca's form stepped forward and held out one hand to the boy. With a blank expression on his face, the boy extended the coat.

Lifting her eyes to the sword, Amaliya fought to regain control of her body. Her mind felt terribly lucid, but her limbs were weighted and immobile.

The sound of helicopters, sirens, and screams rent the air, but an eerie calm filled the bystanders who had delivered the final ring to The Summoner. Taking the coat, The Summoner withdrew the ring from the pocket.

"No!" Amaliya cried out.

Seconds later, she caught sight of Cian hurtling over the heads of the crowd that had brought the ring.

"Ah, look who's here. But too late," The Summoner said.

The golden ring spiraled out of The Summoner's hand to join the other twelve hovering overhead. There was a bright flash of white light that illuminated the entire area like a nuclear bomb. Amaliya was instantly blinded and covered her face. A loud noise like a sonic boom followed, and the glass windows of the Navigators exploded.

When she was finally able to see and hear again, Amaliya lifted her face to see The Summoner standing over her with Bianca at his feet. Handsome, cruel, and nude, a halo of golden light surrounded him. Above him hung the complete Sword of Lucifer. Its elegant hilt was encrusted with jewels, and its sharp blade glinted in the ethereal light it cast.

"It's time," The Summoner said to her.

Then the ground opened and started to swallow the world.

Cian flew over the heads of the crowd, aiming for The Summoner. He could clearly see Amaliya standing just behind Bianca's possessed body in a circle of black SUVs. Etzli, dark witches, and other beings were also gathered in the ring that was protected by the power emanating from the floating rings in the form of a sword.

Amaliya screamed just as Bianca withdrew the ring from Galina's coat. Cian was almost to The Summoner. Drawing his obsidian blade, Cian prepared to attack.

The explosion caught him just as he descended. The concussion sent him spinning through the air and crashing through the remains of a pillar, destroying it completely. Landing among the ruins of the overpass, Cian growled with anger and agony. His broken bones started to mend as he fought the blindness that had seized him. Unable to hear or see, he pushed himself to his feet and staggered forward. Pumping his blood power into his broken body, he repaired the damage.

"Dad! Dad!" Cassandra called out to him.

He spun toward the direction of her voice, his vision still blurred but rapidly returning. Cassandra was hopscotching over cars and hunks of the overpass with Aimee close behind.

The ground rumbled beneath his feet.

Twisting about, Cian saw enormous fissures spreading over the ground and the remains of the interstate. The earth lurched violently, then began to crumble. In horror, Cian watched people, vehicles, and debris disappear into the massive sink hole.

"Fuck!" Cassandra screamed. "Fuck!"

The cracks spread toward where Cian stood, and he leaped into the air just as the ground gave away. Darting backwards, he barely caught Cassandra and Aimee before they tumbled into the cavern opening below them. Lifting the women into the air, he swung over the growing chasm.

Across from the expanse, he caught sight of Lucifer's complete sword glowing brightly in the night. The Summoner in his true form stood directly beneath it with his arms spread out. Behind him was Amaliya clutching Bianca in her arms.

A redhead stepped forward and raised her hands. Within the cavern, the walls shuddered and formed a long sloping path to the floor far below.

In a long procession, The Summoner and his people started downward.

Aimee and Cassandra clung to Cian, observing the destruction. In silence, the three descended into the darkness.

Samantha ran behind Jeff, weaving between vehicles. The cataclysmic sounds ahead were terrifying in volume. It sounded like the end of the world. Debris littered the ground, and dirt filled the air.

"There it is!" Benchley was running along another path through the stopped traffic with his sister hot on his heels.

Eduardo loped along in full were form. No one said anything to him about exposing his true nature. The world was ending. Samantha supposed seeing a were-creature was the last of everyone's worries. Those people still alive were running away and not paying attention to the small group of people rushing toward the devastation. Baptiste was just ahead them, pumping his arms as he sprinted. He was in the best shape out of all of them due to his regular runs. Samantha now wished she had kept up her running regime.

Baptiste reached the Mini Cooper first and peered inside. "She's here!"

When Samantha saw the woman inside, she was struck by how absolutely gorgeous she was with her dark hair and big eyes. She looked strikingly like Cassandra and not much older than her daughter.

"Galina, it's us!" Benchley bent into the car to hug her.

"Oh, Benchley!" Galina cried out. "I remember you!"

Samantha yelped as the ground lurched under her feet, knocking her into the car. Jeff grabbed her. They both lost their balance and fell to the blacktop.

"Oh, shit!" Baptiste exclaimed, hands held out trying to keep his balance as the road trembled.

Samantha and Jeff fought to get to their feet just in time to witness the remains of the interstate falling into the massive chasm opening beneath it.

"Get Galina out of here!" Samantha shouted at Benchley.

"I want to fight!" Benchley protested.

"No! Go!" Samantha shoved the big guy. "You have to get her away from here."

Benchley's mouth twisted in frustration, then he nodded. Grabbing Galina's arm, he heaved her into his arms. The blood from Cian granted him strength and swiftness he didn't usually have. He rushed toward the van.

Alexia drew her pistols out of her backpack and took a deep breath. "We're going in, aren't we?"

"Yeah," Jeff sighed.

"I'll see you down there." Samantha closed her eyes, summoning her powers. Her magic instantly spread out from the core of her being and filled the air around her. The sparkling mist of her magic was a comfort amidst the bedlam. She summoned the ghosts to her side and felt them rushing to answer. When she reopened her eyes, they were glowing white with tiny black specks spiraling within them.

"Sam, wait!" Jeff cried out.

"I love you, babe, but I gotta get down there. The Summoner fucked up by not killing me. I'm The Phasmagus, and I'm about to show him what that means."

The rush of spectral beings zoomed over the cars like a milky-white fog and caught her up in their arms. Riding the crest of the massive wave, Samantha was swept up and over the crashed cars.

The gigantic crater below was filled with darkness and death, but Samantha wasn't afraid anymore. The Summoner couldn't control the ghosts, but she could.

The sparkling wave of phantasms descended into the sink hole, carrying her into the darkness.

The Mayan temple was nothing more than a ruin. It had been swallowed long ago by the earth. Maybe it had been sheltered in a cavern all that time, but now it lay exposed to the fine rain falling from the storm clouds above. The walls covered in glyphs and elaborate stonework lay in shambles. The heads of stone serpents were broken in pieces, but a few still snarled at the base of the remains of the temple.

Crumpled cars littered the floor of the cavern. Bodies lay broken all around the temple, blood oozing along the rocks and pooling in the dirt. None had hit the desecrated temple, which didn't surprise Amaliya. The black magic of the sword would protect everything but the human innocents.

Their descent was in silence. Much to Amaliya's relief, the sword had released its hold on her and allowed her freedom of movement. She knew she could not strike out yet, or else she would meet with failure. Amaliya clutched Bianca to her side, supporting the smaller woman. Clearly overwhelmed, tears streamed over Bianca's cheeks. Failure weighed heavily on both of them.

Amaliya couldn't use her necromancy or The Summoner would seize her power and use it against her. That left her vampire abilities to fight with. It made her feel weak, but she trusted herself. She could and would find a way out of the situation. Plus, she had seen Cian, which meant the others were coming to help her fight. She had hope, which was enough to keep her walking into the dark behind her creator instead of foolishly trying to flee.

The Summoner strode before them. Etzli was behind. The witches, demons, were-jaguars, infused humans, and elemagus finished off the procession.

The Sword of Lucifer soared over the center of the broken temple and illuminated the ruins with its golden radiance. The top of the building had broken away, but a flat surface remained.

The slope that the elemagus had formed was firm beneath her, but Amaliya kicked off her heels anyway. The dirt was frozen beneath her feet. Everyone always associated black magic, demons, and Lucifer with flames and heat, but all she felt was a marrow-deep cold.

When they reached the base of the temple, The Summoner easily scaled the broken steps rising to the platform. Amaliya followed. Keeping a tight clamp on her necromancy, Amaliya focused on her desperate, but only, plan.

A giant serpent hewn from stone lay in pieces in the center of the temple floor. The head was massive, with a gaping mouth and ornate stonework creating elegant, gruesome designs over its surface. The sword hovered just above it. The black witches strode ahead of the group and took their positions in a circle around the head. Raising their hands to the sword, they began to chant.

"Bianca," The Summoner said, extending his hand to her, "it's time to usher in the new world."

With a whimper, Bianca lowered her eyes, understanding now what her fate was to be. "I knew it. He always wanted just you, Amaliya."

"No, you can't." Amaliya protectively shoved Bianca behind her.

The Summoner's blue eyes focused on her, cruel and demanding. "Amaliya, we discussed this."

"Get the girl," Etzli ordered from behind Amaliya.

Amaliya twisted about, snatched Etzli's bone dagger from her waist, and slashed her throat in one swift movement. Etzli gasped in shock, her fingers gripping Amaliya's shoulders. Amaliya was aware of the others descending on her but ignored them. Thrusting the dagger into Etzli's heart, she shoved the woman to the ground. The shock on Etzli's face was satisfying, but not as much as the feel of her heart clutched in Amaliya's fingers.

"Bye, bitch," Amaliya hissed.

Amaliya yanked her hand out of the woman's chest and shoved the organ into her mouth. She swallowed the bloody thing as the were-jaguars hauled her away from Etzli's body.

"No!" Gregorio cried out, falling to his knees beside Etzli.

Blood dripping from her mouth, Amaliya smirked at The Summoner.

With an angry howl, he grabbed Bianca, who was staring in shock at Amaliya. Etzli's blood power surged into Amaliya a second later. It took her a few seconds to find the red thread of Etzli's power mingling with her own, then Amaliya summoned all the blood from Etzli's body. In a mighty gush, it exploded out of the hole in Etzli's chest and splashed over Amaliya and the six were-jaguars clutching her. Taking advantage of their shock, Amaliya wrenched free of their slippery grip. The blood soaking the were-jaguars turned into a supernatural vice as Amaliya attempted to utilize Etzli's power over blood. The were-jaguars thrashed about in an attempt to break free of the blood encapsulating them while Amaliya struggled to contain the vampire blood magic. Etzli's power was foreign to her, but Amaliya was good at winging it. She finally yanked the red thread of power taut in her mind's eye and was rewarded when Etzli's blood tightened around the were-jaguars and popped them like ticks. As their destroyed bodies fell, Amaliya kicked Gregorio down the stairs of the temple, and he vanished into the rubble.

The murk lit up with a red glow, and the demons turned toward Amaliya, their hands aflame.

"Shit!"

To her surprise, Aimee landed in front of her, and the witch lobbed balls of white magic at the demons. They immediately scattered. Cassandra appeared, silver knives flashing as she fought her way through a cluster of Etzli's vampires charging up the broken stairs toward them.

Then Cian was there, handsome, fierce, and armed with his obsidian dagger. She wanted to drag him into her arms and kiss him, but she had to save Bianca. She raced toward the serpent's head where The Summoner was attempting to hold down Bianca, and Cian followed in her wake. Bianca had bought them some time by actually fighting against The Summoner. The slender girl battled savagely, kicking and punching, and to Amaliya's relief, was not using her necromancy.

It had been a huge gamble, but Amaliya had believed that The Summoner would be too arrogant not to want to be in his true form at the end of the world. That meant he'd utilize the power of Lucifer's Sword to manifest himself and abandon Bianca's body. To create his body in the greater world, she'd assumed that he'd have to utilize most of the power of Lucifer's Sword and hoped that the drain on the sword's magic would be too great to also keep her captive. She'd been right.

It hadn't been until they were almost ready to leave the mansion that she had finally remembered the advice Innocent had whispered to her in her dreams.

Trust yourself.

Amaliya planned to do exactly that.

"Finish the ritual!" The Summoner barked at the black witches. Reaching over his head, he gripped the hilt of Lucifer's Sword.

"I've got the witches!" Cian shouted.

"I've got The Summoner!" Amaliya answered but immediately knew she was too late.

The Summoner swung the sword toward Bianca's throat.

A great white sparkling mist billowed into view. Riding the wave was Samantha, eyes glowing, body shrouded in the power of the dead. Amaliya gasped as the ghosts bore The Phasmagus down on The Summoner. Samantha struck the sword from his hand a split second before it was going to strike Bianca. The look of shock and anger on his face was extremely satisfying, then The Summoner launched himself at Samantha.

The Sword of Lucifer arced through the air, and Amaliya ran after it, tracking it with her eyes. Blood flew through the air as Cian killed the black witches, darting around their bursts of magic with eerie swiftness. Orbs of white fire flashed, driving back the demons rushing to help their masters. The glint of silver blades revealed Cassandra's brutal dance of death through the vampires and infused humans.

Amaliya lashed out, and the hilt of Lucifer's Sword slapped into her palm. Twisting about, she sprinted after The Summoner. The ghosts had lifted Samantha out of his reach, but he was scrambling up the broken walls trying to catch her. Not a vampire, not human, not a necromancer, he was confined to his false form.

Bianca, much to Amaliya's surprise, was closing in on him, scampering up behind him, clutching at his ankles and bare feet to drag him off. The blonde girl climbed rapidly and with purpose, but he kept out of her grip. So consumed in anger, The Summoner had made a mistake. Unarmed, his pursuit of Samantha was futile.

Hovering just above him, The Phasmagus goaded him on. "C'mon, fucker!"

The power of Lucifer's Sword called to Amaliya, demanding blood, vengeance, and release. She intended to give it what it wanted. Amaliya hurled herself into the air, flying toward The Summoner, the sword in her hand ready to swipe off his head.

The Summoner paused in his climb, recognizing his folly. Eyes locked with Amaliya's, he read her intent as she swooped toward him. With a wicked, triumphant smile, he blinked out of existence.

The sword cut through where he had perched seconds before. Spinning about in the air, Amaliya searched for The Summoner.

"Where is he?" Amaliya shouted at Samantha.

"I don't see him," Samantha floated in the cloud of phantoms. They held her aloft as the phasmagus searched for The Summoner.

"Let's play, shall we?" Bianca's voice snarled below.

Looking down, Amaliya saw the other woman's eyes glowing brightly.

Then the bodies of the many humans The Summoner had slaughtered rose to their feet.

CHAPTER TWENTY-NINE

Jeff scrambled down the makeshift stairs Baptiste had summoned. The steps made of bedrock and dirt were steep, forcing him to descend faster than felt safe. Jeff kept fearing he'd miss a step and fall. Baptiste led the way, Jeff followed with Eduardo on his heels, and Alexia took up the rear.

Water poured from broken pipes, the reek of sewage filled the air, and gas lines burned like torches along the walls of the chasm. Below, the bright sparks of magic illuminated the remains of the old Mayan temple. The greatest light came from the luminescent cloud of ghosts that held his fiancée aloft. Samantha looked nothing like the sweet, bullheaded girl he'd first met. With the spirits surrounding her and her power flowing in great glittering waves around her, she looked like a goddess.

"Your girlfriend is amazing," Baptiste said, observing the same view.

"Are we winning?" Alexia asked.

"Hard to tell," Jeff admitted.

It was difficult to track everything that was happening. Cian was on a killing spree, Cass was dodging stone spikes being thrown at her by a redhead, and Aimee was holding off a horde of demons while flitting around in the air and hurling magic bolts. Amaliya was holding a beautiful, terrifying sword while flying toward The Summoner.

Arriving at the bottom of the cavern, Jeff ran across the muddy surface. The drizzle, water, and sewage were turning the ground into sludge. Eduardo surged past them and leaped into the fray.

"I got the elemagus," Baptiste said, swerving off to confront the redhead.

Summoning some of the fire from the flaming pipes above, Baptiste hurled it at the elemagus fighting Cassandra. Her head jerked in his direction, and she thrust out her hand. Baptiste barely avoided a stone spike that erupted from the ground. The other elemagus barely avoided the fire ball and then charged Baptiste, abandoning Cassandra.

Jeff gripped the silver stake in his one hand tighter and lifted the pistol in the other. The demons were herding Aimee into a corner. The modified bullets in the gun contained vanquishing spells. When used on any other creature, they'd have the impact of a normal bullet, but on demons it would send them back into the abyss. Taking careful aim, he started to fire. He grinned when the first demon he hit winked out of existence.

From behind a large rock, a mortal young man bolted toward the stairs Baptiste had created. He clutched an iPad to his chest and ran like a scared rabbit. Jeff pondered going after him, but the demons had turned their attention in his direction. Reloading, Jeff was glad he had allowed Cian to infuse him. He was much faster doing the task than ever before. A demon barreled toward him, hands aflame. Jeff slapped the clip home and raised the pistol. He fired, and the demon vanished.

"Out of my way!" a voice shouted behind Jeff.

Twisting about, Jeff saw the young man rushing Alexia. She started to raise her gun but thought better of it when she must have realized he was unarmed and mortal. Instead, she pistol whipped him, then kicked him into the bottom stair. Striking him two more times in the back of the head with her foot, Alexia seemed satisfied that he was unconscious and ran to join Jeff.

"I think we got this," she said with a gleeful smile.

Then a second later, the dead bodies littering the cavern climbed to their feet.

"Shit," Jeff sighed.

The dead didn't just rise, they were pulled apart and knitted together by sinews of darkness into new, terrifying creatures with bones for teeth and claws. The giant monsters rushed Amaliya, intent on stopping her.

"Oh, hell!" Cassandra cried out, leading the charge into battle.

The dhamphir spun through the air, aiming for the closest creature. She landed on the mushy ground and drove her blades through its torso, ripping it in half. Blood sprayed her as she twisted about, just missing the swipe of a huge clawed hand. Hacking away at the creature, she had no idea how to kill it but knew she had to keep it away from Amaliya until the necro-vampire could finish off The Summoner.

Nearby, Cian fought another creature, his black blade cutting off the claws of a multi-limbed creature. A grim expression upon his face, he fought with a brutality that was familiar to Cassandra. All her life she'd been afraid she was like her father. Now she realized she was very much his daughter in every way.

At last, it didn't scare her. It empowered her.

With a gleeful shout, she decapitated the monster she was fighting and charged the next one.

Leaving the bodies of the thirteen witches in his wake, Cian raced after his daughter to face off against the monstrous beings made of the bodies of The Summoner's innocent victims. Just before he leaped off the temple platform, he caught sight of Amaliya for a split second. She was a vengeance goddess, eyes glowing red, covered in blood, wielding the terrible sword, and fighting to save them all. In his heart, he knew she was the only one who could actually kill The Summoner, and he had to allow her to do just that. Though a part of him wanted to fight the battle for her, he knew his place was with his daughter and the others keeping back the army of creatures that The Summoner had created to stop Amaliya.

Slashing and hacking at the claws of the terrible flesh and bone creations of The Summoner, Cian kept them from charging Amaliya. If she wasn't using her necromancy, there was a reason for it, which meant he had to kill the creatures himself.

The bone claws of one of the monsters raked his chest, and Cian cried out in pain. Recovering, he darted around the creature and lopped off one of its arms.

Daring to steal a glance at the temple, he saw Amaliya confronting Bianca's possessed form. With dread, Cian realized that Amaliya would have to do the one thing she'd been desperately trying to avoid.

Amaliya had to kill Bianca.

Jeff and Alexia dispatched the demons with carefully aimed bullets while somehow still managing to avoid their flaming hands. Baptiste sent the red-headed elemagus flying with mighty gusts of wind, then called lightning bolts down on her flailing form. One struck her and shot her into the wall of the cavern. The redhead fell to the muddy ground, her body sizzling and smoking in the rain.

"That was one tough bitch," Baptiste gasped, clutching his arm. Stone spikes had struck it, and one protruded near his shoulder.

They were on the outskirts of the major battle between Cian, Cassandra, Aimee, and the massive creatures made out of the flesh of humans. Eduardo had one of the smaller creatures cornered, howling gleefully as he tore it apart with his teeth. Jerking the head of a dark-haired woman out of the torso of the creature, the were-coyote dashed away like a dog with a toy. Darting around the creature, Eduardo howled with delight and tugged another head out of the monster. The coyote gleefully played with the creature, ignoring the massive battle behind him.

"Uh," Baptiste grunted.

"Jeff?" Alexia said, her eyes widening.

Reaching into his messenger bag, Jeff yanked out a clip with silver bullets. Slamming it into his pistol, he raised the weapon and aimed. One shot sent Eduardo to the ground, his head blown apart.

"Let's finish this," Jeff said, gesturing to the epic battle before them.

The three of them charged forward.

Growling with frustration, Amaliya landed near the stone serpent. The dead witches littered the stones, their blood slipping along the cracks to pool around the head. The sword in her hand froze her fingers but sent pulses of warm delight through her. It wanted blood.

Amaliya's mind was a whirlwind of thoughts and half-formed plans. There was no way in hell she was going to kill Bianca to get to The Summoner. Too many people had died already, but if she didn't kill Bianca more would die.

The Summoner in Bianca's body smiled. "Do you really think you can best me?"

"Yeah," Amaliya answered, lifting the sword. "I got this."

"I have Bianca." Dropping to the floor, The Summoner bent over and plucked a jagged piece of stone from the debris. "The witches cast the spell. The sword is formed."

"I have the sword!" Amaliya brandished it.

Bianca's delicate form in the white gown looked so harmless against the grotesque backdrop of the cavern. A hint of her innocence remained in her features as The Summoner used her hand to raise the stone to her throat. "All that's needed is the blood of a necromancer."

"No!"

Slitting Bianca's throat ear to ear, The Summoner grinned at Amaliya, twisting Bianca's face into something inhuman and terrible. Blood gushed out of the wound to paint the white gown red. The blood slid over the ground toward the gruesome stone serpent head with its snarling mouth and cruel eyes.

"The ritual is complete," The Summoner declared.

The Sword of Lucifer sang in her hand, its thirst for blood sated. Amaliya stepped back, the sword slicing through the air. A rent formed in the fabric of reality. A void of endless darkness lay just beyond the tear.

"Don't move, Amaliya!" Samantha shouted. "It's opening the abyss!"

Unable to move, Amaliya watched in horror as Bianca's life spilled onto the ground. She was trapped, unable to move the sword and fight The Summoner. Even the slightest movement of the sword opened the gash further.

Below the temple, her friends and love fought the massive monsters of flesh and bone. Spears of earth and ice revealed where Baptiste fought. Gunshots echoed through the darkness. Ghosts swirled through the battle, tearing apart the creatures only for the golems to reform. Samantha drifted above the fray, directing her ghosts.

"Samantha!" Amaliya cried out, then dared to awaken her necromancy.

The bond between them instantly flared to life, darkness and light intermingling. In a split second, understanding passed between them. Samantha closed her eyes, and Amaliya shut her own.

Instantly, the world of the ghosts opened before Amaliya. Tethered to Samantha through the fine sinew of their power, she released her physical form.

Amaliya's body crashed to the ground, the sword slicing through the air to create an even greater opening to the abyss.

In the world of ghosts, she could clearly see The Summoner wrapped in Bianca's slim form. Wings of darkness spread out behind Amaliya's ethereal form as she hurtled toward Bianca. Samantha landed behind The Summoner and Bianca, beautiful in her otherworldly body. The Phasmagus grabbed The Summoner as Amaliya latched onto Bianca. In the spectral world, it was clear that Bianca was close to death, which loosened her bonds to The Summoner.

Together, they ripped the two apart.

The Summoner gasped as he was torn from Bianca's body. His astral body flailed between The Phasmagus and Necromancer, but in this world, Samantha ruled. Amaliya released Bianca's spirit body and seized The Summoner. Amaliya and Samantha dragged him toward the opening to the abyss. The sword had torn through both the physical and spiritual realm, revealing the darkness beyond.

"No! No! You can't do this!" The Summoner cried out, terror in his face.

"You wanted the abyss. You got it," Amaliya snarled.

"We're done with you," Samantha added in her perky way. "Ciao!"

Together, they hurled him through the rip, his scream of horror immensely satisfying as his sprit vanished into the void.

"Finish it," Samantha said, turning to Amaliya, her white eyes burning.

Opening her physical eyes, Amaliya scrambled to her feet and flung the sword through the rip in the air. It vanished into the abyss, and instantly the tear vanished.

The wet, fleshy splatter of The Summoner's creatures falling apart filled the eerie silence.

"Did we do it?" Alexia's voice echoed in the massive chamber.

Amaliya ran to Bianca's side and crouched next to the girl. Dragging Bianca into her arms, she drew her tongue over gash in her throat. It took several swipes to finally stop the bleeding, but it wasn't healing.

Cian kneeled next to Amaliya. His shirt was in shreds, and deep wounds were healing. "I'll feed her," he said, immediately opening a vein.

"I can't let her die," Amaliya said, stroking Bianca's fine blonde hair with her bloody fingers. "I just can't. Too many have died."

His hazel eyes meeting hers, Cian nodded. "I know, Amaliya." Holding his dripping wrist over Bianca's mouth, he let his blood pour into her.

The cabal drifted into view one by one. The dhamphir was covered in blood and dirt, and a nasty cut was healing on her cheek. The witch was just as grungy and had a few scorch marks on her clothes and bit of singed hair but appeared whole. Baptiste's left arm hung limply at his side, a jagged spear of rock sticking out of his bicep. Jeff was dirty but otherwise unharmed. Alexia was covered in blood and chunks of flesh.

"One of those things fell apart on me," she explained, seeing Amaliya's look.

Samantha joined them, her eyes still glowing. A mantle of ghosts clustered behind her. Among them was Roberto, looking very satisfied.

"Benchley?" Amaliya asked, fear creeping into her.

"He's with Galina. They're safe," Jeff assured her.

Amaliya noted another was missing, too. "Eduardo?"

"He's dead." The coldness in Jeff's gaze when he looked at her explained the whole story in one second.

"You killed him!" Amaliya gasped.

"He was a serial killer."

Amaliya took a second to absorb that truth, then said, "Oh, that's why I was attracted to him."

"Serial killer?" Aimee exclaimed, the conversation finally registering. "What?"

"Oh, that makes total sense," Alexia said, continuing to wipe off the fleshy bits from her skin and clothes. "That head thing he was doing was creepy."

"Amaliya, you need to give her blood, too," Cian said, drawing her attention back to Bianca. He was pale and drawn from giving so much of his own. "I think we can save her."

Nodding, Amaliya ripped open her wrist with her teeth and started to feed Bianca.

"She's still here," Samantha said, crouching next to Amaliya. "I can see her settling back into her body."

Amaliya gently stroked the girl's cheek with her grimy fingers. "She tried to save me."

"And now you saved her." Cian kissed Amaliya tenderly. "You're amazing, you know."

Nuzzling his lips, Amaliya relished the feel of his kiss. She loved him so much it was a physical pain inside of her to think of how close they had come to losing each other.

"We should probably get out of here," Jeff suggested.

Above them, sirens wailed and spotlights from circling helicopters skimmed over the sinkhole's walls.

"How do we explain this?" Amaliya wondered.

"We don't have to explain anything. Follow me," Baptiste said, gesturing to the group.

Cian lifted Bianca into his arms, and Amaliya slid her arm about his waist, leaning against him. The rest of the group fell in behind them. When the dirt wall split apart before them, forming a tunnel, no one was really surprised.

Baptiste flashed a wide grin. "I have talents."

Together, they filed into the narrow passage. It was a little disconcerting as the earth parted before them and closed behind them as they walked. The pathway gently sloped upward until at last the ground divided to reveal the dark silhouettes of trees against the night sky.

Amaliya pulled herself out of the earth, briefly reflecting on the first time she had emerged from a grave in the woods. Sweeping her gaze from Cian to the others gathered around, she smiled. Unlike the first time, she was no longer alone. She had a purpose. She had love. She had friendship.

And she had saved the world.

Epilogue

December 24, 2012

The chill wind buffeted Bianca as her scooter zipped down Congress Avenue toward downtown Austin. Ahead, the pink granite state capitol building glowed white in the lights. Bundled in a new white leather jacket and a matching pink knit cap and scarf, Bianca giggled as her passenger, Alexia, sang along, badly, to Mariah Carey singing about what she wanted for Christmas. It was hard to hear the music emanating from the phone clutched in Alexia's hand over the wind, but Bianca relished the gloriousness of the moment.

She was free.

She had a friend.

She was alive.

Bianca had volunteered to take her brand new scooter (courtesy of Cian) out to grab some last minute items for their Christmas Eve celebration. Alexia had also opted to go along. They'd found a Walmart that was still open and had taken the side roads to get there, giggling and singing the whole way.

Bianca still couldn't believe she was alive. During the dark, terrible days of her possession and imprisonment, she'd been convinced she was doomed. She had known that in the end The Summoner had truly wanted Amaliya at his side, not her. That knowledge had prepared her to die.

Instead, she was alive.

Cian had used so much of his blood to bring her back from the verge of death that he had become her new creator. It had surprised Cian and Bianca when they had realized they now shared the bond of a creator and fledgling, but he had quickly stepped in to guide her through the dark life. He was kind to her in a way The Summoner never could have been. She understood why Amaliya loved him so much. Cian made her feel safe and strong. It was odd to go from being an orphan to a slave to a part of a family of vampires.

Though the vampires were presently sleeping in Jeff's attic, they would soon be moving into a new house that Cian was having modified to suit their needs. Bianca would even have her own room decorated to her taste, but Amaliya had made it clear she could sleep with them whenever she wanted. After being alone most of her life, Bianca found comfort in sleeping with the other two vampires through the hours of the day. Surprisingly, she no longer awoke during the day, and her necromancy powers were waning. Cian suspected they might disappear altogether as his blood continued to alter her vampire nature.

That thought thrilled Bianca.

All her life she had dealt with the spirits of the dead, and now she was free of them. If she had to live as an undead creature, she preferred the simplicity of just being a regular vampire.

Alexia continued to sing along to yet another song.

Bianca zoomed her scooter around a corner and toward Jeff's Victorian. Her scarf fluttered behind her, and the cool air kissed her cheeks red. It was Christmas Eve. She had a family, a home, and a future.

She had tried so hard to save Amaliya, but in the end Amaliya had saved her.

"You are mutilating that poor bird!" Samantha stomped her foot and frowned at Jeff.

"Excuse me, but my turkey cutting skills are excellent," Jeff responded, holding the carving knife over the golden roasted bird.

"Doing it all wrong. So wrong."

Jeff kissed her nose. "Well, deal with it. We're getting hitched. You're signing on for the whole package. Besides, I have to put up with the cat and the ghost." Jeff gestured to Beatrice sitting at his feet waiting for more turkey skin and then Roberto.

The ghost was washing dishes and looking decidedly grumpy about it.

Samantha grinned, lifting her eyes to the ceiling. "True."

"Why haven't you sent him on to his just reward?" Jeff asked, leaning toward her. He adored her cute face and twinkling eyes.

"He's afraid it's in the burning place."

"I'd rather go to hell than do your dishes," Roberto groused.

"Oh, shut your face," Samantha shot back.

Jeff returned to carving the turkey. "I have the craziest life."

"And you love it." Samantha plucked a bit of turkey from the pan and fed it to her cat.

With a grin, Jeff had to admit she was right.

"Did I do that right?" Galina frowned at the setting on the dining room table.

Cassandra craned her head to check. "Yep. Everything is right. Fork, knife, spoon all in the proper places."

Setting crystal goblets at each setting, Aimee bestowed a sweet look on Galina. "You're doing very, very well."

"Do I set a place for Cian, Bianca, and Amaliya?" Galina pursed her lips, her eyes filling with tears.

Cassandra slipped behind her mother and gave her a little hug. "The vampires are going to join us but not eat. Don't set anything for them. They're here for conversation."

"It's been a very long time," Galina said, her eyes settling on the notebook open on the table. "Cian moved on."

Kissing her mother's cheek, Cassandra wished her mother didn't hurt so much over Cian, but it was safer for her in Austin than anywhere else. Until they were sure that all of The Summoner's forces were wiped out, they all had to be very careful. It was awkward to have her mother and father in close proximity, but they were both trying very hard to be cordial.

"It's all good, Mom."

"It *is* good." Galina nodded her head. "It is. You and Aimee are here with me. Your friends are very nice. The house is beautiful. And your father loves you. Plus, I'm going to make you cookies tonight."

"See! Life is perfect!" Cassandra gave her mother one more squeeze.

"I'll start now!" Galina smiled at her lovingly, picked up her notebook, then hurried to the kitchen already forgetting she had been helping to set the table.

Aimee sidled around the table and wrapped her arms around Cassandra. Her kiss was sweet and loving. It always made everything much better when Aimee held her.

"It's all going to work out, you know. It always does," Aimee assured her.

"As long as we're together, I'm not worried," Cassandra answered.

"I'll never leave you. Ever. You're stuck with me." Aimee kissed her again.

Cassandra couldn't imagine anything more wonderful.

Cian tangled his hands in Amaliya's hair as he came hard inside her. Gasping, she bit his bottom lip and rolled them over so she was on top. Her wild black hair in her face, she was gorgeous. Every time he thought he couldn't love her any more than he already did, he discovered he was wrong.

"What time is it?" she gasped.

Keeping himself firmly inside her, he shifted his legs, edging toward the end of the bed where the bed stand sat. He'd had the king-sized bed and bedroom furniture delivered weeks before. The attic was now much more comfortable, a welcome departure from the one day he had spent alone in it. Grabbing his cell-phone, he checked the time.

"We have thirty minutes before the dinner," Cian answered, then read the message from Bianca. "Bianca will be back by then with Alexia."

"Then we have time for one more roll in the fuckin' hay." Amaliya rotated her hips over his, a seductive grin on her face.

Already aroused, Cian grunted, cupped her full breasts, and rubbed her pierced nipples with his thumbs. "We have to shower and dress still."

Sliding up and down his cock, Amaliya smirked. "We'll just attend naked."

Flipping her over, Cian answered, "I'm fine with that."

"Fuck me," she ordered.

He did.

Dinner was far removed from Samantha's usual Christmas Eve celebrations with her family. She sat next to Jeff at the end of the table sneaking bites of turkey to Beatrice while the conversation around the table was increasingly loud and bawdy.

The three vampires sat at the opposite end of the long table with glasses of wine in front of them. Amaliya wore her usual black tank top and jeans, while Cian looked handsome in a dark red shirt. Bianca's slim form was tucked into combat boots, rolled-up jeans, and a plaid shirt over a tank top. She looked young and cute. The twin buns on either side of her head had delighted Benchley. He had called her a "blonde Princess Leia." Samantha sensed there was a bit of flirting going on between Benchley and Bianca, but she wasn't quite sure how that was going to fare considering that the three vampires slept together.

Samantha strongly suspected that they were *not* just sleeping together and watched their interactions like a hawk. Amaliya teased Samantha if she even dared broach the subject. Samantha knew she'd never get a clear answer, so it drove her a bit nuts. She'd come a long way from being her old judgmental self, and it wasn't her sex life, but she couldn't imagine sharing her bed with anyone else but Jeff. Jeff was her everything.

Amaliya caught her eye and winked.

Samantha stuck out her tongue.

Bianca laughed and chatted with Baptiste about Louisiana, the state they were both born in. Baptiste, still angry with Rachoń for her betrayal, had surprised everyone by staying in Austin. It was uncertain if he would return to his home. Samantha hoped he stuck around. He was a part of them now, and it was hard to imagine him not being with them.

Benchley and Alexia yanked the wishbone apart. Benchley ended up with the bigger piece, which resulted in a tug of war. Aimee intervened, granting them both a wish, or so she claimed.

At Cassandra's side, Galina just smiled and looked confused most of the time. Cian appeared uncomfortable whenever Galina looked at him, but Samantha supposed it was Cian's fault in the end. She loved the bastard, but he had messed up more than one woman during his long life. It was obvious from how he interacted with Amaliya that he had learned his lesson and found his happiness, but he was going to have to deal with the fallout of his past.

Meanwhile, Samantha had a wedding to plan in the spring and a life to look forward to. Stealing a look at Jeff as he chatted with Cassandra, she felt utterly content. She finally had her happy ending.

Roberto appeared in the doorway carrying the Christmas cake Samantha had toiled over for hours. With his head held high, he strolled to the table and dropped the cake with a thunderous clap onto the surface. Frosting and bits of cake splattered everyone.

"Cake is served," he intoned.

"Food fight!" Benchley hollered.

The following madness was nothing like the dignified gatherings of her family.

Samantha loved it.

"Oh, my gawd! You went the wrong way again!" Bianca exclaimed, waving her hands at Benchley.

"I know! I know! I got confused!" Benchley mashed the buttons on the controller, and Bianca laughed with delight.

Curled up on the sofa next to Cian, Amaliya watched Benchley playing a video game while Bianca sat on the arm of his chair trying to give him directions. Amaliya was glad not to have to watch television. The cabal had been obsessed with watching all the news footage on the devastation in San Antonio. The media theories as to what had actually happened were surprisingly tame considering that a Mayan temple had been discovered at the base of the massive sink hole that had destroyed the area. Amaliya suspected the authorities were trying to keep everyone calm. Rebuilding was going to be hell, and the traffic in San Antonio was going to be heinous for years to come. The destruction of the major thoroughfare was going to affect the city for some time to come.

"Bench! No! Not that way!" Bianca howled with laughter.

Bianca looked far removed from the shell-shocked vampire that had woken up on the way home to Austin after The Summoner had been defeated. Amaliya had been a little disappointed with Bianca's fading necromancy, but she was pleased that Cian was being such a gentle guide to the young woman.

Baptiste sprawled on the loveseat, favoring his still-healing arm and eating the popcorn Aimee was attempting to string for the Christmas tree. Cassandra sat on the floor with her arm slung over Aimee's lap. Galina was in the kitchen with Alexia making cookies. Jeff sat in a chair sipping eggnog while Samantha sat on his lap and texted her parents on her phone.

Cian's fingers gently stroked Amaliya's leg. She was tempted to drag him back upstairs but reminded herself it was a special occasion and she was a guest in Jeff's house.

Happily, the vampires would soon be moving out to their new place. Cian had also purchased a house a few blocks away for Cassandra, Aimee, and Galina. Amaliya couldn't wait to be in their own place again so she could play her drums as loud as she damned well pleased and smoke without having Samantha giving her the evil eye.

Wrapping her arms around Cian, Amaliya nestled her lips against his cheek. He grinned at her and kissed the tip of her nose. The pride and love she saw in his eyes every time he looked at her made her glow with happiness. She had spent every night since the big battle showing him how much she loved him. He had returned the favor in spades.

Alexia wandered into the room with a plate of cookies, one firmly tucked between her teeth. Setting it down on the coffee table, she observed the mad scramble by the non-vampires to grab the tasty treats.

"So now that we've saved the world, celebrated Christmas, and are looking forward to a non-apocalyptic 2013, what the hell are we going to do with ourselves?" she asked.

"I don't know about y'all, but I'm going to do a little bit of traveling," Amaliya answered.

"Oh? Where to?" Baptiste munched on his cookie, his maroon eyes watching her curiously.

"Yes, where to?" Cian twisted about to gaze at her.

"Houston and Dallas," Samantha said, looking up from her phone.

"Huh?" Benchley shoved a cookie in his mouth. "Why?"

Bianca handed him a napkin for his mouth, pointing to the crumbs.

"To kill some bitches," Samantha answered for Amaliya.

With a wide grin, Amaliya said, "Right on, little bitch. You in?"

"Fuck yeah, bitch-face." Samantha gave her two thumbs up.

"Who are we killing exactly?" Aimee lifted her eyes from the string of popcorn she was diligently working on between cookie bites.

"Courtney and Nicole," Cassandra declared, nodding her head as she figured it out. "Those two bitches."

"And all their asshole servants." Amaliya crossed her legs and folded her arms over the swell of her breasts.

"Exactly why?" Cian tilted his head. "All the vampires abandoned us. Why them specifically?"

"Because I promised those bitches I'd come for them for betraying humanity.

I'm going to keep my word," Amaliya responded, flipping her hair back from her face and giving him a defiant look.

"I'm in," Bianca volunteered, holding up her hand.

"I've got nothing else to do. I'm in." Baptiste raised his good hand.

"I like a good fight." Cassandra lifted hers high over her head.

"I go where the hot dhamphir goes." Aimee added her vote, raising hers, too.

"C'mon, you guys. We just saved the world. Can't we chill for a bit?" Benchley gave them all a surly look.

"We'll go after the New Year." Alexia raised two hands.

"Fine." Benchley grudgingly raised his.

Jeff looked at Samantha for guidance. "So?"

"Well, duh. They were total asshats. We're so in," Samantha retorted, waving her arm over her head.

"The hot blonde and I are game," Jeff said, lifting a hand.

Tilting his head, Cian gave Amaliya a slightly exasperated look. "So...are we taking over Texas now?"

"Sure." Amaliya shrugged. "Why not?"

"Raise that hand, Cian!" Samantha urged. "Do it!"

With a chuckle, Cian raised his hand. "Okay. Fine. Let's do it." Leaning toward Amaliya, he whispered, "You have corrupted us all."

"Oh, I'm just starting," Amaliya promised him with a grin.

ABOUT THE AUTHOR

Rhiannon Frater is the award-winning author of over a dozen books, including the *As the World Dies* zombie trilogy (Tor), as well as independent works such as *The Last Bastion of the Living* (declared the #1 Zombie Release of 2012 by *Explorations Fantasy Blog* and the #1 Zombie Novel of the Decade by *B&N Book Blog*), and other horror novels. She was born and raised a Texan and presently lives in Austin, Texas with her husband and furry children (a.k.a pets). She loves scary movies, sci-fi and horror shows, playing video games, cooking, dyeing her hair weird colors, and shopping for Betsey Johnson purses and shoes.

You can find her online at rhiannonfrater.com

Subscribe to her mailing list at tinyletter.com/RhiannonFrater